N
GOES UNPUNISHED

A Noir Psychological Suspense Thriller

BRYAN QUINN

A NOVEL IN SIX PARTS

Copyright © 2020 Bryan Quinn

Print ISBN: 978-1-64719-024-8
Epub ISBN: 978-1-64719-025-5
Mobi ISBN: 978-1-64719-026-2

All rights reserved. No part of this publication may be reproduced, stored in a retrieval system, or transmitted in any form or by any means, electronic, mechanical, recording or otherwise, without the prior written permission of the author.

Published by BookLocker.com, Inc., St. Petersburg, Florida.

This novel is a work of fiction. Names, characters, places and incidents are products of the author's imagination or are used fictitiously. Any resemblance to actual events or locales or persons, living or dead, is entirely coincidental.

Booklocker.com, Inc.
2020

First Edition

About the Author

Bryan R. Quinn, a life-long student of history, earned a BA in American History & Politics from McGill University and a Computer Electronics Diploma from Herzing College, which comes in handy when he has to troubleshoot inevitable computer problems. Yet, despite his expertise with digital technology, he still relies on his wife to operate the coffee machine. Bryan lives with her in Canada.

Bryan won an Honorable Mention Award in the worldwide 85th Annual Writer's Digest 4000 Word Short Story Competition in 2016.

NO GOOD DEED GOES UNPUNISHED is Bryan's second novel. His first novel THE PACKAGE, an historical-contemporary conspiracy thriller, has garnered international acclaim.

Follow Bryan on Twitter: *@AuthorBryan*.

Acknowledgements

Producing a novel is not a solo endeavor and so the many contributors must be acknowledged.

First, my loving wife who supported me in every way. Next, Todd Engel for his brilliant cover design. Then, my publisher Angela Hoy at BookLocker for packaging my novel and putting it the hands of book retailers.

Finally, I extend a heartfelt thank you to my friends and fellow writers Sandra Johnson and Wendy Waters for whipping my novel into fine shape. May the muse be with you always.

But greed of gain can often make men fools

- Sophocles

Beginnings

Belonging to the Mafia was like standing over a trapdoor—the bottom could fall out anytime, anywhere, on anyone, without warning. From the highest rank to the lowest, no member of the Mob was safe. Fate lurked around every corner, behind every door, under any circumstance. Like it or lump it, there was no escaping it or stopping it.

Normally tucked in the back of his mind, this sobering truth preoccupied Bronco, a forty-something mobster with nothing to lose and everything to gain. His boss had ordered him to snuff out a loyal underling for the greater good of the family. Nothing personal. Simply business…Family business…And no one else's business.

And all the while Bronco skulked in the dark, littered alley like a common thief, doing his best imitation of stealthy in his snakeskin boots, barely succeeding at it. Though imitation wasn't his forte, killing *was*. And despite appearances, his overabundance of caution didn't spring from any sense of fear, even though he lived a life steeped in violence, rather, it sprang from what—or more precisely who—lay ahead.

The advantage presently his would be lost if his minions hawking their merchandise at the other end of the alley caught him spying. He might lose face. He couldn't let this happen; it would undermine his fearsome reputation, a reputation he had spent decades cultivating. But these concerns were secondary. His primary concern was carrying out the don's command.

Untroubled by this order, Bronco wondered why as he skirted piles of rubbish, his nose wrinkling at decomposing garbage and God knows what else. He dismissed out of hand right versus wrong, the conventional moral ball and chain shackled round the neck of the typical Jane and Joe. Morality had never hindered him in the past, so this couldn't be why. He carried the line of self-enquiry further. Could his indifference be due to his indispensable capacity to inflict mortal injury upon his fellow man—and the odd woman—without remorse or regret? He mulled it over. The pain of others rarely nudged his conscience, so this must be why. Bronco congratulated himself for this insight, never dreaming the fatal scheme he was putting into play tonight would boomerang.

He continued to weave his way toward Pepe's Tavern, a place he often called his second home, its shoddy decor and even shadier clientele oozing a certain *je ne sais quoi*. But ambiance was the least of it. Besides quenching his undiscriminating thirst for cheap alcohol, the wayward tavern doubled as a convenient waystation for resolving family issues away from nosy law men, issues like snuffing out a loyal underling.

Bronco arrived at the alley's end in silence and settled in the shadows next to the tavern, a ramshackle structure whose crumbling bricks and cracked mortar evinced neglect more than age. Erected in the South Bronx long before he had popped into the world, the tavern was now a seedy hangout for members of the Cabreezi crime family, a notorious neighborhood haunt locals darted past on their way to someplace safer, to someplace saner. Walk-ins never happened.

Unsure if the building might cave in, Bronco restrained himself from leaning his hulking frame against it, and he peered from the shadows to check on the street action, his pitiless black eyes scouting left and right. He bided his time, he was in no hurry.

Distrustful by nature, but also due to his profession, he wasn't above spying on his crew from time to time. A *caporegime*, or captain, in the Cabreezi gang—the muscle in control of the market for banned substances and illicit liaisons in this part of town—Bronco maintained tight rein on a crew of soldiers, drug pushers and prostitutes. But keeping a low profile wasn't easy; he stretched over six feet and was built like a pro wrestler, thanks to pumping heavy iron every day.

Although foot traffic was sparse on this overcast night, the street teemed with idling vehicles, several luxurious. Drivers chatted up his girls and bargained with his dealers, like every other night. Poorly lit, the strip was anything but a regular shopper's paradise, more of a market for those who wished to obliterate the unrelieved *ennui* of modern life through chemical and carnal diversions that offered the illusions of paradise. Back in the days of Prohibition, the Noe-Schultz gang of bootleggers held sway in this neighborhood, but vices had changed and so, for better or worse, the Cabreezi gang provided services to gratify them.

Satisfied with the pace of illegal commerce, Bronco retraced his path through the heaps of malodorous garbage and slipped into his gleaming low-slung ride, a charcoal Chrysler 300S. He cruised around the block and parked down the street from the tavern. A jolt passed through his people while he progressed along the uneven sidewalk opposite them. Moving into a cone of feeble light carved out of the semi-darkness by the tavern's overhead lamp, he gave his crew one last hard stare before pulling on the door handle with his meaty hand. Message transmitted and received.

Boisterous voices spilled into the street and, despite the citywide ban on smoking in public places, a wave of air reeking of stale tobacco smoke let loose by the open door assaulted his sensitive nose. His face screwed up. There were some things he couldn't control. Setting aside his irritation, he plunged into the dim interior, smoke and all. Members of this private club didn't care about a whole gamut of regulations, let alone an anti-smoking one, and neither did the city health inspector. But this paperclip pusher had been paid not to care, so he didn't count.

Over on the left, in a corner behind the bar, a Yankees game blaring on a flat screen TV anchored above shelves of bottled booze competed with the energetic chatter of the all-male clientele enjoying the contest of skill between batter and pitcher. They paid Bronco no attention, mesmerized by the luminous action on the tube. Beefy forearms crossing his pneumatic pecs, the bartender, a fellow iron pumper, gave Bronco a respectful nod as he lumbered by the bar on the wooden floor worn shiny with wear, then resumed watching the game.

At the rear of the room on the right, among the shadows, Bronco spied his underling through the foggy haze hauling on a cigarette. A wiry hustler in his early twenties, his hair tangled and his jawline untouched by the caress of a razor for what must be several days, the kid waited alone in one of the cracked red vinyl booths fixed to the wall decorated with sports memorabilia from a bygone era. He stiffened at Bronco's approach, as did most people in his presence. Those who didn't often regretted it.

Bronco watched him take a final drag on his cigarette for none of his minions dared smoke in his company. He had witnessed his mother die one breath at a time from lung cancer brought on by smoking multiple packs of cancer sticks per day. He had no desire to follow her act of slow suicide. Tilting back his head, the kid blew out a final plume of smoke while he hurriedly stabbed out the butt.

Unexpectedly, the door to the men's room in the far corner opened, seizing his concern, and a triangle of light spilled into the darkened alcove followed by one of the regulars. Bronco threw him a look, the kind of look that could knock his teeth out from across the room, and the fella's head dropped as he scampered back to the bar to rejoin his buddies.

Bronco scraped to a halt and squeezed himself onto the spongy banquette opposite the kid, and cheap vinyl groaned at his bulk. An empty glass frosted with a residue of beer foam rested on the ring-stained table and a pile of cigarette butts lay squished like miniature accordions in an improvised ashtray fashioned from a mini-tinfoil cup, the sort that might have once held a butter tart or some other sugary confection. No hellos or handshakes were exchanged. This was a business meeting, not a social gathering. And besides, they weren't equals on the scales of life.

"About time you arrived. Where you been, man?" the kid said. "Like, I'm down half a pack of smokes."

Anyone else displaying such nerve would've earned him a cuff upside the head, but Bronco let it slide. He possessed a soft spot for him; they had both experienced violent episodes in their adolescence. What's more, the kid's days were numbered.

"I can't figure out why I let you talk to me with such a lack of respect," Bronco said.

"'Cause you got a big heart?" his quip punctuated with a toothy grin.

"I got to hand it to you," Bronco's tough persona dissolving in snorts of laughter, "you know me better than I know myself."

Untrue, but there was no harm in letting the kid think so.

What could be relief passed over the underling's face. He checked around then leaned in, "Don't worry," he whispered. "Your secret's safe with me." He gave his boss a wink to seal the deal and settled back.

Bronco's shoulders shook with another bout of amusement. When he regained self-control, the kid was regarding him with expectation.

"So, what do you want with me this time, big guy?"

"That's what I admire about you. You don't waste your breath with useless small talk."

"'Cause, like, there's other places I'd rather be than this dump."

Bronco quirked an eyebrow and rested his weight on the table, his leather jacket creaking in concert. "The decor doesn't do it for you?"

The kid fiddled with his pack of cigarettes, his lips twitching with unspoken thoughts and counter-thoughts, and Bronco enjoyed watching his minion squirm. He coughed up an answer and he coughed it up quick. "This place could stand some upgrades. I mean, check out the damn ashtray for chrissake." He held his breath.

Bronco's stony demeanor softened. "Had you going there for a second, didn't I?"

The kid exhaled. "You got me, big fella. Now can we get down to business or do I, like, have to get rough with you?"

To the din of cheering in the background—the home team must have scored—Bronco ignored his jest and in a loud voice said: "Take care of this," and his hand whipped out of his jacket.

Part I

Several Weeks Earlier…

Chapter One

Centi-billionaire Nelson McCormack, America's richest man at the relatively young age of forty-two and senior partner and majority shareholder at McCormack & McCormack, an uber-prosperous Wall Street investment firm, rode the walnut-paneled elevator in a state of anticipation to his twenty-first floor penthouse on Central Park West. The grandiosity of his home never failed to thrill him, the kind of luxurious lodging envious plebs only set foot in to clean or to cook.

He could easily afford a place on Park Avenue but *les parvenus vulgaires* had spoiled the exclusive cachet of that address ages ago. Besides, Central Park West was where old money resided and reproduced. The first part of this compact he enjoyed in spades. To his frustration—and his wife's—he was still working on the second part.

The rising compartment halted its ascent without a lurch and the door whisked open onto eleven thousand square feet of marble, mahogany and marquetry. His eyrie occupied the entire top floor of his co-op apartment building and lent him commanding views of Central Park. But the visual feast would have to wait, his magnificent home lay in darkness. Odd.

Denied his daily dose of architectural eye candy, Nelson's face fell, and he paused a beat before stepping onto the red and black marble floor of his palatial residence. *Lava floor* he called it. Because any visitor's gaze falling upon its fiery-like surface usually burned with envy. Crossing the threshold into his sanctuary, he caught the aroma of the evening meal, and the elevator door shushed behind him, shutting out the sole source of light.

Somebody forget to pay the electric bill?

No one was present to greet the master of this domain. It was futile to call out his wife's name, especially if she were on the other side of their cavernous home. Navigating in the gloom, he laid his weathered Finlay briefcase on the Chippendale side table, shrugged out of his wrinkled Burberry trench coat and hung it from memory in the double-wide closet. Per his routine, he visited his office and deposited his briefcase on the inlaid marquetry desk fashioned from handcrafted mahogany. Thousands of lights sparkled beyond the floor-to-ceiling windows like so many diamonds. But he didn't linger to admire the urban view for he sensed a game was afoot.

He exited his office and crept along the marble hallway decorated with avant garde canvases and sculptures rendered by artists he couldn't tell from cartoons. His wife, Sharron, with the help of Nora, an interior designer, had curated the artwork to speak subtly to their membership in high society, but to his mind, the paintings and sculptures screamed, rather than whispered, their belonging to the One Percent. He didn't dare share this opinion with his wife. She hadn't polled him for it.

"Come out, come out wherever you are," he said in a rasp to heighten the tension of the game.

Nelson and Sharron were childless—not for any lack of effort—and so they weren't above acting silly when the mood suited them, like tonight. He slunk his way past the living room and rounded a corner towards a soft glow flickering from the dining room.

"I see light." Passing through the archway in a slight crouch, he waggled his fingers in the air.

"Gotcha!" Sharron said, grabbing him from behind.

Nelson wheeled around and gave his thirty-seven year-old wife a tight squeeze. "You're better at this game than me."

"Your clunky brogues don't help. A cowbell would be quieter," and they smothered their laughter in the fusion of their lips. Her fingers dragged his well-groomed cinnamon-colored hair while his hands roamed the smooth hills and valleys of her still firm figure. She pressed against him and purred.

Mid-kiss, Nelson opened his eyes and wondered about the burning candles on the dining room table, their lambent flames reaching for the bronzed coffered ceiling. He unlocked his lips from hers. "What's the occasion?"

She stroked his patterned Hermes silk tie, then raised her hooded emerald eyes to him. Her lustrous blonde hair, twirled atop her head, was styled the way he preferred it. "I had Renalda prepare your favorite dish for dinner: duck tartar with juniper, mustard, radish, beets, and wild black rice."

Renalda, their live-in Filipina maid, could be heard rattling around in the kitchen beyond the swinging door separating the rooms. She was probably cleaning up.

"Must be special."

Sharron returned him a coy smile.

"You want a glass of wine?" He detached himself and advanced on the well-dressed table.

"None for me, Nels."

"Since when?" he asked, wiping the spout of the '73 Chardonnay Chateau Montelena with a linen napkin. He didn't wait for her answer. "Did Kim talk you into another crazy diet?" He replaced the bottle in the silver ice bucket.

Kim was Sharron's best friend, and she had sampled every diet and exercise regimen on the planet. And then some.

"Wine isn't healthy for babies."

"You're my baby, so you're allowed to drink." He sprouted a lascivious leer. "How else can I ravish you later?"

"I am...but our baby isn't."

He pulled a stunned expression and seized up for an instant. "Wait a minute. Are you telling me you're pregnant, after all those miscarriages?"

"Close to six weeks."

"Why didn't you tell me sooner?"

"With my track record, I didn't want to give you false hope, like all those other times."

Candlelight danced in his eyes and his mind hummed with the pleasure of impending fatherhood. He tabled the crystal wine glass and pulled her into his arms again. "This calls for a celebration," he said with gusto, his face inches from hers, his delight mixed with relief. The pressure's off, he told himself. I've done my duty. I can stand down now.

"What are you grinning about?"

"Me, grin?"

"Out with it, Nels."

"After countless innings, I finally scored a home run. I think I deserve a timeout." He rubbed her nose with his.

Laughing, she carried the baseball metaphor further. "I guess you can give your bat a rest—for now." Then a devilish look captured her. "But conserve your strength. You're going to need it for future late-night feedings."

"A job for a nanny."

"Typical male!" She gave his chest a playful swat. Just then an idea lit her up. "We have to call our parents. They'll be thrilled."

He pursed his lips. Your mom can stop nagging us now about producing a grandchild. But he kept this irritation to himself. He didn't wish to spoil their evening by dragging *her* into their celebration.

Maybe Sharron read what was behind his eyes for she stepped to the table laden with covered dishware and said: "Let's eat first. The food's getting cold. I had to practically flog Renalda into preparing this feast."

"A slight exaggeration, Baby?" he said in defense of their maid. "Renalda never gives me a hard time. She's paid to serve us." And if she were younger, she could serve me in a whole different capacity.

"It's a good thing I'm in charge of the help. They'd walk all over you if you were the boss."

Nelson ignored her comment and patted his stomach absent the flesh of success despite his affluence. "It smells so good. I'm starved." He helped Sharron into her high-backed chair swathed in burgundy and gold silk damask. He seated himself at the other end of the lengthy table and raised his crystal glass, candlelight glittering in it. "To our future progeny. May our child carry forth our good names and be a worthy heir to us," he laid on thickly.

Sharron giggled. "When did we become bluebloods?"

"We have enough money to buy a royal title from a down-in-his-luck duke."

"British royalty doesn't have the prestige it used to. The current crop of commoners have cheapened the cachet of the Windsors."

"An aristocracy of middling mediocrity. On second thou—"

"Where's Renalda?" She gritted her teeth. "Ring the damn bell."

Nelson rode her squall of erratic temper with calm and jingled a little silver bell. Renalda, a still handsome dark-haired, middle-aged woman wearing a maid's modest black and white uniform, promptly appeared.

"We're hungry. Serve us," Sharron ordered.

Nelson sympathized. "Mrs. McCormack informed me you prepared my favorite dish."

"Mr. McCormack, it is my pleasure," she said in Filipina-accented English. It came out as: *Meester MeeCormack, it ees my pleasor*.

"I'm grateful to you."

"I pray for health of your little one."

Bowled over. "You're aware of this news already?" he asked while he reproached his wife with his eyes.

"I told *you* to keep it a secret."

Renalda ignored her mistress.

Nelson set aside his annoyance. "We've waited so long for this moment to arrive." He faced Sharron again. "And we'll spare no expense to ensure our child grows up in a safe and healthy environment."

"Enough with the useless chatter," Sharron said.

With deliberate movements, Renalda, a sly smile on her lips, served them dinner.

Between mouthfuls Nelson asked: "Did your doctor say it's okay for you to continue working?"

"My job isn't strenuous, Nels."

He conceded her point. "What about your power walks?"

"I need to stay in shape for the sake of the baby."

"I know, but I'm concerned for both of you. I'm surprised your doctor didn't confine you to bed."

"My doctor said we'll take my pregnancy one trimester at a time."

"Your doctor knows your medical history better than I do."

"She does, so drop it."

Parsing her statement for hidden meaning was unnecessary, so he changed subjects. "Imagine, Baby, we'll have one of our own to helm the family firm when I retire."

"What makes you think our child will follow in your footsteps? He or she might want to be an artist or a musician."

Sharron's response was so unexpected he couldn't process it.

"A McCormack has always occupied my great-granddaddy's chair."

"Maybe so, but I hope there's room in your great-granddaddy's grave to roll over should your company tradition become a thing of the past."

Nelson dropped the matter. There was nothing to be gained by arguing about a hypothetical. "How's the duck?"

"A touch gamey."

"Wild meat has a unique flavor."

"I'm glad one of us is enjoying it."

"It's an acquired taste, Baby." Memories of duck hunting with his father among the bulrushes of a pond in upstate New York flashed by.

"Why can't you eat chicken like everyone else?"

"Because I'm special."

"You're *special* all right," she said in her best Church Lady voice.

He laughed. "Good one!"

Pleased with herself, she asked: "What's the plan for this evening?"

He played with his food before answering. "I'm feeling hopeful, so how does planning our baby's bedroom decor sound to you?"

"Great idea." She barely paused a breath when she said: "I'll give Nora a call. She can brainstorm with us."

Nelson did his best not to allow his disapproval to show itself. He put on his game face. "Isn't it a bit late to call her?"

"The self-employed don't keep regular hours, Nels. Not if they want our business." She practically danced in her seat. "Hurry up and finish so we can start."

So much for *our* celebration. He smothered his unhappiness. "Go ahead and get the ball rolling. I'll join you when I'm done."

"It'll be a ton of fun." Pushing herself away from the table, she suggested: "Let's have dessert in the den."

"I'll inform Renalda."

"Don't be too long." Then she disappeared.

He didn't count on being consulted for his decorating ideas. But it would be expected of him to gush over Sharron's and Nora's design choices once they were decided. And to pay for them.

"The hoops a husband has to jump through for the sake of marital peace."

When done eating, he rang the silver bell. Renalda materialized moments later.

"Yes, Mr. McCormack?"

"The boss wants dessert served in the den."

A smile almost made it to her lips before she nodded her compliance.

Nelson looked to the archway then back at her. In a guarded voice he said: "I apologize for my wife's behavior, Renalda. I appreciate all you do for us."

"I no mind, Mr. McCormack. I use to it."

"Her pregnancy is playing with her hormones," he offered as an excuse. "I'll mention to Mrs. McCormack to lighten up."

She returned him a blank look.

Nelson clued in. "*Lighten up* means to take matters less seriously."

A light went on in her eyes. "I understand now. You good man, Mr. McCormack"

"I hope so." He finished with a wink and left.

He entered the den and found Sharron in animated conversation with whom he guessed must be Nora. She paid him no attention. He pulled his mobile from his rear pocket and sat opposite her. His thumb swiped the screen several times until it found the Dark Web app. He entered a long password and waited for the video to start. Cheering erupted from the phone and, in a panic, he hurriedly lowered the volume. He glanced over at his wife and her eyes were shooting daggers at him. He mouthed her a silent apology. A no-rules fight-to-the-death was in progress on the tiny screen. He settled back to watch the bare-knuckled mortal combat while Sharron enthused over Nora's suggestions. It was going to be a long, lonely evening, but the fights would keep him entertained, especially the gruesome finales. He was thankful to be a spectator. He couldn't imagine what it must be like to be one of the fighters in the ring, brawling to keep his head.

Chapter Two

Meanwhile, worlds away, in a grittier part of town, Tommaso "Rommy" Romano, a loyal senior soldier in the Cabreezi gang, sat in his partner's rolling car and gazed out the spotless windshield at graffiti-tagged buildings, abandoned businesses, and overgrown fenced-in lots, parading by like props in a post-apocalyptic movie. The urban blight stirred up treasured memories of his youth.

"I can't believe how much this hood has changed since I was a kid," he of thinning hair and red-veined nose said to Bronco, sitting alert behind the wheel, the outlines of his harsh features limned by the glow of the dashboard. "There was a time when such blight"—Rommy waved toward the street—"was a common sight throughout the Bronx."

Bronco grunted, his attention focused on the dark road ahead.

Rommy sat in contemplative silence for several beats, savoring distant recollections in the rearview mirror of his mind. "We used to play a game when we were kids to keep ourselves amused while my parents shuttled us around town in the family minivan. It was real simple. The first one to spot a scrapshack earned a point. A piece of cake at the time." He dragged out a sigh. "Nowadays, you have to search real hard for a building worthy of a wrecking ball. Whatever happened to urban decay?"

"Gentrifrication is what happened," Bronco said, unaware of his mispronunciation.

"I don't know what that prissy word means but I bet it involves screwing the working man and putting affordable housing out of his reach."

"The American dream is a house of cards built on a foundation of unpayable debt."

Stunned, Rommy faced him. "Aren't you a fountain of knowledge this evening?"

"Don't be fooled by the news spinners, Rommy. Lowlifes in the tens of thousands are overdosing every year because America passed its best before date decades ago. Hope and opportunity are slogans, not realities, for most people."

Rommy stared at Bronco for an extended beat. "Yeah, but it's good for business. Those lowlifes can't flee their miserable circumstances, so they escape them temporarily with the right fix."

Bronco shot him a rare grin.

Rommy changed subjects. "Ever wonder why they call this crib the 'Big Apple?'"

Bronco's face scrunched up. "What's with you? You got a thing for city slogans? Yesterday, it was Chicago and its broad shoulders."

While Rommy stewed, jazz trumpeter Chet Baker, the "prince of cool," playing quietly on the radio, filled the tense space with syncopated rhythms as they cruised west along East 135th.

"It beats yacking about shoptalk twenty-four-seven," he griped to the windshield. "And it's 'big shoulders.'"

Bronco gave a shrug as if to say, "Whatever."

Undeterred, Rommy carried on with his spiel. "New York got its nickname from a horse racing reporter name John Fitz Gerald—and, no, he's not related to the famous writer." As if he'd know, Rommy sneered. "Anyway, while on the beat in New Orleans in 1920, Gerald supposedly overheard a couple of stable hands talking about an impending trip to the 'big apple.' Turns out they were referring to our fair city because in horse-racing circles it was considered big league. Gerald liked the phrase so much he included it from that point on in his sports columns."

"You don't say."

Encouragement? Whatever is was, Rommy seized upon it. "The nickname was eventually embraced by jazz players for the same reason jockeys did: you weren't in the big leagues until you performed in the Big Apple."

Enthusiasm must then have taken hold of Bronco. "It sounds better than Big Swindle," he said. "I mean, Big Apple is more inspiring than Big Swindle."

"Or Big Deal."

Bronco twerked an eyebrow at him. "Here's the thing. A red apple beats the image of hordes of suckers failing to make it big in this town."

"Yeah, the dreamers keep settling here to take a bite out of the apple."

"Only to discover the remains of a core crawling with worms."

"But this doesn't stop them dreamers from fighting over the rotting remains."

Bronco carried it further. "We got to fight our way into this world. We got to fight for our share in this world. Then we got to fight to protect our share."

"We crawl and scrape for our slice of the apple, no matter how chewed up it is. Take that homeless dude over there," Rommy said, pointing.

A hatted man garbed in what appeared to be several layers of frayed clothing had laid claim to a derelict storefront nook, a refuge from the elements. A dented shopping cart filled with his personal possessions was parked on the sidewalk. A layer of cardboard provided him a mattress of sorts.

"He's seized his piece of the American Dream," Rommy continued as they drove past. "A place to call his own for the night. And it's rent-free."

"Yeah," Bronco agreed. "Some individuals can't hack the nine-to-five circus. Juggling a job, paying bills, staying clean, so they drop out."

"Sucks to be poor in this city."

"Sucks to be poor, period."

"Yeah."

Talked out, they settled into companionable silence while the mean streets slid by.

Just then Bronco slammed the steering wheel and Rommy jumped three inches in the air.

"What's gotten into you?"

"Nothing."

"So, you almost broke the steering wheel because...it was in the way?"

Bronco stared straight ahead. "Nico's in the way. He's a bamboo shoot beneath my fingernail."

But what he didn't say was Nico was a roadblock in his efforts to win the undivided respect of the don. If Nico was removed from the scene, Bronco's own bright light would catch the don's sole attention. So he imagined.

"If he weren't Cabreezi's spawn, I'd whack him."

Bronco shot him a predatory glare. "Dangerous talk. One word and you're on ice."

Ignoring the truth of his dispensability, Rommy said: "But you wouldn't."

"Overconfidence killed the cat."

Rommy let his blunder pass. "We've been crewing together for what?"—he paused to calculate—"Seventeen, eighteen years? And in all this time you never tipped no one off to their blind date with doom."

"I'm going to have to change partners."

"What for?"

"Predictability."

"Predictable's beneficial," Rommy said to assuage him. "Beneficial for me. It keeps me out of trouble. Know what I mean?"

"I do, and it means you could be withholding vital info."

Rommy balanced on danger's edge. "Whoa, Bronco. Remember the time I shared with you news of Louie skimming the family?"

"Don't remind me of your no-good brother."

"He got his due because of me." *And maybe you will too.* Hot revenge smoldered in him.

"It couldn't have been easy to whack your own blood."

Rommy turned away. "Rules are rules," and he balled his brawny fists in his lap until they hurt.

"If you hadn't, you'd be garden compost too."

Rommy's thoughts zoomed back to the night his younger brother was fed feet first into a meat grinder, an inch at a time, while Bronco managed the controls. He suppressed the urge to shiver. Louie's screams still gave him occasional night terrors despite the passage of nearly three years. Sadists. Every one of them. But not him. Staying alive was important to him, no more, no less than the next fella. Sacrificing his own brother was his ticket to salvation.

"You did the right thing," Bronco said as though getting a read on Rommy's inner turmoil.

"I'm glad he was my only brother."

Bronco snorted at his gallows humor, and he swung the car left off of Walton Avenue onto East 146th. Rommy joined in the laughter.

No use anguishing over spilt blood, he consoled himself.

"Did I ever tell you the don appreciated your loyalty to the family? He said you were a stand-up guy."

No greater compliment could be paid to a fella.

"It was generous of the don to say so." But the praise didn't erase Rommy's guilt for having helped convert his brother into chopped liver. Nothing would. "You know, to this day I still can't figure out why Louie acted so stupid," he lied.

"Stupid is as stupid does. Leave it at that."

Rommy detected an unspoken warning in his partner's words.

Silence descended once more and Chet Baker played on.

"Keep what I'm about to tell you to yourself," Bronco said.

"I don't tell nobody nothing. Not even Rosie."

"The gooks have a contract out for Nico's head."

"Do you have to call them names?"

"Oh, that's right. Your daughter married one of them."

This was damn nearest to an apology Rommy would ever receive from his partner.

"What'd he do?" Rommy asked.

"Nico killed Johny Thai's brother a few months ago."

"Over what?"

"Dissed him, I heard."

"Figures."

Bronco took umbrage with Rommy's dismissive attitude. "*Respect* is what separates us from the animal kingdom."

"I thought it was exercise, but what the hell do I know?"

Bronco threw him an odd look. "All to say the gooks may take care of my problem for me."

"We can pray, can't we?"

"I'm not a praying man. Praying didn't help my mother, so I chucked it in."

"Me neither. Lots of people fall off the holy wagon."

"I didn't fall. I jumped."

His quip got a chuckle out of Rommy.

"Here we are," Bronco announced, parking in the darkness beneath the smooth concrete belly of the Major Deegan Expressway which snaked away into the gloom.

"Where's here?"

"We got to take us a little walk."

They alighted from the car and the horn beeped twice, affirming the doors were locked. Bronco and Rommy strode with purpose in the gloom and traffic rumbled and roared above them.

"Did you know, in the 1920s, the Noe-Schultz gang relocated the headquarters of its growing bootlegging operation from the Bronx to East 149th in Manhattan?" This from Rommy.

"What are you now, a tour guide?"

Rommy ignored the jibe and plowed on with his tale. "I watch the History Channel. Anyway, Jack 'Legs' Diamond, the leader of New York's Irish Mob, felt challenged by this bold move, so he launched a bootleg war against the Noe-Schultz gang."

"Ancient history."

"Noe died of infected wounds from an assassination attempt committed by a member of the Jewish Mob."

"I'm not worried. We're not a war with any rival family, so we'll probably die of boredom."

"New York has a fascinating history of crime. Maybe when we're six feet under, historians will immortalize us like they did with Capone and Luciano."

"Only if our descendants become historians." Bronco laughed at his own wit.

Rommy gave up on his hope of being celebrated by historians. "Are we close?" He scanned left and right while his hand gripped a gun in his coat pocket. Bronco stared straight ahead, unconcerned with their surroundings. Both were packing but it wasn't much consolation; other armed thugs prowled this part of the Bronx.

"You'll see."

Bronco stopped at a steel door and pressed a buzzer.

"What?" a hollow tin-can voice asked over the intercom. That's it. One word.

"Bronco," he growled.

A metallic *click* resounded and Bronco pulled the handle. "After you."

Rommy peered into the dark void, then back at Bronco. "What is this place?"

"Patience," he said with a rare mischievous smile, and he urged him on with a toss of his head. Rommy's throat bobbed before he plunged into the murk, and his bulky partner clomped behind him. Out of nowhere yellow light and the roar of a blood-thirsty crowd burst into the unlit corridor up ahead.

The knot in Rommy's gut loosened. A huge doorman in a black suit, shirt, and tie placed his frying pan-sized hand on Rommy's chest to prevent him from joining the rowdy crowd inside. When Bronco entered the scene and said: "He's with me," the doorman removed his outsized appendage.

Surrounding a small sunken ring, delirious men crammed onto steep bleachers cheered on two bloodied fighters exchanging bare-knuckled blows in a battle for survival. A burly valet escorted Rommy and Bronco to a private ring-side booth.

"What is this?" Rommy shouted at Bronco.

"Human cockfighting," he yelled back, his thumb extended.

Caught up with the baying crowd, they abandoned themselves to the frenzied slugfest.

There were no timed rounds. The opponents fought until one of them could no longer stand. But the brutal tournament didn't end with a simple knockdown.

Shaking his head later in the parking lot, "Unfrigginbelievable," Rommy said to Bronco on their way back to the car.

"Quite the show, heh?"

Rommy remained too astonished to reply. He had seen his share of inhumanity in his life but he had never witnessed a beheading, let alone multiple beheadings in one setting. Three matches had been fought. At the end of each, a sword on a velvet cushion borne by a masked bikini-clad female was presented to the winner who sealed his victory by beheading the loser with the sword. If this wasn't carnage enough, the victor paraded the bloody head around the ring for the pay-per-view audience watching on the Dark Web.

"With the popularity of MMA fighting and the money it generates, Don Cabreezi upped the ante and created this fight fest for fans who crave it savage. Each fight earns him tens of millions of dollars from a worldwide audience," Bronco said.

"Who're the fighters?"

"Desperate young men seeking to escape the dungholes of Asia, Africa and Latin America. They're easy targets. We fill their heads with dreams of living here, the land of the free and the home of the brave and other such drivel."

"Human trafficking."

"It's a growing concern. Our grunts are skilled at producing refugees, and we're skilled at finding them refuge. Short term of course."

"Of course," Rommy said, no sarcasm in his tone. *Is there no bottom to this hell?*

"The next phase of this venture is a female edition. It'll top the male cockfights."

"No doubt."

His comment went unacknowledged, for Bronco was too busy shadowboxing. "Women are dirtier fighters than men." Despite being a hefty guy, he moved like a dancer in his snakeskin boots.

"I wouldn't know."

He lowered his fists. "You will soon." He swatted Rommy on the back, almost knocking him off his feet.

"Those fights"—Rommy motioned rearward with his head—"explain the headless bodies in the news."

"Got to dump them somewhere."

"How do you keep this operation under the radar?"

"*Omertà.*"

The Mafia code of silence. The implication was not lost on Rommy.

Bronco carried on, "The spectators are made men and the goombahs disposing the bodies aren't connected to the fights, so they're none the wiser."

"And nobody's filing reports for missing illegals," Rommy finished for him.

"You catch on quick."

Rommy offered a modest shrug. "Comes with the territory."

"The don's a genius."

Rommy weighed other choice words to describe Cabreezi but sharing them with Bronco would probably earn him a place in the ring. The don could do no wrong in Bronco's eyes. He was Cabreezi's boy, like a second son.

"He has a flair for business."

"I'm in the mood for pizza," Bronco announced.

How can he be hungry after what we just witnessed? Nothing phases this mook. "Sure, Bronco. Beheadings stimulate my appetite."

"Me too," he said. "We'll get extra pepperoni."

Chapter Three

In the beehive of the Central Park Precinct, Senior Detective Terrell Ambrose, he of gray steel-wool hair and bulbous face, bent to retrieve the police bulletin from the printer tray. Scrolling through digital text on a screen wasn't real to him. He was old school. He appreciated the tactile sensation of holding a piece of paper and perusing words printed in black and white. "Tree killer," whispered those behind his back too timid to tell him so to his face. Bulletin in hand, he read while he trundled back to his desk. Swear words traveled to the tip of his tongue and stopped there. Over thirty-two years on the force and he still hadn't seen the entire range of people's inhumanity to their fellow citizens. When he believed he had, a perp short one rocker on his mental rocking chair committed a crime to top all others. Until the next time.

"Heads up," a passing colleague cautioned him in the corridor.

Ambrose ignored the collegial warning. Back at his desk he glanced up from the paper at his partner Camila Sandanos, she of long black hair and smooth complexion.

"From your expression, I'm guessing nothing good?" she said.

He nodded in way that suggested grim news was coming. "Three more non-Caucasian headless bodies discovered overnight."

"Not again," her face said. "Which precinct?"

"Not ours, thank God." He laid the printout on his desk facing his partner's and folded his beefy but still muscular frame into the government-issued office chair. "The 34th drew the short stick this time."

"Lucky them—and us. Our case backlog can't handle anymore murders. How many headless victims in total now?"

"I stopped counting when the Feds took over."

"You know what's strange?"

"No."

"Decapitated corpses showing up in threes at a time."

"So."

"*So*, this tells me there's a fight club operating in this city."

Ambrose assumed a contemplative pose. "Could be. Every coroner report mentions the injuries to the hands and faces of the victims are consistent with hand-to-hand combat."

"And what's even more peculiar, they're non-Caucasians."

"Some enterprising white supremacists are running a private fight-to-the-death competition?"

"It wouldn't surprise me what with the significant uptick in white extremism." This earned her a grim nod from Ambrose. "Let's suppose we're on the money. How do we explain the absence of leaks about this underground fight club?"

The senior detective reclined and focused on the ceiling. Maybe the answer was written in the stained white tiles. Sounds of the office intruded into the conversational void. A possible answer came to him and he lowered his gaze. "Secret membership?"

"I was thinking along those same lines."

"But if it's secret, how does one join?"

She picked up a pen and spun it with her index finger over her thumb, like the Maverick character in *Top Gun*. "Invitation only?"

"People trusted to keep their mouths shut." He envied her dexterity with the pen. He had tried her trick many times but couldn't get the hang of it.

"An exclusive club of like-minded barbarians."

"Do we have any such clubs in our fair city?" Ambrose posed the question in a knowing way.

"The Italian Mafia. The Russian Mafia. The Irish Mafia. The list's as long as it's notorious."

"Any rumors circulating?"

"None of our informants is singing a tune worth listening to."

"And the Feds aren't a gusher of info either," Ambrose complained.

The pen stilled. "*Naturalemente.* They covet the glory for themselves."

"They haven't ruled out a serial killer committing these beheadings."

"A dubious theory," she said. "Unless the serial killer has a partner or two."

"I'm of the same mind."

"The Feds have their work cut out for them."

"No pun intended?" he asked.

"Sometimes an expression cuts both ways."

He pantomimed an explosion. "Anyway, this case is out of our jurisdiction, so let's not waste any more time busting our heads over it." He slid the bulletin aside and leaned on his forearms. "Bring me up to speed on the Cabreezi surveillance."

"Our watchers reported no unusual visitors overnight."

"You think he's aware we're casing his building?"

"If I were in his Guccis, I would assume so and take prophylactic measures."

Detective Ambrose had it in for Cabreezi like Agent Eliot Ness had it in for Al Capone. Several years back, one of Cabreezi's soldiers had shot and killed his long-term partner. Although the soldier went to prison for life, Ambrose held Cabreezi responsible for the death of his friend and colleague. He vowed from that day forward he'd clip Cabreezi's wings and lock him up in a steel cage. Exacting revenge was the solitary obstacle standing between him and his long overdue retirement party.

"Pro-fi-what?"

"Prophylactic," Sandanos repeated. "It means preventive."

"Birth control?"

She bobbed her head, trying not to chuckle. "Sort of. In Cabreezi's case it's a matter of dodging *in flagrante delicto*."

"If this means catching him with his pants down, I'm all for it."

Camila tossed out a laugh. "Luckily for him adultery isn't a crime, otherwise, he would've been in prison long ago."

"Let's slip a word to his wife and maybe she'll can him for us."

"She's aware of his philandering. It's on the tapes."

"I must have skipped that part," and he pulled on his bottom eyelid. "Then why doesn't she throw the bum out?"

Sandanos shot him a "Are you crazy?" look.

"What I'd say wrong?"

"His wife is from the old country—devout Catholic—so divorce is out of the question."

Ambrose's chest heaved. "I don't understand why women suffer in silence. If I so much as gave another woman the once-over, Shanice would castrate me."

"The city should hire her to neuter the tomcats in this precinct."

"She'd be glad to be of service."

"So where were we?"

"We were discussing the matrimonial harmony of the Cabreezis." Ambrose waved his hand to continue.

"The don maintains his wife in style. Nice clothes, nice vacations, nice homes. For some women these things are sufficient recompense."

"More akin to an unholy compromise."

"Separate bedrooms keeps it civil."

"They also ensure a decent night's sleep."

Sandanos questioned him with her eyes.

"My snoring kept Shanice awake for years," he explained. "Earplugs helped. But once the kids moved out, she exiled me to a distant bedroom."

"Poor Shanice."

"Why do women get all the sympathy?"

"Because men deserve all the grief. What could be better?"

"I hope I'm around when you're married so I can counsel your husband in the techniques of marital self-defense."

"Not a chance!"

Ambrose swallowed a mouthful of black coffee and changed course. "I suppose we should tackle our caseload."

"Got to keep the taxpayers happy."

"Not to mention *Hizzoner* who's pinning his re-election on lowering major crime," he muttered.

"Don't look now but here comes the lieutenant," Sandanos whispered.

Ambrose resisted the urge to peek behind him. "Time for our morning pep talk."

"Ever wonder whose side she's on?"

"The one who rips the smallest chunk out of her behind."

Sandanos coughed to stifle her snickering.

"Good morning, *detectives*," their superior officer said, stopping at the end of their desks. They identified the ice in her tone.

"Morning, Lieutenant," they said in unison like cooperative schoolkids, fake smiles planted on their lips.

"I know you know what I'm about to say but I'll say it anyway." But not before she scowled at them. "I got chewed out again by the captain who was chewed out by the police commissioner who was chewed out by the mayor. So now it's your turn," she said, flicking her eyes from one to the other.

"Hold on there, Lieutenant," Ambrose said, raising his palm to forestall her. "If you chew off any more of my butt, there won't be any cushion left."

Sandanos couldn't help burst out laughing, and, much to their amazement, so did the lieutenant.

"Score one for you, Ambrose," the lieutenant said through her tittering. When it had subsided, she added: "Do your best," and walked off.

The coast clear, Sandanos and Ambrose exchanged a high-five. "Your wisecrack spared our *derrieres* for another day," she said.

"Laughter is a tonic for whatever ails us."

"Let's get to work before the lieutenant nails us."

"Yeah, let's."

Chapter Four

Lorenzo, a low-echelon hood in the Cabreezi family, met Yolanda the old-fashioned way—through an online dating site. She was a psychology major in her senior year at NYU. He wangled a date out of her with the promise to participate in a psychology test. Whatever it measured, he must have passed; she joked the test determined he wasn't a serial killer. If only she knew, he had informed her on their first coffee date.

Much to his surprise—and ego—his lack of higher education didn't affect his chances with her. Having a job and an apartment were in his favor, and his sense of humor sealed the deal. Several months later, their relationship deepened and Yolanda hinted around about living together.

"Why maintain two apartments when we can share the expenses of one?" she had suggested all innocent-like in the afterglow of coupling one evening.

A perfectly logical and reasonable but dead-on-arrival proposal demanded a perfectly logical and reasonable but evasive answer.

"Smart thinking, Yolanda. But I'm the marrying type of guy, so shacking up would cheapen our relationship," he wanted to say, but didn't. (She might call his bluff and then he'd find himself in much hotter *and* deeper water.) So Lorenzo ducked and dodged whenever she broached the subject of creating a nest for two, and the effort made him dizzy on occasion. A kind of sport for him. Then she got pregnant. And the stakes soared skyward. But he held his ground, slippery though it was. He wondered if her getting knocked up was to trap him into a long-term relationship. Pretty evil if she did. She swore she had taken the pill daily, but he still harbored doubts.

The pressure to cohabit grew heavier as Yolanda's belly grew bigger. And she laid on the guilt.

Our child will need his father, she never failed to remind him.

Our child? Was he really going to be a dad at twenty-one years of age? Unless something terrible happened to the fetus, changing dirty diapers was his destiny. Where to turn to for help? His mother was dead and his father was a ghost, so he couldn't ask them for advice.

He had no siblings either. And seeking religious counsel was a non-starter for he could predict what those pro-family ministers would tell him in solemn tones:

"Assume your responsibilities, young man, for the sake of the child."

Lorenzo figured they wouldn't care to hear what *his* emotional needs were.

So here he was three years later in Yolanda's living room and not any wiser. His mind continued to meander while she lacerated his conscience with her sharp tongue. This wasn't the first time, but he bet it was the last. He watched her lips move but he heard no sound.

Stalemate best described their relationship. The fault was his. He stood accused of paternal neglect. Guilty!, the jury proclaimed. No weaseling his way out. Sentencing was next.

A long-time building, this day of reckoning didn't surprise him. But why it had taken so long to reach this stage did. Must be due to Yolanda's coming to the conclusion he couldn't be reformed. And she was so right. The hardships a mother endured for her child. Give her points for perseverance.

A framed picture of Ali, their three-year-old son, snagged his attention. Had it already been three years? *Damn*. Another year and he'll be in pre-K. And you won't be there to wave to him when he enters the school. Loser! He searched in himself for the sentiment of paternity and came up empty. Shame on you, he scolded himself. Self-reflection was often a stepping stone to self-correction. Not so with him.

He hadn't bargained for a son when he hooked up with Yolanda. But mistakes happened. He couldn't tell her this. Why couldn't he do the moral thing and be the father Ali deserved? He needed no time to answer his question: Freedom! Glorious, selfish freeee-dom. And he hated himsel—

Her shrill voice yanked him back to the present. "Look at me when I'm talking to you."

He ceased daydreaming and examined her. Anger contorted her face but it didn't diminish her beauty.

"You're either a full-time father or you're out of our lives," Yolanda said.

The options she presented were stark, one no less awful than the other. He sensed his days of being a hound were hurtling toward a shameful end. A doghouse loomed on his immediate horizon. Committing hari-kari was the honorable thing—the manly thing—to do, but he didn't wish to create a mess on her living room carpet. Besides, she hated his guts, so why spill them at her feet?

He rasped his stubbly pale face with his hands and let them flop into his lap. "I guess I should go."

She thrust forward in the armchair, eyes bulging. "Go?" she challenged. "Slink away is more apt." She ached for him to take a stand. To be responsible. To man up. Alas, he wasn't the kind of man she needed.

"I'm sorry, Lan," he said in defeat. "I can't be the man you wish me to be."

"Ain't that the truth!"

Lorenzo unfolded his lanky frame from the couch. He felt beaten. The tongue-lashing eliminated whatever fight in him he might have possessed. "Take care, Lan. I'll be in touch."

She shifted to watch him go, and he didn't see her tears brimming.

Lorenzo exited the lobby of the Yonkers apartment building and sniffed the balmy October air perfumed with the pungent scent of decomposing leaves. Hands in his jacket pockets, he lingered on the cement pathway in the glow of street lighting and contemplated his next move. Too dejected for companionship, he summoned an Uber cab to whisk him back to his apartment on 35th in Hell's Kitchen.

Lorenzo entered his darkened home, pried off his running shoes with his feet and hung his jacket in the hallway closet. No pet greeted him. His job didn't permit furry frills. This was partly true. The real reason was to avoid any responsibility for a dependent creature. When it came down to it, feeding and grooming himself taxed him. Both efforts met the standard of good enough. Barely.

He grabbed the last Corona from the fridge, padded to the living room, and flopped onto the couch. A twist of the cap and a *pst* broke the silence. He tilted his head and felt the cold amber liquid burn a trail down the length of his throat. His thoughts switched to the top—or nadir—of the day.

Women are so needy. Why can't they separate their feelings from sex? Would be *so* much smoother if they did. No guilt, no phony lines, no promises to call. Unzip, dip and skip. Smiles and high-fives all around.

He took a long swig of beer and rested the perspiring bottle in his lap. You're expecting *way* too much. But the way society's going, I might live to see my wish come true. His flight of imagination soared. Got to stay positive. My dream girl's out there somewhere.

Done with fantasizing, he reached for the TV remote laying on the table.

There's always the realm of fantasy women to compensate.

Chapter Five

Following the fights, Bronco dropped Rommy off at his apartment in Yonkers and now he coasted into his darkened driveway on Florence Street in Floral Park and killed the engine. He alighted from his car and closed the door with a gentle *clunk*, not wanting to disturb his slumbering neighbors. Respectful behavior was the price of remaining inconspicuous in a borough inhabited by middle-class clock watchers. His neighbors believed he worked the night-shift at a private security firm (a story he had told them when he relocated to this street years ago). It explained his rare daytime appearances. Hiding in plain sight was the cleverest way to conceal his true profession.

Standing beside the car in front of his two-storey cottage, thick arms hanging at his sides, he savored the crisp nocturnal air scented with freshly clipped grass. Tyrone, a teenager living three doors down, must have given the lawn mower a workout earlier. Deep night was Bronco's favorite time. Quiet reigned—except for the chirping of crickets—and so did anonymity. The nine-to-five routine tended to curb owlish pastimes in this neighborhood. His sniff of nighttime air indulged, Bronco dug out his wallet and removed forty dollars. Up the brick path he strode to the small covered porch and he slipped two of Ol' Hickory into the mailbox. Tyrone would fish for them later in the day on his way to school. He grabbed his mail and lingered on the concrete stoop while his eyes roved the street. No suspicious cars loitered.

Bronco entered his home and changed the alarm system setting to Stay mode. A meow greeted him, and he felt Rufus brush by his leg. He scooped up the Persian cat, crossed the hallway into the living room and flopped into his leather armchair, which complained at his bulk. He tossed the clutch of letters and flyers onto an occasional table. With Rufus in his lap, the mail could wait until daylight, after he had slept.

"Did you miss me?" he asked his feline friend in a soft voice, stroking its thick charcoal fur.

Rufus purred his reply.

Bronco surveyed his domain in the darkness. Neat as a shiny nickel. No clutter. No bric-a-bracs. Just clear open surfaces. The way it should be. Some people's homes brought him to the point of depression what with their junk on every table and shelf. No clean lines to admire. No open surfaces to place a book on. Clutter from floor to ceiling. Made him want to swallow a bottle of Prozac.

None of his possessions would be out of place in any of his neighbors' homes. Not even the Beretta laying on the table next to his chair. Especially the Beretta. The quality of his furnishings might be superior, but a sofa was still a sofa and a lamp was still a lamp. Purpose had nothing to do with price. But comfort? Not always. He recalled the modern furniture store he visited alone in Manhattan last year. Expensive but delicate *objets d'arts* designed for pansies desiring to impress folks. Flimsy furniture wouldn't survive a day against his bulk. He snickered at the memory.

Then Bronco's contemplations drifted to the solid wood furniture his papa used to craft back when America manufactured goods. Goods of much better-quality than low-cost, low quality junk produced by foreigners. His papa had been fortunate. He retired with a healthy pension before American manufacturing was packed up and shipped south to Mexico or to overseas sweatshops. Those were the days. A time when things were built to last and employees were fairly compensated for their labors. So he believed.

Rufus let out a meow.

Bronco came out of his reverie and discovered he was petting him too firmly. "Sorry, buddy." He changed positions in the chair. Maybe the politicians will bring the factories back, he thought, and, with them, jobs. And maybe Congress will cut the deficit, he scoffed. Unlikely, politicians' promises being as reliable as an Amtrak train. It was stupid to think the past could be undone.

All Bronco had ever wanted in his former life was to be a woodworker like his papa had been. From a young age, he had set his mind on following his old man's footsteps. The smell of sawdust was like ambrosia to him. But life intervened. An assault charge landed him a stretch at Spofford, the former juvenile detention facility in the Bronx. Bronco was a minority in this penal institution. To say life was rough for Bronco would be an understatement. Incidents happened to him, unspeakable incidents. Upon release, all dreams of being a woodworker had vanished. He didn't resume his last year of high school studies.

For several years he drifted, trying his hand at an assortment of odd jobs. And in the course of this varied employment, he discovered a liking for bouncing patrons from bars. Working as a bouncer gave him a sense of power over people, a power he sorely lacked while doing time at Spofford.

Then Cabreezi, an up-and-coming hood who was shopping around for muscle, popped into Bronco's life and propelled it in a new direction. But not in the way he expected. Bronco had come to Cabreezi's attention through word of mouth. He tracked down Bronco at a bar a friend of his owned on Third Avenue in the Bronx where Bronco was working as a bouncer. He was taken by Cabreezi's flashy clothing and shiny wheels, trappings any young man whose sap was running high would covet for himself.

Over a beer at the bar, Cabreezi informed his prospective acolyte of the two avenues open to a young man hungering for respect: create something people will remember you for when you're dust, or build a reputation people will talk about generations from now. The first way took too long, Cabreezi explained. You were usually dead before the masses noticed your talent and only if the self-appointed *think-they-know-better* elitist scum deigned to inform them. The second way to gain respect was quicker and easier, but you had to operate under the legal radar, he said with a glint.

Bronco clued into Cabreezi's inference, having once belonged to a street gang, his springboard to earning a fearsome reputation not only among fellow gang members but among rival gangs. Even now, after the passage of decades, the memory cheered him. So he had hitched his high hopes to Cabreezi's rising star and said to hell with the life of a lowly bouncer.

But now here he sat, feeling cheated. Not for the first time either. And probably not for the last. Sure, he had secured a formidable standing in the family, but beyond it, he was a nobody, another enforcer, and he had risen high, as high as Cabreezi had allowed him to. Meanwhile, the don reaped the lion's share of the family's lucre. Didn't seem fair. Bronco's loyalty to his boss, on the other hand, was far stronger than his desire for recognition. Not once did Bronco conspire to tip the scales in his favor. He figured he owed Cabreezi. Owed him for snatching him from a life of endless drudgery. Deserting the don or the family wasn't an option, unless he wished to dig his own grave. He couldn't quit the Mob. Uh-uh. But the Mob could quit him—for good.

Bronco brooded over his fate.

"Beats tossing people out on their arses, hey, Rufus?"

Silence answered him. He sat in the dark until drowsiness overtook him.

Later, he suffered a fitful sleep.

Like every other night.

Part II

Two Weeks Later…

Chapter Six

Yolanda's younger and only sister Teagan, frizzy-haired and aged beyond her twenty-one years, outfitted in faded jeans and a navy blue sweatshirt topped off with a jacket, shuffled without purpose in dirty white sneakers along upper Broadway, near 138th. Her eyes darted left and right, up and down, catching nothing noteworthy in the blighted borough of Manhattanville, its best days seen only in history's rearview mirror. The urban landscape, though bleak and uninspiring, and her fellow New Yorkers, though poker-faced and indifferent, were no more blameworthy for her dismal mental state than they were for the sunless sky above. In a city of millions, Teagan was friendless.

Not entirely true. Teagan hung out with a circle of male "friends" at the gack house (similar to a crack house), but they used her body to pay for the drug she craved. So they didn't really count, did they? She lost connection with the friends she had grown up with and with the new ones she had made at City College, before she dropped out. Crystal was responsible for the estrangement of her former friends. A male college friend had introduced Teagan to her. Crystal was now her best friend. How she loved Crystal for the friendship high she gave her. How she loathed Crystal for the hold she exerted on her. A love-hate relationship forged in Hell.

Teagan couldn't identify what drew her to the opaque window and caused her to stop on the cracked sidewalk. Maybe it was the word *Hope* stenciled on the glass, which began the phrase: *Hope Is a Helping Hand*. Or perhaps it was the collage of colorful images stark against the drab storefronts bookending the building. Whatever it was infused her with a sense of hope, a sentiment Crystal never offered her. Intentional or not, Crystal prevented her from experiencing hope. Some friend.

Teagan checked around. It was doubtful anyone in this neighborhood would recognize her. But still. Passersby ignored her, or pretended to.

What could it hurt? she asked herself before she yanked on the handle with her nail-bitten fingers. A bell jingled.

Unaware of what awaited her, she stepped inside...and was blown away by the tasteful decor. Comfortable-looking armchairs rested against the walls of the reception area painted in muted tones of lilac gray. Abstract art hung on the walls and soft instrumental music played in the background—the kind she'd expect to hear at one of those exclusive New Age retreats in the Poconos, a hotspot Manhattan millionaires too stressed out from counting their loot escaped to, endeavoring to reconnect with their inner lives, if they existed.

She felt better already.

Then it dawned on her why the window wasn't transparent. Every junkie in town would crash this place.

She noticed a large plate of softball-sized muffins resting on a table positioned in front of a row of armchairs. Her mouth salivated. Crystal suppressed her appetite when she was around, but she had gone away for a couple of days, so Teagan's hunger had returned. In fact, she was starving.

A dark-haired, middle-aged woman sat at the reception desk, pleasantness upon her pale features.

"Welcome, dear. They look yummy, don't they?"

She talking to me? Teagan resisted the urge to acknowledge the receptionist, mesmerized by the muffins. Her stomach grumbled.

"Please take a muffin. They're homemade. One of the counselors bakes them. She uses GMO-free organic ingredients."

In her present state, Teagan didn't care if they were prepared with GMO-free organic mud. She craved one.

"Dope!" was all she could voice, still amazed at the upscale setting surrounding her. She felt like Alice must have felt when she passed through the looking glass. She reached over, grabbed a muffin and a saucer and was poised to take a bite when the receptionist said: "It's more comfortable to eat sitting."

So Teagan sat. She resisted the urge to stuff the muffin into her mouth; she tried to eat it in a civilized manner. Despite her best efforts, crumbs spilled from her lips like hailstones. She didn't care. Impressing folks with proper table manners was the least of her present worries. While she gorged, she inspected the reception area again. The place was spotless, nicer than most of the homes of friends she had once visited, back when she was *persona grata*, before she met Crystal. She was tempted to lick her fingers but instead she reached for a napkin provided and wiped her mouth and each finger clean. Crystal hadn't completely dehumanized her.

"Tasty wasn't it?"

"My compliments to the baker."

"What's your name, dear?"

"Teagan...or Teag. Either one's okay with me." She crumpled the napkin into a ball and dropped it onto the saucer resting on her knees.

The receptionist wrote her name. "Nice to meet you Teagan. My name is Rhonda."

"Never met a Rhonda before. Congratulations on being the first."

"And what is your last name, if you don't mind me asking?"

Teagan hesitated to reply. *Maybe I've stumbled into one of those secret clinics where evil doctors harvest homeless peoples' organs and sell them to Chinese tycoons and Arab sheiks. Good luck with that...Who would want* my *organs?* Paranoia was one of the many snags of hanging around with Crystal. To hell with Crystal. Teagan gave caution the old heave-ho.

"Ryan," she said at last, placing the saucer back on the table.

Rhonda scribbled some more. "So Teagan Ryan why did you stop by today?"

Here come the questions. Teagan shrugged, then chewed her chapped lower lip for a moment. "Nothing specific. I mean, the colorful window display stopped me in my tracks. What is this place?"

"It's an addiction treatment center."

Teagan's bloodshot eyes popped. "You kidding me?"

"We take our work seriously."

"This place must be private," she guessed, taking it all in.

"Yes and no," Rhonda said, playing with her pen. "This center is privately funded, but open to the public free of charge."

"Dope!" Teagan said again. "Someone has deep pockets."

The receptionist smiled at her comment. "One way of putting it."

"So, like, what does a person have to do, you know, to enroll here?"

"A prospective candidate has to meet with a counsellor to determine their suitability for our treatment program."

"If it's free, why can't anyone join?"

"It may be free, Teagan, but we have a limited number of counsellors whose time cannot be wasted with candidates who aren't willing to work hard to overcome their addiction."

"I get you." Teagan mulled over this information. "Do they lock people in?"

"No. But if a person leaves before the treatment deadline expires, he or she cannot return. A candidate must be firm in their decision to improve." Rhonda assumed an air of compassion. "Are you ready to work on yourself, Teagan?"

She contemplated the floor. You have no place to go. Mom and dad are dead. Yolanda's apartment is off-limits. The gack house is a dump. You're out of options, girl. She fastened Rhonda with her eyes. "I'm ready." She didn't know if she was, but she hoped to crash here for a few nights. If the food was good and the treatment regimen not too strict, maybe she could hack it. Time would tell.

Joy lit up Rhonda's face. "Music to my ears." She ditched her pen. "Sit back while I check the counsellors' availabilities." Her hands moved to a computer keyboard. Above the sound of clicking keys, she made small noises to herself.

"Here we go. I found someone," she said in a sing-song voice, staring at the monitor. "Let me give her a ring."

While Rhonda spoke quietly into the phone, Teagan tingled with what she guessed must be excitement. She wasn't sure since she hadn't felt this way in so long. The prospect of seeking help was always at the back of her mind, but Crystal somehow talked her out of it each time she mustered the courage. Well, Crystal wasn't in charge anymore.

"Your counselor is on her way. She's tough, though, so don't say I didn't warn you." The pen moved in Rhonda's hand again, then she held out a business card to Teagan. "Hang on to this, dear. You may need it in the future."

Teagan gave it the once-over before sliding it into a rear pocket of her jeans and returning to her seat. She squirmed in anticipation. Someone cares. Tears welled. She smeared them with the back of her hand.

"I'm so happy for you, Teagan. You're taking the first step on the path to a new life."

A side door opened, interrupting them, and a blonde-haired woman of medium height and slim build sheathed in designer jeans and a loosely belted blouse strode into the room like she owned it. Truth was, her husband did. His charitable foundation paid the treatment center's bills.

Blondie addressed Rhonda first without acknowledging Teagan's presence. Not even a glance.

"So, Rhonda, who's next?"

There was no pleasantness in her tone.

Teagan got a sinking feeling in her belly.

Rhonda stood up behind her desk and performed the introductions.

Teagan jumped to her feet. Blondie gave her the once over, then greeted her with a tight smile and a formal greeting. Her expression said, "Not another one." Teagan felt like she had been strip-searched.

"P-pleased to meet you too, Sharron."

"We'll see." She nodded to Rhonda and whirled towards the door.

Teagan remained immobile, deliberating what to do.

Rhonda motioned vigorously for Teagan to follow the counsellor, and she gave her a wink as she hurried by.

Teagan managed to catch the door before it automatically closed. Up ahead, her designer heels clicking on the tiled floor and her curvaceous figure swaying from side to side, Sharron strutted, and Teagan saw her duck into an office on the right. Muted voices floated in the corridor as Teagan plunged deeper into the labyrinth.

She sure plays rough, like Rhonda said. Was her behavior an act to rattle her, to test her response to adversity, or was this woman, like, simply a bitch? I guess I'll find out soon enough.

Sharron was seated when Teagan entered.

"Shut the door and be seated," Sharron ordered, her hands busy sorting folders on her well-organized desk.

Teagan obeyed and sat in a chair, facing Blondie, her enthusiasm for the program beginning to wane with each passing moment.

Finished shuffling folders, Sharron edged forward and grasped her forearms on the desk. "So, when was the last time you got high?"

Teagan flinched at her accusatory tone. "Umm, two days ago."

Sharron's gaze didn't waver, nor did she blink. "What's your drug of choice?"

"Meth."

A haughty grin cracked Sharron's stiff demeanor. "Bingo!" She unfolded herself from the desk. "I figured so. You could stand to gain a few pounds." She chuckled. "Lucky you. Not many women have your underweight issue."

Teagan fidgeted in her chair. "Meth suppresses my appetite."

"*Suppresses.*" Sharron's eyebrows arched. "Such a *big* word. Your fellow meth heads use this word at the gack house? Oh yes, I speak the lingo of the street," she said, reading Teagan's mind.

Hot tears stung her cheeks, and Teagan fought the urge to wipe them. "I didn't come here to be humiliated, miss."

"Humiliation is part of the treatment program, honey," she said in a little-girl voice. "We obliterate the candidate's defenses, then we rebuild the person within."

"I-I don't..." Her voice trembled. "I came here seeking help. How does degrading me help?"

Sharron's features contorted themselves, and she shot forward in her high-backed chair. "You're not in control here, Teagan. I am!" She wagged her finger at her. "Billions of dollars taken from honest, hardworking taxpayers have been spent on trying to lift addicts like you out of the gutter for decades. But instead of living productive lives, you resort to drugs because it beats holding a job and contributing to this great city of ours."

Teagan sat rigid for a moment to gather her courage. "You don't know the first thing about me. I didn't choose to be an addict. A classmate sold me some pills to help me stay awake during exams. I didn't know they were meth. I got hooked. I want to get clean so I can finish college, like my older sister did."

Sharron dismissed her objection with a wave. "How do you pay for your drugs?"

Hesitation hovered in the air. Sharron drummed her fingers on the desk.

Teagan lowered her head. "I-I do them favors."

"Oh." Sharron wetted her lips. "Who's *them* and what *kind* of favors."

More hesitation. "I...I give out sexual favors to pay for my drugs."

"They must be desperate," Sharron said. "What kind of sexual favors," she pressed, inching closer, a layer of huskiness in her voice.

Teagan shot up. "This is too weird. I'm out of here."

"See what I mean?" Sharron said, tossing her hands in the air. "When the going gets tough, the addicts get up and go."

"I'm not quitting the program," Teagan said, her jaw clenched, tears trailing down her face. "I'm quitting you!"

"Good riddance, quitter."

But Teagan wasn't done with Sharron. "I don't know what your game is, lady, but I do know you suffer from a superiority complex. You slum around the inner city treating drug addicts because this work probably gives your empty life some meaning. Something to brag about to your equally empty high-society friends over cocktails and caviar." The full-on shock animating Sharron's face was priceless. Teagan tore out of the office and half-walked, half-ran toward the door at the far end of the hallway. Her life might have taken a healthier direction had she veered left, instead of right, when she bolted from Sharron's office. Tears blurring her vision, Teagan pushed through the fire exit and found herself in a back alley strewn with debris. Anger and shame seized her. The alley swirled in her vision. Teagan felt her resolve weaken. Crystal's voice whispered in her ear.

Her head buzzed with desperation, closing out the rest of the world. She stumbled along the alley and dug out of her jacket pocket the smartphone her dealer, Reggie, had provided to her for free. She could only use it to call him, or he would take it away from her. Teagan kept her side of the bargain. She speed dialed his number. Several anxious rings later, then a comforting male voice.

"Tea-gan. Where you been, baby?"

"I need Crystal. Now! She's-she's the only friend I have."

"Where you at?"

Teagan gave him her coordinates.

"Don't worry, baby. Crystal is on her way."

Chapter Seven

On his way home from the office, another profitable day of whipping markets worldwide under his belt, Nelson ordered Sam, his long-time chauffeur, to drop him off at the corner of Columbus and West 77th. He had planned for this moment earlier in the day to fulfill a promise to Sharron. He released Sam for the remainder of the night then alighted from the hushed interior of the glossy black Lincoln Town Car into the raucous urban street scene.

Friday evening had arrived at last in the Big Apple and the streets teemed with pent-up human fodder discharged from corporate servitude, raring to let loose with their weekend pass. Nelson marveled at the spirit of revelry in the autumn air—people laughing, people talking, people flirting—but he couldn't relate to it, having never been an inmate of the capitalist system. Born into wealth, he didn't have to work. Instead, he chose to work. The richest man in the country, according to the magazine that tracked the wealth of the uber-rich, he aspired to be the richest man in the world. And he was well on his way. Nevertheless, the energetic vibe of his fellow citizens caused a frisson of excitement to surge through him. Then it was gone. And he was neither better nor worse for the experience.

Nelson refocused his attention on tonight's daring assignment: gratify Sharron's pregnancy-induced craving for charcoal-grilled meat topped with dill pickles. Strange how hormones could transform a devoted pescetarian into a ravenous red-meat carnivore. Two weeks had passed since she announced her pregnancy and all was well. So far. The next week was critical. Sharron had never carried a pregnancy past the ninth week.

Happily, a gourmet burger shack was located a short city block from his place, so fulfilling his quest would not require a sortie through the backstreet warrens of this urban jungle. An added bonus, it was safe enough for him to travel the rest of the short way home on foot from the eatery and enjoy the mild fall weather.

He opened the door of the restaurant to a babel of foreign tongues and accents and joined the conga line of fellow carnivores, a rare event for him. Most times, he enjoyed meals with Sharron prepared by Renalda. This brief field trip would do him well, if only to mingle with the natives of his fair city and satisfy his latent anthropological curiosity. Adopting a neutral expression, he examined his fellow citizens up close and personal, foraging for their daily sustenance, and it all seemed so exotic, so foreign...so...safari-like!, he decided upon. Their accents and mannerisms, their bizarre tattoos and neon hair colorings, their facial ornaments and outlandish clothing. Oh! what a wild spectacle. And his eyes watered at the wonder of it all. For one incredible moment Nelson felt at one with the little people and was glad for it.

"Sir, can I help you?" a distant female voice asked. "Sir!"

Startled out of his contemplation, Nelson moved forward and placed his order with a gal who sported more body piercings than his tailor's pin cushion and more facial lacquer than a drag queen. Hard to believe a real person existed beneath the dangerous hardware and war paint, he marveled. Where did the fresh-faced American food service worker disappear to?

Potential hires sporting facial spikes or excessive makeup or visible tattoos never advanced beyond the first interview at his company. It was an unwritten rule, one he had devised. His clients were conservative and expected their wealth to be managed by employees who displayed a conservative appearance. Individuality was fine for companies producing video games.

The odor of fast food fading behind him, his bag of gourmet burgers clutched in one hand and his briefcase in the other, he sauntered east on West 77th toward Central Park West, drinking in the heady scent of decaying leaves wafting in the air from the floodlit grounds of the American Museum of Natural History, the autumn foliage ablaze with artificial golden light. The picturesque setting reminded him of a Thomas Kinkade painting. At this precise moment, he realized he had never visited the museum even though he lived around the corner from it for...well, too long. He would have to remedy this oversight. God forbid his cultural philistinism should be exposed to New York's elites.

As he walked, a ticking sound interrupted his musings. Nelson glanced down and noticed his right shoelace had come undone, the brass aglets slapping the concrete sidewalk with each stride. He knelt to retie it. About to rise, he spied a tan leather wallet lying in the shadow of the gutter. Luckily for the owner, the wallet was still in pristine condition, otherwise, Nelson wouldn't have touched it. The wallet couldn't have lain there very long, not more than a day, he guessed. He remained squatting and unfolded it, ignoring the thick wad of Franklins slotted in the middle of the billfold while he hunted for an address.

A driver's license will do.

Mr. Vito Cabreezi. 510-12 West 77th.

His name seemed familiar. Nelson absentmindedly tapped the wallet against his hand. Enlightenment soon dawned. The Mafia don! The sudden recognition caught him off-guard. He scowled at the thought of living around the corner from a mobster. Then he remembered Russian gangsters had purchased apartments over on Park Avenue. The neighborhood had gone to hell.

Nelson looked to his right at a wall of rusticated limestone stretching skyward. To his surprise, he realized he was squatting in front of the address, and between the gaps of passing pedestrians, a liveried doorman hung back in the well of the bright lobby and beyond him another man attended behind a counter. He was tempted to replace the wallet; his burgers were calling to him. Instead, he thought, What could it hurt?, and he allowed himself to be swept away by a spirit of do-goodism. Maybe it had something to do with the electricity of TGIF in the air. Whatever the impulse, it was Vito's lucky day. Nelson gathered his possessions and marched towards the frame of light carved out of the dark façade.

"Good evening, sir," the concierge addressed him from behind a marble counter. Looking more like a bouncer at bar, he had the proper sense to recognize Nelson was a sir, after all, his clothing screamed Sir! The concierge sported an enquiring look, intimating he knew Nelson wasn't a resident.

"I found a wallet. Does a Vito Cabreezi live here?"

"He does. He owns this building."

The revelation caught Nelson off-guard. "Oh," was all he could express. Crime does pay it seems.

"Mr. Cabreezi will be most grateful to you for your honesty."

Nelson shrugged it off. "Is he on the premises?"

"No. He departed less than an hour ago."

He digested this bit of news while the concierge read his mind.

"I'll contact Mr. Cabreezi so you can speak to him."

"Grand idea."

"What is your name, sir...?" Star struck, he said, "Are you *the* Nelson McCormack."

"The one and only."

The revelation seemed to tickle the concierge, like he was in the presence of a celebrity. "You look different in person."

"Hopefully, for the better," Nelson said with haughty pride.

The concierge laughed.

"Time is a wasting," Nelson prodded him.

"Of course, sorry, Mr. McCormack." He dialed a number on the courtesy phone at his station while McCormack parked his belongings on the counter and inspected the Italian decor with a critical eye.

Part of the second floor had been removed to create an atrium. Large arched mullion windows faced streetside to permit the ingress of natural light. Marble columns—their distinctive order eluded him, for he couldn't distinguish Corinthian from Colonial—mounted around a marble pool soared to the ceiling. Water flowed from an amphora held by a semi-clad female marble statue centered in the pool. Potted Cyprus trees and exotic flowers strategically placed completed the indoor tableau, an attempt to invoke ancient Rome. Too much gilt and veined marble, he sniffed.

The doorman spoke Italian into the handset, then passed it to him. "Mr. Cabreezi wishes to speak with you."

Nelson cleared his throat. "Good evening, Mr. Cabreezi."

"Mr. McCormack, I can't tell you how indebted I am to you."

Nelson identified a faint Italian accent beneath the New York patois. "Think nothing of it."

"How can I repay you?"

Repay me? He bit off a laugh.

"Mr. McCormack?"

"This one is on me," he said.

"Well, then, thank you again. And, Mr. McCormack, if you ever require my help with *anything*, please don't hesitate to contact me. Ask Luigi to give you my personal number. Oh! I almost forgot," and he chuckled. "Please leave my wallet with Luigi. Good night, Mr. McCormack." A busy signal transmitted down the line.

He returned the receiver to the doorman, then the wallet. He didn't bother to get the don's phone number. "I guess we're done here." McCormack tendered a toothless smile.

"A good evening to you, sir."

Nelson exited the building into the twilight, the don's offer of help still preoccupying his thoughts. As if a man in my position would ever get into bed with the likes of him, he smirked. I can buy any help I need. The nerve of him. He's only in the business of making self-serving offers. Nelson then thought of his great-granddaddy. Laundering bootlegger money back in the Roaring Twenties was fine for him; he needed it to build the firm. But those dirty times are history and will remain so, so long as I'm in charge. Leaves rustled in the gutter and his brief, but irksome, encounter with a member of the Mob was brushed aside by his desire to be with his wife.

In a mild state of dread Nelson rode the elevator to his floor enveloped by the aroma of charbroiled hamburger and spicy dill pickles. He hoped Mr. Smythers, a snooty neighbor he ran into on the elevator more often than anyone else in the building for some unfathomable reason, wouldn't intrude on his swift but odorous ascent. Nelson pictured Smythers, a latter-day John Houseman, gazing down his long pointy nose at him with hooded eyes, his countenance exuding disdain for daring to poison the rarified air of the elevator with the Bohemian bouquet of takeout food. Scandalous!, his whole being shouted. Smythers didn't have to utter a word. Why speak when he could wither you with a look of contempt? Nelson willed the elevator to rise faster, higher, in hopes of evading the non-verbal censure of his haughty neighbor.

To his relief the elevator halted its ascent on his floor without a hitch. Nelson thanked his lucky stars for the uninterrupted ride and entered the foyer of his sanctuary.

As usual there was no one to greet him, the master of his domain. He placed his briefcase on the Chippendale side table and balanced the bag of burgers on top of it. God forbid he should stain the surface of this rare antique with hamburger grease. Sharron would pull a temper tantrum. He shed his trench coat and hung it lopsided on the hanger. His hunger momentarily greater than his fear of Sharron's disapproval, he left his briefcase and embarked on a quest for her.

Distant voices drew him toward the den.

He entered the cozy room—the size of volleyball court—dangling the bag of burgers. Sharron was reclining on the distressed leather sectional, eyes glued to their wall-sized television. "Hi, Baby. Dinner is served."

She gave him her full attention. "About time. This carnivore is starved for meat," she said, while she lowered the volume on the TV. She had given Renalda the night off.

Consternation clouded his face. He searched for a suitable spot to place the burgers on without causing a fuss. Spying The Wall Street Journal lying on the sectional, he spread it out on the center table and placed the food on top of it, and all the while Sharron was scrutinizing him with gimlet eyes. God forbid he should soil the table.

He pulled the table closer to them, then sought her approval before emptying the contents of the bag onto the newspaper. Awarded a nod of consent, he passed her a thick burger swathed in a paper wrapper damp with the sweat of meat and a box of crispy fries.

"God, I hope it tastes as good as it smells. My mouth is actually watering," Sharron said while she unwrapped her burger.

To the sounds of paper crinkling and subdued TV voices, they munched on their burgers and fries.

"What were you watching?" Nelson asked, speaking around the food in his mouth.

"An alien invasion of the U.S."

"They finally made a movie about the illegal immigrant invasion of the Southwest?"

Sharron gagged on her food in laughter. She swallowed hard. "I hate it when you joke while I'm eating, Nels. But a good one nonetheless."

He gave her a thumbs up. "The aliens served their purpose of discrediting the former maverick in the White House," he said between bites."

"Pawns for the greater good of the nation," Sandra piled on.

"Yup. Voters are so easily duped by slogans that pander to their petty parochial prejudices. And thank God for this because the pliable tool in the Oval Office is serving *our* interests once again."

Nelson didn't believe in God, but it never stopped him from invoking His name whenever it suited him.

"But at the same time the little people no longer respect us. They used to want to be like us. Now they gripe about our wealth. As though we don't deserve it," Sharron said.

"We can thank the former chump in the White House for devaluing the currency of respect for our class. He gave wealth a bad name."

"A bullet would have been too good for him."

"Believe me, Baby, we considered that scenario, but it would have triggered Civil War 2.0."

"For all his blubber and blather, he couldn't stop the shotgun blast of millions of mail-in ballots and software *glitches* the second time round."

Nelson burst out laughing. Then he tabled his burger and licked his fingers. "Thirsty?"

"Grab me a bottle of Fillico."

Sourced from a natural spring in Kobe, Japan, at more than two hundred dollars a bottle, Fillico bottled water was one of the most expensive on the planet. Sharron consumed it by the case.

"What are you having, Nels?"

"It was a profitable week so I'm going to celebrate with a Stella Artois," he said, heading toward the wet bar on the honey-colored bamboo parquet floor.

Nelson settled back on the sofa and glanced at Sharron, her lips and fingers glistening with hamburger juice. "How was your day at the clinic, Baby?" he asked, twisting the cap off the green bottle of beer, and carbon gas escaped into the air making a *fst* sound. He chugged a swig of fermented hops and barley extract while he waited for her to finish chewing.

She rolled her eyes for dramatic effect and wiped the corners of her mouth with her pinky before admitting her day was dreadful. "To top it off, a potential client stormed out on me."

"A first time for everything. Who was the client?"

"A young Black girl. In her early twenties, if my memory serves me correctly. Hooked on meth."

"Her and hundreds of thousands of others, Black, white and every useless eater in between," Nelson interjected. "We need a major war to get rid of those lowlifes. And it's coming."

"Give it a rest," she chided him. "*Anyway*, when the questions got too personal, she accused me of degrading her." Anger reddened her cheeks. She tabled her burger and wiped her mouth and fingers with a paper napkin provided by the takeout joint. "The nerve of her. Here I am trying to help her recover from her addiction and she repays me with ingratitude."

"Don't take your day job too seriously, Baby," he said to console her. "Your time at the clinic is for optics only. Charity work burnishes our public image."

"I *know*, but it upsets me nevertheless when they give up on themselves."

"Are you sure you're cut out for this work?"

"The job takes its toll on me, but I'm not a quitter."

"I admire your spirit, taking one for the team," and he raised his bottle of beer in salute to her. "My Baby's not a quitter." Just then a noble gesture grabbed hold of him. "Why don't you hire an assistant to manage your paperwork so you can spend more of your time counselling?" he said.

Her face beamed. "Can I, Nels?"

"I just said you could."

"Being the wife of the principle donor has its privileges," and she giggled her delight. Then she frowned until Nelson caught sight of it.

"What, Baby?"

"I don't wish to sound ungrateful...."

"Don't be coy. Out with it."

"I'll need a bigger office to accommodate an assistant, but the ground floor is maxed out."

"Good point." He digested this setback for a moment. A solution popped into his head. "We'll just have to shrink your fellow counsellors' offices so you can ease your workload."

That Sharron carried half the caseload of her coworkers was a non-issue for him. If it was within his power to make her happy, he did so. Nothing was too good for his wife.

Sharron lunged at him and gave him a squeeze. "You always know what I need without my having to ask for it," she whispered into his ear.

"You can't afford to burn out, then you'll be of no benefit to our *cause*."

Sharron resumed her place, contentment radiating from her. "Care to watch the rest of the movie with me?"

"Sure." He slid beside her. "I predict the aliens will be evicted."

"If only the aliens occupying our country could be evicted."

"We're working on it, Baby," he said, taking another swig of premium beer before putting his arm around her. "But we may have to resort to internment camps first like FDR did during the Second World War."

Sharron stopped mid-chew, her jaw dropping like an unchained drawbridge.

"Baby, the birth certificate of this republic was written in the blood of our forefathers," he explained. "War gave birth to this great nation. Martial valor is the highest virtue. We're going to make America great again, the old-fashioned way." He paused for effect. "Through war."

Chapter Eight

While McCormack was exchanging goodbyes with the concierge in the lobby, on the topmost floor above them, Vito Cabreezi, attired in a charcoal gray *Cad and the Dandy* tailored suit from Savile Row—he eschewed the flashy suits of his own kind, part of an effort to adopt a more WASP-ish image—cradled the gold-trimmed black 1920s-styled Bakelite phone receiver with delicate care, as if it would detonate on contact with the base. His eyes glowed amber beneath a crown of well-groomed pewter hair sculpted to the right, and from the opposite side of the polished expanse of his elephantine desk—large enough for a game of billiards—they pinned his consigliere, Paco Delonzo, whose meaty face was a picture of anticipation.

"Serendipity has brought us luck," Cabreezi said, twirling a diamond-encrusted ring on his sausage-like pinky. A diamond Rolex adorned his right wrist and a thick gold bracelet rattled on the other.

Delonzo, his black hair slicked rearward on his block-shaped head, offered him a look that said, "I'm listening."

"I never expected to see it again, but my wallet was recovered right outside this building. By an honest man. In New York," and he raised his palms as if to say, "Who would believe it?"

The consigliere shifted his muscular bulk in the overstuffed leather armchair, a manifestation of the masculine character of the office decor. "I'm intrigued. Don't keep me in suspense."

Cabreezi steepled his fingers and rested his fleshy chin on them. "The caller—forgive me, Mr. McCormack—was on the other end."

A light went off in Delonzo's head. "The richest man in the country? Your pleasure makes sense now."

The enormous potential of this chance encounter was not lost on both of them.

"Here's the best." The don allowed a measured pause to heighten the tension of the moment, and Paco fixed his reptilian eyes on him. "He laughed at my offer of reciprocity."

"The *nerve* of him. He must be arrogant if he believes he's above dealing with a man of your...sterling reputation." He couldn't put too fine a point on it.

"Sterling? Not golden?" Cabreezi chuckled at his inflated valuation of himself. "It's doubtful he hasn't heard of me," he said with the conviction of someone aware of his own notoriety. "But on the outside chance he's ignorant of my *noble* standing in the community, he'll soon discover it," and there was menace, not amiability, in his tone.

"The fool has no reason to feel morally superior to us. The impacts of his investment practices are much more destructive than those of any conquering army."

"This ought to be good," Cabreezi offered; his consigliere was inclined to judge matters in a novel way.

Paco smiled his appreciation. "On a macro-level, his kind have wrecked entire economies with their financial weapons of mass destruction."

"So true. Tens of millions of people were ruined by the global financial crisis engineered by those Yids and WASPs over a decade ago. Including many of our own people who lost their life savings."

Cabreezi neglected to mention his real estate empire had gorged on distressed properties during the real estate crisis.

"And not one of them shysters stood before a judge," Paco pointed out. "Instead, the banks were fined four weeks' worth of profits with no admission of guilt. Rich man's justice," he said, scowling with contempt.

"Those crooks don't run traditional rackets," the don said as though speaking to a tenderfoot. "They offer innocent investors government-approved swindles wrapped in the solemn investment lingo of credit default swaps and mortgage-backed securities."

"And they pay no sales tax on those financial transactions."

"And the grasping Fibbies are at perpetual war with us to seize our assets in order to offset the loss in tax revenue."

"Politicians are nothing more than a bunch of double-dealing bums in bad suits incapable of doing real work." Paco adopted a commendatory expression in salute of his original turn of phrase.

"Why else would they insist on maintaining a monopoly on violence if not to protect their income extraction rackets from the fury of the common man?"

"We should form a government. Our problems would then be solved," Cabreezi said.

"We certainly dress better."

"But the barracudas and their lackeys in government wouldn't allow it."

"Al Capone said it best when he said: 'Capitalism is the legitimate racket of the ruling class.'"

"And the ruling class hates nothing more than a competing economic system."

"Thing is, we don't compete with them. We complement their system with goods and services they are unwilling to provide to those who crave them," the consigliere said.

"Supply and demand. People demand, we supply." Cabreezi flapped his hand in irritation. "But that's *so* old economy. I've always itched to make a killing in the financial arena. And we may have found our entry ticket."

"Am I correct in assuming you wish to add an investment vehicle to the family's portfolio?"

"You have a talent for words, Paco."

He acknowledged the praise with a humble nod before asking: "What do you propose?"

"I'd kill to beat those swindlers at their own game. Choke them with their own greed!" Cabreezi's face darkened and he punctuated his declaration with an emphatic smack of his fist against the desk. But his rage subsided as quickly as it had come on. He leaned forward, rested his bulging forearms on the desk and in a calmer voice said: "I want you to get inside McCormack's life. Dig around. Tear it inside out and upside down. Find his Achilles heel. No man ever got rich the honest way. We will teach this arrogant prick never to look down on his betters again."

An ambitious and yet cautious man, Paco had risen in the ranks to his current position—and no higher would he ever go—by toadying to his superiors. So he couched his doubt about the don's plan in awe-like innocence. "You believe he can be brought to heel?"

"A desperate man and his arrogance are soon parted."

"Machiavelli?"

The don shook his head no. Then, as though on the verge of revealing a deep, dark secret he didn't want the walls to hear, he hunched forward and in an undertone said: "Cabreezi."

Through his energetic laughter, his consigliere said: "Don, you are a comedian at heart."

"It's a talent I can fall back on should I ever lose my day job," and he joined in the good humor of the moment.

Paco checked himself and resumed their previous discussion. "When should this investigation begin?"

"Right away," Cabreezi said.

"I know just the man for the job." He then tacked on, "You'll soon have your own pet Wall Street trader at the end of a short leash you can yank on at your leisure."

"An apt metaphor, Paco." Just then an outlandish idea seized hold of him and he felt compelled to express it out loud. "You could be a writer should you ever lose your day job," and they both shared another hearty laugh.

"I could write material for your comedy routine. And the material wouldn't have to be funny. What customer would dare sneer at your riffs?"

"Only a dead one."

"You'd be a hit without breaking a sweat."

"Enough, enough" Cabreezi pleaded between gasps of laughter, slapping the desk.

"As you wish."

Once Cabreezi composed himself, he said: "Paco, the straight man is not supposed to upstage the comedian."

"My apologies. I couldn't resist the opening."

"We're a pair, aren't we?" There was rare affection in these words.

"A pair of snake eyes lethal enough to loosen our enemies' bowels with one look."

"Should I shoot you now or later?" he said between belly laughs.

Paco laughed along with him. He managed to squeeze in: "How about never?"

"Done."

A ringing phone interrupted their jollity.

Paco answered his mobile, his amusement still not under control. "What is it, Milo?" He listened and bolted upright, his aspect transforming into rough granite, all signs of humor gone. "*Grazie.*"

"What now?" Cabreezi asked.

"It pays to have an ex-CIA operative on the payroll," Paco gloated, since it was his idea to hire Milo. "This building is under surveillance."

Hot anger boiled Cabreezi's blood. "My nemesis has no respect for taxpayers. He must be a few handcuffs short a bordello to think I would conduct my business affairs in the open."

Paco grew wary. "Ambrose is raring to nail you."

"All he will do in his desperation to nail me is to whack his thumb with his own hammer, if I don't do it to him first."

"Let us keep our focus on the bigger picture, Don," he said to calm him. "Retaliation will bring unnecessary heat upon us."

Cabreezi pinned him with those amber eyes of his. It was a rare occasion when he accepted advice from others. This was one of them. "Good point. Personal vendettas have no place at the top." He waited a heartbeat. "But I would not be displeased if someone were to do me a favor."

Paco communicated his understanding with a simple nod as if to say, "Thy will be done."

But it would be one of those rare occasions when Paco ignored his boss' will.

Chapter Nine

The burgundy Chevy Malibu rolled toward the East River along Hunts Point Avenue at a leisurely pace. The driver was in no hurry, nor were his two passengers. A red light at Spofford, the border between suburbia and the industrial zone in the South Bronx, brought the vehicle to a temporary halt. Other than that it was in need of a wash, there was nothing remarkable about the ride to warrant a double-take. It was just another nondescript car passing through the downscale peninsular neighborhood on the way to someplace else.

To the soothing rhythms of John Coltrane's tenor sax flowing from the satellite radio station, Frankie, a second-string crew member, said from the passenger seat: "So, Rommy, Nico gonna show?"

His wrist hanging limp on the steering wheel, Rommy stared through the windshield, concentrating on the empty roadway. A lot of quick planning had gone into this meeting ever since Bronco revealed the contract on Nico's head weeks ago. Rommy saw an opportunity to curry Bronco's favor and so he had grasped at it like any minion would.

"No reason not to." He broke contact with the road and checked the rearview mirror again.

"Why so sure?" Mattie, another low-echelon crew member, shot out from the back seat.

The traffic light turned green, Rommy hit the gas and the car jerked forward. "The greedy prick hates his old man. He jumps at every chance to screw him over." To confirm his opinion, he reminded his backseat doubter of an incident in the not-too-distant past, and this reminder satisfied his doubt.

"Why doesn't the don burn him? If Nico were my son, I'd whack him six ways to Sunday."

"You don't have a son, Frankie, so it's easy for you to talk tough," Rommy said.

"Son. Daughter. Who cares? Nobody screws me and lives to brag about it."

"Except your old lady," Mattie said.

He and Rommy shared an energetic laugh while Frankie scowled.

"Laugh all you want." He turned to the passenger window and sputtered: "A guy can't get no respect."

Mattie patted him on the shoulder. "You're always setting yourself up, Frankie Boy."

He tossed his shoulder. "Screw you, Mattie."

Rommy favored Frankie with a brief sideways glance. "Like I was saying, it's damn near impossible to kill your own flesh and blood no matter how many times they stab you in the heart."

"No wonder you're such a bleeding heart," Frankie said, and Mattie split his sides.

Rommy joined their humorous exchange. He could suck it up as well as he could dish it out.

The Malibu cruised through another intersection to deserted Halleck Street bordered by covered fences and business fronts—remnants of industries that had once sprawled across the cityscape but had since been squeezed into the butt end of this peninsula. Not a soul trod the sidewalks at this late hour. It wasn't the place for a night-time stroll—unless the stroller planned for it to be their last. Rommy swung the car right on Ryawa Avenue, drove a few hundred feet, pulled next to the curb beneath a burned out streetlight and killed the engine—and with it Coltrane's mellow sax.

"Why're we stopping here?" Frankie asked. "The meeting place is up ahead."

"I know, bub," Rommy said as though speaking to a child. "There might be security cameras on the property."

"Oh," was Frankie's reply.

"Oh," Rommy repeated to emphasize his forward thinking. "Now shut your cake holes and put your ball caps on. Try to stay alert."

They poured out of the vehicle and each of them checked their surroundings, the habit of men who lived lives submerged in violence, for violence could always boomerang without warning. The night air was crisp and cool. Nothing out of the ordinary pinged their senses. They closed their doors without rousing the dead and headed west on Ryawa, Rommy in the van and Frankie and Mattie bringing up the rear. The sidewalk trembled. A large diesel truck rumbled toward them, and the cab spasmed in sync with the engine ratcheting through the gears.

"Should we waste him, Rommy?" Frankie said.

"Who?" he said over his shoulder.

"The truck driver. Three guys on this street at this hour might stick in his memory."

Rommy spun around on a dime. "You're a real dumbass." Frankie wilted under his glare. "I ought to whack you right here and put you out of my misery."

"Take it easy, Rommy," Mattie broke in.

"You wanna bring the whole frigging police force crashing on our heads?"

"No."

"The driver's no one to worry about. He's from California, you dumbass!" Rommy said.

"How you know?" Frankie asked, mystified.

Rommy regarded him as though, of all the dimwits in the world, he was the dimmest. "I read the frigging license plate, bub."

"Oh," was his sheepish reply.

"Oh," Rommy repeated. "It'll take him at least twelve days to complete the round-trip. Provided he comes back this way. The news might never reach him."

"Look who got told," Mattie interrupted.

"Killing isn't the solution to every problem," Rommy said to both of them. "Sometimes a frigging dose of common sense is enough."

Distorted shadows kept pace with them in the pools of yellow light cast by aged street lamps, and their footfalls clopped on broken cement and crunched down hardy weeds. Yards from their destination, Rommy held up his hand and the three of them came to a sudden halt. Spot lit by a streetlamp, he faced his partners and said in a low voice: "The next address is our rendezvous. Act loose. Nico can smell a rat a mile away." He turned on his heels without waiting for their confirmation.

A gap in the covered fence up ahead indicated Nico had been first to arrive. A skeleton of a concrete building under construction poked high above the enclosure. Rommy passed through the open gate first with his backup in tow. He spied Nico's glossy black souped-up Audi parked next to the unlit and unmanned guard house. Rommy surmised Nico had probably told Pucci, the night watchman, to take a hike.

"Nico," Rommy called out into the darkness.

"Over here."

A tall human form emerged from the shadows of the construction material piled around the site.

Rommy strained to remain unruffled in the presence of a man exuding the aura of a coiled cobra. They met halfway to the sound of shoes crunching gravel. "Great to see you, Nico." He didn't extend his hand. He knew better. Nico didn't shake hands with underlings.

"Who's the posse?"

Rommy followed Nico's gaze. Frankie and Mattie were busy admiring Nico's wheels. "Hey!" he shouted at them. "Keep your stupid eyes on the street." He turned back to Nico. "They're supposed to be our lookouts," and he compressed his lips.

"Skip the pleasantries and cut to the chase."

"The Red Tiger gang needs our network to distribute its product."

"What's wrong with their own?"

"The Fibbies have been rolling it up. Johny Thai is willing to call off his headhunters if you deal him in."

"You heard about the contract the gook has out on me?"

"I'm surprised he's still around to admit it."

"Not for much longer," and Rommy wondered at this remark. "So, why'd the gook reach out to *you*?"

"We have mutual contacts." Rommy hoped the expression conveyed an air of sophistication.

"How are they importing their product?"

"Frozen fish."

Surprise lit up Nico's features. "Go on."

"Before freezing the captured fish on the high seas, the crewmen gut them through their mouths, then stuff their bellies with bags of heroin. Drug-sniffing dogs can't detect it. Pure genius, don't you agree?"

"Passes the stink test so far."

"Our wholesaler at the fish market down the road will buy the catch of the day, then we'll purchase and distribute it throughout the city."

"Appears you've thought of every contingency."

A self-satisfied smile broke out on Rommy's face.

"Except." There was danger in this single word.

Rommy's mouth drooped for he sensed the conversation had taken a deadly turn, and he felt his bowels loosen.

As if he had heard his thoughts, Nico said, "Dogs might not smell a rat but I sure as hell can. Call your boys over here."

Oh, Christ, Rommy thought. A long second ticked by.

"Now!"

He lurched and was about to call out to them when Frankie and Mattie scurried over on their own, Nico's growl having drawn their interest.

"Are you goombahs in on Rommy's plan?"

They regarded one another. Mattie answered first. "We were given the outlines, Nico."

"Sounds legit," Frankie said.

"You can't tell legit from lasagna." They shifted their feet. He raked them with scornful eyes. "What a bunch of loose crumbs. The gooks would sooner sweep the likes of you off the table than work with any of you salami slingers."

"Yesterday's troubles, Nico," Rommy said. "Johny needs our help and he's willing to pay for it."

"I burned his brother a few months back." They shrank from his murderous gaze.

"All is forgiven," Rommy said with a confidence he did not feel. "Johny shelved the contract he put out on you. We're on the same side now."

"A personal vendetta can't be bargained away. Not by them. Not by us."

"So what are you saying?" This, from Frankie.

"Johny Thai miscalculated in hiring you to fulfill the contract on my head." In a flash of movement, a knife appeared in his hand. "Don't move or I'll gut you."

"Nico!" a voice behind him commanded.

He jolted. "You too, Pucci?" he said to the guard who had snuck up behind him. "I'll double whatever they're offering you."

Pucci didn't let the offer stand for a heartbeat. "A meat hook is the only payment I'll collect from you."

"You're not as stupid as you look," Nico replied.

Like any man low on the totem pole, Pucci saw his shot at power and he seized it. "And you're deader than you look. But tomorrow I will be alive and kicking. So shut your dirty pie hole."

"Steady, Pucci," Rommy said, hearing the threat in the watchman's voice. "Drop the knife, Nico."

Realizing the gig was up, and not being suicidal, he let the weapon slip from his grasp; it clattered on the ground.

"Grab his arms," Rommy ordered.

Frankie and Mattie, both far heftier than Nico, moved to subdue him.

"Keep your gun trained on his back," he directed at Pucci. "Take him over there," Rommy pointed with his finger. They moved deeper into the shadows while Rommy stooped to retrieve Nico's knife. "Far enough."

He stood before Nico, a picture of cocky defiance. "We may be a bunch of crumbs, but sometimes the crumbs are the tastiest part of the meal. Especially to someone with hunger in their belly. We crumbs do the dirty work and get paid peanuts. So tonight's our ticket to a grand banquet with all the trimmings."

"You won't get away with whacking me."

"I waited a long time for this, Nico. You set my brother up. He was skimming the family for your benefit. But he kept his mouth shout about it to the end. Except for me."

"He told you?" Nico said, disbelief in his tone.

"You squeezed Louie, you prick. If he refused to play along, you would've whacked him. Screwed if he did, screwed if he didn't."

"The fate of low men in our line of work."

"Nobody will miss you, Nico. There'll be a lot of fellas cheering tomorrow when news of your execution does the rounds."

"My father won't rest until he has his revenge." He thrashed against his captors, sensing what was coming.

"Hold him tight," Rommy commanded the two men. "An eye for an eye, Nico. Say goodbye."

Chapter Ten

Amidst loud voices and louder music, Lorenzo paid the waitress for their beers, his gaze lingering on her swaying backside as she swished away to serve other customers in the popular sports bar. He unpeeled his eyes to rejoin his baseball-capped friend.

"Where were we?" he said.

"We were talking about your ex-significant other. Appears you escaped with your freedom intact," Mitchel answered.

"I slipped out before the prison door clanged shut."

"But you still have to pay child support. It's the law."

Lorenzo shrugged. "Not a problem. Like, I'm willing to pay for my freedom if it means escaping the drudgeries of fatherhood."

Mitchel diverted his attention to the big-screen TV. A hockey match was airing. "We rarely hang out anymore."

"I feel your pain, bro."

"You shouldn't ignore your friends when you start swapping saliva with a girl."

"You know how it is." Mitch probably didn't. He had never been in a long-term relationship, but Lorenzo gave him the benefit of the doubt, anyway. "I'm a free man now."

"Yolanda had you wrapped around her finger like thread around a spool," he said, twirling his finger. "You unraveled every time she crooked her finger at you."

"You slay me, bro. But not anymore she doesn't."

"Yeah, you finally wised up."

He played with his beer bottle. "Fatherhood would cause any footloose guy to flee." He laughed at himself.

Mitchel's eyes went wide with astonishment. "Dude! I'm so proud of you. High five."

Their palms smacked in the neutral zone above the table.

"Out with the used, in with the new," Lorenzo said.

"You're treading in fertile territory now."

Lorenzo sat up. "Someone on your radar?"

"Take a peek at the brunette dish behind you in the red blouse, the one standing with her two friends." While Lorenzo was giving her the once over, Mitchell said: "She's been scoping us since we arrived."

"Dibs on the girl in red."

"Not so fast."

"May the best man win."

"Don't be so sure."

"I'm not sure. I'm convinced."

Mitchel's mouth twitched. "Doesn't she get to decide?"

"Miss Red already has. But she doesn't know it yet."

"You a mind reader?"

"It's Psychology 101," Lorenzo said. "You put the idea in her head and let her think it was hers to begin with. Works every time."

"You learnt something useful from your ex." His tone assumed a competitive edge. "Head games aside, humor is the way to a woman's heart."

"Got you beat in that department too."

"You're on," Mitchel said.

Lorenzo caught Miss Red's eye, gave her a winning smile and saluted her with his beer bottle. She returned his gesture with a nod, then huddled with her friends. They arrived at a quick decision and sauntered over to his table, bringing their drinks with them.

Only two chairs were available, so Lorenzo said to Miss Red: "I'll give you my chair if I can sit in your lap."

"Like, in your dreams."

"Okay, then you can sit in mine," and he pushed himself away from the table.

"I have a better idea." Her eyes twinkled with devilry. "Why don't *you* sit in your friend's lap?"

Without missing a beat, Lorenzo said: "I would—except doing so might excite him."

Mitchel favored him with a withering expression while the three girls snickered.

Having demonstrated he was the alpha male, Lorenzo offered his seat to Miss Red and went to fetch another chair. Returned to the table, Mitchel introduced him to their new acquaintances.

Detecting their different accents, Lorenzo asked: "So where y'all from?"

"We're on vacation from Wisconsin," Beverley—Miss Red—lied.

"So what are y'all doing here on a Saturday night?" he threw out to them.

Beverley answered for her friends. "We're, like, looking to hook up."

Lorenzo's eyes popped out of his skull, no less than if he had won the Powerball lottery, and he noticed Mitchel was busy reinserting his own. They remained speechless, too shocked to express their windfall. Oh my god! My prayer has been answered. My dream girl has arrived, Lorenzo exulted.

Beverley added: "You don't live in your parents' basements do you?"

Both of them suffered mild concussions in their haste to shake their heads no. Mitchel wasn't completely honest. He occupied a bedroom on the first floor of his parents' home.

Zeroing on Lorenzo, Beverley said to him: "What do you do for a living?"

"A little bit of this and little bit of that."

"Ooo. A mystery man," she cooed.

"The only mysterious thing about Lorenzo is his gender," Mitchel said.

The girls cracked up and Lorenzo pulled a face at him. "Actually, I work in accounts receivable for a family firm. I chase after delinquent accounts."

"You don't look like the accounting type," Beverley said. Before he could reply, she suggested: "Let's finish our drinks and go."

"Where we going?" Lorenzo asked, puzzled.

"Your place."

"Of course. Duh," and he ground his finger into his temple.

Mitchel waved his hand. "Can I come too?"

"Wouldn't be the same without you," Beverley answered for Lorenzo.

They finished their drinks and piled into a cab on 9th Avenue.

They spilled into Lorenzo's apartment, giddy with expectations. "You have anything to drink?" Beverley asked, heading for the kitchen, while Lorenzo and his guests settled in the living room.

Fortunately, he had gone shopping in the morning. "All I have is beer."

"Beggars can't be choosers, I guess."

Beverley rummaged in the fridge while Lorenzo and Mitchel gabbed with her friends.

"How if we split a beer?" Lorenzo heard her call out to him from the kitchenette.

He gave her a thumbs up.

"How about you, Mitch?" she asked above the buzz of conversation.

"Just a beer, please. No glass."

"Coming right up," she said. A few seconds later: "Where do you keep your glasses?"

Lorenzo told her.

"Could one of you gals grab Mitch's beer?"

Blonde-haired Anne responded to her request.

Much to Lorenzo's pleasure, Beverley squeezed beside him on the couch, holding his beer, her chest pressed against his upper arm.

"Let's get this party started." She clinked glasses with Lorenzo. "Drink up," she said to him over the rim of her glass, and a trace of—wickedness?—flashed in her eyes.

"Play some music," auburn-haired Meredith, the third girl, said.

"Any preference?" Lorenzo asked.

"Eighties music makes my pulse race."

"I thought I did," Mitchel called out.

"To be determined," and she winked at him.

"Quiet everyone." When silence ensued, Lorenzo said: "Alexa. Play music from the nineteen-eighties."

"Louder," Anne said.

"Alexa. Increase the volume twenty-percent...Better?"

"Perfect."

"Let's dance for the boys," Beverley suggested. She tabled her glass.

Lorenzo got Mitch's attention and gave him the thumbs up and Mitchel responded in kind.

The girls put on a show for their attentive male audience of two.

"This is too good to be true," Lorenzo shouted out to them; they responded with seductive dance moves. He noticed Mitch sitting mesmerized, grinning like the Joker, his ball cap askew on his head.

The music pulsed, the boys drank and the girls gyrated. Soon, Lorenzo wondered why the lyrics sounded garbled and why the girls appeared distorted, like images reflected in a funhouse mirror. He tried to shake it off, but lacked the motor control to do so. Mitch appeared to be equally immobilized. Laughter erupted in the room, deep and drawn out, far away. It wasn't his own. Then a contorted face appeared before him.

"Sometimes, 'too good to be true' really is, sucker," Beverley said to him through his mental fog.

"Get his wallet," another voice spoke.

Hands tugged at his front pocket. He tried to resist, his arms refused to respond. Someone waggled his bank card in front of his face.

"What's your PIN number?" Beverley asked.

Lorenzo struggled to focus. A slap stung his cheek. The question came again. Another slap. Garbled voices, then something thin tightened around his throat.

"If you don't give us the number, we'll strangle you," Beverley said.

His eyes bulged in panic. He concentrated. The five digits slurred passed his lips in slow motion. Satisfied, they moved on to Mitchel who received a similar treatment.

"Nice doing business with you boys," was the last thing Lorenzo heard before he blacked out.

Lorenzo came to with a hand patting his cheeks and Mitchel cajoling him to snap out of it. He flicked away Mitchel's hand. "What the hell you doing, bro?"

"Waking you up."

He found himself lying sideways on the couch, then confusion grabbed hold of him. "I don't remember getting drunk." His half-empty glass of flat beer on the table confirmed this.

"Bitches drugged us," Mitchel said.

Lorenzo massaged his temples. "Explains the pounding in my head and the upset in my stomach."

"Me too."

"What time is it?"

"Almost two-thirty in the morning."

Lorenzo sat up and wooziness and nausea overcame him. He lay back and stretched out on the couch. "What happened?"

"We, like, got rolled." Mitchel plopped himself into an armchair.

"What are you talking about?" He glanced around, confused. "Where'd the girls disappear to?"

"They probably left hours ago. And with our bank cards."

Lorenzo's right hand shot to his front pocket. The telltale bulge was flat. "My wallet's missing!"

"It's by your feet."

He retrieved it and rifled through it. His bank card and cash were gone. "Bloody whores!"

"Better call your bank, pronto. Then we have to report this theft to the police."

"No we don't."

"Why not?"

"Me and the cops, like, have a history."

"But what about me?"

"The girls shoved off with our scratch. The cops won't recover it, so what's the point of filing a report?"

Mitchel didn't wish to surrender so easily. "We can give the police a description of the girls so they don't pull this crap again."

"Do you care if they pull this caper on some other sexed-up suckers?"

Mitchel bent to the humor of their plight. "We got played like a couple of pathetic frat boys in heat."

"Looking for *love* in all the wrong places," Lorenzo crooned.

"We got rolled but not in the sack," Mitchel carried it further.

Unexpectedly, their laughter began low and built to a bellyaching crescendo.

"That felt good," Mitchel said.

"I needed a good laugh—even if my gut didn't," Lorenzo said, holding his stomach. "You see my phone anywhere?"

"Here," and Mitchel passed it to him.

Lorenzo let a whoosh of air. "Glad they didn't steal it."

"We could've, like, hunted them down if they had," his friend pointed out.

"They'll collect their comeuppance one day."

"Karma can be a bitch."

Changing subjects, Lorenzo said: "Did you call your bank?"

"Yeah. I'm fifteen hundred bucks poorer, my daily limit."

"I'm not sure what mine is. I guess I'll find out soon enough. Here goes."

Mitchel lounged in the armchair while Lorenzo explained to a customer service rep what had happened. After answering several security questions to confirm his identity, he discovered how much lighter his bank account was.

"Cancel my bank card and send me a new one." More questions. "Thank you for your help."

"So how much scratch did they relieve you of?"

"The sleazy whores stole two grand."

Mitchel let out a low whistle. "Comes to thirty-five hundred bucks in total. Not bad for a night's work."

Anger slitted Lorenzo's eyes. "Them no-good bitches better pray I don't see them again or I'll work them over in the worst way."

"And I'll be there to help you," Mitchel said, slamming his fist into his palm.

Chapter Eleven

Standing in the shadows at the construction site, Bronco shrugged at the abrupt busy signal as if to say, "Don't blame me for spoiling your evening." He slipped the sleek smartphone back into the pocket of his crinkly leather jacket. He had delivered the grim news about Nico to the don who had listened to it in stunned silence and then hung up on him. No surprise.

Bronco hated to be the bearer of bad news, but better it came from him than from the police. He resumed his inspection of the body of Cabreezi's son, Nicola, also known in the family as Nico the Knife, sprawled on its back on a patch of gravel stained with congealing blood, grinning up at him like a ghoul from hell. Except the macabre grin wasn't on Nico's puffy face; it was inches lower, where his throat used to be, now a dark gash in the gloom. *Necklacing*, the Mob's term for such a gruesome killing, was a fitting end for a wise guy who had lived by the sharp edge of a steel blade.

Killing the sole heir to the family firm was someone's way of sending the head of the family a message—a very potent message: you could be next. Security would be tightened around the don. Fewer people would be privy to his movements. His transportation was bulletproofed and so were his fedora and overcoat, but a determined assassin could overcome those obstacles with the requisite firepower.

"As if I don't have enough crap to deal with," Bronco murmured to himself while he contemplated the ghoulish grin. "What were you up to, Nico? A little side-dealing?"

It wouldn't be the first time a mobster tried to set up a racket for himself outside the purview of the family. Cheating the family was an act of betrayal and those who betrayed their *paisanos* paid for it with their lives. But the don's son? He was above this decree—unless the don said otherwise.

With the demise of Cabreezi's heir, Bronco savored two details: 1) He would no longer stand in Nico's shadow. The don would now recognize his value and contributions to the family. He hoped. 2) He would no longer have to clean up after Nico. His mind coasted back to the time Nico carved up a barber like a Christmas turkey for nicking him during a shave. Mistakes happened. Not with Nico they didn't. Then to the time Nico ran a car off the road. The driver had cut him off. Fortunately, the driver survived the accident. For each of these outrageous incidents, apologies were offered, hush money was passed around and medical bills were paid by the family, and the victims were 'urged' to accept these payments without complaint. No charges were ever laid.

Man, the guy did some crazy stuff. A real badass like his old man, Bronco chuckled to himself.

Nico, a made man and thus "untouchable," according to Mob rules, was being groomed to replace the don, but this plan was obviously off the table now. A succession crisis was the least of the family's problems. The immediate challenge: hunt down the killer. Somebody had declared war on the Cabreezi family and it was Bronco's job to find him and those who provided the support for the hit. Then take revenge on them. Maybe a contract killer had been hired to do the job or maybe it was a member of a rival family who had perpetrated this grisly deed. Either case didn't matter. The killing would not go unanswered—could not go unanswered. This would signal weakness. Whoever had drawn the knife across Nico's throat surely calculated the family's response to this brazen act.

There was also the faint possibility the murder was random. But two factors dispelled any such notion in Bronco's estimation: first, the vicious nature of the slaying, and, second, Nico's smartphone was missing. Bronco's search of the body had come up empty. The missing device told Bronco the killer was a professional, making his job of playing detective more difficult. Professionals rarely left clues behind. The killer was probably miles away from here by now, seated in a plane, the murder weapon carefully ditched during the getaway.

Bronco twigged the killer had grabbed Nico's phone. But why...? The family's strict policy of speaking and texting in code eliminated any possibility of finding valuable data on the phone. Then the answer came to him in a flash of inspiration: The meeting between Nico and his killer must have been arranged via the unit. Purloining the phone was the killer's way of erasing his digital tracks. When you smelled something fishy, you didn't think sardines.

Someone Nico probably trusted lured him here; otherwise, why come to this construction site at night on his own?

Bronco cast around in the somber light. Heavy mechanical beasts rested in silent repose on their haunches, ready to spring into action at the turn of a key, and stacks of construction materials cluttered the place, ready to be nailed, screwed or bolted into place. The building site, controlled by the family, was friendly territory, so Nico must have felt safe coming here by himself. He was no coward, but showing up solo oftentimes emboldened treacherous rivals.

Nor was his slaying a matter of being in the wrong place at the wrong time. The odds were against it. Nico came here to deal. And Nico suffered a final judgement for doing so without the don's knowledge. Bronco continued his examination of the body. A fan of *Law & Order* and *CSI* reruns, he gave free reign to his imagination, visualizing how the killer immobilized Nico, who was no featherweight, while dealing the fatal stroke. Bronco conjured a scenario. He imagined himself behind the victim, his left arm around Nico's throat, while he completed the lethal cut with his right hand.

It was then he realized his reenactment didn't fit. The wound was above the larynx. Which meant the killer could not have tucked his arm under Nico's chin, the most effective position for restraining a victim. He puzzled this out. Maybe there was more than one guy on the other team...Three guys? Two to hold Nico and one to deliver the *coup de grâce*? He cottoned to this scenario a whole lot more.

A later autopsy would prove him correct.

This killing's looking more and more like a setup, Bronco decided. He snapped alert. Boots crunching crushed stone announced the approach of Pucci, the night watchman, returning from his rounds. Bronco had spoken to him earlier and he admitted to seeing nothing and hearing nothing. Nico had ordered him to take a hike when he arrived, Pucci had said. Fat chance the guard hid behind a cement column in the unfinished structure to satisfy a forbidden curiosity. What with Nico's rep, no one dared flout his orders. Bronco recalled their earlier conversation as the guard drew near:

"Nico show up alone?" he asked the taciturn guard who nodded in the affirmative. "Where'd you disappear to during Nico's head-to-head?"

"I hid at the rear of the building and hauled on some smokes to kill time."

Bronco ordered Pucci to guard Nico's body while he went for a look-see. He snooped around and discovered the guard's cigarette butts ground into the dirt. It never hurt to verify a statement.

"When did you return to your post?"

The guard pushed his cap back before answering. "Nico told me to give him half an hour, so I did."

Bronco weighed the man's words and believed them. "What'd you do when the time was up?"

"I didn't return the whole way at first," the guard said. "I hung back at the corner of the building," he indicated with a toss of his thumb.

Once again on guard, Bronco asked: "Then what'd you do?"

"The lot was clear, so I figured Nico had finished up. When I was coming back to the guard house, I saw Nico's body lying on the ground." The guard was grimacing now. "I-I damned near tripped over it." Worry crept into his voice. "I'm not in trouble am I? Tell me I'm not."

Bronco heard fear mixed with pleading in the guard's petition and he let him marinate in it for a couple of beats before saying: "Only if you're lying."

"I swear on my mama's grave it's the truth," he sputtered. "I had no clue about what was going to go down. But if I did, I would have done something, anything to save Nico's life."

"Sure you would have," Bronco said with feeble conviction to let the guard stew some more.

"You gotta believe me, Bronco. Tell me you believe me."

He had sent Pucci away on his rounds to give himself time to investigate the murder alone. Now once more the guard was at his side, wordless, apprehension apparent on his pudgy face.

Pointing to Nico's body, Bronco said: "Whoever did this is going to pay." Then he eyeballed Pucci. "And whoever helped is going to pay even more."

The guard's throat bobbed. Then: "Christ! I almost forgot." He flicked on his flashlight he was carrying and directed the shaky beam of light at the stony ground leading away from the body. "What do you make of these?"

Bronco concentrated on the circle of illumination. He grabbed the flashlight out Pucci's hands, startling him, and crouched, balancing on the pointy ends of his snakeskin boots. "Well, well, well, what have we here?" Outlines of several pairs of dark footprints—probably caused by stepping in Nico's blood—trailed off toward the street. So my hunch was on the money. He straightened up and his knees cracked in protest. "Be sure to show these prints to the cops when they arrive," and he passed the flashlight back to the guard.

No congratulations. No clap on the back. No atta boy.

"You got it, Bronco."

"And don't say a word to the cops I was here. *Capiche*?"

"My lips are sealed."

You had to pick tonight to conduct your shady affairs, Bronco telegraphed to the corpse. Guess you weren't a Yankees fan. If not for the presence of the guard and respect for the dead and such sentimental crap, he would've given Nico a solid kick. There were some lines he wouldn't cross.

The call from Pucci had come during the overtime inning. The Yankees had two men on base, two outs and a 3-2 count.

Bronco would have to content himself with viewing the highlights later.

"I'm out of here." Bronco made to go but he stopped himself and poked his index finger in Pucci's spongy chest. "Don't leave town. *Capiche*?"

The guard shook his head vigorously.

Bronco regarded Nico's body one last time. To hell with you. He gave it a kick in the ribs and stalked off while Pucci looked on, open-mouthed.

Chapter Twelve

Rommy dropped Mattie and Frankie off at their pre-arranged meeting place and high-tailed it for home. He had taken a calculated risk bringing these two mooks in on his plan, but he couldn't have pulled it off without them. They weren't the sharpest knives in the butcher block, but they listened to orders, so he trusted them to keep their traps shut. Should be a snap. But if torture was added to the mix, then all bets were off. Stay cool and no one would be the wiser. Least of all Bronco.

As a precaution, he warned them not to flash money around or buy any big-ticket items with the cash they had received for the hit on Nico. Obvious details to any rube, but Rommy wasn't one to leave anything to chance. Sometimes, the most obvious thing taken for granted becomes the trigger for one's downfall. Per his orders, they also left their mobile phones at home in case Cabreezi retained a telecom insider to access their phones' GPS tracking software.

As he raced through the darkened streets against the clock, Rommy reviewed his actions to determine if he had overlooked something in his state of extreme jumpiness. Once they had left the construction site, he removed the battery and SIM card from Nico's phone and dropped them into a sewer near their parked car. Check. Then he tossed the phone out the window several streets back, a gift for a lucky vagrant. Check. Whatever was in the mobile's memory storage was password protected, so it would have to be wiped clean for re-use. Check. He had ordered Pucci to call Bronco forty-five minutes after their departure and not a minute sooner. He forced the guard to repeat his order. Check. This gap should give him ample time to arrive home before Bronco called, barring an unforeseen delay. Rommy expected him to call after he had informed the don. He hoped for a safe journey to his pad in Yonkers.

His checklist completed, he congratulated himself for covering the gamut of hazards he could think of. Only one hazard remained on the list; he would take care of it when he got home. Breathing easier now, his hands loosened their grip on the steering wheel. He checked his speed and relaxed his foot on the accelerator. A quick glance in the rearview mirror calmed him further. No blue and red flashing back there. A speeding ticket would spoil the timing of his entire plan, not to mention leaving behind a paper trail.

"Where you been, Tommy?" Rosie said to him from the kitchen when he came through the front door. "You had me worried." She held onto a cloth and sets of dishes rested on the faux wooden counter. If she wasn't fussing around in the kitchen, she'd find another place in need of an imaginary cleaning. Their place was so tidy it could pass an army boot camp inspection. He hung his jacket in the closet before replying.

"Remember way back when you were supposed to be at the movies with what's her face—"

"Vickie was her name," she interrupted.

"Vickie. Yeah," he said without any conviction. "Anyway, you were canoodling with me instead in the backseat of my papa's car."

Color rose in her cheeks. "Not in front of the children, Tommy."

"And when your old man asked you how the movie was, you lied to him with a straight face?"

"I hated lying to him," she said with a hint of regret. "May the Virgin forgive me." She crossed herself.

"It was a long time ago, Rosie. Besides, I made an honest woman of you."

"Should I lie again?"

"I promise you won't have any regrets this time."

His pledge mollified her. "Since you put it that way...."

"Just as I would have been a dead man if your papa had found out about us that night long ago, tell anyone who asks I was with you the whole time tonight, and we watched TV together. Okay?"

"What's going on, Tommy?" she said it frightened.

"The less you know, the better it is for you, Rosie." He came to her and gripped her shoulders gently. Lowering his eyes to hers, he said, "I avenged Louie's murder tonight."

Her hand flew to her mouth. She recovered quickly. "Murder? You said his death was an accident."

"It wasn't."

"Why are you so certain?"

He broke eye contact and examined the far wall without seeing it. The guilt of his brother's murder had weighed heavily on his conscience these past three years and he gauged whether it was time to unburden himself. If there was anyone he could trust, it was Rosie. Her voice interrupted his meditations.

"Earth to Tommy."

Rommy gazed into her searching violet eyes, eyes that had lost none of their allure in forty-plus years of marriage. His mind teetered between withholding the truth and telling it. "I was there, Rosie. I witnessed his killing." His arms slid around her ample girth and he squeezed her. Trying but failing, he couldn't stop his emotions from erupting. His body trembled, and he held onto Rosie for dear life. He felt her struggling against his tight embrace.

"You're smothering me, Tommy."

He released her and stared at the floor to avoid meeting her gaze. "I can't tell you more than this. For your own safety. So let it go."

"You tell me you witnessed your brother's murder, then you tell me to let it go, like it was nothing?"

"It was either him or the both of us. Louie got himself into trouble with some—some bad people."

"What kind of trouble?"

"It doesn't matter now, Rosie. Please let it go."

The uncommon pleading in his voice must have struck a chord with her. She dropped it.

"I have one last question."

He heaved a sigh. "I'm listening."

"Are you—we—in danger?"

He answered without hesitation. "No." He was banking on Bronco not searching too hard for Nico's killer since he had no love for Nico.

As though a switch had flipped inside her, she asked: "Care for a cup of coffee and a piece of apple pie?"

"Ah, Rosie. You're the best gal a mook could ever hope for."

While he was making his way to the dining room, his phone rang on the table where he had placed it earlier and he felt a chill gush through him. Only one person would call at this hour.

Time to walk the tightrope.

Chapter Thirteen

Nelson was watching the morning news on one of the many TVs suspended from the ceiling while putting the elliptical machine through its paces when Deeanna Patella, the company's Chief Investment Officer, sauntered into the executive gym, wearing painted on black tights and a neon-pink sport bra, attire leaving little to the imagination. His heart skipped a beat, so did his feet, almost launching him into the electronic console. He hoped she didn't notice the effect she had on him.

Deeanna did.

"Good morning, Nelson," she said in a Latina-accented voice, climbing aboard the treadmill in front of him. "Deep into your grunt-and-groan session I see."

In more ways than one now that you've arrived, he thought, poker-faced. "I certainly am," he agreed. "But I wish there was an easier way to stay in shape."

"Oh, but there is," she replied, naughtiness glinting in her eyes.

He decided to play along. "Enlighten me."

"Vigorous naked mud wrestling."

Nelson stumbled into the console and cursed himself. They weren't on such familiar terms, so her comment staggered him. Deeanna smothered her giggles while Nelson recovered. At a loss for words, he debated with himself. How far should he take her remark? Should he err on the side of caution or let loose with a witty comeback? Slow on his mental feet, he couldn't summon a clever retort quick enough, so he threw the ball back into her court.

"Define vigorous."

"Loads of sweat and lots of gasping."

His jaw dropped. Once again she undercut his self-control. The sheer boldness of her! Is she making a pass at me? And if she is, does this constitute sexual harassment? Wait. She's not in a position of authority over me. These questions and more whirred through his mind. Deeanna activated the treadmill before he could reply. He couldn't help but admire her assets, assets a blind man could not help but gawk at.

His CIO was a nut he had been trying to crack open for ages. She had missed—or was it ignored?—his every discreet advance. With the way she was behaving, maybe his stealthy campaign to seduce her was finally gaining traction.

Nelson was certain, even though there was no way to prove it, his CIO was swinging her hips in an exaggerated fashion. Not that he minded. What hot-blooded male in the prime of life would? Was this for his benefit? Was she teasing him? But to what end? He hungered to squeeze the forbidden fruit swaying beyond his reach.

Deeanna's change in her self-contained behavior baffled him. She usually kept to herself in the gym. Other than a polite greeting, she didn't socialize. What had brought on this...this transformation? He puzzled it over. Was she finally succumbing to his charisma? Nelson fancied himself a charmer of women. Although he was no duck in the looks department, his vast wealth catapulted him to the top of the heap in the adultery stakes. He wouldn't be the first man to overestimate his sex appeal, nor would he be the last. Ego goeth before the abyss.

Straining to concentrate on the blow-dried news reader whose main journalistic qualification was her stunning beauty, his eyes drifted downward despite his best efforts. He resolved to count to ten to check himself. He counted to eight on the first attempt, but he admitted to himself he had cheated when he reached six. So he gave it another try. He made it to five this time. The next time it was three. He capitulated on the final test of self-discipline with the excuse gawking at Deeanna's *derriere* wasn't sinful since it was unavoidable.

Time flowed and its passage went unnoticed by Nelson so immersed was he in his fantasy. His heart pounded and not from physical exertion. Deeanna's feet slowed on the treadmill and Nelson came out of his trance. She dismounted and dabbed at the sweat on her exposed upper chest with a white towel, drawing his attention to the nestled swells of forbidden flesh. Deeanna didn't mind his glazed concentration.

"Could you spot me on the bench press?"

I'd wrestle a grizzly bear for you, baby. He played cool. "Do a couple of warm-up sets first, then I'll come and spot you."

"Smart idea."

Out of the corner of his eye, he observed her sashaying to the free weight section.

Pretending to listen to the news, he instead kept his ears attuned to any utterance from Deeanna.

"Okay, Nelson, I'm ready," she called out to him. He ignored her. Wouldn't want her to think he was hanging on her every word.

"Nelson!"

He jumped. They had the gym to themselves, a possible explanation for Deeanna's off-character behavior. Nelson dismounted and joined her. Two ten-pound plates hung on the Olympic barbell for a total weight of sixty-five pounds. He could press the same poundage with one hand easily.

"I'm impressed," Nelson said to stroke her ego.

"My goal is ten reps," she informed him. "As much as possible, let me do the work on the final two reps." She ducked beneath the barbell and lay flat on the bench.

Nelson couldn't help but admire the view. Her pecs flexed with exertion, and so captivated by the swelling vision below him, he failed to notice her struggling with the weight.

"Nelson," she managed to squeeze out.

He snapped out of his trance and sprang to her assistance. He placed his index fingers beneath the bar and pulled up, letting Deeanna do most of the pushing. Her arms trembled, and the barbell landed with a metallic *clang* on the upright supports.

"Thanks," she said, a bit out of breath. She remained in the supine position on the blue vinyl bench.

Her chest rose and fell in a steady rhythm, mesmerizing him.

"See anything you like?"

He checked his caution and replied: "What's not to like?"

She tittered at his remark. "You're such a charmer, Nelson."

His conceit swelled. "Sharron says so too." No sooner were the words out of his mouth when he grimaced inside. Mentioning a wife was such a romance killer.

"She's one lucky woman."

"I guess she is."

"You're too modest, Nelson. You're still quite the catch," and she gave him a wink. Before he could comment, she said: "Stand by." She pressed and lowered the bar for all it was worth, and Nelson stood mesmerized, persuaded her praise for him was genuine. He helped her on the last couple of reps, then she sat up on the bench.

"My pecs feel pumped." She flexed them for his benefit. "What do you think?"

If I told you, the #MeToo movement would have me castrated. "Good definition," was all he allowed himself to say.

Deeanna stood and wrapped the towel around her neck. "Thanks for the help, Nelson." Her finger traced a serpentine vein on his bicep.

He suppressed a shiver from her delicate touch. "Anytime, Dee."

"Time to hit the showers," she announced.

Nelson undressed her as she swayed toward the female locker room. What I'd give to teach *her* the meaning of vigorous, he fantasized. He shook himself and resumed his workout, but his heart wasn't in it. Deanna had made an opening move. Now the initiative rested with him. How should he proceed?

Chapter Fourteen

"Watch your speed," Rommy warned Bronco. The cityscape flickered up the windshield in bright flashes while they raced over the Manhattan Bridge toward Little Saigon, and the inky East River swirled in the darkness far below. "We can't have the cops on our tail."

"You worry too much," Bronco said above the throaty growl of the engine, as he wove in and out of the late evening traffic.

"Flying off half-cocked isn't wise."

"Wisdom's got nothing to do with it." Bronco sat rigid in his seat, his knuckles bloodless on the steering wheel. "We're showing Johny we aren't scared to confront him on his own turf. He won't be expecting us, so he won't have time to fabricate a tale."

"But we aren't sure he carried out his threat against Nico."

"And we can't say for certain he didn't."

Rommy felt a frisson of fear quiver up his spine. Would Johny betray him to save his own skin? He gave the snag some hard deliberation. Nah, he wouldn't dare, he concluded. Johny would seal his own fate if he did. Rommy had to play it cool. Cooler than he ever had. He would be Mr. Frigging Ice, if the situation called for it. He hadn't anticipated Bronco leading the charge into enemy territory a mere twenty-four hours after the murder of Nico. His parents must have known what they were doing when they named him.

He beheld the hard-edged skyscrapers on the black horizon, lit up and nowhere to go, each structure trying to outstretch the other. Christ, what a jam! This car was the last place he cared to be. Especially next to a man who would squash him like a bug if he cottoned on to the truth. But when the summons from Bronco came, he couldn't beg off with an excuse even though it was Sunday. Sick days weren't a perk in the Mob.

"We can't storm his crib and accuse him of murder, Bronco. What proof do we have of him killing Nico?"

"The contract he put out on Nico's head is proof enough."

Rommy laid down his cards prudently, one at a time, so Bronco couldn't examine the entire hand he was holding. "There are other folks besides Johny who wanted Nico dead. You didn't shed tears over his death and neither did I."

"Personal feelings aren't part of the equation." He shot a glare at Rommy, then shifted his attention back to the roadway. "That's why I'm a capo and you're not. I can put aside my likes and dislikes for this job."

The man's not human, Rommy thought. Hell, if I were in charge of this investigation, I wouldn't search too hard for the killer.

"Where were you last night?"

Rommy detected more than curiosity in Bronco's question. "I was home with Rosie. Where else would a guy my age be when not on the job?"

"That's your story?"

"Yeah, and I'm sticking to it, if that's all right with you?"

"I had to ask."

"No trust in this God-forsaken family."

"If I were to trust anyone, and I don't, it would be you, Rommy."

"Thanks. I guess" The tension of the moment bled off. "What's the plan?"

"Make chop suey out of Johny and feed it to him."

Rommy wished to, but didn't dare, point out to him the illogic of fulfilling such a threat. Nevertheless, he admired its viciousness. "This isn't the time to be launching a war."

"They started it," Bronco snarled. "So I'm going to finish it. Tonight!"

"Jesus, Joseph and Mary, we can't go in there with guns blazing. There's more of them in there than us."

Bronco didn't pause for a second to consider Rommy's warning. "This is America, not Vietnam. The gooks have no allies here, only enemies. They'll kowtow to us or they're fried rice."

Unable to reason with him, Rommy gave up and gnawed on his lower lip, the city blurring by his window, and they rode on into the night.

Little Saigon was true to its name, a u-shaped neighborhood that ran east along Grand Street to Bowery and southward to Hester, then west on Hester. Bronco squeezed the car into a spot on Bowery.

Their objective was on Hester, around the next corner. He beheld Rommy. "Ready?"

"Would you care if I wasn't?" he wanted to say. "Ready as ever," he replied instead. Ready as ever to get the hell out of here. He hoped his tone didn't betray his false bravado.

They alighted from the car and Rommy scanned the street, a habit of his profession. A little paranoia never hurt no one. Due to the lateness of the hour, awninged shops, many sporting foreign characters, were shuttered for the night. Foot traffic was thin. A black cat scurried past him on the sidewalk. An omen? He furtively crossed himself out of superstition. It paid to be cautious, even though he and Bronco weren't expected. They hot-footed to *Johny's Takeout*, an eatery where special customers got more than takeout. Their footballs resounded in the near-empty street and light, spilling from their target ahead, pooled on the cement.

Bronco barged into the starkly lit restaurant like he owned it and Rommy brought up the rear. Scents of exotic spices filled the air. A thin elderly Vietnamese man waited behind the counter outfitted in a white smock smattered with a Pollockian-palette of food stains. A smile deepening his roadmap of wrinkles, he asked: "What you genelmen want for eating?"

Taking charge of the conversation, Bronco barked: "We not hungry. We here to see Johny."

"Johny no here."

Out of patience, Bronco whipped out his Berretta and pointed it at the man's head. "I no have time for games. Go find him. Tell him Bronco here. Chop, chop."

The man's happy expression did not waver, even for a moment. "I go see." He scurried through a doorway hung with strings of beads. They hadn't ceased rattling when Mr. Smock reappeared. "So sorry. Johny now arrive," he lied to save face. "He see you now."

The man lifted a wing of the counter so they could pass through. Bronco fairly tore aside the beaded strings which Rommy wrestled with in Bronco's wake. They marched through a storeroom into a dim office furnished with black leather-and-chrome furniture.

"Saving money on electricity, Johny?" Bronco said to a lean Vietnamese man seated behind the desk, his prominent shiny cheekbones emphasizing his sunken charcoal orbs. Two dark-suited Asian men, their hands clasped in front, flanked his chair.

Johny's mouth curved upward. "Only the shadows know what hides therein."

"Let's cut to the chase. You ordered a hit on Nico. He died of a nasty neck gash last night. Two plus two equals gook."

"Please take a seat," Johny gestured. "You too," he said to Rommy.

Rommy made to move but stopped himself when Bronco remained standing. "We're not here to socialize. Did your men ice Nico? Simple question. Simple answer."

"Typical white American. You roar into my restaurant and threaten an employee of mine with a gun. Then you charge into my office like it were yours." He leaned forward in his chair. "Note to Bronco. You are *not* the Pentagon and I am *not* a rickshaw peasant." Johny spoke in a measured voice, but his words scorched the room.

"You boat people should learn your place."

"Where's that?"

"Steerage."

"Like you, I was born here. So I sit where I damn well please."

"You still didn't answer my question."

"I don't take orders from wops."

Bronco launched himself forward, an enraged bull seeing red. He skidded in his tracks when Johny's guards drew Uzis on him.

"If you had possessed the manners to pose your question politely, this display of testosterone would be unnecessary." He motioned to his men to lower their weapons. "On my mother's grave, I give you my word none of my men came near Nico."

Bronco snorted.

"One more point." Johny moved into the glow of the lamp on his desk. A jagged scar marred his left cheek. "I placed no contract on Nico's head. It is a malicious lie invented to provoke bad blood between us." Johny changed tack to lower the temperature in the room. "Are you familiar with the Latin expression *cui bono*?" He didn't wait for a reply. "It roughly translates into *who benefits*? So ask yourself, Bronco. How would I benefit from the murder of Nico?" Johny's logic momentarily silenced his adversary.

Bronco took an audible breath. "When I'm done with whoever iced Nico, they'll be nothing but fish bait." He turned to Rommy: "Let's go."

"Ask the cook for an order of *banh beo*," Johny said to their backs. "It's not too spicy."

"We're no further ahead," Rommy said, once again seated in their ride.

"He's lying," Bronco said. He fired up the engine and gave it a shot of gas. The muffler rumbled. "When I sort out this affair, bodies will fall."

Rommy's blood iced. "Johny sounded truthful to me."

"His mother isn't dead."

"Says who?"

"We have an ex-spook on the payroll who passes us info on demand."

Rommy stared straight ahead. God forbid Bronco should catch a glimpse of the naked terror in his eyes.

Paco and I are going to have to advance the timetable, he said to himself.

Chapter Fifteen

Peaches and pie, peaches and pie, not all is obvious to the naked eye.

Where did this strange rhyme come from? Sharron, clad in a thick Turkish cotton bathrobe, wondered while she critically appraised her delicate features in the bathroom mirror. She pushed on her cheeks with her index fingers. The corners of her lips moved up. She released her cheeks. Her lips fell. She repeated the action. Stay up! she commanded them. Once more, she evaluated the glossy eight-by-twelve photo of her younger self tucked into the edge of the mirror's frame. Snapped eleven years earlier, the photo did justice to her then tight-skinned face.

Mouth's starting to droop. She glared at the mirror. Then she duplicated the same procedure on her eyebrows. Eyelids too. The corner of her mouth twerked. Maybe it's time. She moved back from the mirror. You can't stay young-looking forever, girl. This depressing but candid truth was shortly replaced by a happier one. But Nelson's money can help you prolong it. Her face brightened, her mind made up. Time to give Kim a call. The cosmetic work Kim's doctor had performed was flawless. Of course, Sharron would wait until after the baby was born to undergo the scalpel.

Content with her decision, a decision she had been debating for months, she snatched the photo from the mirror and replaced it in the top drawer of the Brazilian rosewood vanity unit. Done with her beauty inspection, she applied a touch of blush to her cheekbones and jawline and mascara to her almond-shaped eyes. She stood back to assess her handiwork. Satisfied with her artistry, she exited the bathroom and strode to her walk-in closet, as large as a middle-class bedroom.

Sharron had been born into wealth, so every domestic item from her earliest memories was large. A large bedroom. A large family home. A large in-ground swimming pool. A large sedan. A large summer home in the Hamptons. A large yacht. And a large staff to manage the household. Life had always been large and she enjoyed living it in this fashion. How could she not?

Her family's wealth had insulated her from the worries that preoccupied the minds of the little people, worries such as student loans and mortgages and car payments. She never worried about her next meal, only the exclusive restaurant it would be consumed in. Life had always been easy for Sharron, a Cinderella existence.

She selected a black dress created by Canadian designer Danzel Lew whose women's fall collection was creating waves in New York's fashion world. The dress was fabricated from synthetic material (polyester)—as were many of his sartorial creations—but this didn't faze her. Most important to her was the *look* and, man, did Danny-boy know how to clothe the female figure—for those fortunate to have one. And Sharron possessed one. She loved how his clothing made her feel girlish and feminine at the same time.

Once dressed, she admired herself in the full-length freestanding mirror, turning this way and that way. Her tummy bulged a little. "Good enough to eat," she predicted Nelson would say when he saw her, and she bared her dentist-perfect white teeth and growled at her reflection. She let out a self-conscious giggle.

"What's so funny," Nelson asked, entering their closet.

"Nothing and everything, Nels." She spun away from her reflection to face him. "How do I look?" She modeled her dress for him.

"Guess what's for dinner?" He approached her with hunger in his eyes, passion still very much alive in their union of fourteen years.

"Save your appetite for later, big boy. We have a schedule to keep."

"Then how about a kiss to tide me over?"

"Lucky for you I haven't applied my lipstick."

"Lucky for both of us."

"Do you still love me?" she asked post-kiss, playing with his tie.

Seconds rolled out. "Let me get back to you," and he failed to contain a grin.

She gave him a playful swat on the chest. "Be serious."

"Okay, okay. What was the question again?"

She cocked an eyebrow in mock annoyance at him as if to say, "Last chance, buster."

He grasped her tenderly by her bare shoulders and locked eyes with her. "I love you more today than I did yesterday and I'll love you more tomorrow than I do today."

"Am I still beautiful?"

"You're more beautiful today than you were yesterday and you'll be more beautiful tomorrow than are today."

"You're just saying that to please me."

"Baby, beauty, like diamonds, has many facets. Your beauty is more than skin deep. You grow lovelier each day. Especially since you've become pregnant. You have this—this healthy glow about you."

"Even so." She faced the mirror again. "I'm going to make an appointment with Kim's doctor."

"Which doctor?" he said to her reflection.

"The cosmetic surgeon."

"Uh-uh. No way, Baby. Over my dead body," he said, shaking his head.

"Do you prefer cremation or full burial?"

Mirth flashed upon his face. Firmness resettled. "I prefer your not resembling a clown fitted with a perma-smile and slitty eyes."

"You get what you pay for. Kim's doctor is the best. You wouldn't have had a clue if I hadn't told you."

"Kim was one of the lucky ones. Consider what happened to that actress after her nose job. No one recognized her. And I'm sure she didn't patronize a discount surgeon."

"She was unlucky."

"My answer is still no."

"What does no mean?"

"It means I won't pay for it."

"I'll use my own money then."

"I won't sleep next to a mannequin."

"I made my decision, Nelson." She crossed her arms. "It's my face and I'll do with it as I please."

"Fine. Don't expect me to feel sorry for you if the doctor botches the job."

"He's one of the best in the country," she said, doing her damnedest to put a positive spin on her decision.

"Famous last words."

"Why can't you support me in this?"

"Why can't you age naturally?"

"You're one to talk, Mr. Gym Rat."

"There's a world of difference in maintaining one's appearance with weights than maintaining one's appearance with a scalpel. You don't see me injecting steroids to gain big biceps, do you?"

She could concede his sensible point, but her desire to preserve her beauty was worth any price. "I've thought long and hard about this procedure, so I'm not giving in."

"This makes two of us. I will not support your vanity project." He checked his watch. "Get dressed. You know the Vice President doesn't like to be kept waiting and neither do I."

"Do I ever."

Nelson appeared to be on the verge of responding, but instead he spun around and stomped out of the closet.

"That didn't go well," she said to her reflection in the mirror. "Men," she huffed. "They don't get it. Our self-worth is bound up in our self-image no matter how hard feminists argue otherwise."

With her fingers, she pushed on the corners of her mouth. "Better. Hold that pose." She removed her digital support and beheld her plastic smile. "If you don't feel it, fake it, gir—"

"Let's go!"

Sharron jolted at his angry voice. She rushed to finish her preparations before her husband burst a blood vessel.

Chapter Sixteen

From his side of the busy street Lorenzo stared up in contempt at the towering limestone apartment complex, its columns of checkerboard lights soaring into the night sky. Anger and envy churned in his gut. His mama used to spend long hours in buildings like this, scrubbing the palatial homes of the idle rich. From Monday to Friday, she would return in the evening to their one-bedroom apartment in Hell's Kitchen dead-tired and dispirited. Lorenzo accepted her fatigue. The toll physical labor took on her body was tolerable. But he refused to accept the humiliation his mama's clientele heaped upon her day after day.

His mother slipped and broke her leg at work one morning in an apartment undergoing renovations. It didn't heal. The leg became infected. Long story short, she died of gangrene. Lack of insurance killed her. And so did lack of money. Suing the owner of the apartment was out of the question. Try to prove causality without a high-priced lawyer.

Life progressed from bad to worse for Lorenzo. Having never known his father—a ghost for all intents and purposes—and having no close relatives nearby, Lorenzo became a ward of the state. It placed him in a foster home for the duration of his youth. Despite his difficult formative years, he managed to scrape by in his studies and graduate from high school. Life had dealt him a tough hand, but the callous rich had made it even tougher.

The rich are different from everyone else. He recalled this line from a high school English class. The writer who penned it—quotations weren't his strong suit—must have rubbed shoulders with his mama's clients. Why mountains of money made rich people believe they were better than everybody else mystified him. Did the rich assume Fate favored them with wealth due to their *exceptional* humanity?

His target lived in this complex, according to the address written on the back of a photo given to him by Bronco weeks ago. Lorenzo wondered if his mama had ever worked in this building...What did it matter? The occupants were scum. Just then Lennon popped into his head. He was an exception to this rule. Lorenzo adored *The Beatles*. The lyrics weren't vulgar and the band members wrote songs that stood the test of time, unlike today's crop of fly-by-nighters. Did Lennon's killer stand out in the cold too, plotting the murder, resenting the rarified glow radiating from those tall glittering windows?

Lorenzo didn't own a gun. Nor did he ever plan on owning one. Fists were his weapons of choice. A killer he was not. He didn't possess the killer instinct. At least he didn't believe he did. Bronco paid him okay money to give upper-class clients a beating when they fell behind on their loan payments. The workload was easy—if beating people for a living was considered easy. Rarely did the borrowers fight back, for they knew Bronco lurked in the shadows behind Lorenzo, the front man. But when they resisted, they regretted it. One round with Bronco was enough to remind them who was boss in this town.

Wealthy high-stakes gamblers and drug users comprised most of his clientele, losers who couldn't control their compulsions. But the family didn't care about its clients' urges. The only thing it cared about was the juice—the interest on the money these losers had borrowed. So long as the exorbitant interest was paid monthly, the family would roll over the loan each month. More money was earned from juice than from the original loan. Bankers bet on this. And so did the Mob. Only difference, bankers' bled borrowers dry without legal consequence.

Lorenzo studied the entranceway, then the striped crossing, the designated strip of pavement where a pedestrian could legally traverse to his side of the street. Cars raced by in both directions while he schemed. The punishment wouldn't take place here. Too public. He would shadow his quarry and act when the opportunity arose. Nothing like surprise to soften up a target. Sometimes they froze in terror. Other times they fled. Fleers posed a problem— Lorenzo wasn't much of a runner. Running away pissed him off no end and netted the debt delinquent a round in the ring with Bronco. Stupid people. You can run from the Mob. But not for long.

Satisfied with his reconnaissance, Lorenzo melted away and retraced his path. His body craved pillow-time. This job—it's how he referred to the licks he dished out—would be different from the other ones he had done for the family. Never had he the pleasure of dishing out discipline to a member of the super-rich. His quarry might mount a defense. But doing so would be futile.

When he had learned the target of this job, he joked to Bronco he would do the job for free to avenge his mother's death such was his hatred for the uber-wealthy. Lorenzo smirked at the recollection while he trudged homeward. Of course he didn't mean it. Like every other low-life, he needed the cash.

Then a warning from his conscience pinged him. *Revenge is mine sayeth the Lord.* His mama used to recite this biblical verse whenever he complained about a kid bugging him at school. He didn't wish to flout his mama's holy advice, but since she no longer lived in this world, he wasn't disobeying her if he took revenge on her behalf, was he?

He stuffed his hands in his jacket. Right and wrong had never been an issue with any of his prior jobs. What was different this time? he wondered...Maybe because none of his previous jobs had been personal. He gave a mental shrug.

"This one's for you, mama," he whispered into the night air.

Chapter Seventeen

Nelson and Sharron arrived late at the Darlingtons' apartment. Poised to ring, he stopped himself when, for what seemed like the hundredth time, Sharron asked his opinion of her appearance.

"Relax, Baby, you're going to knock 'em dead."

She radiated appreciation. Finally.

He rang the bell. A thin-haired tuxedoed butler swung open the door with flourish and a din of voices made merry with alcohol poured into the hallway. British expatriates, the Darlingtons had fled John Bull's exorbitant tax regime for the saner Uncle Sam system. They had refused, however, to leave in their wake Old World customs. A butler was one of these.

"Welcome, Mr. and Mrs. McCormack." He tendered a slight bow. "Won't you come in?"

This came out more like a request than a question.

"Thank you," Nelson said, allowing Sharron to enter ahead of him. It amazed him how the butler remembered their name.

Sharron left her overcoat with the butler.

Nelson felt the temperature rise when he entered the high-ceilinged grand salon decorated with cream-colored satin wallpaper shimmering with reflected light. Body heat, he surmised. Subdued lighting leveled the playing field somewhat between the *have looks* and the *have nots*, and classical music played from a source he couldn't discern. Men and women, talking loudly and clutching glasses of liquid courage for dear life, crammed the salon, many with lips peeled back in artificial glee, others with faces fixed in solemnity, as though grave problems besetting the world were being solved in this very space. The early birds studiously ignored the latecomers.

Nelson searched for familiar faces when he caught site of Lily Darlington steering a zigzag course toward them through the islands of chatty guests. Help was on its way. Lily earned her keep authoring best-selling crime thrillers. You wouldn't know it, though, her sweet demeanor a camouflage for the cold, calculating mind that lurked behind her innocent exterior. Her husband, Bryson, owned a money-printing shop flogging equities and bonds. It was often said they were a pair of killers, she in the book market and he in the stock market.

Lily and Sharron blew air kisses past each other's cheeks to avoid tattooing the other with lipstick.

"You look yummy, darling." Darling came out as *dolling*.

Coming from green-eyed, raven-haired Lily, this was a compliment. If anyone could compete with Sharron in a beauty contest, it would be her.

"You look good enough to eat too," Sharron said.

They giggled like school girls. Waiting to be acknowledged, Nelson continued searching the crowd for familiar faces, and, since she was worth the risk, his roving eye gave Lily a surreptitious thrice-over—once wasn't nearly enough.

"Nelson, how nice to see you again."

Pretending to be interrupted, he acknowledged her with mock surprise, as though he had more important matters demanding his attention. "Oh! Lily. The pleasure's all mine." He squeezed her proffered hand.

"Vice-President Stanson is holding court in the library," she said, knowing this would be music to his ears. Far be it for anyone to ever accuse Lily of inviting incompatible guests to her *soirées*. Somehow, she knew everyone's likes and dislikes and prepared her guest list accordingly.

Flapping the back of her hand at him as though shooing away a child, she said: "Away you go, my dear." She refocused her interest on Sharron. "Come with me. There's a best-selling author you should meet." Lily hooked her arm around one of Sharron's and conducted her toward the marble fireplace on the far side of the salon where Wallace Whitcomb held forth in a circle of attentive listeners hanging on his every word, *bon mots* apparently spewing from his mouth like pearls from an oyster bed.

"Wally!" She interrupted him mid-sentence. "This is my dear friend Sharron McCormack. If you treat her well, she may deign to buy one of your trashy novels and tell her important friends all about it." Heads swiveled toward the pair of them with wide-eyed astonishment.

Palm on his chest, he feigned mortification. "What remains of my ego just struck the floor."

His audience laughed like trained seals, no funnier line having been uttered in ages.

Wallace extended his hand to Sharron. "Pleased to meet you."

She returned his firm handshake and his steady gaze. "Please tell me about the trash you write."

His avid listeners held their breath. Meanwhile, a grin had sneaked its way onto Sharron's mouth. Wallace took notice of it. "You got me," and he laughed at his own expense. His hangers-on joined him.

Sharron struck a haughty pose and said: "Tell us, Wally. Do you employ a ghostwriter?"

"God forbid I should stoop so low and cheat my readers."

"Glad to know because readers like me pay a premium for the works of bestselling authors. Employing ghostwriters robs the buying public of the trust they are purchasing the writer's own words and not those of a second-rate scribbler."

"Problem is," Wally explained, "top-selling authors are contracted to deliver a novel every year to maintain public interest and to generate revenue."

"I don't see how this contractual obligation jus—"

"Sharron!" Kim squealed. "There you are."

Ignoring Wally, she pivoted in the direction of her best friend's voice. "Kimmy!"

They exchanged air kisses. Kim drew Sharron away from a relieved Wally and his circle of sycophants into an open channel between islands of guests.

"You look *so* hot in your little black dress."

"Don't I," Sharron agreed. "It's a Danzel Lew creation."

"Guess what?" In her haste to tell Sharron her good news, Kim didn't allow her to respond. "My firm finalized an M & A deal today. I stand to make millions. Isn't the law grand?"

They had remained best friends since their hell-raising days at Harvard. Brown-eyed and auburn-haired Kim stayed single, however. It was impossible to swing a partnership in a major law firm in record time while being a dutiful wife.

"A celebration is in order," Sharron said. "And what better way to celebrate than to go spastic with the plastic?"

"Can't wait," Kim said, trembling with excitement. Recomposed, she asked: "Where's Nelson?"

Sharron leaned in, "He's scheming with Stanson and his pals in the library." She tossed her friend a conspiratorial wink. "They're plotting a war with Iran. Keep this to yourself."

"Let's hope they're successful. War is good for some of my firm's clients," she confided. "You know, every time I hear the calls to bring our troops home, I get this uncommon urge to flush a toilet."

Sharron barked a laugh before she stifled it. Heads torqued in their direction while they tittered like a couple of sorority sisters.

Serious once more, Kim said: "Did you hear about the mass shooting in Brooklyn earlier today?"

She nodded her head in the affirmative. "Thank God those shootings aren't committed in our part of town."

"The high cost of living keeps the riff-raff at bay."

"At the back of my mind, there's a frightening scenario of a servant going postal on me."

"You too?" Kim said, saucer-eyed. "I'm careful not to push the hired help too far. They could smuggle a gun into my home."

"It would be the height of ingratitude if one of them attacked us," Sharron said archly. "After *all* we do for them." Her aspect darkened when she spoke these words.

"Anger against the wealthy is at a fever pitch. I wonder if the hired help harbor sympathies for those crybaby looters and rioters."

"Why would they? We pay them well. They receive free accommodation and two weeks paid vacation. What more could they want?"

"Everything we own?"

An angry snort escaped Sharron. "These self-entitled slackers can bloody well earn it like we did."

Kim lowered her voice and leaned in, "Guess what I've been batting around."

"A ball?"

She stifled a laugh, then became serious again. "We should pack a gun on our speed walks through the park. It's pretty deserted in the morning."

"I've never touched a gun. But I can imagine myself posing as a pistol-packing mama." For kicks, she cocked her thumb at Kim and mouthed *Pow*! Kim stumbled and clutched her chest as though she had been shot.

Recovered, Kim said: "I'll text our buddies later about gunslinging."

"Maybe we're being paranoid." Sharron stroked a lock of hair at her collar bone. "The park is safe. Security cameras are positioned everywhere."

Did she say this to convince herself, or Kim?

"Don't be too confident, girl," Kim said.

"We train in a large group, so we have safety in numbers. Who would dare attack us?"

"Predators pick off the weakest member of the herd."

"You read too many of Lily's books."

Kim feigned offense while she reached for a flute of bubbling champagne from a passing waiter. She imbibed more than a sip. "Mmm. A tonic for my stressful day."

"I'd join you if not for—" She palmed her tummy.

"I'm so happy for you," Kim gushed. "How's the little one doing?"

"So far so good. Ten weeks and counting."

"A record, isn't it?"

Sharron nodded. "The god of fertility is in my corner."

"Have you considered cutting back on our power walks?"

"Exercise is beneficial for a pregnant woman's health. And the baby's," she appended.

Kim scanned the crowd then faced Sharron again. "I want to kick off my shoes and let loose."

"Appears I'll have to pull chaperone duty tonight."

"Keep the champagne away from me. I'm in the mood to par-ty." Mischief glinted in her eyes.

"Girl, you always were and still are the life of the party."

"And you always were and still are strait-laced. Cheers!" Kim raised her glass in salute to her.

"When are you going to slow down and get hitched?"

"When I find a man who is willing to let his career play second fiddle to mine."

"So, never, in other words."

"Not never. Unlikely." Over the rim of the champagne glass, Kim asked: "Any eligible men here?"

"You prowl and I'll hold your leash."

"Deal!"

Part III

Ten Days Later…

Chapter Eighteen

Beneath a pinking early morning sky, a gaggle of women in constant but not-ready-to-admit-losing battle with time and gravity gathered near the 77th Street Stone Arch in Central Park. Outfitted in the latest skin-hugging workout gear, they were anxious to kick off their daily weekday rite of passage: speed walking the Bridle Path—so-called because it doubled as an equestrian trail.

Slim legs and round backsides were on full display thanks to a hi-tech sheath of thin black material worn not for personal comfort, but to incite pangs of jealousy in the hearts of their luckless sisters condemned to suffer the flaws of their less-than-favorable genetic endowments. And to add insult to injury, what genes and strenuous exercise couldn't forestall on these speed walkers, the best cosmetic surgeons money could buy did.

Junior, hiding in the woods, something he had done for several mornings past, kept his sights trained on one particular woman. She had captivated him ever since their paths had virtually crossed in a smoky bar weeks ago. He had been obsessed with her ever since. The feeling wasn't mutual though—for an obvious reason: she wasn't even aware of his existence. An uptown lady like her wouldn't give a lowtown slug like himself the time of day.

He was okay with this. Really. If she wouldn't give him a second glance, he would give her something a whole lot more memorable. Yessiree. Uppity wench deserved a comeuppance. She can fling her *flang* and flang her *fling* and not put out a *thing*. Have it your way, lady. Daddy's coming for you.

Once they had exchanged greetings and blew air kisses at one another, enough to inflate a hot air balloon, the women got going, legs striding, arms pumping, hips swaying in the brisk autumn air. They surged away and formed into pairs. Junior waited several long moments, then he approached the edge of the path and stole a glance both ways before sneaking out of the woods. He soon came up to speed—but not without effort—in faded black sweatpants (sweatpants he often slept in) and scuffed-up red canvas sneakers, the standard attire, not of an aspiring athlete, but of an unrepentant couch potato. He followed the female posse from a discreet distance, doing his damnedest not to fall behind. Maybe today would be his lucky day. His aching joints and muscles hoped it would be. Notwithstanding the pain, Junior was exercising and experiencing the great outdoors, items not on his bucket list.

He hadn't progressed very far when speed walking took its toll on him. His breath came in gasps. Keeping up with the female pack on the gravel path taxed what little endurance he enjoyed. Walking wasn't his thing. Neither was exercising. The closest he ever got to a gym was the one he passed by in the neighborhood on his way to the pool hall. His idea of a workout—if it could be called such—involved shooting a game of pool and hoisting cold brewskies with his fellow layabouts. Smoking didn't help his lack of physical conditioning, either.

Junior did his best to keep the women in sight. To his advantage, genetics helped him more than optimal health hampered him. Six feet plus and lean since adolescence—even sinewy—his legs comprised more than half his height. So what he lacked in physical conditioning, he compensated with a yard-long stride.

Between gaps of sporadic conversation, the speed walkers inhaled and exhaled with measured breaths, oblivious of their being followed. They might not have been so relaxed if they knew who was stalking them in this idyllic sylvan setting. Attacks in Central Park were rare, and they typically involved a lone female. This fact, plus their combined number, granted the women a degree of invincibility and permission to lower their collective guard. The *safety-in-numbers* mantra had been drilled into them from an early age and, in most cases, this conviction was sensible.

Soon they were approaching Summit Rock—the woods thickened here and the trail circled back on itself up ahead—when Junior's posture stiffened, but he didn't break his stride. Ahead, a woman had detached herself from the pack and strode off the path into the woods. *His* woman. He marked the spot. He performed a quick check of the trail now glowing amber behind him. Still deserted this early in the morning. He continued for several more yards. Then he veered into the woods near where the woman had left the trail and skulked through the undergrowth and trees.

Slanted sunlight burned through gold and crimson foliage thick in places, and he moved aside branches blocking his way with a minimum of noise. A soft breeze soughed through the treetops. Untethered leaves wobbled earthward through the air and settled gently on the ground. He ventured deeper into the woods and hissing coming from ahead caught his attention. He approached the area with stealth.

Crack!

The snapping of the branch went off like a rifle shot in the quiet. He froze, his foot resting on the broken branch; the hissing stopped instantly.

"Who's there?" The words trembled with existential terror.

Partially obscured by the bole of a stout tree, his target was desperately yanking up her shimmering Lycra tights. Without further regard for stealth or caution, Junior narrowed the gap between them. Birds shrilled and scattered in fright. Poised to scream, the woman froze instead, paralyzed with overpowering fear.

His leg lashed out. Air whooshed from the woman and she doubled-over, but did not maintain this posture for more than a second, the force of his knee driven into her face flipping her onto her back, leaving her nose broken and bloodied. Heavy foot blows pummeled her head, her torso, her arms.

The woman's struggle to fend off her attacker soon waned. Her defensive blocks ceased and her eyes fluttered. Discordant moans and grunts broke the tranquility of the forest. Junior wiped his mouth with the sleeve of his jacket and stood back to assess his deed.

"All in a day's work."

The woman's chest expanded and contracted, he was glad for it. His cautious eyes swept the woods. Stillness reigned. He kneeled and said in a voice with what sounded like glee: "Sorry to do this to you, lady, but you pissed off the wrong person." He copped a squeeze before his victim went limp.

Wasting little time, Junior pulled a black New York Yankees ball cap from a pocket and snugged it over the black beanie atop his head.

To complete his transformation, he reversed his jacket. He was about to don a pair of sunglasses when he heard female voices calling out: "We're back!" Cold fear surged through him.

"Shit!"

He moved fast but carefully in the opposite direction through the woods speckled with sunlight. Before emerging from the woods, he peeked from behind a large tree and scouted both ways. A bend in the path hid his position from the women up ahead. Just then a woman's scream pierced the air. Immobilized by terror, he felt the hair on his neck stiffen. Time to skedaddle. He fairly flew across the path and plunged into the woods on the other side. Despite the brutality of his deed, he sported a grin while he ran. Mission accomplished, he congratulated himself.

A crow cawed.

Chapter Nineteen

Cabreezi stared red-rimmed at the framed headshot of Nico in his grip. Several days had passed since he buried his son. His wife was inconsolable. Tired of her emotional venting, he shipped her off to Sicily to be with her sisters. He was glad to be rid of her. Even though they spent little time together, when they did, it was tense enough without having to cope with the added loss of their beloved son.

Would she be still sad for him if she had known the *real* Nico? He had always treated his mother with love and affection and she reciprocated. Not so with his father. Cabreezi didn't raise the future head of a major crime family with pablum and pacifiers. Hell no. He had drilled obedience and fear into his son from birth. The family required a man of iron at the top, not someone in touch with his *feelings*.

An urgent knock interrupted his grieving.

"Speak!"

The door cracked open. "Don Cabreezi, have you seen the news?"

He palmed his face to wipe away the telltale signs of his grief. Then he kissed the photo and tucked it in a drawer. "What could be more important than my grieving?"

Paco eased his way into the room and took his seat facing the desk. "H-How are you, Don?"

Cabreezi sagged. "My heart's in a vice."

If Paco was astonished at this revelation, he didn't announce it. It was rare for the don to emote. "We miss him too."

Cabreezi's curiosity overcame his sorrow. "What are the men saying, Paco? Tell me," he ordered.

Off-balance, Paco coughed into his hand to buy himself time to think. "They're miserable over Nico buying it so young. He was your strong right arm."

The don's features brightened for the first time today. "I wasn't aware Nico had their respect."

Paco lied: "The men considered Nico a younger version of you."

"Really?" Cabreezi was beaming now. "So Nico's firm upbringing paid dividends."

"Well, you know what they say."

He shook his head no.

"The hand that disciplines the son rules the family."

"Clever saying. I never heard it until now."

"Because I just made it up."

Their eyes met and, unable to control their amusement, they busted a gut.

"Paco, I'm not supposed to be laughing while I'm in mourning."

"Nico's living it up on the other side as we speak, so don't feel guilty, Don."

"You believe so?"

"The soul of any murdered person gains a free pass to Heaven. Purgatory is waived."

"You a priest now?"

"No. I gave a generous donation to the bishop in your name and asked him to pray for Nico's soul."

"Yes, yes. Charity erases sins."

The thing is, Nico didn't make the donation, so whose sins were forgiven? If asked this question, Cabreezi would be unable to answer it, religion not being his strong suit. He swallowed Paco's good deed without any second-guessing, ignorance being the cousin of deception.

"It pays to have a man of God on your side," Paco said.

"I couldn't agree more." Cabreezi, serious once more, leaned on the desk. "So what about the news you announced earlier?"

Paco came alive. "It concerns McCormack's wife."

"The name rings a bell," Cabreezi said.

"McCormack returned your wallet weeks ago."

He snapped his fingers. "Now I remember."

"She was attacked in Central Park this morning."

No surprise registering, Cabreezi said, "Let us tune in to the news."

"As you wish."

He pushed a button on a remote device and the giant TV screen on the wall to his left came to life. His consigliere adjusted his chair so he could view the picture square on.

"If you've just joined us," the female morning anchor said, her voice appropriately grave, "today's top news story concerns the attack on the wife of billionaire investor and philanthropist Nelson McCormack. Sharron McCormack was found by her fellow speed walkers in Central Park early this morning unconscious and brutally beaten."

"Who would do such a terrible thing?" Cabreezi said to the TV. "Women aren't safe in broad daylight in this God-forsaken city."

"A real husband wouldn't let his wife out of his sight. New York's a dangerous place," Paco added.

"Violence is the way of the world," Cabreezi said.

"Perhaps you should call him and express your condolences."

"Yes, yes. Good suggestion, Paco." He remained focused on the newscast. "Maybe we can help him."

"Ask him when you speak to him."

"You're full of grand schemes this morning."

"You honor me, Don."

"I can picture how terrible Mr. McCormack must feel. If someone so much as ogled Donatella, I'd whack him seven ways to hell."

"And I would torture the prick—slowly and painfully," Paco said.

"The law criminalizes vigilantism." Cabreezi left this statement floating in the air.

"Only if the police catch you."

"Good point. You don't require legal help if you haven't been caught. If I were Mr. McCormack, I'd hire a private mercenary to find and avenge my wife's attacker."

The screened blanked and Cabreezi swiveled to face Paco who was shifting his chair once more.

"Such a sad world. So much violence and hatred," the don said. "I hope Mr. McCormack's wife recovers. I'd love to catch her attacker."

"Wealthy WASPs won't ask for our help unless they're desperate," his consigliere pointed out.

"Any idea why?"

Paco snorted. "Because we're wops."

"Pity."

"For them."

They shared a chuckle.

"If the police don't find McCormack's wife's attacker, he might become desperate for help and seek us out," Cabreezi said with a note of hope.

"This could be the Achilles heel we've been searching for," Paco said.

"Yes, we'll take advantage of it should the opportunity present itself." He gave his consigliere a crafty smile. "Leave me now, Paco. I need to be alone."

Paco came to his feet. "Of course, Don."

Cabreezi waited for the door to close. He withdrew Nico's picture from the drawer and set it on the desk. "If only the dead could talk." Tears dampened his flushed cheeks.

Chapter Twenty

The investment firm of McCormack & McCormack occupied an imposing cloudbuster, one of many that formed the high-walled concrete canyons in lower Manhattan's financial district, the pulsating heart of the investment world and prime real estate singularly devoted to the pursuit and acquisition of wealth, both licit and ill-gotten. Founded back in the freewheeling era of the Roaring Twenties by McCormack's great-grandfather, Patrick "Paddy" McCormack, the firm got its head start laundering money from the Noe-Schultz gang's bootlegging operation, a dark family secret passed from father to son. McCormack & McCormack constantly strove to project a corporate image of impeccable probity. God forbid the photo of Paddy and "Dutch" Schultz shaking hands should ever come to light.

The firm had moved locations in this fabled district several times in its history, its fortunes growing from strength to strength. Although its former headquarters on Wall Street had been demolished decades ago, having been replaced by a more grandiose architectural monument to greed, the firm was one of a handful of investment houses in the twenty-first century still possessed of a historic connection to its former address. A testament to the lucrative track record of the firm's financially astute and, dare say, lucky senior managers.

Fashioned from the same mold of his forebears, McCormack, the majority shareholder of the firm—every McCormack had been since its founding—was holding court in the wood-paneled boardroom with his compliance team beneath the stern countenance of former senior partners whose likenesses were captured for posterity in vibrant oil tones on smooth Utrecht linen (the medium of choice for portrait artists since it retained its natural oils, preventing the canvas from becoming brittle and causing the paint to crack). Bathed in bright daylight, *grâce à* floor-to-ceiling windows that faced the rising sun, the well-appointed space was blessed with a commanding view of the muddy East River to Brooklyn. But McCormack had more important matters to deliberate than the million-dollar panoramic view on offer to him.

He and his senior executives were reviewing with painstaking care the latest rules that had trickled from the U.S. Securities and Exchange Commission like so much water from a leaky faucet, an annoyingly steady *drip, drip*. Every quarter, the SEC issued new rules and regulations, or updates to same, to stop shady investment schemes brainiacs had conjured to enlarge the already obscene profits of their respective firms. In an endless game of cat and mouse, the SEC was always playing catch up. When one scheme was banned, or regulated to the point of unprofitability, another money-making stratagem was hatched. McCormack's brokerage firm had to stay on top of these changes or run the risk of being non-compliant and incur financial penalties, a consequence to avoid at any cost.

Planted at the head of the conference table, he looked up from the leather-bound agenda and concentrated on Deeanna seated to his left two executive-styled chairs down from him.

"So, Deeanna," he said to his CIO decked out in a tailored gray power suit, "what's the deal with the rule change to security-based swaps (SBS)." McCormack worked with his bespoke suit jacket off; he didn't fancy wrinkling it. But he kept his shirt sleeves buttoned. Wouldn't want to crinkle the ridge of those razor-edged creases so painstakingly fashioned by his Bangladeshi dry cleaner. The creases appeared sharp enough to shave the CIO's naked glossy gams tucked safely beneath the table away from McCormack's wandering eye.

Prepared for the question, she answered: "In a nutshell, under this rule, the publication or distribution of SBS price quotes wou—"

"Please excuse my interruption," Abigail said, a grim air about her.

An unwritten rule at McCormack & McCormack, no employee should *ever* interrupt a boardroom meeting unless for an emergency. So, when McCormack's middle-aged executive administrator burst into the sun-splashed room, all eyes focused on her with a *this-better-be-good* message flashing in them.

"What is it, Abby?" McCormack asked in the tone of one who knew she wouldn't disturb their meeting for a trivial reason.

"The police are holding for you on line three." Her speech conveyed a degree of disbelief, as if to say, "Why would the authorities be calling *you*?"

"The police?" Abby confirmed his response with an uneasy nod while worry and surprise rose in concert in McCormack's being. He felt cold fear surge from his gut to his extremities. Had they unmasked his double-dipping trades in his offshore account? He quickly dismissed this paranoid idea. The police wouldn't call to broadcast such an announcement, he wagered. No. They'd barge in here, waving subpoenas, throwing their weight around, full of themselves for capturing an uber-wealthy bigshot with his greedy hands trapped in the cookie jar. He stopped debating himself when he realized his executive team was staring at him, waiting for him to answer.

He was on the verge of responding when Cornell, a partner, beat him to the punch. "Didn't I tell you not to snub the invitation to the policemen's ball earlier this year," he joked to McCormack.

Laughter rippled around the conference table, reducing the atmosphere of tension in the room.

"Give us your best imitation of a perp walk," another executive kidded.

"I know the name of a good lawyer," offered another.

Laughter erupted at this sally. McCormack ignored their gibes. "Seriously, what do they want?" he said to Abby above the merriment, hoping his voice exuded calm and innocence.

"They refused to disclose the purpose of their call." She stood rigid by the towering wooden door, her discomfort obvious what with a dozen pair of eyes focused on her.

He quirked his mouth and came to a decision. "I'll take the call in my office." McCormack folded the agenda, rose from his seat and acknowledged his colleagues huddled around the conference table, a blend of concern and curiosity on their faces. "Sit tight people. I'll be right back."

He didn't know it at the time but it would be longer—much longer—than he ever expected before they would reconvene.

Chapter Twenty-One

Later that same day Rommy's sweaty palms wrung the steering wheel of the stolen parked car as though they were wringing out a wet towel. Not a good time to lose his nerve. A case of the jitters could get him killed. He wished to be any place other than Little Saigon, but he had a job to do—a job the family knew nothing about. And if he pulled it off, he'd be a hero. But if he failed, well, he'd be less than zero. Failure wasn't an option.

"It's now or never," he whispered *sotto voce*.

He flung open the car door and struggled to exit, even though the seat was positioned fully back on its rails.

"Rosie's frigging lasagna is going to kill me before anything else does," he complained as he squeezed out from behind the steering wheel. He slammed shut the door, came around the hood of the car, stopped on the sidewalk and studied his surroundings, paranoid of being spied upon. He stood out like a scarecrow at Christmas in this corner of the city. Oblivious to him, Asian-American shoppers, many clutching bags, went about their business.

His chest heaved and dropped before he set off at a brisk pace under a bright sky toward Johny's restaurant. Rommy did his best to appear nonchalant, letting his arms swing at his side, while another part of him wished to run pell-mell in the opposite direction. But Johny was waiting for him. Rommy had arranged this meeting to warn the kingpin of a grave danger. Ostensibly.

He spied Johny's storefront through the throng of humanity and he felt his heart thump harder than on his wedding night.

Steady, big guy, steady.

He tensed his upper-body muscles until they screamed for release. When he could endure the pain no longer, he ceased tensing, and his pulse resumed its normal rhythm. Rommy came abreast of the door and, gritting his teeth, he tugged on it and hustled himself inside. Once again, a wall of exotic scents hit him, and Mr. Smock was bustling about behind the food counter. He checked out the newcomer. If he recognized Rommy, his innocent expression belied it. Several weeks had come and gone since Rommy's last visit, so the passage of time might have erased the cook's memory of him.

"What I do for you?"

"Tell Johny Rommy has arrived."

"I go check." He scurried through the beaded doorway.

"He's expecting me," Rommy shouted to his retreating back. He concentrated on the swaying strings of beads while his gut roiled.

Mr. Smock reappeared. "Johny see you now." Like before, he raised a section of the counter to let Rommy pass through.

Rommy took his time in the gloomy passageway, mouthing words of courage to himself. He entered the dark lair of Little Saigon's kingpin; nothing had changed. Bodyguards stood rigid on each side of him.

Yards beyond the threshold he halted and broke the silence. "You a frigging vampire, Johny. A little daylight won't kill you."

Johny's cheeks creased. "Who needs light when I bask in the glow of your saintliness?"

Rommy snickered. "Don't mind my halo."

It was Johny's turn to snicker. "Please take a seat."

So far, so good, Rommy reassured himself. He eased his bulk into a leather-and-chrome chair unsure if it could support his weight, and it stretched in protest. Dispensing with further pleasantries, he skipped to the end. "We have ourselves a situation, Johny."

"Oh...."

"Bronco knows your mother ain't dead."

"So."

"*So*," he dragged out. "Last time we was here, you swore on your mother's grave you weren't lying."

"A minor detail."

"Details get people in our line of work killed. And your moves are being monitored."

Johny drummed his well-manicured fingers on the desk. "Why are you telling me this?"

"Duh?" his eyes fairly shrieked. He leaned forward. "In case you've forgotten, we're partners in crime. I help you, you help me. *Capiche?*"

"Is Bronco coming for me?"

"He's planning to off your mama per Cabreezi's order. An eye for an eye crap." This ought to jolt him.

Johny's eyes saucered and his fingers ceased drumming. He shot to his feet, his fists supporting his upper body on the desk. "You people are animals." Rage contorted his features. "You would kill an old lady!" Spittle flew from his mouth.

"I have no part in this—this insanity," Rommy said, palming the air in a begging off gesture. "I'm here to warn you. Consider my visit a courtesy call."

"You took a chance coming here." His statement hung between them before he spoke again. "I-I thank you for this." He took his seat again, his anger spent.

"I hope to hell I haven't painted a target on my back."

"What will you do if this surveillance you spoke of takes note of your presence here?"

Talk of surveillance was just that—talk. Paco had ordered an end to it days ago. Rommy sensed his counterpart was probing his loyalty. He had anticipated such a question and therefore had prepared a logical answer. "Bronco sent me as his, uh, emissary. Between you and me, he fancies no role in Cabreezi's vendetta. His procrastination is driving Cabreezi crazy. Killing an old woman would blacken Bronco's code of honor on the street. It's a moral stain he's not willing to live with." Rommy laid it on thick, but not too thick.

Johny stared into space for a long moment. "Honor among criminals. Who would have thought?"

"Hide your mother someplace safe. Send her back to your country," he suggested. "She'll be safer there, won't she?"

"America is my home," he seethed.

Rommy winced.

"We have nothing more to discuss," Johny said, a signal their meeting was over.

Unfolding himself from his seat, "Good luck," he said to the kingpin.

Johny dismissed him with an angry flick of his finger.

Rommy shrugged it off. While he progressed toward the front of the restaurant, a warm surge of triumph overcame him. This ought to flush the little prick out of his lair pronto.

Chapter Twenty-Two

Its red lights flashing and siren blasting, the southbound ambulance flew by Junior sitting in the backseat of a yellow cab rolling north on Central Park West as traffic noise quickened and the morning rush hour thickened. The high-pitched sound soon faded from earshot.

"Serves her right."

He turned to face the front again, grinning.

"Serves who right?" the driver asked him.

Junior thought up a suitable answer. "No one you know."

The driver shrugged. "If you say so."

Junior settled back in the seat. Snooty bitch got what she deserved, that's what. Junior idled his mind and watched the urban scene pass by the passenger window. He changed cabs several times along his get-away route. Several blocks before his final destination, he told the cabbie to pull over. Again, he paid the driver cash. Before exiting the cab, he removed his jacket and ball cap and left on the beanie. Security cameras were everywhere these days.

Junior waited on the sidewalk until the cab became lost in traffic. Only then did he plan to lay low until the furor over his deed flamed out, however long it took.

Chapter Twenty-Three

They were waiting for McCormack in the reception area of the emergency department at Lenox Hill Hospital on the Upper East Side. *They* were Detectives Terrell Ambrose and Camila Sandanos. The police had informed him his significant other had been whisked here by ambulance.

Ambrose, outfitted in a scuffed tan leather jacket, must have recognized McCormack for he waved him over, and a baby's wail rode above the low buzz of voices as McCormack waded through the crowded room.

Ambrose formed the proper introductions, then he said to McCormack: "Your wife was admitted to the Intensive Care Unit a few minutes ago," words the veteran homicide detective had delivered one too many times in his protracted career. "She's out of danger, according to the doctor."

McCormack bit his quivering lower lip and forced himself to ask: "How badly is she hurt?"

Sandanos, average in height and wearing black slacks and an olive jacket, assumed command of the interview. She grasped McCormack gently by his elbow and steered him toward a row of empty seats at the rear of the emergency room. They could speak in semi-private here. Despite the demands of being a homicide detective, her angular, unlined face did not mirror the stresses of her profession.

"Can I interest you in a coffee, Mr. McCormack?" Ambrose asked, his eagerness apparent.

Fetching coffee was a tactic he and Sandanos had developed over a few years of solving crimes together for, once on his way in search of java, she would disclose the grave news to McCormack alone. They had discovered folks expressed their feelings more freely when she was the bearer of bad news, especially if the person was male.

"It's pretty good here," Ambrose hastened to add to sweeten the offer. He had spent many thankless hours in this emergency room, so this entitled him to tender such a favorable recommendation.

McCormack awarded him a grateful nod, and they watched him leave in search of the coffee vending machine.

Sandanos cleared her throat to signal her intent to have a word and this got his attention. She clasped her hands on her knees and leaned toward him. Fastening her eyes on his, she said: "Your wife was severely beaten. She was unconscious when found off the Bridle Path in Central Park by her friends. She entered the hospital in the same state. Her left arm was broken and so were several ribs we were told. There were no signs of sexual assault. This is what we know for certain. You'll have to speak with her doctor to learn the full extent of her injuries."

There were no suspects at this time. Authorities would have to wait for his wife to regain consciousness to determine the identity of her assailant, provided she had snagged a glimpse of him before blacking out.

"I-I'm trying to process why someone would do this to my wife."

"There might not be a why, Mr. McCormack. Sometimes, these attacks are for random kicks."

"Random kicks?" The word *kicks* came out close to a strangled yelp. "What kind of sicko gets his jollies beating up a defenseless woman?"

"In my line of work this type of crime isn't unusual."

An ill expression came over him. "I'm glad I don't have your job."

"Do you have any idea who might hold a grudge against your wife?"

"Are you putting me on?" his pained eyes silently communicated.

She tried a different tack. "Did your wife ever mention being threatened?"

He studied the polished tiled floor for some time. Then he faced her. "My wife is a volunteer counsellor at a drug addiction clinic on upper Broadway."

"Wouldn't be the first time an angry addict has attacked a counsellor," she said to him.

"You mean this kind of crime has happened before?"

"Such assaults usually take place on or near the premises. Not in public areas far from the treatment center."

"I hope you catch the SOB before I do." He felt his blood boil.

"I understand your anger, Mr. McCormack, but please let us do our job. We would hate to have to arrest anyone for vigilantism."

McCormack sulked.

Ambrose returned with the coffee. "Here you go," and he passed a cup to McCormack. He caught the glance cast by Ambrose at his partner, and she told Ambrose with her eyes the disturbing news had been conveyed. "How you holding up, Mr. McCormack?"

"When can I visit my wife?" This came out as a plea.

"Your wife's injuries will take some time to diagnose and patch-up."

"How's the coffee?" Sandanos said to sidetrack him.

He toasted her with his cup. "Not bad, actually."

"A piece of information in our possession may have a bearing on your wife's attack," Ambrose said.

He stiffened. "I'm listening."

"What I'm about to divulge is confidential, so it cannot be repeated, Mr. McCormack, under pain of prosecution."

Nelson beheld them in consternation.

"You were spotted entering and leaving the premises of the Cabreezi residence on West 77th on Friday, October 10."

Shock registered on Nelson. "You're spying on him?"

Ambrose patted the air. "Keep your voice down."

"Can you tell us why you were there?" Sandanos said.

Ambrose interjected: "You're under no legal obligation to reply. But your answer could aid our investigation."

"I have nothing to hide," he said. "I stopped to tie my shoelace and I found Cabreezi's wallet in the gutter, so I returned it."

Ambrose and Sandanos exchanged wide-eyed amazement.

"Did you meet with him?" Sandanos asked.

"No, but I spoke briefly with him on the courtesy phone. He thanked me for my good deed."

"How polite of him." This, from Ambrose.

"You believe a mobster had something to do with my wife's attack?"

"We have to chase down every lead no matter where it takes us, Mr. McCormack."

"What would he gain from having one of his goon's attack my wife?"

"You're a very wealthy man," Sandanos pointed out.

"Cabreezi isn't panhandling for pennies, detective."

"True." This, from Sandanos.

"If he contacts you again, please inform us," and Ambrose handed him his contact card.

"So you understand, Mr. McCormack," Sandanos added, "you're not legally obliged to do so."

McCormack glanced at the card then at both of them and signaled his agreement.

The detectives got to their feet, indicating the interview was over. They wished his wife a speedy recovery and promised to contact him should a break in the case arise. A round of handshakes and they were off.

Several agonizing hours had expired since his earlier meeting with the detectives. Despite the passage of so much time, their conversation still swirled around in his head while he paced back and forth on the shiny tiled floor outside the ICU. Other visitors sat, some patiently, others anxiously, waiting for news of their loved ones.

Nelson was grateful Sharron's parents lived out-of-state. He couldn't deal with their angst in his present mental condition. Dealing with his own was enough for him. There was nothing they could do for Sharron in her present state anyway and he didn't want their company. They would probably blame him for their daughter's misfortune. He had ordered his own parents to stay away.

His huddle with Ambrose and Sandanos had prepared him psychologically, to some extent, for what he was about to encounter. But he couldn't stop himself from obsessing over the brutal daylight attack on his wife in Central Park. Like most New Yorkers, he assumed the park was safe during daylight hours. Hadn't the former ghoul of a mayor cleaned up crime years ago?

He heard his name being called and registered a doctor was trying to get his attention. He stopped pacing to give the doctor his total concentration.

"Mr. McCormack?"

"How's my wife?" he asked, no attempt to hide the desperation in his voice.

"She's stable. Her injuries are significant but not life-threatening. She suffered a concussion but there are no signs of brain damage."

"Oh, thank God," he breathed out. "What exactly are her injuries? The police mentioned a broken arm and several ribs."

"She also sustained a broken cheekbone; reconstructive surgery will be necessary once she's healed."

Nelson felt his features harden. No amount of reconstructive surgery would suffice should he ever his hands on the punk.

The doctor glanced at the ground, then back at him. "Your wife also suffered a miscarriage. I'm very sorry for your loss. For both of you," he tacked on.

Nelson paled at the news. "Can I see her?"

"Yes, but for a few minutes only. She's still unconscious."

Ashen-faced, he headed for the ICU, and a cheerless female voice paged doctors over the intercom system while medical personnel zoomed back and forth along the polished hallways with a sense of urgency, tension in their aspects. Smiles were as rare as winter robins in this wing of the hospital.

He slipped through the doorway and entered the ICU. A nurse at an island station in the center of the facility gave him the number of the cubicle his wife was occupying. He fixated on the white curtain shielding the narrow space while the room seemed to recede into the background.

McCormack steeled himself, every fiber in his body tensing in expectation of what awaited him on the other side of the flimsy material separating him from his wife. He ducked behind the curtain and his heart broke at the vision of his unconscious wife. Like so many tentacles, a spaghetti of wires and tubes sprouted from her body to electronic monitors, and they blinked and beeped in the cold, impersonal language of metronomes, a discordant lullaby only a comatose person could ignore.

The ache in his chest and stinging hot tears could not compensate for the helplessness he felt at the sight of purple blotches and welts on her face. He took hold of Sharron's small, delicate right hand—the other was encased in plaster—and caressed it with his thumb.

"Baby, how many times did I tell you chasing parked cars isn't a good idea?" He stopped himself. *Where did this come from...? Must be my nerves.*

A hot flush of rage reached his head, the extent of his wife's injuries more extreme than he had imagined.

The police better catch your attacker before I do, he seethed.

Images of a man being torn limb from limb screened in his mind.

The curtain rustled behind him; he ignored it. A nurse peeked in and whispered: "Mr. McCormack, sorry for the interruption, but your wife needs her rest."

He nodded his understanding with vacant eyes. Then he concentrated on Sharron. "Don't worry, Baby. The police will catch the bastard who did this to you," he assured her through gritted teeth. "Rest and get better, Baby." He gave her hand a tender squeeze.

And the machines continued to blink and beep their life-affirming signals unmindful of their sterile surroundings.

Chapter Twenty-Four

Sandanos steered the late-model Chevy Impala away from the hospital with Ambrose in the shotgun position, and they advanced in fits and starts in the stop-and-go traffic on Park Avenue as they progressed southward toward their precinct on 85th.

"You know what gets me?" Ambrose said, while at the same time wondering why there were so many cars on the road. Doesn't anyone work at this hour?

"A chili dog?"

He patted his ample girth. "Now that you mention it, I hear the faint ringing of the lunch bell," and he chuckled. "Hunger aside, the randomness of life unsettles me. One minute you're out for a morning walk and the next minute you're fighting for your life in an emergency room."

"I don't put stock in randomness. Stuff happens for a reason."

"Explain yourself."

"McCormack's friends said she left the path to urinate, right?"

"Yeah."

"While she's doing her business, she's attacked by a woman-hater who's out for a stroll in the woods at the same time? Uh, no."

"Too coincidental?" He executed a leap of logic. "Are you wagering she was targeted?"

"The vic—" Tires squealed; they pitched forward only to be jolted by their locking seatbelts. Sandanos swore like a pirate through clenched teeth. "Should we write him up?"

"And be late for lunch?"

"You and your appetite."

Once again they were rolling, and his partner's hands were tight on the wheel. She picked up where she had left off. "Anyway, the vic's husband has a cordial chat with Cabreezi, then a little under four weeks later his wife is lying on a hospital gurney. There must be a connection we're not spotting."

"Your theory's so shaky the car is quivering."

She shot him a droll look. "I'll admit my hunch isn't worthy of being presented to a grand jury, but I can't shake the feeling

McCormack's phone call with Cabreezi and his wife's assault are linked."

Ambrose wasn't entirely convinced, so he decided to play Devil's advocate. "Okay, so supposing your hunch isn't a stretch. What does Cabreezi gain by having one of his goons rough up McCormack's wife?"

"I'm still working on it. When I come to a conclusion, I'll fill you in."

"I hope McCormack calls us if Cabreezi contacts him."

"If Cabreezi does, it won't be done through normal channels. We haven't scored any incriminating conversations during five months of phone-tapping."

"Your hunch might be a longshot, but it's worth pursuing."

"Thanks, partner."

An idea popped into Ambrose's head. "Continuing with your theory, if the wife was a target, it's safe to say she must have been followed."

"The security cameras ringing the park will tell a tale. If we get lucky, the perp might appear in one of the video feeds."

"The techies have their work cut out for them. I predict overtime in their immediate future."

Sandanos nodded in agreement while she maintained her focus on the traffic.

Depleted of novel theories, they drove in meditative silence to the honks and beeps of cars and trucks and to intermittent police chatter crackling on the radio, and sunlight and shadow striped their vehicle while it rolled by buildings reaching for the sky like outstretched fingers. Before long this quiet state was interrupted by Ambrose's grumbling stomach.

"What are we going to have for lunch?" he asked.

"We have reports to complete, so once again it appears takeout is on the menu."

"Bennies?"

"Only if I order," she said. "The last time you ordered, the spicy food burned a hole in my gut and places further south."

Ambrose offered up a sheepish grin. "Bennies has a reputation for unclogging the pipes."

Serious again, Sandanos said: "We have to protect each other's back on this case, Terrell. We can't allow it to spin out of control. An attack on a rich white woman is red meat for the get-tough-on-crime gang in the media and Gracie Mansion."

Ambrose appreciated her worry. "They can lather up with self-righteous indignation and soak in it for all I care. A replay of the Central Park 5 fiasco isn't going to happen on my watch. Trust me on this." He was policing at another precinct when the later-to-be-exonerated suspects in that case were collared and falsely imprisoned because they were Black in the wrong place at wrong time.

"The lieutenant is probably pacing in front of our desks, expecting an arrest warrant to be delivered once we arrive."

"I hope she's wearing a comfortable pair of shoes." Ambrose said these words with an air of exasperation. "If she doesn't go by the book on this case, she can assign it to Laurel and Hardy."

His partner burst out laughing. "Good luck to them."

Laurel and Hardy were nicknames pinned on a pair of detective colleagues who enjoyed a reputation for bumbling. "Those two couldn't find pepperoni in a pizza palace," Sandanos joked.

"There'll be no effing rush to judgement if I have anything to say about it." Ambrose was careful not to swear in the presence of women, part of his strict moral code.

"People will accuse you of sloth."

"Folks can mouth off until their jaws seize," he growled. "My arrest record speaks for itself. Not *one* collar of mine has ever been set free for sloppy or dishonest police work."

"There's always someone lurking in the shadows, waiting to knock a hero off his perch."

"They have a long wait ahead of them. I'll be fly-fishing before any such thing happens."

If Sandanos had anything more to add, she kept it to herself.

Breaking the comfortable silence again, Ambrose gestured at the tall buildings. "Look around you, Cam. The greatest concentration of wealth is located in this spot, on this tiny speck of land. The rich don't live like the rest of us. They build their castles so high in the sky or so far from the road the grit and grime of ordinary life never soils them. Their view of the world is immaculate. No dirty smudges on their windows. Segregation, separation, seclusion. A trifecta only the rich can afford."

"Where's this cynicism coming from?"

"Common folk are assaulted every day in this city, but nobody holds a press conference for them. You can bet *Hizzoner* is huddling with his handlers to hone his get-tough-on-crime message in time for the six o'clock news tonight."

"I hear you. Prepare for the feces to roll downhill."

"Success breeds jealousy. My critics have been trashing my reputation since I was a rookie, but I keep reeking like a bed o' roses."

"They don't call you 'Ambrose the Rose' for nothing."

"Ain't dat da truth."

"Here we are," Sandanos said as the car bounced over the curb of their precinct parking lot. "Next up: our meeting with the lieutenant."

"Suddenly, I've lost my appetite."

"Makes two of us."

Chapter Twenty-Five

Following his day-long visit with Sharron at the hospital, Nelson returned to his penthouse in a mental fog. Thanks to his senior partner position, he had at his disposal a Lincoln Town Car and a personal chauffeur; otherwise, he may not have reached home under his own power, or in one piece. The drive to his place had been a blur of shape-shifting pedestrians, neon-lit shop fronts and glowing street lights streaming past the rear passenger window.

Renalda met him at the elevator door out of uniform.

"Mr. McCormack, I see news. So terrible what happen." She wrung her hands. "Who do such a crime? How is Mrs. McCormack?" The questions came rapid-fire.

"She—she was unconscious when I left her." He felt his legs wobble and willed himself to stand straight, and Renalda's hand sailed to her mouth. "But the doctor assured me she'll fully recover."

"I pray for her."

He gave her a wan smile, not being much of a praying man, nor a religious one, religion having never played a prominent role in his life. "Pray for both us." Petitioning a remote god who would allow such a calamity to happen was beneath him.

"I made dinner. You want me fix you a plate?" There was an echo akin to motherly pleading in her voice.

"Uh, thank you, Renalda, but I'm not hungry." He left her in the foyer staring after him. He needed to be alone with his anguish.

Limned by ambient light from the surrounding cityscape, Nelson sat rigid in a high-backed leather chair in his unlit office and spun his smartphone in circles on the mahogany desk, obsessing over the wanton violence that had torn asunder their lives. The bastard killed my future heir. He busted up my wife's beautiful face. Appears she'll obtain her wish for cosmetic surgery, but for all the wrong reasons now. The bastard's going to pay. He's got to pay. He can't get away with this.

He pounded the desk with his fist, the mobile device jumped.

One moment you're on top of the world and the next you're in a dark pit of despair. How can anyone prepare for such a sudden reversal of fortune? he asked himself. The fact is you can't. You've got to roll with the punches. He sniffed in contempt. Sure. Easier said than done. Your child dies. Roll with the punches. You lose your legs in a car accident. Roll with the punches. Whoever gave this dispassionate bit of advice probably never experienced an ounce of real tragedy in their smug existence.

His smartphone burst to life playing the theme from *Mission Impossible*, and it jolted him out of his self-pity. It hadn't stopped ringing since word of the savage attack on Sharron had gone the rounds on the six o'clock national news. Friends and family had been calling all evening to express their horror and their well wishes. He oriented the radiant screen to determine who was phoning. Private caller it read.

He wavered.

What's one more call?

"Enable speaker," he said to the phone followed by, "Answer."

"Hello?"

"Mr. McCormack?"

The accented voice sounded familiar. "Speaking."

"This is Mr. Cabreezi. I tried to contact you earlier but your line was busy. Not hard to understand why. How are you?"

Nelson bolted upright in his chair. "I...I'm—"

"You must be suffering terribly. I caught what happened to your wife. It's all over the news. Please accept my sympathies."

McCormack spoke in a rush. "I-I can't fathom how someone could be so vicious, so cruel to another human being. She went to the park to exercise. With friends. In broad daylight." Anguish crept into his voice. "It's so..." Too distressed to think straight, jumbled words bounced around in his head, preventing him from completing his response. Maybe the words to describe with precision the senseless assault on his wife didn't exist. He bowed his head and massaged his temples with his thumb and forefinger.

"Mr. McCormack, I won't keep you. If there's anything I can do, and I mean *anything*, please contact me."

"Thank you. Thank for your...concern, Mr. Cabreezi. I have to go now."

"My sympathies. A good evening to you."

"And to you...End call." He gazed in amazement at the phone lying on the desk. What a generous man. Who would have expected such an offer coming from *him* of all people? I guess some mobsters possess a soft spot. He barely knows me and yet he offered to help. In what way? I wonder. He resumed spinning the phone. A man with his resources would be useful in a sticky situation. But I don't deal with wolves, so I don't expect I'll resort to his kind of help.

It never occurred to him to ask himself how Cabreezi got his private number.

He rolled his chair back from the desk and his eyes played over one expensive object d'art to another until they landed on a bronze triptych on the opposite wall of his hallowed space. Three panels of burnished metal depicted a tableau vivant of medieval battles in bas relief. Swords slashed and spears punctured and axes hacked. One could almost hear the cries of battle ringing out from the hammered panels of copper-tinged metal so realistic had the ruthless scenes of war been rendered. He had commissioned this work of art to commemorate his earlier days as a mercenary take-no-prisoners commodities trader. So he had pictured himself.

Finding no solace in the violent imagery, he rotated his chair and stared out the floor-to-ceiling windows overlooking Central Park. Dotted lines of ghostly white light wound their way through the black rectangle of lawn and forest bordered by an amber glow radiating from evenly-spaced street lamps. From twenty-one stories above, the scene below seemed serene, safe. But who could tell what evil lurked in unlit places. Forget the dark. Evil wasn't bound by it. The brazen daytime battering of his wife was proof enough.

But not proof enough—contrary to law enforcement speculation—her assault was an exceptional act of violence perpetrated by a guy who got his kicks assaulting women. He shook his head in disbelief. Of the millions of women in Manhattan, the bastard had to choose my wife...Did Sharron remind the attacker of someone who did him wrong in the past, causing him to direct his misplaced rage at her? What god did she piss off to deserve this? He groped for a motive to explain this senseless attack. Randomness didn't cut it for him. Everything happened for a reason.

There was his inner voice pinging him again.

He deliberated the import of its message. Then of a sudden words Sharron had mumbled in her state of unconsciousness while he stood by her bedside earlier flashed through his brain.

Sorry to do this to you, lady. But you pissed off the wrong person.

He smacked his thigh. Someone had it in for Sharron. This must be the motive for her assault. Pieces of a puzzle tumbled into place in his head until a clear picture emerged. Her attack hadn't been random after all! A sense of exhilaration overcame him. He jumped up and fished through the pockets of his suit jacket covering the back of the chair.

"Got it." He held up the detectives' calling card like it were a talisman. He tapped the phone and said, "Dial." Then he read off the number printed on the card. "Enable speaker," he said again. The phone rang until a female voice finally answered.

A standard greeting, then she asked: "How can I help you?"

"Put me through to Detective Ambrose, please."

"He's off-duty. But I can relay a message to him."

His exhilaration faded as quickly as it had flared. Damn. The police need their downtime too, he accepted. McCormack identified himself, then dictated Sharron's cryptic words to the disembodied voice on the other end.

"Thank you, sir. Detective Ambrose will try to contact you tomorrow."

"End call," Nelson said, and he hoped his wife's unbidden disclosure signposted the first breakthrough in her case. It was his single hope and he clung to it for all it was worth.

Chapter Twenty-Six

Leave no loose ends.

If ever there was a lesson Rommy had picked up from Bronco, this was it.

Johny was a loose end. He could tie Rommy to Nico's murder.

In a parked stolen car, Rommy maintained nervous vigil. Beneath a black ball cap his eyes remained glued to the side-view mirror, checking for Johny's Beemer to roll up Charles Street in Greenwich Village where his mama lived. Shade from a tree kept the car's interior cool. He had hightailed it here after leaving the restaurant, hoping his ploy would play out to his advantage.

So far, so good, Rommy encouraged himself. The street was devoid of pedestrians. Today was his day to be a hero. Or a zero. He was betting on the former. Time would tell.

Rommy wagered Johny wouldn't waste any time coming to his mama's rescue, human nature being predictable—at least in his mind—between sons and their mothers. And parked across the street several car lengths ahead another hot vehicle held Frankie and Mattie. Both cars' GPS devices had been disabled. Stealing a ride was getting harder all the time.

Rommy watched and waited. Traffic was sparse. Minutes unwound. Then he came alive. A familiar shiny grill grew larger in the mirror. "Get ready," he ordered into a walkie-talkie. He stowed the device in a jacket pocket with a gloved hand. He cranked the engine and put the car in gear, his foot resting on the brake. His tongue lapped his parched lips.

The Beemer crept closer. He deserted the mirror and glanced over his shoulder. Now! his brain screamed. His foot stomped the gas pedal, the car lurched and broadsided the passing BMW. Absorbing the full impact, the front passenger door crumpled, and the sorry ass next to the door was flung into the driver. German engineering ceased forward motion in a crunch of buckled metal and a crinkle of shattered glass.

Rommy scrambled out of his car, pistol drawn. He noticed Frankie already blasting away at the windshield. Rommy emptied his weapon into the rear passenger window, exploding it into jagged shards. Johny cringed in the back seat. Their eyes met, and the kingpin's face mimed disbelief.

"No loose ends," were the last words on Earth he heard before Rommy pumped him full of lead. Johny ceased twitching, and his killer yelled: "Let's roll," to Frankie. Rommy scrambled over the hood of his disabled vehicle and piled into the getaway car, Mattie at the wheel. Only seconds had elapsed.

Tires smoked on dry pavement, and the vehicle shot out from the curb screeching bloody murder. "Take it easy on the gas," Rommy said from the backseat. "We don't wanna draw the heat toward us." The engine revved lower and laughter erupted as the smashup receded in the rear window. Nothing stirred back there. A calculated gamble, and it had paid off in spades, he congratulated himself. One problem solved, another one soon to follow. Facing frontward now, he said: "What's so funny, Frankie?"

His jumpy laughter brought under control, Frankie twisted around in his seat. "We just whacked a trio of rice eaters in broad daylight and you're worried about speeding. Too funny," and his snickering resumed.

Rommy pondered his partner's comment for a beat. "Excuse me for my sense of irony." Then a tremor of laughter rippled outward from his belly. He felt the tension drain from his body, like pulling a plug.

"We got them gooks cold," Frankie said.

This earned him a swat to the back of his skull.

"What the hell?" Frankie complained.

"You forget my son-in-law is Vietnamese, or maybe you don't care? Whatever. He treats my daughter like a queen. Anymore racist remarks and I'll whack you right here. *Capiche*?" Rommy gave him another swat for good measure.

Mattie eyed Frankie rubbing his head and sneered. "Serves you right."

"Put some tunes on," Rommy commanded.

Frankie responded with alacrity. Classical music blared from the radio.

"Jee-zuz. Change it."

He found a rock station. "Better?"

"Much."

They drove the rest of the way to the rendezvous without talking, each one lost in his own private fugue. Rommy reloaded his gun out of sight to the sound of drums crashing, guitars strumming, and a heavy-metal band screeching about a highway to hell. Once done, he held the weapon in his lap and watched the urban scene pass by in shade and in sun.

"Almost there," Mattie announced to no one.

Rommy readied himself. The car bounced over the sidewalk, rocking them, and rolled into the dim interior of an abandoned building. He blinked several times to adjust to the gloom. Two cars lay ahead. Mattie drove a tight u-pattern to face the exit and stopped alongside Rommy's ride. He killed the motor.

"End of the road at last," Rommy said.

Before they could acknowledge him, he put a bullet in each of their skulls, and a gruesome mixture of blood and brain matter splattered the dash and windshield. He leaned forward to check their pulses. Two bullets had been enough. Another problem solved. He would ditch the gun enroute to his place.

About to slide out of the backseat, his ears ringing from the close-quarter gunshots, Rommy grabbed one last look at his partners-in-crime slumped in their seats. "Sorry, boys. No loose ends."

Part IV

Months Later…

Chapter Twenty-Seven

Christmas had come and gone and the New Year was almost a month old. Seated beside Sharron on the white upholstered sofa in their living room—spacious enough to hold a tennis match—Nelson was doing his damnedest to encourage her to venture outside other than just to the psychologist since her assault last fall. This was an essential step toward her mental rehabilitation her doctor had recommended. Sharron's physical injuries were on the mend but her psychological wounds refused to heal.

"Baby, it's been months since your attack." He tried to check the frustration creeping into his voice. "You can't remain in seclusion forever. If you cling too tightly to the past, you'll lose your grip on the present."

Trapped in the memory of the brutal incident that imprisoned her in their home, she recoiled and her body shrunk into itself. "He's still out there, Nelson. And so long as he is, I won't feel safe. I-I can't leave here until he's behind bars."

"But you won't be alone," he reassured her. "Your friends will be with you the whole time. They won't leave your side. They promised."

"They mean well." Tears brimmed. "Except they didn't protect me in the park, did they?"

"You're not being fair," he wanted to tell her but decided not to; it was fear speaking on her behalf, not reason. "A private security guard will be tailing you," he added.

No reaction. He reached for her hands and he sympathized with the fear he saw in her eyes. A sense of helplessness overpowered him and he hated himself for it.

"Why me," Sharron complained. "I didn't deserve this. I help the dregs of society overcome their addictions and this is how I'm repaid. There's no justice in this world." Tears spilled out.

All this wealth, he thought, and it couldn't shield us from criminals. Unable to hold her petrified gaze any longer, he looked past his wife to the view beyond the floor-to-ceiling windows. Puffy flakes of snow swirled past, blurring the outlines of the urban vista in a gauzy white tempest, and for a brief moment he felt himself inside a giant snow globe.

He refocused. A man had a duty to protect his family and show no mercy to those who harmed any of its members. Problem was, he didn't have the contacts needed to find his wife's attacker. No scumbag, no revenge. He nibbled his lower lip and mentalized this hurdle...A memory of a conversation popped into his head. He ceased nibbling.

But there *is* a man who can help.

He faced Sharron with what must be resolve. "I met someone a while ago who can render us the justice we deserve."

"A private detective?"

"No. Someone much more resourceful. A man who owes me a big favor. But he operates outside the law," he explained.

She implored him with wild eyes. "I don't care if he's Hannibal Lecter. The bastard killed our unborn child. He must be punished!"

Her vehemence unsettled him but it also stoked the fire of vengeance in him. "I have to go for a walk, Baby."

"Where are you going, Nels?"

"To get help."

"Now?"

"Would you rather I wait?"

Sharron sagged. "Do you what you have to do, but don't be gone too long."

"You'll be fine, Baby." He kissed her on the forehead. Consternation creasing his brow, he left her on the sofa and hurried along the hallway to the bedroom, determination in his step. He pulled on a heavy wool turtleneck sweater, then covered it with a grey hoodie. He rummaged through their closet for his Yankees baseball cap. Finding it, he pulled it low on his head. An old pair of tinted glasses completed the picture. He pulled the turtleneck over his chin and swept the hood over his head. He grabbed a look in the mirror. Hope this disguise works, he said to his image.

Nelson exited his residence into a winter wonderland. Large snowflakes swirled through the air and coated the sidewalk in a downy white mantle. Puffs of snow erupted with each footstep he took. An excited young boy danced around, trying to catch snowflakes on his tongue while his mother looked on with joy. Nelson smiled at her and waggled his fingers at the boy. Rolling tires hissed by on wet pavement, and he kept his head low as he rounded the corner of his street. *They* were out there, watching. He hoped his disguise would fool them. A fleeting twinge of foreboding poked his gut as he approached Cabreezi's building. The same concierge manned the counter and he scowled at McCormack as he approached.

"Can I help you?"

McCormack noticed the lack of a *sir* anchoring his question. "I'm Mr. McCormack. We met a few of months ago, last fall. I returned Mr. Cabreezi's wallet."

Luigi paused a moment. Recognition then flickered in his eyes. His hardcore demeanor changed instantly. "You found his wallet again?"

Surprised by the unexpected wit coming from a guy whose features were a few rounds short a knockout, Nelson laughed out loud. "No, no." He leaned on the counter in a conspiratorial fashion and motioned for the Luigi to come closer. In a low voice, the billionaire said, "When I spoke with your boss last time, he extended an offer of help. The time has arrived."

Luigi nodded knowingly.

"Is there a number where I can reach him?"

Luigi held up his finger. He put the courtesy phone to his ear, dialed a number and spoke Italian into the instrument. He nodded several times then hung up.

"Mr. Cabreezi is delighted you called on him for assistance. He is most eager to help you," he said while scribbling numbers on a message pad. A sound of paper tearing and then Luigi slid a small piece of paper across the counter to Nelson. "You may contact my boss at this number. He's waiting for your call."

Nelson rushed home to his office. He vocally dialed the number scribbled on the slip of paper. The phone rang and rang. And then it rang some more. Come on. Pick up for chrissake, pick up, he willed while he paced back and forth, contemplating the vibrant pattern on the Persian rug, each foot sinking with every stride. A familiar voice finally answered. He stopped his perambulation and his head shot up.

"Mr. Cabreezi, it's—this is Nelson McCormack."

A slight pause communicated down the line, then: "Yes, I remember you now. The investor."

"You possess a sharp memory."

"I always remember those who did me a good deed."

He felt encouraged. "I hope I'm not disturbing you."

"Not at all."

"Is your line secure from eavesdropping?"

"Should it be?"

"I'll answer your question when you answer mine."

"It is."

"The police have your place under surveillance." *It doesn't hurt to ingratiate myself with him.*

"You sound so sure."

"A certain detective told me in confidence."

"Why are you telling me this?"

He blurted out: "I need your help."

"I hope I'm in a position to render you help."

"It's like this, Mr. Cabreezi. My wife—she was physically assaulted in Central Park last October."

"Yes, I remember this tragic assault."

"The police have a partial description of her attacker but no leads."

"How is your wife?"

"Her physical injuries have healed but she's still terrified. She won't leave our place. Her attacker—this psycho killed our baby. He has to pay for what he did to her—to us!"

"I understand your despair. The streets of this city aren't safe for our women. And the police are incompetent. They couldn't find bark on a tree."

McCormack would have laughed if he weren't so stressed. But Cabreezi had provided him an unintentional opening. *Here goes nothing.* He'd convey his request with as much delicacy as he could muster. "So true, but you...A man in your position has—has ways of solving problems the old-fashioned way. Ways of keeping scumbags off the streets for good."

"What kind of man do you suppose I am, Mr. McCormack?"

Damn. He cringed at having possibly offended him. "Sorry. I meant no offense, Mr. Cabreezi."

"None taken."

"I assumed you held the power to put matters right. Since our justice system can't. Please forgive my assumption."

"If you're asking of me what I think it is, then you're asking for a significant payback."

For the first time in his life Nelson felt himself at a disadvantage. Having to deal from a weak position was foreign to him. "Perhaps, Mr. Cabreezi. But never mind. I'll figure it out myself."

"You give up too easily."

"Does this mean you'll help?"

"Friends help friends, yes?"

Relieved, McCormack replied: "True friends do."

"Listen, I cannot guarantee you results. Your wife's attacker may have skipped town," he cautioned. "But I'll put the word on the street. Maybe we'll flush him out."

"I can't thank you enough."

"You helped me in the past. It is only proper that I return the favor."

"I'm so grateful. Thank you, Mr. Cabreezi—from both of us."

"I'll be in touch." The connection broke.

McCormack pumped his arm. "Yes!" For a beat in time, he was one with the medieval fighters depicted in the wall-mounted bronze triptych opposite him. He strode into the living room a little taller and rejoined Sharron on the sofa.

"What did your friend say?" she asked, a ray of hope shining in her eyes generated by her husband's upbeat deportment.

"He offered us no promises, but he said he'd do his best to hunt down your attacker." He embellished the conversation a bit for the sake of her mental well-being.

A glow of appreciation flooded her features. She reached for his hand and gave it a tight squeeze. "Thank God there's someone who believes in frontier justice."

"It's good to have friends in the right places. Revenge will soon be ours, Baby." He touched his lips to her smooth forehead.

"How much is this guy costing us?"

"Not one penny."

Nelson didn't know how wrong he was.

Chapter Twenty-Eight

Paco watched his boss place the phone on its cradle, his countenance beaming contentment. He had only listened to Cabreezi's side of the conversation with McCormack but he had overheard enough to conclude two plus two equals five. Maybe more. No harm in being hopeful. Optimism never killed no one.

"I might be wrong, but your expression tells me *buona Fortuna* has once again bestowed her favor upon you."

Enthroned behind his desk, Cabreezi, sporting a crafty smile, interlaced his fingers. "You aren't," he confided. "As you must have heard, Mr. McCormack was on the other end. Remember him?"

Paco nodded yes.

"He asked for my help in finding his wife's attacker. I can't imagine why? Can you?"

"*Certamente.*"

Cabreezi indulged his consigliere with a gesture to continue.

"A wise man once said: 'A desperate man and his arrogance are soon parted.'"

The don couldn't hide his pleasure. He burst into a hearty laugh. "We'd make a great comedy team."

"I can picture it now," Paco said, describing a marquee in the air with his hands. "Cabreezi and Delonzo. On Broadway."

"A side act to keep us busy in our retirement."

Paco broke the spell. "Except men in our position aren't allowed to retire. We die on the job."

"Quite right. For better or worse." Cabreezi cleared his throat, a signal to return to more grave matters. "Mr. McCormack is very much aware of the kind of man I am. But to a point," he tagged on.

"If only he knew the real you."

"Lucky for us he doesn't, otherwise, he'd have gone someplace else for help." He leaned back in his chair and steepled his hands. "Such is his misfortune."

"Putting a bug in his ear when his wife was assaulted was a stroke of genius." The consigliere was referring to Cabreezi's offer of help to McCormack on the day of his wife's attack.

"Not to mention an act of compassion."

They both stared at each other for a beat, then their laughter spilled out.

"An act of compassion," Paco repeated, and he banged the padded arm of his chair in mirth.

The don carried it further. "Only exceeded by my gentle bedside manner—provided it's a bed of concrete."

"You slay me, Don Vito."

"I hope I never have to," he said with a beguiling smile holding infinite lethality.

Cabreezi liked to remind his underlings of their expendability from time to time to keep them in their place. The omnipresent threat of violence—abrupt and pitiless—not loyalty, was the singular blunt instrument necessary to compel absolute obedience to authority in such a predatory and hierarchical organization. In ordinary human relations, the path of loyalty typically flowed both ways. But in Cabreezi's line of work, loyalty flowed upward, not downward. The fact was, a man in his position had no real friends, only minions.

Paco sobered up instantly. He was the person closest to the seat of power in the Cabreezi crime family, except such proximity put him within arm's reach of the man who exercised this power. "So do I," he said, accompanied by a nervous laugh.

Message received.

"Back to business." Tapping his steepled fingers, Cabreezi said, "We have to fasten a chain to McCormack's neck and keep it there."

"And at the same time he must be muzzled so he doesn't whine when we give his chain a yank."

"Astute point," he said in the manner of a benediction.

Paco gave a slight bow of his head.

"Besides life, what does a person cherish most?" Cabreezi asked.

"Money?"

"One must have freedom to enjoy money, no?"

Paco conceded his argument. "We'll limit his freedom?"

"Correct," he informed his right-hand man. "A pet dog can only roam the length its leash permits. We'll lash McCormack to us with a leash fashioned from fear."

"A leash he'll think twice about severing," Paco finished.

"Men of McCormack's stripe are not martyrs. They are self-styled Masters of the Universe. Their ability to sway world financial markets grants them a feeling of god-like power. But we'll show him who the true master is." His eyes narrowed and his face darkened.

Paco drew back into his overstuffed chair. Sitting in the company of Cabreezi was like facing a restless lion. His boss was at his most dangerous when seized by a fit of megalomania. In his favor, no weapons were in sight.

But would he stoop to use the telephone?

He had witnessed Cabreezi beat a caddy senseless on his private golf course with a four-iron because he had fluffed a drive. The beating didn't stop until he had spent his power lust. Or was it until the metal shaft had bent beyond repair?

He ceased recollecting when he realized the don was fixing him with a severe glare. If evil were incarnate, it would resemble his boss. "What did you have in mind, Don?"

Cabreezi collected himself and his features softened. "A prospect must rub out at least one mark to join our esteemed club." He chuckled at his inflated portrayal of the family business. "Problem is, no one of McCormack's class would ever dream of being a member of our club of his own free will, let alone commit murder. His ilk commit murder of the legal kind, like destroying other nations' economies."

"But for every glitch there's a solution," Paco said.

"It's the rare person who would resist killing a stranger, especially if refusing to do so jeopardized his own life."

"Take a life to spare his own."

"Precisely."

"I admire your reasoning, Don."

This earned him a gracious smile. "We could offer up his wife's attacker as bait. It might not be enough to entice McCormack to meet our membership terms, but I wager it would be sufficient to lure him to our lair. Then we'll have him."

"A worthy plan."

"I'm glad you agree."

How could he express otherwise? "How do we go from here to there?"

"Get the guy who rearranged the missus' face and use him as bait."

"We'll get to him before the cops do."

"*We* had better," Cabreezi said, and to Paco's mind the *we* sounded more like *you*.

Chapter Twenty-Nine

Sucking furiously on a cigarette, worry lines fixed in place, Lorenzo paced back and forth in the living room of a bolt-hole in Port Morris maintained by the Cabreezi family. He had been cooling his heels here since a job he had completed. Bronco forbade him to leave the place until he was needed again. The isolation made him antsy. Many a time he craved a stroll in the fresh air, except he wasn't sure if one of Bronco's underlings was watching the joint. Risking his life was too high a price to pay for certainty. To disobey Bronco's orders would be reckless—enough to earn him a one-way ticket to the emergency room, no expenses paid.

Patience, he told himself. They can't keep me here forever, can they? Why not?

There were only so many movies Lorenzo could watch, so many websites he could read and so many songs he could listen to. Staring at the same four walls day in and day out for weeks on end would give anyone an acute case of cabin fever. He was no different. To add to his malaise, he couldn't take the edge off his isolation with a beer or two or three. Bronco worried about his getting drunk and jeopardizing *the* plan. Whatever *the* plan was.

But being cooped up was not without a rare highpoint. The climax of his lockdown, so far, had been the wall-to-wall coverage of the sensational crime committed against the wife of America's richest man. The victim fit the bill for his revenge fantasy. He thanked his lucky stars his mama's premature death had been avenged, if only vicariously. The story had faded from the news, as crime stories eventually do, even though the attacker was still at large. In the end, to his mind, justice had been dispensed. Not in the genteel manner of the courtroom, but in the savage manner of the street.

He took another quick drag on his cigarette, spewed out a plume of smoke and switched to other pleasant thoughts. Yolanda. Bodacious Yolanda. She wasn't taking his calls or answering his text messages sent from his personal phone. (Bronco had confiscated his phone provided by the family, but he didn't bother to check him for a personal phone. Dumb mistake.) She had meant what she said all those months ago. She and Ali were off-limits to him. Women were experts at erecting an impenetrable cone of silence around their lives. Impenetrable? Probably. But insurmountable? He could either climb over it or undermine it. If he ever flew this coop, he would beg Yolanda for another chance. These past months had provided him the solitude and the time to think things through, to decide what was important to him.

And he had decided to do something radical, something dangerous, something unexpected. It even surprised him when the idea first pinged him. He planned to quit his current gig and start a new life with Yolanda and Ali far from New York. Take a stab at a new life in Colorado. "Go west, young man," spoke to his inner longing. The Rocky Mountains, with their snow-capped peaks, called to him. Boulder's ruggedness was tops on his list. There shouldn't be too many wise guys operating in this city, he reckoned. Maybe he would take up skiing.

He had saved enough money to stake himself for at least a year. It was worth a shot. He was so done with his old life. Finished. Kaput. He relished a fresh start. First, he'd cut his mop of hair real short, grow a bushy beard and bulk up in a gym to alter his identity. Once the personal makeover had taken effect, he'd search for a job, but not in the service industry. Driving a forklift in a distribution center appealed to him. Warehousing was out of the limelight and low-key. Exposure to the public should be minimal in such a work environment. All things considered he was small-fry, so he figured the family wouldn't search too hard for him. Wishful thinking? Not really. More like hopeful planning.

Once he was settled there, he would send for Yolanda and Ali. If she balked, he'd go it alone. It didn't cost him anything to fantasize while he waited for freedom to knock. A life without a goal was like a plane without a flight pattern. If he didn't know his destination, he'd never arrive. He had weighed his options. Sure, being a small-time hood had its benefits: okay pay and flexible hours, but, at the end of the day, what did he have to show for his efforts? Bruised knuckles? He examined his hands. Definitely not the hands of an artist. Scars crisscrossed them. Each had a story to tell. None worth crowing about. Crude reminders of a young life not well-lived.

Time for a change, he vowed to himself. Once I'm released from this joint, I'm out of here.

He continued pacing through the haze of smoke, working off his nervous energy, while his lips moved in silent conversation with himself. Gently falling snow frosted the metal fire escape that chopped up his view beyond the window. There wasn't much to look at.

What is Bronco waiting on? Contact with his boss over the apartment's corded phone had been sporadic. Usual questions about food, drink and smokes. Whenever he asked Bronco about quitting this prison, he repeated the standard answer: "We'll let you out of your cage when we need you. Until then, sit tight and stop your griping."

Easy for Bronco to say. He wasn't cooped up in a one bedroom rat-hole for months on end. Uncaring prick. Man, how he'd love to give the big guy a kick in the *cajones*. Problem was, he'd probably hurt his foot, Bronco's *cajones* being made of brass and all.

His cigarette drawn down to the filter, Lorenzo stopped pacing and flopped onto the couch, his default posture. There was no use ringing up Bronco on the apartment phone, the only person he was allowed to call on it. He wouldn't pick up. Caller ID must be the worst invention *ever*. He fumbled for the remote on the table. At least the propeller heads had the good sense to invent Netflix. Where would we be without it? he griped.

Chapter Thirty

Nelson's brief but inciting chat with Cabreezi yesterday had affected his slumber. He had tossed and turned the whole night, plotting the pain he yearned to inflict on his wife's attacker once captured. Sharron slept on throughout his restless nocturnal torment without a whimper of protest. The sleeping pills were doing their job, though, she still experienced sporadic nightmares despite months of therapy. He glanced at her in the early morning light, nestled beneath the sheets, her blonde hair splaying over her scarred face onto the white goose down pillow, her breathing deep and regular.

He was happy her nightmares were less frequent now. Sharron's cognitive psychologist had taught her mental exercises to deflect her attention away from cascading negative thought patterns. At a thousand dollars per hour, the months-long treatment was starting to bear fruit. Nelson didn't care about the money. He'd pay any price to restore Sharron to sound mental health. She was worth it.

Lying in bed, Nelson harbored no doubts Cabreezi and his boys would catch the prick. The Mob always got their man. Its eyes and ears were omnipresent. So the movies would have him believe. If the silver screen didn't hold up a mirror to reality, it probably reflected a version of it. He was banking on this. To believe otherwise, well...Whether his notion was based on fact or fiction wasn't something he was planning to explore in any depth. A positive frame of mind never killed anyone.

He locked his hands behind his head and replayed the revenge fantasies that had plagued him during the night. To fantasize about wreaking vengeance on a criminal was one thing, but quite another when presented with the opportunity to do so. Was he supposed to beat the scumbag to a pulp with a baseball bat while a couple of Cabreezi's goons restrained him? Or maybe they'd blindfold the guy and tie him to a chair so Nelson could lay into him with leather-gloved fists, you know, like they did in the movies. Put the fear of death in him and make him swear to never assault anyone again. Then what? Dump the guy in a ditch on a rural road outside the city? But exposure to winter weather might kill him. Or not.

What did he care?

Nelson sensed his moral dilemma required more deliberation. He stared at a spot on the ceiling, and the sun rose higher in the sky. They couldn't set the scumbag free, he finally decided. Too risky. The thug could go to the cops…A desperate act only a suicidal person would commit. So he dismissed the idea. They couldn't imprison the thug forever though…Maybe they could starve him to death. Wouldn't take more than a couple of weeks at most, he calculated. Or why not shoot the scumbag in the back of the head and bury his body in a construction site? The dark hole his train of thought was plunging into repelled him.

Stop moralizing, he berated himself. The guy thrashed your wife and killed your unborn child. It's time to man up.

The uncomfortable truth hung heavy in the air. It was far easier to kill someone in the heat of the moment than execute him in cold blood. If he had been present the day Sharron was attacked, Nelson didn't doubt he would've gone berserk on the scumbag without regard for his own safety. He would've reacted—violently. And to hell with the notion of right and wrong. Whether he had a chance of besting the punk was beside the point, especially when his wife's life was threatened. But killing a guy, even if he was a no-good thug, in a cool frame of mind was a scenario Nelson had played repeatedly in his head with no acceptable moral outcome. Despite his outrage at the violence done to his wife, he wasn't persuaded he could conjure the killer instinct necessary to exact retribution when the time came. He hated himself for his lack of nerve.

His inner conflict reminded him of a movie where a homeowner was given the opportunity by a psychotic cop to avenge the thief who had broken into his house and threatened his wife with a knife. Gung-ho until the moment he came face-to-face with the criminal, the homeowner, instead of going Rambo on the guy, chickened out and witnessed the cop beat the perp senseless with a billy club.

"How much do you love me?"

"Huh?" He twisted his torso toward Sharron who was appraising him with one drowsy eye, her hair pushed away from one side of her face, the other half pressed into the pillow.

"How-much-do-you-love-me?" she drew out.

"I would die for you."

She stirred at his words. "Would you kill for me?"

"Without hesitation."

If only she knew the truth.

"What were you thinking about?"

Should I tell her? I can't divulge I'm having second thoughts about pummeling her attacker. "I'm imagining how to punish your attacker once he's nabbed."

"Make him suffer in the worst way," she hissed.

Nelson started at her viciousness.

"He must die a horrible death for what he did to me—to us."

"My friend and his associates will introduce him to the hurt locker. You can bet on it."

"How can you be so sure?"

"They aren't boy scouts, Baby."

"Who is this *friend*, Nels?"

For a second he debated revealing Cabreezi's identity. He decided to protect it. "He's really more of an acquaintance than a friend. It's best if he remains anonymous."

"If he's just an acquaintance, then why did he offer to hunt down my attacker? What's his stake in this affair?"

Fair questions. "He's repaying me for a good deed I did on his behalf months ago." Nelson then told her the story of finding Cabreezi's wallet—without revealing his identity—while on the jaunt home from the burger shack last October.

Sharron bolted to a sitting position. "You hired a member of the Mob to find the guy? Are you crazy? Those people kill for a living."

"First, I didn't hire anyone. Second, you don't find killers-for-hire in the Help Wanted ads. Third, he owes me a favor, so I'm not in his debt. Fourth, I distinctly recall your saying: 'I don't care if he's Hannibal Lector.' You remember saying this, don't you?"

"You weren't supposed to take me literally."

"Beggars can't be choosers, Baby. You work with whom volunteers."

She remained skeptical. "He's risking his neck for you because you found his wallet?"

"His offer to help may seem a little over the top from your perspective, but identity theft is a serious hassle," he pointed out. "Especially for a man in his position."

"I hadn't considered that angle."

Nor had he until this instant. "I guess preserving his identity means a lot to him."

"And to everyone else," she added.

"I'm not worried, Baby. So you shouldn't either," he said to allay her uneasiness. "He's a straight shooter." In more ways than one.

"Be sure to thank him for me when the deed is done."

Nelson marveled at his wife's cold-blooded resolve. He wished he possessed it in equal measure. "You don't seem the least bit conflicted about what's going to go down."

Eyes glacial, her voice remained buoyant. "It's real simple, Nels. He killed my baby. A life for a life." She finished with a thin smile.

"Remind me to never cross you."

"Let's keep this secret between ourselves."

"I can't wait to put this ordeal behind us so we can move on with our lives."

"You talk as if you've done all the suffering?"

He pondered for a moment the legitimacy of her remark. "You flinch every time I approach you, Baby. We haven't made love in months."

"Be patient, Nels. I'm still healing."

He reached over and stroked her cheek, and Sharron didn't withdraw. "Love is patient." She purred while he fantasized about Deeanna's curves. He mentally shook himself.

"I'd better get ready for work." He gave her a kiss on the cheek and scrambled out of bed. "Need anything from the store while I'm out today?"

"How about peace of mind," she said, sliding back under the protection of the covers.

He counteroffered with: "Would you settle for a pound of flesh?"

"Only if it's from you know who."

"Just a matter of time now, Baby. Just a matter of time," he repeated, the bathroom his destination for a quick shower and shave. "Though I doubt there'll be a finger left by the time my friend is through with our guy. But we can always hope." His humor evaporated by the time he reached the master bathroom and he found himself once more in a sober mood. *I can always hope I won't have to do any dirty work. Carving the Easter ham is all the butchering I can stomach.*

Chapter Thirty-One

Sharron stepped from the gleaming Lincoln Town Car onto West 75th while the liveried chauffeur held the rear door for her and took her outstretched white-gloved hand. No words of gratitude passed her sealed vermilion-painted lips. Although Sharron could have walked to her psychologist's office—it was just two streets south of hers—she preferred to be driven, given her chronic state of fear.

"Don't leave till I'm inside," she said to the chauffeur. This came out more like a petition than a command.

"Yes, ma'am."

Sharron loitered on the sidewalk for a moment, clutching her purse, and stared up at the four-storey brownstone, her mood as somber as the overcast vault of sky. "Let's get it over with," she murmured to hearten herself. One deliberate step after another she climbed the concrete flight of stairs to the lacquered oak door.

"Please have a seat, Mrs. McCormack," Jeannine said, coming around her desk and taking an opposite chair. She wasn't on a first-name basis with her patient. Sharron's choice.

The patient slid off her white gloves and placed a matching purse beside her—God forbid it should touch the well-trod carpet. She took her time settling into the chair, fussing with her cream-colored Chanel pantsuit to distraction.

Jeannine was used to this grooming routine, so she read her notes until her patient settled in. She cracked the ice with: "How was your week?"

"Dreadful."

The psychologist's eyes telepathed: "Not again." She waited for her patient to elaborate.

Oblivious, Sharron said: "You see this outfit?"

Jeannine signaled with her head.

"It cost a fortune. Probably more than the crummy dry cleaner who ruined it earns in a month. But did he care?" When her doctor didn't emote, she frowned at her *less-than-edge-of-the seat* interest. Undeterred, she persisted in piling rhetorical dirt atop her petty molehill. "Would you believe he substituted the wooden hanger I gave him for this suit with a metal one? The negligent fool claimed he lost the one made of wood." She rolled her eyes. "My busy maid had to steam out the creases in my pants caused by the metal hanger."

"Why do you assume the dry cleaner was lying?"

"I didn't say he lied."

"But you implied it."

Her *just-below-the-surface* irritation on the rise, Sharron replied: "He comes from one of those shi —one of those foreign countries where corruption is rampant and people lie and cheat to get ahead."

"Could not this same accusation be leveled against this country and its citizens?"

Sharron jolted as though she had been clouted. "Americans respect the law," she sputtered. "At least white Americans do." In a flash, she regrouped. "Aren't you supposed to listen and let me do the talking? My husband told me you come highly recommended. I'm beginning to wonder." Why didn't he hire a white shrink?

"Mrs. McCormack, our assumptions compel us to make judgements. And if these assumptions are based on opinions and not facts, they lead us to formulate erroneous and at times harmful judgements."

In the charged atmosphere, her anger boiled over. "I didn't come here to be lectured to by a Bla—by you!"

"You were going to say, 'a Black,' weren't you?" She denied Sharron the opportunity to respond. "Is your position in society threatened by my being a professional women of color?"

"No, no." She waved her off. "Don't be so defensive. People get so riled up over nothing these days."

"Was the man who attacked you Black or white?"

"You already know the answer."

"I want to hear it from you."

Sharron fidgeted in her seat. "It happened so fast."

"Black or whi*t*e?" Jeannine said with heavy emphasis on the *t*.

She let out low whimper. "He was white as best I could tell."

"And did his *whiteness* have anything to do with the crime he committed?"

Sharron played dumb. "I don't understand your question."

"Did the man commit his crime because of his whiteness?" Jeannine pressed, impatience seeping into her voice.

"I suppose not."

"You don't sound certain."

Sharron fidgeted again. "My thinking is muddled from taking sleeping pills."

"Are you afraid of white men, Mrs. McCormack?"

"Heavens no. Our friends are white." The words spilled out of her mouth before she could catch them.

"So your recurrent fear of being in public isn't predicated on a fear of white people?"

Sharron shook her head. "My attacker is still on the loose. I have a right to be afraid. I'd be insane not to be."

"Would it be logical for him to attack you in public a second time?"

She shifted her gaze to the window beyond her doctor's head. A squirrel crawled in the branches of a tree. Then Sharron tagged the psychologist with her eyes. "He might try to kill me to prevent my testifying against him."

We can hope, her expression hinted. "A fair assumption."

"*Thank you*," Sharron said in her best Church Lady voice.

"But what is the probability of your fear coming true?"

"I don't play guessing games."

"Mrs. McCormack," Jeannine said, tapping her pen on her notepad. "Every day we deal in probabilities when our feet hit the floor and take our first step of the day. Our conscious mind doesn't acknowledge these probabilities or else we wouldn't get out of bed in the morning. We are sustained by the daily hope nothing harmful will happen to us, but sometimes the law of probability decides otherwise."

"Someone should rewrite the law."

The therapist smiled broadly at the comment and Sharron let out a giggle. Before long, it morphed into laughter, dissolving the palpable tension in the room.

"Finally, we're making progress," Jeannine said after Sharron's laughter had subsided. "I'm glad you have a sense of humor. It can help you overcome your trauma."

"Being assaulted is nothing to joke about."

"I agree," her psychologist said. "But if you can laugh at your fear, then you can conquer it, instead of it conquering you."

A spark of interest lit her up. "How do I achieve this state of mind?"

"I'm so glad you asked."

Part V

Two Weeks Later…

Chapter Thirty-Two

It was another slow evening at Pepe's Tavern in the Bronx. Bronco and Rommy sat alone at the bar, nursing their beers, listening to an anchorwoman's patter on the squawk box.

"In other news, the Justice Department and the Securities and Exchange Commission are establishing a task force to investigate the infiltration of organized crime into Wall Street. This is cause for concern. The integrity and transparency of America's national securities exchanges are at risk of manipulation."

"The bosses are branching out? Who would of thought?" Rommy said.

"It's old news." Bronco said it with the air of someone who wanted you to think he knew more than you did. "The law is always playing catch-up with us. We survive by staying one step ahead of it."

Rommy wondered at his remark, but Bronco wagered he wouldn't probe. Like any other minion, Rommy had learnt knowledge was power and this power can be lethal. Asking too many questions invited suspicion. And suspicion invited reprisal, deserved or undeserved. It was best to listen and keep one's mouth shut. An obedient soldier had a better chance of surviving another day.

"What kills me, Rommy, is the government's lack of concern for the scammers who run Wall Street. What a sick joke, heh?"

"Real sick."

They each chugged another swig of beer in confirmation and resumed watching the news.

"Turning now to our top story this evening," the pretty blow-dried brunette newsreader said, an appropriate grave expression fixed upon her face, "Nelson McCormack, America's wealthiest man and husband of Sharron McCormack, who was brutally assaulted while speed walking in Central Park last October, is offering a one-million dollar reward for the identity of her assailant. Contact the police immediately if you have any information about this crime. Mrs. McCormack sustained severe head injuries as well as broken ribs and a broken arm during the assault. The mayor's office once again condemned this heinous attack. Here's Mayor Gordon Banks himself."

The broadcast cut to a silver-haired patrician positioned behind a thicket of microphones. Whenever an issue dealt with law and order, the mayor was possessed of the annoying habit of flanking himself with stern-faced uniformed cops to project a tough-on-crime image. Tonight was no different.

"The attack on Sharron McCormack was not an attack on one woman but an attack on all women. Let me assure the citizens of our fair city the police force is doing everything in its power to apprehend the perpetrator of this vicious assault. Until such time, again we ask female New Yorkers to remain extra vigilant, especially when venturing out alone in Central Park."

The mayor sported the satisfied look of someone who had spouted the perfect soundbite to be quoted ad nauseam by TV talking heads. He couldn't resist the opportunity to mouth more boilerplate platitudes about stricter sentencing and the need for more police officers before stepping away from the microphone.

Bronco couldn't help but smile at the newscast and out of the corner of his eye he noticed Rommy regarding him with a mixture of curiosity and apprehension. "Out with it, Rommy."

He hesitated for a beat. But orders were orders, so he asked: "What's so amusing?"

Bronco stiffened and his stool creaked. The report had revived hard memories of his youth in the Bronx when he was forced to join a gang to protect himself from other street hoods. He faced his partner. "Those uppity rich people are insulated from crime while slobs in the trenches of life got to put up with it day in and day out." His lip curled back when he said it. "I did a stretch of hard time in Spofford because of one of them snot-nosed blue bloods. My papa couldn't afford a high-priced lawyer to plead my case. My accuser's fancy-pants lawyer filed all kinds of legal motions to bleed us dry. I copped to a lesser charge to save my papa from financial ruin." His eyes narrowed and his face flushed at the memory.

Rommy perked up. "You did time at Spofford? How come you never mentioned this to me before?"

Because unspeakable things happened to me, he couldn't say. "The joint was filled with spics and spooks—" Rommy winced "—I had to watch my back every second. The place was a jungle. Survival of the fittest. But I was a survivor. I shivved a few cons to stay alive." Hot rage radiated from Bronco.

"Jeez."

"Yeah, *jeez*." His expression cooled. "If just one of them champagne swillers tastes the fear average people go through every day in these mean streets, then I going to grin till it hurts," and he replanted a smile on his clean-shaven face.

"Maybe they should hire us to protect them," Rommy said.

Bronco gave him such a severe look it could split granite. But in the next moment his body heaved with laughter and what must be relief relaxed Rommy's features.

"That's rich," Bronco allowed. "Real rich," and he clapped his partner on the shoulder, almost sending him into orbit.

Caught up in the humor of the moment, Rommy piled on: "Or maybe we can help catch the guy who committed the crime. I could use a cool million."

If only you knew, Bronco thought. "She's worth so much more, Rommy. A lot more. I'm sure McCormack would even sell his soul for her."

Rommy's eyes expanded but he didn't comment. "So what's on the agenda tonight, Bronco? We gonna clip someone?"

Although the sophistication of organized crime had soared in the digital age, there was still a demand for old-fashioned methods of dealing with the competition when it overstepped its bounds. Methods such as brute force and blunt trauma. No amount of computing power could compete with a high-powered rifle or a pulverizing fist. The virtual world dealt in bits and bytes, but the real world still dealt in brawn and bullets.

"That's what I respect about you, Rommy. You're a real stand-up guy." And he meant it. "We have a job to do tonight, but we're not going to whack anyone."

Some of Rommy's enthusiasm vaporized. "It beats sitting here warming these bar stools like toads on lily pads."

Bronco drained his beer, wiped away the foam moustache with the back of his hand and banged his glass on the bar. "Let's go." He nodded to the barkeeper.

Rommy gulped down the last of his beer and wiped his mouth with the sleeve of his jacket. "What's the job?"

They both headed for the door, Bronco in the lead.

"On orders from the don, one of our underlings rates a *spring cleaning*," Bronco said over his shoulder.

Oh! Rommy's face mimed.

Spring cleaning was a Mob euphemism for eliminating human evidence.

"For insurance purposes," Bronco said in answer to his partner's unasked question while he pulled on the door.

"Whatever you say, Bronco," he said, stepping onto the cracked concrete sidewalk.

The night had deepened.

"That's why I picked you for this job. You'll keep your trap shut." Bronco's pride swelled at the sight of his Chrysler 300S parked down the street. Every hood in the vicinity recognized these wheels belonged to him, so he wasn't surprised to find his ride unmolested.

"There's not much else for someone with my...my limited skillset to do." Rommy laughed at himself.

"Anybody with an ounce of dignity earns his living any way he can. So don't sweat it."

This dose of street wisdom must have struck a chord with Rommy for he walked a bit taller.

Once they were settled in the car, Rommy asked: "Who're picking up?"

"The *cugine's* name is Lorenzo Benini." The powerful HEMI V-8 engine rolled over with a throaty rumble and the littered roadway lit up with overlapping cones of stark illumination.

Bronco studied the urban scene through the windshield for a bit when Rommy asked: "What'd the two-bit loser do that we gotta bring him in?"

"What he was told."

Rommy stared out the passenger window. "Damned if you do, damned if you don't. A guy can't win for obeying the rules of the game."

"Working for the Mob is a dead-end job." Bronco laughed at his rhyming double-entendre and gave his partner a friendly nudge in the arm with his elbow. "So soldier on and keep your nose clean."

Chapter Thirty-Three

Lorenzo lounged on the tatty sofa in the bolt-hole, limned by the glow from the flat screen TV, a bag of Cheezies in his lap.

"You're going to wake up the neighbors with the TV blaring away."

Lorenzo jumped a few inches off the sofa, and Cheezies erupted from the bag. "Jee-zuz, Bronco. Can't you knock like everyone else?" he said, picking the orange puffs off his lap and putting them back into the bag.

"What are you watching?"

"Rambo Two just finished."

"That pussy's no match for Tony Soprano. He'd kick Rambo's butt to Vietnam and back again, wouldn't he?" He gave Rommy a nudge with his elbow.

"Whatever you say, Bronco."

"Kill the TV. I hate shouting."

Lorenzo complied.

"Now le—"

"Anyone for Cheezies?" Lorenzo held out the bag to them.

"No thanks," Rommy said. He pulled a face. "They gum up my teeth and stain my fingers orange."

"I'm with Rommy."

"Suit yourselves." Lorenzo rolled up the bag and placed it on the table positioned between himself and the TV. "To what do I owe the pleasure of your visit," he asked, the words rolling out on a layer of fear.

"Pack your stuff. We're going for a ride."

"A *ride*?"

"We have another job for you."

"Cool. I've been holed up in this crib for months like a prisoner. So where're we going?"

"Yours is not to question why. Yours is to do or die. *Capiche*?"

"Shakespeare?" Rommy asked.

"Who else but the Bard?"

Rommy regarded him with esteem, his ignorance of Shakespeare easily impressed.

"Awright. Awright," Lorenzo broke in. "I dig the spiel. You're following orders." A desperate thought came to him. "Is the don happy with me?"

"He's doing somersaults. So quit yakking and start packing. Chop, chop." He clapped his hands for emphasis.

Lorenzo sauntered down the hallway to the bedroom, flicked on the light and stuffed his meager possessions into a sturdy nylon backpack. He tucked an envelope bulging with the money from his last job in the back of his pants under his shirt. He didn't know if he should worry. Bronco did say the don was pleased with him. A positive sign? Don't be naïve. Into the pocket of his jacket he shoved a switchblade he had concealed in his backpack.

"Chop, chop," he heard Bronco holler again from the other room.

"*Adagio bidagio*. I'm coming," he hollered back. He indulged his desire for a last goodbye. An unmade bed, a drawn blind. Not much else to admire. He strode to the window and raised the blind. Night had fallen. He knew what he would find: a thirty-foot drop to the street below. He might survive the jump, but his legs wouldn't. Then the fire escape came to his awareness. But it could only be accessed through the living room window. He'd never make it. Despite his bulk, Bronco could move like a linebacker. Lorenzo flicked off the light and returned to where Bronco and Rommy waited wordlessly. He searched their faces for signs of deceit but all he found were benign expressions. Still, something didn't feel right, like a t-shirt worn backward. In the past, Bronco would call to give the all-clear signal, and Lorenzo would pack up and head for home. This time was different. Why the escort?

They're up to no good, his streetwise voice cautioned him.

"You collect all your stuff?" Bronco asked.

"There wasn't much."

"Then what took you so long?"

"I folded my clothes. I'm not a slob, you know," he said with pretend annoyance.

"Whatever. Let's roll."

"Where we going?" Lorenzo asked again, slinging the backpack onto his shoulder.

"A place to die for."

"I hope it's not a cemetery."

"It's called operational secrecy." He moved aside and gestured with his hand for Lorenzo to head out. "A guy who digs Rambo should appreciate the importance of operational secrecy."

"Sure, Bronco." He slid by them as though sliding by a pair of hyenas, their micro-expressions as unreadable as a doctor's prescription.

Bronco was the last to leave. Lorenzo heard the deadbolt click into place behind him, a signal the fan was on, the feces flung, and only a matter of time before they met mid-air. A sight he didn't wish to witness.

He led the way down the stairwell passed scuffed walls and bent railings, and dust balls eddied in the corners of each landing. Cleaning staff didn't come with this downscale accommodation. Lorenzo descended the stairs at his leisure, planning his escape in his mind. Once they reached street level, it would be too late.

Downward they marched and their shoes clanged on the metal treads.

Two flights left. Think, man, think.

"Hey," Bronco called out, "if you go any slower, we'll be going upstairs."

Rommy coughed a laugh.

"My knee's bothering me."

"Maybe you've been knocking knees with the wrong kind of broads in all the wrong places," Bronco joked.

Lorenzo couldn't help but crease up at his comment. Humor wasn't Bronco's strong suit, but he pitched a zinger once in a while. Get hold of yourself. One flight remaining, then the gig is up. He developed a limp to stall for more time. I can't outrun Bronco. But I bet I can outsmart him. A ruse sprang to mind. It's worth a try, he told himself. Better to go down fighting than whimpering.

He pushed on the panic bar and cool night air greeted him. Bronco's low-slung transportation, parked snug against the curb, gleamed. Lorenzo faced Bronco who was coming through the main door after Rommy.

"Front or back?"

"Take the backseat," Bronco ordered. "Rommy rides shotgun."

"Can never predict the hostiles we might run into on the trail," Rommy said in his best cowboy drawl.

"Suit yourselves." Lorenzo pulled on the door handle before Bronco pushed the button on the key fob, preventing the lock from disengaging. Rommy had already opened his door and was wedging himself into the front passenger seat.

"I pulled too soon," he said to Bronco over the roof of the vehicle with an embarrassed grin. "Try it again."

Same result.

"Leave the handle alone, you stupid schmuck," Bronco said, sliding into the driver seat.

Lorenzo waited for Bronco to close his door, then he pulled on the back door again. He yanked on the door then yelped in pain, hobbling away from the car, favoring his right knee.

"What the hell's wrong with you now?" Bronco shouted at him through the open door.

"I banged my sore knee with the edge of the door."

"For chrissake get in or I'll toss you in myself."

He saw Bronco face the front and crank the engine. It growled to life.

It's now or never.

Lorenzo raced for the mouth of the alley yards away. Crates and rust-streaked barrels—remnants of whatever commerce had once been transacted here— greeted him when he burst from the throat of the alley. Stacked in tall drunken piles on a gravel plot sprouting patches of dead weeds, the barrels and crates formed the crudest sort of refuge for a desperate man on the run.

He hurled his backpack against the foot of a tall weather-beaten wooden fence and ducked behind a haphazard stack of barrels. Thank God the snow had melted. No tell-tale footprints to follow, like so many bread crumbs. Ten or fifteen seconds later—it felt like a second to him in his panicked state—footsteps pounded by on the gravel then skidded to a halt. Pebbles rattled. He cringed in terror of being discovered. Bronco could run like a linebacker but he was no pole vaulter. Lorenzo heard him swear. Shoes crunching on gravel receded in the opposite direction. He counted to five hundred. Real slow. He wouldn't swear to it on a stack of his mama's *crespelles*, but he thought he heard tires squeal while he was counting.

Four hundred ninety-eight...Four hundred ninety-nine...Five hundred.

He slowly poked his head around the barrel. The yard appeared empty in the faint starlight. He got to his feet in slow motion and came out from behind his place of concealment. So far, so good. He retrieved his backpack and permitted himself a fist pump.

The throat of the alley, darker than the yard, dared him to enter it. Steel garbage containers and plastic recycling bins lined one brick wall. Faint streetlight at the far end of the alley beckoned him. He found his courage and plunged into the void, hugging the bare wall of his former sanctuary. A critter scurried away at his approach, he cringed.

"Stupid rat," he muttered.

When he reached the mouth of the alley, he squatted and peeked around the corner of the building. If anyone was waiting for him, his low profile presented less of a target. The empty parking spot comforted him. He remained squatting for several long moments, glancing up and down the empty street.

Time to go.

He uncrouched and was about to take a step when cold fingers tight on his neck stopped him. His blood froze.

Chapter Thirty-Four

Earlier that same day Nelson swung away from his laptop and studied the boat traffic on the sun-sparkled East River from his corner office perched on the top floor of his company's building. Tour boats, ferries and tugboats plied their way through the mud-colored saltwater estuary bordered by parks, highrises and roadways. Two agonizing weeks had dragged on like a disputed presidential ballot count since Cabreezi offered to help and still no word from him. Not even a simple text message to say the manhunt was making headway. He hated being left in the dark. Too accustomed to having data at his fingertips provided by his legions of employees, the information blackout was driving him mad. So mad he had posted a million-dollar reward to light a fire under Cabreezi.

And still he hadn't heard from the don. Nelson looked away from the window with a tic of annoyance and returned to the crude oil futures market report he had been studying earlier. His commodities team had prepared the report, and it forecast global spare capacity of petroleum to increase in the long-term given the economic downturn caused by yesteryear's covid scamdemic, as he termed it, and recommended buying oil futures contracts at lower prices in anticipation of lower demand in the years to come.

Nelson tilted back in his chair and steepled his fingers. The oil price depended on the Kingdom of Saudi Arabia, the linchpin of America's energy strategy. So long as the kingdom remained in the US orbit, the price of oil could be manipulated. It had been this way since President Roosevelt guaranteed King Abdulaziz's place on the Saudi throne in a one-on-one meeting aboard the USS Quincy in Great Bitter Lake, Egypt, on February 14, 1945.

Should the current Saudi puppet step out of line as King Faisal did with his instituting the oil embargo in 1973, resulting in his being assassinated in 1975 by a cousin and the price of oil being set in London and no longer in Riyadh, the current puppet could just as easily lose his throne to one of the many contenders in the Saudi royal family. As a former Libyan colonel bluntly put it to a former

Saudi king at an Arab League meeting: "The Brits put you on your throne and the Americans keep you there."

So far, the Saudi leader was dancing to the tune composed by US puppet masters. For how long? Time would tell. But should he develop a sense of independence, well, McCormack would reap the financial windfall of a higher oil price resulting from the ensuing geopolitical turmoil.

Nelson leaned forward and reached for his Mont Blanc fountain pen. The analysis was solid and unimpeachable. His commodities team rarely got it wrong. He was certain they had gotten it right this time too.

He pushed a button on his phone console to summon Abby. Her eight-year employment anniversary date was approaching fast, he suddenly remembered. Nelson had a good head for dates. In contrast to many of his peers, he had a master's degree in history from Harvard, far more valuable than an MBA in his line of work. His investment account bulged with tens of billions of dollars in equities, proof of this thesis. Geopolitics, not charts and graphs, drove markets. Always would.

Understanding how the lessons of the past informed opportunities in the present furnished him an unbeatable edge in grasping the seeming randomness of the markets. The reason his organization was top-heavy with political scientists and historians in possession of master's degrees and higher. Number crunchers quantified. Social scientists analyzed using lateral and critical thinking. All new hires in finance and investment had to pass the 'petals around the rose' puzzle in three tries or less. Most of the job seekers with a finance background failed the test.

Abby bustled into the office, her skirt swishing while she marched on the plush Persian rug toward his imposing walnut desk, her digital personal assistant in hand, ready to take notes. He would make her anniversary memorable, like he did every year.

"Abby, send this report to Dick Durban with my compliments."

"Right away, Mr. McCormack," and she took possession of the report. "Will this be all?"

"Your employment anniversary is coming up. I'll dream up something special for your tolerating me all these years."

She waved him off, but his humility touched her. "It has always been a joy to serve you Mr. McCormack. I couldn't imagine working for anyone else."

"And I couldn't imagine anyone else but you to keep me on track."

"Speaking of which."

Nelson perked up with expectation.

"Your three o'clock massage is next."

On-site massage therapists were a company perk enjoyed by the lowest employee.

Nelson bent his neck side to side. "A neck massage is in order. Show her in, please."

Abby turned to go.

"Please hold my calls until we're done."

She gave him a nod and exited as quietly as she had entered.

The massage therapists plied their trade in a dedicated room on a floor far below his own. Senior executives, on the other hand, were entitled to personal visits from a therapist. Nelson removed his tie in preparation for his neck massage. He heard a polite knock.

"Come in!" his voice resounding in the cavernous space.

Charlene sauntered in pushing her portable chair. She wouldn't win any beauty contest, one of the reasons HR had hired her. Maybe even the principle one. This, to prevent his employees, whether male or female, from fantasizing during a massage session. But her fingers worked magic on his neck muscles and this is all that mattered. His trapezius muscles were sore from the heavy dumbbell shrugs he had performed in the executive gym.

"Go easy on my traps, Charlene. I trained them hard yesterday," he said while he eased himself onto the chair.

"I can feel the tension in them."

He yelped. "Gently, I said."

"You iron pumpers are a sensitive bunch. My female patients are much more stoic."

Not one to let a riposte go unchallenged, Nelson said: "Maybe it's because we have more muscle mass and less body fat to knead."

"*Sor-ry*," she corrected him. "Women handle pain better than men. Women give birth while men give out cigars." A throaty giggle ensued.

"Can't argue with you on that point."

Her fingers undid the knots in his neck and he enjoyed the bliss of the moment.

"Can I tell you something in confidence?" she asked.

"Sure." He sensed reticence on her part. "What you tell me is confidential," he said to encourage her to speak up.

"Miss Patella made a pass at me," she blurted out.

Deeanna Patella? The firm's Chief Investment Officer? "*Really?*" And his *really* came out more like: "How could she be attracted to *you?*" Fortunately, she couldn't see him wince at his own remark and he hoped she didn't catch the insult his question conveyed. Too late for a take back. So Deeanna swings for both teams, he mused. Who would have thought?

"What should I do?"

Nelson pivoted in the massage chair and she retreated a step. "The firm has a zero tolerance policy for sexual harassment. But an accusation won't necessarily stand up in court. The burden of proof is upon the accuser. Other than your word, Charlene, do you have concrete proof to bolster your case?"

"I ignored her come-ons in the past, but I recorded our last session together on my phone."

"When did this incident take place?"

"Yesterday."

"You have your phone with you?"

She nodded yes.

"Would you play it for me?"

Showing no reluctance, she produced her phone and swiped it several times to locate the app. Rustling fabric and the occasional sigh issued forth from the device's speaker. Then Deeanna's voice asking Charlene to massage her breasts was followed by Charlene's objections. Deeanna apologized and claimed she was joking. The dialogue ended with Charlene saying she was leaving. More rustling, then a door closed. She stopped the playback.

"Do you wish to take Deeanna to court or do you wish to settle this matter internally?"

"I feel boxed in," she said in a soft voice. "I can't afford a lawyer to fight for my rights."

"What can the company do to make this right for you?"

"I love working here, Mr. McCormack, but I'm afraid of losing my job if I cause a stink about this incident."

"No one's losing their job today," Nelson said to console her. Including Deeanna, he didn't say. So he offered her a proposal. "I will speak to Miss Patella myself. You won't be meeting with her in the future. The firm will compensate you for your pain and suffering. How much money is necessary to put this affair behind you?" He hoped to heaven she would take the carrot.

"I haven't given it any thought," she said.

"Take your time, Charlene," he said, patience in his tone. For someone of her station, he wagered her number would be around a hundred grand.

"I haven't been sleeping well since...since it happened... Therapists are expensive," she added. "Would a hundred thousand dollars be asking for too much?"

He was right on the money. "I agree. Therapists are competing with greedy lawyers in their hourly rates." If Charlene concurred with his condemnatory remark, she kept it hidden. "But your pain and suffering are worth more."

Dollar signs practically danced in her eyes.

"Would one hundred-and-fifty thousand be adequate compensation for your trauma?" Jackpot! she's probably telling herself.

She staggered. "You're—so generous, Mr. Cormack. I accept your offer."

Of course you would. He contained his relief. "I will speak to HR about this settlement later today. A check for the amount we agreed upon and a legal document will be mailed to you by the end of this week." He rose from the chair, signaling their time together was up.

"Thank you for the massage, Charlene. And on behalf of this firm, I apologize for Miss Patella's unprofessional conduct. I can assure you it won't happen again." He rotated his shoulders. "Tension's gone."

"Glad to hear it." She retrieved her chair. "Same time next week?" There was hope laced with uncertainty in her question.

"Of course."

Her features smoothed out. "Have yourself a great day, Mr. McCormack."

"I hope to." He went behind his desk, grabbed his tie off the back of his chair and sat while Charlene showed herself out. "But someone else's day is going to be ruined," he said to the office furniture while he arranged his necktie.

***

Charlene exited Abby's anteroom and stopped in the hallway to text: *mission accomplished.*

Chapter Thirty-Five

Lorenzo squirmed against the calloused hand squeezing his neck like the jaws of a pit bull. "Lemme go, Bronco. You're breaking my fricking neck. Lemme go, you bully."

"I ought to break it but the don wants you brought in alive. Lucky for you," he tacked on.

"Why? So he can kill me himself?"

"Is that why you ran you stupid punk? The don wanted to thank you personally for the way you handled your last job. Here's what running earns you instead," and he walloped Lorenzo upside his skull with his free hand.

"Aayeee!" Lorenzo yelled, and he rubbed the side of his head. "You're not supposed to damage the merchandise."

"The don wants you in one piece. But he said nothing about bruises."

"Awright, awright. I'll quit squirming if you'll stop my eyes from popping."

"I ought to squish your head, punk."

"What did I do to deserve this?"

"What you were told."

"I'm warning you, Bronco. Lighten up or I'm gonna hurt you."

"I'm in no mood for your humor tonight." Lorenzo recoiled from another swat.

No sooner had he done so when Bronco let out a scream unlike any wild animal Lorenzo had ever heard, and he felt the pincer-like grip on his neck release. Lorenzo whirled around and cringed at the sight of a long knife handle jutting out of Bronco's convulsing thigh. A spreading dark spot on his pants surrounded the deep puncture wound.

Backing away, his eyes saucer-wide, his hands spread in a pleading gesture, Lorenzo said: "I-I'm sorry, Bronco. Real sorry, man. But there's no way you're bringing me in alive. Whatever you and the don cooked up no longer includes me. Ta-ta." He turned tail and fled west along East 132nd toward St. Ann's Avenue, the nearest cross-street, and Bronco's voice screaming repetitively in holy rage,

"You'll pay for this," faded as the distance increased between them. Before rounding the corner, he glanced back and saw a pair of legs sticking out of the alley, one of them trembling.

One man down. Glad it isn't me.

As he sprinted up St. Ann's in full flight, arms and legs churning, the 'Doctor' sparked his awareness. A licensed physician and surgeon, the Doctor, so named by the family, was on call 24/7 to treat any medical emergencies sustained by a made man. Bronco's injury will buy me some time, Lorenzo calculated. But not much. Word of my escape will soon hit the streets. And when it does, I'll be a dead man walking.

Lorenzo didn't allow himself to feel sorry for Bronco. He was no friend. Not even a colleague. Just someone who gave him orders. Lorenzo didn't owe him any loyalty. And he certainly didn't owe him his life. Ahead, rectangles of warm yellow light against an inky sky beckoned to him from Bruckner Boulevard, beacons of civilization, but not of refuge.

Lorenzo accepted he couldn't return to his apartment in Hell's Kitchen for the remainder of his sorry life. The don would have it under round-the-clock surveillance until he was picked up—if he was picked up, he corrected himself. But this meant one less goon on the street prowling for him. A point in his favor. The longer he remained in the open, though, the easier to capture him. His above-average height worked against him. Can't blend into a crowd when your head sticks above it. Finding secure shelter from the vortex of violence swirling towards him dominated his attention while he ran, and his backpack weighed him down. Desperate schemes cascaded and collided in his head.

Just then an idea struck him. A bold one. And the more he explored it, the more brilliant it became.

It's the last place in the city they'd search for me.

He scanned the bleak urban landscape while he fled for his life. Unluckily for him, the street was empty of cars to hide behind and businesses were shuttered for the night, offering no nooks for concealment. Panic rose in his throat. Find a spot to hide—and fast. When he came level with Bruckner Boulevard, he stopped and searched for a suitable place of concealment. To his left, he spied a cement staircase jutting onto the sidewalk. It would have to do for cover. He possessed no desire to be a deer caught in the headlights when his pursuers came this way. Lorenzo expected Rommy to circle the block clockwise to find him, and not finding him, return to pick up Bronco and travel this way again.

Lorenzo squatted in the dark corner beside the protective barrier of the staircase, his pulse pounding in his ears, his frosted breath escaping in gasps in the chilly air. No sooner had he done so when a car tore up St. Ann's, its engine's angry roar reverberating ever louder in the deserted street as it approached his location, a match for the loud beating of his heart. Lorenzo risked a peek above the rim of the landing and the red glow of the Chrysler's taillights tore through the yellow light at the intersection, heading north in the direction of the Major Deegan Expressway. He got his breathing under control. The danger had passed. For the time being.

That was close. Too close. He stood and brushed off his sweatpants. *I'm probably the least of their worries until Bronco gets patched up.*

He jogged around the corner and down the street he had just fled up in terror, less desperation in his stride. The dreaded alley soon loomed ahead of him and he slackened his pace, caution once again overtaking him. A dark puddle stained the pavement at the entrance to the alley. Lorenzo skirted it, no remorse tugging at his conscience. Bronco had asked for it.

Back once again in the gravel yard, he put into action the plan he had conceived only minutes ago. He studied the fire escape, the tail end of a metal ladder dangling out of reach. A hook would be grand at this moment...Or maybe not. An easier solution materialized. He shrugged off his backpack and set it on the ground. Then he rolled a steel barrel beneath the ladder and climbed onto it. He stretched for the ladder but it still remained more than a foot beyond his reach. *You can do it.* He leapt and his fingers wrapped around the last rung in a desperate grip. For a moment he hung in empty space, then he plunged, and the rusty ladder screeched in protest at the unexpected tug. His feet landed on the gravel with a *thud*.

Not so hard, he congratulated himself. He slipped his arms through the straps of his backpack and jostled it into place.

About to mount the ladder, prudence asserted itself, and he hastened to manhandle the barrel back to its original place.

No sense announcing his reappearance.

His legs wobbly from exertion and stress, he struggled to climb the cold rungs without slipping off. At the top he scrambled onto the rickety metal staircase and rested. He blew warm breath into his cupped hands. With renewed energy, he hauled the ladder back into place and clanged upward on the metal stairs, counting off the floors until he reached the fourth floor where he climbed onto the grated catwalk, and it complained at him. The window he sought was a few feet away. He hoped it was still unlatched. While living here, he had opened the window from time to time to air the apartment.

He peeked through the window in the weak starlight. "Yes!" The latch was still open, and for the first time in his life—at least in recent memory—he gave thanks to God for his luck. He wouldn't have to break the window to gain entrance to the apartment. But one obstacle still remained: the screen. Too bad. He yanked out the screen and placed its bent metal frame against the wall of the building, hidden from view inside. Although the front door of the building was armed with an alarm, nobody thought of arming the windows. There weren't any portable items inside worth fencing anyway. He pushed up the window, stuck his fingers in the gap and jiggled the window upward.

He tossed his backpack through the opening and entered the room one leg at a time. "Safe at last," he breathed out when his other foot hit the floor. "And warm too." He slammed shut the window to keep out the cold air. In celebration—or was it relief?—he bopped on the carpet, doing his best to disprove white guys can't dance—and failing at it.

Before long, the shakes grabbed hold of him, the icy reality of his dire predicament chilling him to the marrow. He rifled through his backpack like an addict in desperate need of a fix. Amid the tangle of clothing he grasped a pack of cigarettes and heaved a sigh of gratitude. The backpack bounced on the sofa, and the lighter shook while he tried to set alight a cigarette. Several frustrating attempts later, success was his, and he pulled a long noisy drag with his mouth, letting the smoke issue from his nose in a lazy stream, savoring the hit of nicotine.

He paced back and forth in the unlit room, drawing on his cigarette in earnest, the tip glowing bright orange each time he took a drag. When it finished, he lit up another. By the time he extinguished the second smoke, his anxiety had steadied and his body had unwound. He eased himself onto the sofa and, in the empty darkness, contemplated his next move in this lethal game of wits.

He was about to reach for the bag of Cheezies he had left behind on the table when he heard male voices on the other side of the front door. Then a key jiggying its way into the lock. His stomach flip-flopped. He sprang off the sofa and was about to bolt for the bedroom when he remembered his backpack. He grabbed it and raced to the bedroom at the end of the short hallway just before the door opened.

"It reeks like an ashtray in here."

"We won't be here long, so quit your complaining."

"I'll take care of the bedroom. You take care of the kitchen."

Lorenzo cowered in the closet whose door he had left open, hoping no one would bother to peek inside.

A burst of light, then heavy footsteps pounded on the wooden floor.

"Don't forget to check the closet while you're at it," a voice in the next room said.

Lorenzo froze.

"Whatever," a man muttered to himself. Fabric rustled and plastic crinkled. Then: "Nothing but a damn chambermaid is all I am."

Footsteps on wood approached his hiding place and stopped.

Lorenzo cringed inwardly while he pressed his back against an inner wall.

"Boo!" and Lorenzo twitched in the dark.

The man laughed to himself. "Ain't no ghosts in here."

Footsteps plodded away and the room went dark again.

Lorenzo bit his hand to stop himself from emoting.

"Got everything?"
"Yeah."
"Let's roll."
A door banged shut.
Lorenzo poked his head out.

Thin shadows striped the naked mattress and pillow. He went to the window, clutching his backpack, and waited. In the glow of streetlight, two goons exited the building, each holding a plastic bag, and they placed the bags in the trunk of their car. Voices drifted up to him, but he couldn't catch what was said. He watched the red taillights fade out of sight.

Maybe staying here isn't such a good idea after all. He nibbled on his lip. One night and then I'm out of here, he decided.

He turned away, and the bed called out an invitation to sleep. So he did.

Chapter Thirty-Six

The following day Rommy eased the Chrysler next to the curb in front of the don's building on West 77th and killed the engine. He scurried around to the passenger side to help Bronco to his feet, but he shooed Rommy away.

Stitched up but still ambulatory, Bronco ignored passersby' curious glances as he wriggled out of the car, and Rommy waited under the green awning, holding onto a pair of crutches.

The don had summoned Bronco to his lair to account for last night's fiasco. The "black hole"—so-called by the family because an unlucky few had been seen entering the don's building but not leaving it—was the last place Bronco wished to visit. He hoped he would be spared the fate of those aforementioned unfortunates. To maintain a clear head, despite the severe agony in his right quadriceps, he had stopped taking painkillers.

"You won't be chasing any skirts for at least a month," the Doctor had kidded him last night in the small but fully equipped operating room. The knife had missed Bronco's femoral artery by mere millimeters.

Pursuing women was the least of his concerns. Living beyond this day concerned him most. Last night's failure was a first for him in twenty-seven years of serving the don. But Cabreezi didn't keep score. A perfect track record was meaningless. Each new assignment wiped the scoreboard clean. Bronco had never been called onto the carpet, so he had no idea what to expect. He was aware of the don's murderous temper so it would be no surprise if he should leave the building trussed up in the trunk of a car. If such a scenario arose, he would surrender to his fate. Only those afraid to die resisted. He hoped it would be quick and merciful. A bullet in the back of the head would suit him fine. But the manner of his dying wouldn't be his decision.

And there was no guarantee mercy would be on offer today however much he wished for it. A settling of accounts he had participated in a couple of years ago reminded him of this fact. Aluminum baseball bats had been the weapons of choice. (Wooden ones broke.) A soldier had been caught skimming—withholding proceeds of commercial transactions from the family. A big no-no. Bronco and a batting partner started on the soldier's lower body and worked their way up. They had tied the victim to a tree to hold him upright, making the swinging of their bats in a faithful imitation of America's favorite pastime much easier. Once the victim became mushy, they buried his unconscious body—they had avoided any headshots—in the pit the guy had dug next to the tree with his own sweat labor. If the victim was lucky, he died unconscious.

The honk of a horn transported Bronco back to the present. Ahead, the liveried doorman held open the door for him. He stopped at the threshold and beheld Rommy who now stood by the car like the loyal soldier he was.

"Good luck," Rommy called out to him.

Bronco threw him a chin-thrust, performed an awkward pivot and hobbled through the doorway on his crutches.

The elevator ride was the longest one he had ever experienced. A powerful sense of doom pervaded the atmosphere of the constricted space, and the walls pressed in on him. He who terrified others was now terrified himself.

So this is how a condemned man feels.

A chime sounded. The elevator doors slid open and he burst from the elevator as only a man of crutches could, relieved to be freed from his tight confinement. He gathered himself and adopted a brave face. Be humble but show no weakness. At the end of the hallway two men he recognized guarded the wood-paneled door to Cabreezi's office. Their suits strained to confine their bulk.

Maybe their tailor was on a tight budget, and he forced himself to suppress a smirk.

They exchanged greetings devoid of jollity.

"Sorry, Bronco. No disrespect, but we have to pat you down," Riccardo said.

"No problemo."

"He's clean," Antonio said. "Sorry about the leg."

Bronco brushed it off. "The kid's gonna get his and real soon once I'm done here."

"Sure he will, Bronco," Riccardo said to encourage him.

Bronco took his encouragement with a grain of salt for death was the only certainty in their line of work.

Antonio put his ear to the door and knocked once. A muffled voice spoke. He opened the door inward and moved aside so Bronco could enter.

Bronco swung into the office on crutches creaking with strain, and halted a few feet beyond the threshold. The door closed behind him with a soft *click*. The don was hunched over a putter while his consigliere sat on a tan leather loveseat beneath a large abstract painting executed in bold, colorful brush strokes. Not being an art snob, Bronco couldn't discern whether the painting was a one-of-a-kind or a reproduction. Whether it was the former or the latter didn't matter to him. Art was in the eye of the beholder. And he was partial to what the artist had captured in his vision even if he couldn't fathom out the subject matter of the painting.

"Come in, come in," Cabreezi said, his head lowered, concentrating on his putter swing.

Bronco took a few painful hops forward. He hoped the don would make the putt to put him in a better mood.

The putter connected with the ball and it rolled in a straight line toward a metal ring placed about fifteen feet away. Cabreezi stood tie-less, watching the ball roll away while Bronco willed it to sink.

The ball hung on the lip of the ring and Bronco felt his life hanging in the balance. Move! As though it had heard him, the ball tipped into the ring. A wave of relief cascaded through him.

Cabreezi sported a victorious grin and said to Bronco: "Lucky for you I made this putt, otherwise, your fate would have been sealed."

Bronco paled while he plastered what he hoped was a smile of gratitude on his face.

"I'm pulling your leg, Bronco. By the way, how's it healing?" he asked, holding onto the putter.

"It's holding up, Don Cabreezi."

"The Doctor does excellent work."

"No argument from me."

The don approached him and said: "Good to hear. So you won't need these then." He relieved Bronco of his crutches and left him standing in agony. Paco hustled to relieve the don of the crutches and placed them against the armrest of the loveseat to where he had retreated.

Beads of perspiration sprouted on Bronco's forehead despite putting most of his weight on his left leg.

"In which leg did the punk stick you?"

Bronco stared straight ahead, avoiding eye contact with him. "The right leg, Don."

"This one?" And he gave Bronco's muscular calf a tap with the putter.

Bronco nodded in the affirmative.

"And where exactly did he knife you?"

Bronco anticipated what was coming next, so he tensed his injured quads in preparation.

"Here?" And Cabreezi clouted the wound with his putter.

A terrible jolt of agony exploded in Bronco's brain and pinpricks of light danced in his eyes, and he strangled a scream in his throat before it could erupt from his mouth. He felt his armpits dampen and a bead of perspiration tickle his spine.

"You disappointed me, Bronco. You got nailed by a two-bit punk."

"It'll never happen again, Don," he gritted out through his teeth.

"You're my best captain." He patted him on the shoulder and Bronco's heart swelled with pride. "See that it doesn't." He gestured to Paco with his putter and the consigliere returned the crutches to Bronco who, with superhuman strength, resisted collapsing onto them.

"What do we know about this punk?" Cabreezi didn't direct the question to either of them so they both answered at once.

"Let Bronco speak." Cabreezi now sat behind his desk, palming the armrests of the chair.

"His crib in Hell's Kitchen is being watched, so it's doubtful he'll show up there."

The don dipped his head in agreement. "He'd have to be suicidal—or stupid—if he did." He gestured with his hand to continue.

"He has no family and he never mentioned any relationship with a woman," Bronco continued. "Let's spread money around the local flophouses and flush him out. It's winter. He'll seek shelter."

"Sound reasoning."

"We should also monitor the bus depots," Bronco continued.

"Anything else?"

"Give me first crack at this punk once he's captured."

"Granted. But bring him to me alive," the don stressed.

"You have my word. The prick has to pay for what he did."

"Oh, he'll pay. He'll pay in the worst way." Cabreezi promised.

Paco, his hairy upper chest bedecked with a ponderous gold chain, said: "Our network has been alerted to the importance of finding this prick. If he goes to the police, there's no telling what damage he can do the family."

Cabreezi settled his severe countenance on Bronco. "This matter is settled. Do what must be done."

Bronco took this as his cue to leave, but he felt compelled to grovel before the man who had spared his life. "Thank *you*, Don Cabreezi, for allowing me the opportunity to correct the error in judgement I made last night. I won't underestimate an opponent in the future."

Cabreezi acknowledged his contrition with a regal-like nod.

Paco moved to open the door.

When the door clicked behind him, both guards clapped Bronco on the back.

"You're a true survivor," Riccardo said.

"It's a reprieve. But I'll take it."

"It's a happier ending than some unfortunate fellas get," Antonio said. "The don must have a soft spot you."

He has a sadistic way of showing it. "We go back a long way. It must have counted in my favor."

"I bet it did," Riccardo agreed.

After his life-and-death ordeal, Bronco, in no mood for small talk, refrained from replying. He was desperate to put distance between himself and the black hole whose treacherous maw he had narrowly escaped. "Could one of you get the elevator for me?"

"Sure. No sweat, Bronco."

The ride down was the most exhilarating of his life. Rommy was waiting for him in the driver's seat. Bronco tapped on the passenger window with his crutch to gain his attention. Rommy scooted around to his side with alacrity.

"You made it out alive." He affected no attempt to mask the amazement in his voice.

"My life is on loan to me until we catch the punk."

"We'll catch him, Bronco, we'll catch him. This city ain't big enough for him to hide in."

"I hope to hell he hasn't skipped town already or I'll be taking a one-way trip through the black hole."

Rommy grimaced while he helped Bronco into the front seat. "And I'll be right behind you. Guilty by association."

"Paco put our people in play," Bronco said.

"The kid couldn't have gotten far." Rommy swung shut the passenger door.

"Man, it's great to be alive," Bronco said, staring through the windshield at Rommy skirting the hood of the vehicle. He shivered, but not from the cold.

Chapter Thirty-Seven

While Bronco got to work tracking down his wily fugitive with the doggedness of a Doberman, Lorenzo ducked out of the apartment the same way he had entered to make a bank run. It was a calculated but necessary risk. He spent the rest of the new day on edge, his ears straining at every odd *tick* and *thump*. He logged countless trips to the windows and the front door, looking and listening for signs of danger. He was relieved when the curtain of night had descended. Before skipping out of the apartment the same way he had entered, he composed a note detailing the poor living conditions he had endured and left it on the living room table, his way of giving his former associates the proverbial finger.

Beneath a brooding sky, he hauled feet to Bruckner Boulevard and hired an Uber cab to convey him to Yolanda's place in southeast Yonkers, a mixed neighborhood of Irish and Italian families. He didn't trust the cab companies, several of them had been infiltrated by the Mob. No sense taking unnecessary risks with his life.

As luck would have it, he was forced to suffer a rant of the driver, a Canadian expat who complained the whole trip about Americans ruining his former homeland's national sport, this being hockey. One part of Lorenzo's awareness grunted at appropriate moments in the monologue while another part ruminated on what he would say to Yolanda whom he hadn't seen in...must be several months. He had forgotten the exact date of their last get-together. Yolanda probably hadn't. In fact, he'd bet money on it.

Lorenzo interrupted the driver's tirade to tell him to take the Yonkers Avenue east exit off the Eighty-Seven. The driver complied—earning him several angry blasts of horns—and without skipping a beat launched back into his criticism of the NHL commissioner who he compared to a fetid human orifice.

Lorenzo snickered at his imaginative description of the hockey official.

"Take a right on Kimball Avenue," he cut across the driver's droning voice. His gut churned, his destination was near. The Hillview Reservoir soon appeared to his right. No signs announced its location and he couldn't actually see the reservoir, but locals knew the black frost-free fence scrolling past his eyes surrounded the large basin of water out of sight.

How do I worm my way into her apartment? Skeletal trees, stark against the moody night sky, whipped by. With the truth and a dose of humor, he decided.

A little beyond Wakefield Avenue he ordered: "Pull over here."

Here was a parking lot for residents living on the other side of the street. Lorenzo paid the driver in cash and was happy to escape into the silence of the crisp, winter air. He watched the vehicle's taillights fade away to red pinpricks. Good riddance motor-mouth. He shrugged on his backpack and walked back in the direction he had just travelled. On the outside chance his pursuers tracked down the Uber driver, the most he could tell them was the location Lorenzo had exited the cab.

His hurried feet beat a tattoo on the sidewalk. He made his way onto deserted Wakefield Avenue and headed east toward New Avenue. Not a soul was out on this frigid night. All to the better. He bunched his shoulders against the chill, his hoodie and light jacket not rising to the challenge of winter weather.

Brightly lit single-family dwellings lined both sides of the street, and, surrendering to the urge to peep, he noted their well-stocked interiors. Big screen TVs glowed within like giant aquariums, their viewers mesmerized by the changing images trapped behind the matte display. But these scenes of middle-class domesticity failed to kindle warm and fuzzy memories. Instead, nightmares of a drunken foster father terrorizing him and his foster mother replayed behind his eyes. Physical and psychological abuse were his constant companions in his youth. He squeezed shut his eyes for a brief moment to erase these horror-filled images.

When he opened his eyes, he focused on his objective. You still haven't concocted a game plan for gaining Yolanda's good side, he scolded himself. Think, man, think. But no plausible strategy presented itself.

Before he knew it, he reached New Avenue. Gaining his bearings, he headed right, and his stomach churned like a whirlpool.

When he arrived at Scott Avenue, he headed left. Soon enough, the apartment block he sought stood stark against the night sky, its checkerboard pattern of electric light stretching eight stories high.

"Time to rumble."

He crossed the street to the building and pressed Yolanda's number on the buzzer panel.

"Who is it?" Irritation coated her voice.

"Guess who?"

"Guess not, loser."

This is going to be harder than expected. He bit his lower lip.

"I'm not a loser, Yolanda. I left you enough money last time we met to cover your expenses, and I brought more tonight."

"Your son needs a father, a real father. Not someone who pops in and out his life like a jack-in-the-box."

Desperation engulfed him. "Please, Yolanda. I'm in big trouble. Help me out. Let me crash here for the night."

"This is not a hotel."

"Can I at least use the toilet?"

"Use a fire hydrant."

"There's a lineup. Every two-legged hound dog in the neighborhood is gathered here tonight."

"You're so pathetic."

"Don't you mean *sym*pathetic?"

He heard her titter.

"Don't push your luck, buster."

"It's all I got."

The main door buzzed.

He clenched his fists in victory and hissed: "Yes!" He pulled on the door and strode across the spacious granite-floored lobby to the elevators. The tight compartment rose and the noise of his churning gut grew louder.

You've got one foot in the door, so don't screw it up.

On the fifth floor the elevator door slid open. No one was waiting. So far, so good. He headed left out of the elevator and followed the elbow in the corridor to the right. Subdued lighting in the ceiling cast a welcoming glow in the carpeted hallway. He approached Yolanda's door and it dawned on him his appearance was probably less than presentable. Not one for carrying a comb, he smoothed back his bushy hair with his fingers and checked the condition of his clothing.

Macho-ness is in the eye of the beholder, he reminded himself. Keep telling yourself that, you loser.

He entered into a protracted hesitation at her door. He sucked in a lungful of air and let it out. Here goes nothing. Instead of ringing the bell, he knocked. Ali was most likely asleep.

The rasp of a deadbolt sliding back resounded in the corridor. The door opened a crack and a sturdy chain bridged the gap.

Then luscious Yolanda's face appeared. "Well, well, look what the wind blew my way. Male trash," she said through the narrow opening.

"Are you going to let me in and shame me in the privacy of your home or are you going to inform your neighbors how much you hate me?"

"I don't hate you. I'm indifferent to you."

"Of course we're different. So let's discuss our differences in private." He sweetened his offer with a clownish grin.

"You're twisting my words."

Lorenzo stood there, still grinning clownishly.

"You're *so* pathetic." She closed the door on him.

He heard the chain rattle. Then the door reopened, but Yolanda had disappeared into the apartment. He pushed open the door and entered the cozy interior. A tidy kitchen spread away from him and to his immediate left was the combination living-dining room. He bolted the door.

You made it!

About to take a step, he stopped himself and removed his running shoes.

He didn't want to start off on the wrong foot.

He padded in his stocking feet on the hardwood floor into the tastefully furnished living room. His eyes swept the room. The TV was off. A child's firetruck and a ball lay on the patterned carpet in a corner, toys he had purchased for his son on his last visit. Off to his right the cry of his son caught his attention, then Yolanda's soothing voice calming him. He moved toward the hushed baby talk.

"What's wrong with Ali?" he asked in a low voice from the doorway of his son's room illuminated by a baby light.

Yolanda was leaning over the side of the crib, dabbing Ali's forehead with a damp cloth. "He has a fever. His damn daycare is an incubator for childhood bugs."

"Can I help?"

She favored him with a glare. She didn't have to speak. Her eyes spoke volumes: "If you were a real father, I could stay home and raise our son."

He withered from her glare. Not knowing what else to say, he asked: "Does he need medicine?"

"I gave him the last of the liquid Advil. It should lower his fever."

Lorenzo concurred with a nod. "Mothers know best." His experience with childhood illnesses was minimal to none.

Done with her ministrations, she shooed him out of the bedroom, and headed for the living room. He obeyed like an obedient puppy.

"Stop!"

Poised to seat himself, Lorenzo froze mid-motion, a rictus of terror fixed on his face.

"You can't sit on my sofa in those rags."

He scanned the immaculate room. "Maybe I'd better remain on my feet."

"You're in luck. There's a bag of your clothes in the coat closet. I was ready to toss them in the dumpster."

He shot her a look of gratitude, a look that would melt the coldest of hearts. But not hers. "Give me a minute. I'll change in the bathroom."

Minutes later he returned, wearing a pair of faded blue jeans and a gray sweatshirt.

Yolanda gave him the once over before letting him seat himself at the opposite end of the sofa.

Arms folded on her chest, she asked: "So what's this story about being in big trouble?"

Her question caught him off-guard. He cleared his throat to give himself a moment to think. "The people I work for are after me."

"I can picture the kind of criminals you consort with, you being Italian and all."

"Stereotyping Italians?"

Yolanda folded. "You're right. I apologize."

Lorenzo acknowledged her contrition before continuing his tale of woe. "I did what they asked me to do and now I suspect they plan to kill me."

"And so you came here, putting my life and my son's life in jeopardy," she shrilled.

"No, no," he said to calm her. "You and Ali are safe. I never told no one about our relationship."

"There is *no* relationship," she emphasized.

"You and Ali are the only good things to happen in my rotten life." His eyes watered. "I'd never allow anyone dangerous near either of you."

She reached a decision. "You can sleep on the sofa tonight. Then I want you gone from our lives. My son's life cannot be put at risk by your existence."

His hand came out from behind his back, clutching a thick white envelope. "This is for you."

"What is it?"

"About seven thousand dollars." Money from his last job.

"Keep your dirty money."

"Take it, Lan." He implored her with his eyes. "For Ali."

She fixed him with a hard stare while she weighed his offer. Her expression softened. She reached out and accepted the envelope. "Thank you." But her next words informed him nothing had changed between them. "I still want you gone in the morning."

He pressed his lips to signal he understood. "I-I'm sorry, Yolanda. I'm sorry I can't be the man and father you need me to be."

Yolanda's composure cracked for an instant. "I know you are, Lorenzo. But sorry doesn't change the fact you're no good for us."

"Yo—"

She put a finger to his lips. "I'll fetch you a couple of blankets."

He wagged his head, docile-like.

She returned with two blankets. "Don't come near my bedroom," she warned him. "I sleep with a loaded .38 next to me now."

Alarm grabbed hold of him. Whether she was being truthful, he couldn't tell, but he wasn't willing to risk his life to find out.

Her eyes twinkled at him. "Goodnight, Lorenzo."

He watched her curves sway out of the living room, and with her went any hope of reconciliation.

And of hiding here from his many enemies.

Dread overcame him. The reality of being a fugitive lay like a heavy weight upon him. He stared at the ceiling, pondering his fate, when a diabolical scheme appeared on his mental horizon. The more the scheme gelled, the lighter he felt.

He reached over and grabbed a pen and tore a page off a notepad he had spied earlier on the side table. "Dear Yolanda," his note began. He chose each written word carefully. Satisfied with a rereading of it, he folded the letter and stuffed it into his backpack. *This'll fix Bronco's ass real good should I suffer a terminal incident.*

Then he wrote another note. He dug into his backpack and took money out of a white envelope and put the second note in it and sealed it. Using his mobile, he Googled an address and wrote it on the front of the envelope. He placed it with the note. *I hope Yolanda has stamps.*

He switched off the lamp and fell into a troubled sleep.

Chapter Thirty-Eight

Nelson was elbows-deep in analyzing the crushing defeat of the French and Greek navies in the eastern Mediterranean by Turkish naval forces whose geopolitical impact was every bit as momentous as the 1904 Battle of Port Arthur when his office phone rang.

"Miss Patella is here to see you, Mr. McCormack."

"Please show her in, Abby." He replaced the handset. Oh-ho. The she-wolf has arrived. I can't wait to hear her howl. Nelson came from behind his desk as Deeanna entered the office decked out in a navy blue dress suit. Her flawless calves shimmered and flexed while she glided over the carpet.

"Good of you to come, Dee," he greeted her. "We have a delicate matter to discuss," he said, wasting no time on pleasantries. He gestured for her to sit on a burgundy leather sofa beneath a bold-colored avant-garde painting Nelson had christened *Whatever* because it depicted whatever was in the imagination of the beholder. Such was the state of post-modern art in his opinion.

Deeanna sank into the seat, crossed her long satiny legs and swept them back.

"Something to drink?" he asked her.

"Too early in the day for me."

"Don't mind me then," Nelson said. "It's been a rough morning." Admitting to his need for liquid reinforcement didn't seem like a weakness to him.

Ice clinked in a glass at his private bar. When done preparing his bourbon-fueled beverage, he joined Deeanna on the sofa.

"So what's on the agenda?" she asked, twirling a lock of her glossy black hair.

"I'll come straight to the point, Dee." He took a gulp of his fiery drink, grimaced, and placed it on a table before continuing. "This company's policy against sexual harassment is transparent and the penalty for transgressing this policy is equally transparent."

Deeanna ceased playing with her tresses. "How does this concern me?"

"Yesterday, Charlene played for me a phone recording of your making sexual advances toward her."

Nelson saw her mouth the word *bitch*, but her expression did not change, and he wondered at it. Amazing self-control.

"I can explai—"

He stopped her with a raised palm. "Relax, Dee." He reached for his drink, swirled the ice cubes and took another swallow. He eyed her while he tabled the glass. "I wish to avoid a scandal—for your sake." Evil twitched at the corners of his mouth.

"You'll have my resignation today."

"No need to be hasty, Dee. People at our level are under a lot of stress. We're human. Errors in judgement happen."

Nelson studied her reactions. Deeanna's posture relaxed at his justification of her behavior. She went along with it. "It was stupid of me. A moment of weakness. I assure you it won't happen again."

He drove home the issue. "There's still the problem of Charlene's recording. If it ever leaked out, your career would be ruined. You'd never work on Wall Street again."

She broke eye contact to consider this dilemma, and he copped a furtive peek at the naturally tanned cleavage in the vee of her unbuttoned white blouse.

"Have you considered offering her a financial settlement?" she finally asked.

"I have." He let the hook dangle in space.

"I could repay the company whatever amount she accepts."

"What amount would be fair in your estimation?"

She took no time to weigh her answer. "A hundred thousand would be reasonable."

"A nice round number. However, the company is paying Charlene one hundred-and-fifty grand."

"Fine. So it's settled?"

Nelson shifted closer to her. Her intoxicating scent flooded his nostrils, and it aroused him. His marital bed had been barren since the attack on Sharron months ago. "Your repayment could be taken out in trade."

Her brow creased. "You've lost me."

"I possess a desire only you can satisfy."

Apperception lit up her eyes.

"You want have sex with me?"

He shot her a charming smile. "I want a round of naked mud-wrestling with you—absent the mud."

"So there's no misunderstanding between us." She leaned toward him. "If I sleep with you, you'll disappear my indiscretion?"

He misread the desperation in her eyes and he stroked her exposed knee. She did not recoil. "Yes, then you're off the hook."

"I'm so relieved to hear this, Nelson," and a wolfish smile replaced her innocent guise. She reached into the breast pocket of her suit jacket and slowly withdrew a smartphone.

Fingers of icy dread clutched at his guts.

"Shall I replay our conversation, lover boy?" She didn't wait for his permission.

Although muffled, he recognized his disembodied voice and a cold panic rose in him.

"A man's appetites and his money are soon parted," Deeanna said to him in a merry tone when the recording finished. "How much money are you willing to part with, lover boy?"

Nelson remained speechless, and in a moment of clarity, it dawned on him he had been played for a sucker. If Sharron listens to this recording, she'll divorce me in a New York minute and grab half my fortune. He felt his dread transmuting to anger, but he checked it with every ounce of his willpower. "How does five million grab you?" he said through clenched teeth.

Deeanna stiffened. "Your offer insults me. I emigrated from a poor country, but I know the value of money."

He doubled the amount. It came out as a final offer.

"I wonder how much a liberal New York City jury would award me. A hundred million? A billion? I can see the lurid headlines. Can you, Nelson?"

He blanched and swallowed hard.

"Private islands in the Bahamas are a trifle expensive these days, and I have many years of life ahead of me," she pointed out. "Fifty million would ease my pain and suffering."

Nelson's eyes popped.

"You're worth almost three hundred billion. You earn at least ten times the amount I'm demanding on your annual investment dividends alone."

Nelson saw he'd been outmaneuvered. How he'd love to give her a real dose of pain and suffering on a secluded white sandy beach. "You should congratulate yourself. You're the first woman to have outsmarted me."

"And perhaps not the last."

"Clear out of here today if you know what's good for you."

Undaunted by his threat, Deeanna pulled a small white envelope out her jacket pocket and passed it to him.

"What's this?"

"Instructions for depositing my—" she paused to select precise words "—let's call it *severance pay*."

"Get-out," he said with barely controlled fury. He desired nothing more than to wipe the *gotcha* look from her face with the back of his hand.

"Don't ever think of getting even with me, Nelson. I have a cousin in the police force. She knows all about you and me." Deeanna ran her finger lightly down his shirted arm; he flicked it away. "Nice doing business with you."

He didn't know whether she was lying about having a police officer for a cousin, but he wasn't willing to discover the truth. He watched her sashay toward the door and it was all he could do not to throw her to the ground and drag her back to the couch by her hair and show her who was boss.

Reaching the door, she spun around and said: "You'll need to hire a new masseuse too." Then she blew him a kiss and was gone.

Murderous thoughts warred in his brain. He pressed his fists against his temples and a stream of expletives reverberated off the floor-to-ceiling windows. A glass shattered against a wall, leaving behind a Rorschach-like wet spot cleaning personnel analyzed later on without much effort.

Minutes passed. The fog of rage lifted. Clarity resumed. Nelson evaluated his situation and came to the conclusion he had dodged an arrow, but not one sent from Cupid. His reputation remained intact and he had learned a hard lesson albeit an expensive one.

"You got lucky this time, buddy." He pressed back into the sofa. "But not in the way you expected," and he chuckled in spite of himself.

Chapter Thirty-Nine

Lorenzo awoke to the tantalizing scents of frying bacon and filtered coffee. He stretched and yawned before throwing off the blankets, reveling in the familiar aromas of breakfasts past. He swung his legs onto the carpet and brushed back his mop of frizzy hair with his hands while he collected himself. Still dressed in his rumpled jeans and a sweatshirt, he tiptoed to the kitchen and spied Yolanda, an apron tied around her slim waist, manipulating a lime green plastic spatula in a sizzling fry pan.

"Smells awesome."

She started at his voice and whipped around. "I hate it when you sneak up on me," she said, brandishing the spatula at him.

He held up his hands in a warding-off gesture. "What's for breakfast?"

"For you? Fresh air." A laugh escaped her open lips.

His face fell.

She must have caught his expression of woe. "I'm kidding, Lorenzo. I won't send you packing on an empty stomach."

Gratitude erupted on his face. "I'm going to the men's room. Give me a few minutes."

"Don't stink up the place."

Yolanda had prepared a plate for him at the dining room table; the tiny kitchen had no eating space. The sight of his plate, heaped with strips of crisp lean bacon, eggs over hard and a thick stack of whole wheat pancakes, set his mouth to watering, and the bouquet rising from his cup, filled with steaming black coffee, set his nose to sniffing.

"You spoiled me." He seated himself before the appetizing spread.

"Don't let my generosity give you any ideas."

"Why do I feel like a condemned man about to eat his last meal?" he said, smothering his pancakes in syrup.

"Stop."

He contemplated his breakfast. "I played the cards Fate dealt me."

"You could have folded."

"Life doesn't let you. Death or suicide is the only way out. But I'm not a quitter."

"But you're not a winner."

"Thanks for the reminder. At least I'm not a wife-beater like my foster father was."

"True," she conceded.

Lorenzo used the lull in conversation to scoff more food and slurp more coffee.

"Where will you go when you leave?"

He talked around a mouthful of pancake. "Boulder, Colorado."

"How will you live?"

"Looking over my shoulder."

"I wish I could offer you shelter, Lorenzo, but...."

The silence completed the sentence for her.

"No problem. I'll figure something out. I have emergency funds to cover me through this tight spot." He glanced at his backpack before continuing. "Hopefully, it'll be enough to shelter me in a safe place."

"Running from your employers—" she qualified the word *employers* with finger quotes "—won't be easy."

"One more challenge to overcome in my exciting life." He planted a brave smile on his face.

"I wish you well, Lorenzo. Stay out of harm's way."

He recognized the sincerity in her tone and he was glad for it. "Once I find a place to live, I'll send you money when I can."

"Don't worry about us. Worry about yourself."

"I'm happy I got to be with you and Ali one last time."

Her eyes glassed over.

"Do you have a photo of me? A reminder to show Ali who his father was."

She swallowed hard and nodded her head.

"When he's old enough to understand, tell him I love him and I didn't abandon him—or you."

"Stop it," she blubbered.

He stared into space. "You know, I never got a chance to dream like normal kids do. I was always waiting for the hammer to fall. I hope Ali is given a chance to dream and live out his dreams."

"That's in the past. What about now? Do you have any dreams?"

He stilled his fork. "I have one recurring dream," he admitted. "It's kind of weird."

She sensed his reluctance to divulge his dream. "Tell me about it."

He swallowed first before answering. "I pass through some sort of machine and I come out the other end transformed, like I'm a fish swimming through water."

"That *is* a bit weird, especially since you don't like swimming."

"Correction," he gestured with his fork. "I hate swimming in public pools. Gallons of undissolved urine lurking in the water. Yuck." He shuddered and pulled a grimace.

"Why not work at a ski resort when you relocate to Boulder."

His eyes lit up at the suggestion. "There's an idea. I could be a handyman. In his sober moments, when my foster father wasn't beating me, he taught me a few useful skills."

"See, Lorenzo."

"See what?"

"You're dreaming."

"I guess I am. Well, I'll be a—"

Ali's cry pierced the air and sobered up both of them.

Yolanda scrambled away from the table and made a beeline toward her son's room with Lorenzo following in her wake.

"What's wrong with him?"

"His fever's back."

"Give him some more Advil."

"I gave him the last of it last night."

"So you did," he recalled. "How if I trip over to the pharmacy and buy him another bottle?"

"Would you?" There was surprise in her tone.

"Why wouldn't I?" his expression said.

"I'm sorry."

"Let me finish my breakfast, then I'll take a run there."

"Deal. But be quick about it."

Yolanda remained in Ali's bedroom ministering to him while Lorenzo wolfed down the remaining food on his plate. When he was done, he grabbed his jacket from the closet.

"Lock the door," he shouted to her on his way out.

He strode with renewed purpose toward the elevator, a young man in the throes of performing a good deed. Once out on the sunny street, he pushed aside his sense of caution, his son's health uppermost in his thoughts.

Nobody will be fishing for me here. They'll be staking out the bus depots and flophouses. Smart of me to have kept my private life away from them goons.

A honking horn and squealing brakes snatched him from his reverie. He found himself in the middle of Brook River Road, staring at the shiny chrome grill of a jacked-up Ram truck inches from his head. A tremor of fright passed through him. He gave the driver a sheepish wave, and the driver floored the vehicle as if to say, "I'm in a desperate hurry to go nowhere."

Pay better attention to your surroundings, he warned himself.

The pharmacy was steps ahead now. A pall of feminine scents engulfed him when he entered the premises, the entrance giving onto the perfume section. He wound his way to the aisle stocked with every manner of cold and flu remedy—a hypochondriac's heaven on earth.

Finding what he came for, he moved toward the cash registers along the narrow aisle, and fear suddenly gripped his insides. At the top of the aisle, Lorenzo spied Romano, whose back was to him, heading out the store. What the hell! What's he doing in this neighborhood? Did he pick up my trail? These questions and more ramped up Lorenzo's fear as he spun on his heel and moved in the opposite direction. He pulled his hoodie over his head and pretended to inspect the items at the end of the aisle while keeping one eye on the front door. He caught Romano exiting the store.

A sole female cashier was working the morning shift, so the line was long and several customers were pushing carts filled with all manner of consumer goods. Lorenzo shifted nervously in place while he kept his eye on the door. After what seemed an eternity, his turn arrived. He paid for the liquid Advil, and, clutching the bag, he stopped at the exit door and pretended to count his change while his eyes darted left and right. Romano was nowhere in sight.

"Excuse me," a female voice said.

"Oh, sorry."

Lorenzo moved aside so the woman could squeeze by. He used the time to scout some more.

For the second time in as many days he said a prayer and exited the premises.

He hadn't covered much ground when he heard footsteps approaching rapidly on the sidewalk. He checked behind him.

His features pitiless, Rommy was hard on his heels.

Run! his mind screamed. Lorenzo tore off. A car screeched to a halt just ahead of him in the roadway. Before he could react, a bulky man jumped out of the vehicle and grabbed Lorenzo's upper arm in a severe grip, terminating his panicked flight. The man subdued Lorenzo with a punch to the gut. Rommy held open the rear door while the man tossed Lorenzo into the back seat and dove in after him. Rommy hopped into the front and swung shut the door. The vehicle peeled away, tires spinning, engine revving high. Only seconds had passed.

As the getaway car receded into the distance, a bag left behind on the bare sidewalk ruffled in the cold breeze.

Chapter Forty

Yolanda had one ear on her son's wailing and another listening for the door buzzer.

What's taking him so long? Irritation rose in her like magma in a volcano primed to erupt.

She was about to curse him when she stopped herself and cut him some slack instead.

The pharmacy's probably busy and he's stuck in line.

Despite her spirit of tolerance, her irritation continued to build, and Ali's piercing cries increased her sense of desperation and helplessness.

"Ssh, my little angel. A cure is on the way. Daddy will be here with your medicine any minute now."

She glanced at the empty doorway.

Where is he?

Her forbearance wore thin. The thought of killing him when he returned spiked her mind several times.

Ali let out a shrill cry.

"I hear you, angel. Never send a man to do a woman's job."

She checked the doorway again. Her desperation getting the better of her, she jumped out of the chair beside the crib.

"Angel, mommy has to go for help. I promise I won't be long."

She dashed out of the bedroom and rushed out of her apartment.

I hope she's home.

She was Mrs. Romano who lived one floor above. She babysat Ali on several occasions while Yolanda ran errands.

Forsaking the elevator, Yolanda raced up the emergency stairs two at a time to the next floor and knocked on her neighbor's door. It opened and Yolanda was greeted by a silver-haired lady aware her best days were past and didn't hide this awareness behind layers of garish makeup and expensive dye jobs.

"Thank God you're home. I—"

"Come in, come in, dear."

"I'd love to but I can't, Mrs. Romano. Ali has a high fever. I sent my"—she settled on ex-boyfriend—"to the pharmacy over half-an-hour ago to buy Advil. I'm going out of my mind worrying about my son's fever. He needs his medicine."

Yolanda was on the cusp of appealing for help when Mrs. Romano experienced a bout of clairvoyance and said: "I'll come right away."

Yolanda's relief gushed out in a torrent of words. "Thank God. I'm at my wits end."

Mrs. Romano locked her door and bustled behind her young neighbor. "Minutes ago, my husband called me from the pharmacy. He was on his way back when a work emergency came up. He said he'd be home later. Wouldn't it be a coincidence if he and your ex-boyfriend bumped into one another?"

As they entered the elevator, Yolanda asked her: "Your husband went to the pharmacy this morning?"

"Yes. He left around nine. I remember the time be—"

"About the same time Lorenzo left." A hopeful idea burst forth. "Please ask him if he saw my ex-boyfriend." She then described him to her.

"Mr. Romano has a photographic memory. If he saw him, he'll remember him."

"It's strange he hasn't returned by now."

They reached Ali's bedroom.

"I've been putting a cold cloth on his forehead," and she handed it to her. "I hope it's helping lower his fever; it's better than doing nothing at all." She sought affirmation from her motherly neighbor.

"Don't worry, dear. Ali's in good hands. I raised three children of my own and they are still alive and well." She paused to consider. "Although the oldest is developing a paunch like his fath—"

"I have to go, Mrs. Romano."

"Yes, of course. Where's my head?"

Yolanda fled out of the bedroom. She yanked her coat from the hallway closet; the plastic hanger snapped from the violent tug and clattered to the floor in two pieces.

"Dress warm, dear," she heard Mrs. Romano say before she secured the door. She stuffed the jingling keys into her coat pocket.

Yolanda pushed the button for the elevator several times in a frantic but futile attempt to hasten its arrival.

"Come on, come on," she urged. She kicked the metal door. "Why does the stupid elevator always take longer to arrive when you need it most?"

Gratitude washed over her when the elevator door opened and an empty compartment welcomed her. It dropped to the ground floor uninterrupted while she zipped up her coat. She squeezed through the partially opened door, raced across the lobby and shot out the main entrance into the chilly air. She hoped she would catch Lorenzo on his way back. He was nowhere in sight.

Is the pharmacy that busy?

A worm of worry wiggled at the edges of her awareness. The wiggle increased when she spied a small pharmacy bag lying on the sidewalk ahead of her. She stooped to pick it up. Inside was a receipt and a bottle of liquid Advil, the kind for babies.

"This-This can't be," she whispered.

Her world spun and she with it and she felt her stomach in her throat.

"Lorenzo?"

She circled on the spot, eyes wide.

"Lorenzo!"

The horrible reality of his fate finally settled upon her.

"LORENZO!"

Half out of her mind with fear and grief, she sprinted back to her apartment without regard for personal safety, the screech of tires on pavement and the shrill of horns mere background noise to her panicked flight.

Out of breath and her face tear-streaked, she stormed into her apartment and headed straight for her son's bedroom.

"What's the matter, dear?" Mrs. Romano got up from her chair, noticing Yolanda's freaked out condition.

"My ex is in trouble."

"He is?"

"I found this on the sidewalk." Yolanda thrust the package at her neighbor as though it were radioactive. "It contains a bottle of baby Advil."

"You think your boyfriend—" She stopped to correct herself "—ex-boyfriend dropped it?"

"I don't believe in coincidences." She felt herself relaxing now that she could share her suspicions with a person she trusted. "The people he was afraid of must have kidnapped him in broad daylight."

Ali wailed.

"Let's deal with one problem at a time, shall we?" Mrs. Romano suggested in a maternal tone. "Sit him up."

Yolanda obeyed.

"I need a small spoon."

She returned from the kitchen with a baby spoon and her neighbor gave Ali the medicine. "If his fever doesn't drop, you should take him to a pediatrician."

"A trip to the hospital is the last thing I need." Yolanda laid Ali on his back.

"I know. All those germs floating in the air and lying on every surface." Her face screwed up like she had bit into a lemon.

Yolanda supervised her son with concern while she spoke. "Lorenzo—my ex—said the people he worked for were planning to kill him."

"Who did he work for?"

"I'm not sure. We never discussed his job in any depth, but I suspect he worked for the Mafia. Lorenzo is Italian," she added.

"Just as every Irishmen isn't a drunk, not every Italian is a mobster, dear," she cautioned. "Mr. Romano is an anti-theft supervisor. He catches employees stealing from his employer."

"I suppose you're right." Ali comforted, Yolanda faced her now. "But how many employers kidnap their employees?"

"We don't know if he's been kidnapped, dear."

"I can't think straight."

With nothing more for her to do, Mrs. Romano said: "I should leave now. Mr. Romano's lunch won't cook itself." Passing through the doorway, she said in afterthought: "I hope he won't be late."

Yolanda followed her out of the room. "I really appreciate you babysitting Ali for me, Mrs. Romano. I'd be lost without you. And so would Ali," she added.

She warmed to the compliment.

They moved toward the front door.

"Going hiking, dear?" she asked.

Yolanda followed her gaze and felt her heart lurch at the sight of her ex's backpack. "It belonged to Lorenzo," was all she could answer.

Mrs. Romano stopped at the door. "What are you going to do?"

"I'm going to call the police and file a missing person's report."

"I'll say a prayer for you and him."

Yolanda held on to the door. "Thank you for your help, Mrs. Romano. You're a kind neighbor. We'd be lost without you," she repeated, and she planted a grateful kiss on her plump cheek.

"Please keep me informed of Ali's fever."

"I will." Yolanda closed the door gently and leaned against it. "As if I don't have enough on my plate."

She moved to the sofa and scrutinized the backpack propped against it.

What happened out there, Lorenzo?

She crumpled. Oh, God, I sent him to his death. She buried her face in her hands and her body wracked with misplaced guilt. Minutes later, her grief spent and her being calmer, her inner voice told her: you don't know this for certain. She wiped her eyes and regarded the backpack.

What could it hurt?

Curiosity overwhelming her, she unzipped the main compartment and peeked inside. On top of a pile of clothing she noticed a piece of stationary and a sealed white envelope resting on stacks of money. "What the?" she said under her breath. She withdrew the folded paper and the envelope, and she noticed it was addressed to the Central Park Police Precinct. She put aside the envelope and unfolded the paper. Dear Yolanda, it began.

If you're reading this, it's because they found me. I didn't abandon you and Ali. I've done some wrong things in my life so I guess fate has come full circle. Don't search for me and don't contact the police. A waste of time. These people cover their tracks real well. Believe me.

Don't feel sad for me, Yolanda. I don't deserve it. What goes around, comes around. Please mail the white envelope. The police will know what to do with its contents.

The money in the backpack is yours. Invest it on behalf of Ali for his future.

There's something I never told you but now's probably a good time. Bronco, a brute I worked for, is responsible for Teagan's death. He manages a crew of prostitutes and drug dealers in the South Bronx. His headquarters is at Pepe's Tavern. You can find him there most nights. He's a white Italian guy and he's built like a tank. He'll be limping thanks to me. :^) He drives a black Chrysler 300S.

Love you in my own crazy way.

Lenzo

She laid aside the note. Her lower lip began to tremble. Unable to contain it, emotion spilled out of her, and she wept for the man she had once loved, if ever so briefly, and for the man who had fathered her child, a child who would never come to know him. But her grief was soon replaced with smoldering rage with the awareness of who was responsible for her sister Teagan's death.

She swiped away her tears and reached for her smartphone. She speed dialed her brother's number.

"What's up, Sis?"

"Listen to me, Bobby. I discovered who's responsible for Teagan's death."

She heard a sharp intake of breath on the other end.

"Go on."

Yolanda filled him in on Lorenzo's note.

"Where can I find the bastard?"

"At a place called Pepe's Tavern in the South Bronx. Ever hear of it?"

"No, but I'll ask around."

"He's there every night."

"Yeah, well, tonight is his last."

"Bobby, be careful. This thug works for the Mafia."

"The least of my worries, Sis. His ass is mine!"

"Tell him you got a message from Lorenzo, then waste him."

"Lorenzo? You still seeing that loser?"

"It's a long story, Bobby. We'll talk later. Go avenge Teagan."

"Consider it done."

The call ended. Yolanda replaced the phone and wished she could be there when Bobby settled an old score for both of them.

Chapter Forty-One

Miles east of Yolanda's location, Bronco limped toward a blindfolded figure tied to a metal chair in the far corner of a storage space crammed with inventory. Three of his men hovered nearby, talking in low voices. They ceased gabbing when one of them informed the others of his approach.

Bronco walked gingerly on his right leg. He tried not to grimace for the sake of his hardcore reputation. He had spurned the convenience of crutches. They signaled weakness and any display of weakness might give a contender the idea to challenge his position. Bronco couldn't allow this. A display of resolute grit should give any contender pause to topple him from his hallowed perch. And every jolt of agony shooting through his quadriceps reminded him how much he would enjoy torturing his prisoner in the worst way. Revenge would render the pain worthwhile, not to mention the reward the don would extend to him once this nasty business was concluded.

Bronco gazed down at his trussed up prisoner. "Tried to flee, did you?"

Lorenzo returned him a contemptuous smirk. "So we meet again. For what it's worth, I'm sorry about your leg, Bronco. I warned you not to mess with me."

"And I warned you I would make you pay, didn't I?"

"So pay up. I've got places to be and people to see."

"Always the wise ass, heh?"

"Better than a jackass like you."

"This is how you want to play it?"

"I'm not going to beg for my life. I endured whatever my foster father dished out and I'll endure whatever you goons dish out."

"Brave words." Bronco looked to his men for confirmation. They shook themselves loose, needing only a nod from him to take Lorenzo up on his word. But Bronco had a tongue-loosener far more effective than an old-school thumping.

"What were you doing at the pharmacy?"

"I was buying some aspirin. Listening to your voice gives me a headache."

One of his crew snickered only to be cut short by a dangerous glare from Bronco.

Lorenzo's head snapped back from the force of Bronco's backhand, and he let out a yelp.

Bronco addressed the trio of men: "Did any of you find a package on him?"

They glanced at one another with questioning eyes. "No," Rommy said on their behalf.

Bronco faced Lorenzo again. "We found the note you left for us in the apartment. You're a real comedian."

"My foster father used to say the same thing, but you're only half the man he was."

Bronco's aspect darkened. He grabbed a clump of Lorenzo's springy hair and yanked it backwards. "I could break your scrawny neck."

"You probably could, tough guy, but the don wouldn't be thrilled with you. I'm sure he has a better end in store for me."

Bronco regained control of himself and gave Lorenzo's skull a shove. "Lucky for you he does." He swung a chair, placed it in front of Lorenzo and planted himself on it, his forearms leaning on the backrest, his injured leg extended at an acute angle. "Where did you crash last night?"

"What does it matter to you?"

"Maybe you spilled the beans to whoever you stayed with."

"I'm not a snitch."

"No, but you're my bitch now!"

"I always pegged you as a butch."

This earned him another wallop.

He glared at Lorenzo. "One last chance. Where did you stay last night?"

"I got friendly with a warm sewer grate. And if I didn't know any better, I could swear it stank like your place—you being a mangy rat and all."

The men coughed to cover their snickers.

Bronco sighed, his irritation obvious. "You're wasting my time." He rose awkwardly from the chair. "Bring me the pliers." He addressed no one in particular.

Rommy produced them for Bronco.

Bronco snipped the pliers next to Lorenzo's right ear. He didn't flinch. Bronco moved around behind his prisoner. "Eeny meeny miny moe," he sang, tapping Lorenzo's fingers with the cutting tool.

Lorenzo came alert and his bravado deserted him. "Okay, okay, I'll talk."

"You certainly will." He grabbed hold of a pinky and Lorenzo wrenched against his fetters, anticipating what was coming. "Keep him still," he ordered his men.

Two goons sprang forward and restrained their prisoner.

A screech like a hawk bounced off the walls.

"Ready to confess now?"

Blood had drained from Lorenzo's tortured face and he appeared more ready to faint than confess. Bronco gave him a hard slap.

He gasped from the pain, but he managed to find his voice. "A...A friend. Used to...l-live in Yonkers. But he...moved."

"Go on."

"I spent...night behind...apart-apartment building...backpack could still...be...there."

"Which building?"

"Se...Second one from...from corner...near wh-where you...your goons c-caught me."

"These trusty pliers never fail me," and he held them up to admire them. To Lorenzo he gloated, "You talked like I said you would."

"Scr-Screw...yourself!" he hissed.

Bronco pointed at Rommy. "You found him in your neighborhood. Go verify his tale. And call me if it checks out."

"I need a lift back." Rommy couldn't conceal his relief to be rid of this hellhole.

Bronco addressed the driver of the getaway vehicle. "Drive Rommy home." And to the other goon, "Bandage this loser's hand. Keep him alive for the Boss." He sniffed the air, then noticed a puddle at Lorenzo's feet. "And fetch a pail of water and a mop. The pig pissed himself."

He faced his prisoner again and tapped him on the noggin with the bloody pliers. "If you're lying, you have nine more fingers to play with. *Capiche?*"

Despite the agony he was in, Lorenzo rallied himself. "I-I'd watch your back, B-Bronco. Someone meaner...bigger than you has...has you in his s-sights."

"I'm trembling in my boots."

"Remember the name...T-Teagan."

"Who's she?"

"Her...older brother believes you're...you're responsible for her d-death."

"Why's that?"

"'Cause I-I told him you were. A-a parting gift...from me to you."

Unfazed. "What's the name of this big, bad guy?"

Lorenzo fabricated a name to protect his identity. "S-since you're the man with the pliers, there's no use...me h-holding back. His name is-is Tyrone...Gim-bly," he got out.

"And where can I find him?"

"What do...I look like? A fri...fricking spy?"

This earned him another wallop.

"He'll...he'll find you before you...f-find him."

"Why so sure?"

"Ex-marine...s-served overseas. Seen serious shit, so...so h-he ain't afraid of you. And...and if you had half a brain, you'd...be a-afraid of him. He's real badass...c-compared to you."

"I'm shaking in my boots."

Bronco limped to a workbench, grabbed a rag and carefully cleaned the blades of the pliers. He examined them in the light, then he thumbed the sharp edges.

"A couple of fingers more, and I'll have to sharpen these babies." He settled his gaze on the goon tending to Lorenzo. "Need a trim?" He snipped the tool in the air and let out an evil cackle.

The goon kept his head down, pretending to be engrossed in his work of patching up their prisoner. One could never tell when Bronco was fooling.

Chapter Forty-Two

Mrs. Romano looked up from the book she was reading at the telltale *rattle* of a key in the lock. Cheer rose in her. She laid aside the captivating conspiracy thriller about a jaded priest's search for the truth in Istanbul, unfolded herself from the armchair, and greeted her husband at the door.

"Let me take your coat, dear."

"Mmm. Something smells good," he said and headed straight for the kitchen.

"I cooked your favorite, *Spaghetti alla puttanesca*," she said to his back while she hung his coat.

"*Perfezionare*." Perfect. He lifted the lid of the pot of sauce simmering on the stove and inhaled the rising aromatic vapors. "After my tough day, a tasty plate of homemade pasta will hit the spot."

"And there's garlic bread with mozzarella cheese warming in the oven," she said, joining him.

"You're too good to me, Rosie," and he pecked her on the cheek. To her surprise, he held out to her a little brand-name jewelry box.

"For me?"

"For the fairest of them all," he said with flair.

Her eyes moistened and she accepted the box from him. She pried it open and sucked in her breath. "Oh, Tommy, they're beautiful," she gushed. A pair of emerald and diamond earrings transfixed her eyes.

"Does this mean you like them?"

"Like them? I love them." She examined the earrings with wonder, tilting the box this way and that way to make them sparkle. "How did you afford them?"

"I got a bonus from work. Sometimes crumbs fall from the table into my lap."

The roil of boiling water and noodles on the stove broke the magic of the moment.

"Go wash up." She shooed him out of the kitchen.

Minutes later he called to her from the dining room. "I'm ready whenever you are, Rosie."

"There's no one more impatient than a hungry man," she said to herself as she ladled sauce over the thin noodles. "*Aspetta un momento!*"

She set their plates of spaghetti on the table and raced back into the kitchen for the garlic bread. He was swallowing his second mouthful of noodles by the time she returned.

"You couldn't wait for me?"

"Ah, Rosie. I can't help myself. The only thing more irresistible than you is your cooking."

Mollified, she took her seat at the table. "How's the sauce, dear? Not too spicy?"

"*È perfetto.*" It's perfect.

She beamed. "So what was the emergency earlier today?"

"An employee who dealt with valuable inside information was acting suspiciously, so we clipped his wings, so to speak."

"You fired him?"

"In a manner of speaking. He won't be divulging anymore company secrets. We rendered him unemployable."

"You did?"

He took a sip of water before replying. "Sure. A potential employee must undergo a background check. And guess which security company performs this service?"

"Yours?"

He pressed his lips in confirmation. "We simply place a black mark in his electronic file so no one will hire him."

"Kind of mean, dear."

"Not where trust is involved. Businesses survive on trust."

"Since you put it that way, I guess I can sympathize with the company."

"So how was your day?" he asked between mouthfuls.

"I had to babysit our neighbor's son this morning. The young Black girl on the floor below us had to go to the pharmacy for her son's fever."

"Lucky for her you're around during the day."

"While I was there, she told me the strangest tale."

"And?" he gestured.

"She said her boyfriend had been snatched off the street this morning."

"Where? By who?"

"Between here and the pharmacy. She suspects Mafiosi did the kidnapping because her boyfriend is Italian."

"You don't say." He remained expressionless.

"Funny how her boyfriend was at the pharmacy at the same time you were." She then described him. "Does his description match anyone you saw there this morning?"

He sat back and stared into space for a moment. Then he fixed his eyes on her. "I recall a tall guy matching your description. But I'm pretty sure he left the store before I did."

"You didn't see him on your way home?"

"I got the emergency call while I was in the store, so my attention was elsewhere when I left."

"Our neighbor had to go to the pharmacy herself when her boyfriend didn't come back. When she got back to the apartment, she said she found the medicine on the sidewalk she had sent him to buy. Sounds suspicious."

Rommy adopted a contemplative look. "This boyfriend of hers might've bumped into the wrong people today."

"The girl said she was going to contact the police and file a missing person's report."

"Is that right."

"Could the police find him?"

"They'd need a lead. A witness to this so-called kidnapping."

"This used to be a safe neighborhood."

"Rosie, you worry too much. Young people these days get mixed up in drugs and the next thing you know they're on the six o'clock news."

"I suppose you're right."

He plated his fork and spoon and patted his ample girth. "Rosie, you certainly know how to spoil your man."

"I'm glad you enjoyed it, dear."

"But a fine meal isn't complete without a tasty dessert. What's for dessert?"

"Guess," she said while she gathered their dirty dishes.

"Ah, Rosie, you're tormenting me."

"Guess."

"Tiramisu?"

"Keep guessing," she encouraged while she waddled toward the kitchen.

"Cassata?"

"You ruined my surprise," she protested. "How did you guess?"

"Lucky guess."

Dishes clattered in the sink. A tap ran for several seconds. The fridge door snicked shut. Mrs. Romano returned with the fruit-filled sponge cake on a platter.

"Would you like me to do the honors, dear?" she asked.

"Why not? You baked it."

"Large piece or small?"

"Do you have to ask?"

"You've been complaining lately your pants are too tight."

"I'll dial back on my snacking. Now cut a slab of cake fit for a man with my appetite."

"All right, dear. But don't complain to me about your waistline. *Capiche*?"

"Cut the cake, Rosie."

"Patience, dear." Then a notion came to her. "Should I mention to our neighbor you saw her boyfriend this morning? It might help the police with their investigation."

"Listen, Rosie. Don't involve us in our neighbor's problem."

"What should I tell her then?"

"Why do you have to tell her anything?"

"I promised her I would ask you if you saw her boyfriend at the pharmacy."

"Tell her no one matching his description crossed my path."

"I hate to lie to her, dear."

"What'd I just say?"

"Okay, okay. I only wanted to help her."

"You got to know when to back off. Many a person has lost a finger putting his hands where they don't belong."

"I suppose you're right."

"Of course I am. It comes with experience. Now eat your pie and I'll help you with the dishes when we're done."

"That's sweet of you dear, but you've had a tough day. Go put your feet up and I'll clear the table."

"You spoil me, Rosie. I have to make a call first."

"Work?"

"What else?"

"I wish you had a job with regular hours."

"In the security business, you can never predict when someone's going to step out of line." He pushed himself away from the table when he finished his dessert.

"Will you be long, dear? I was hoping we could watch TV together."

"Not more than a few minutes."

"He gives too much of himself to his job," she griped on her way to the kitchen. She leaned on the sink. Wouldn't he be surprised to know he doesn't fool me with his talk of working for a security company? My man's a Mafioso. Best to let him believe I'm a simple gal from the suburbs. What does it matter anyway? His job pays for those nice winter vacations at the company-owned compound in Florida, she reminded herself. Content with this final thought, she dug out the dish basin from beneath the sink and filled it with hot water from the tap. A woman's got to stand by her man through thick and thin, she concluded, and she busied herself with washing the dishes.

Chapter Forty-Three

While Lorenzo wrestled with whatever fate awaited him, Nelson paced on a corner, blocks south of his address. He had received the *call*. Cabreezi practically ordered him to meet him at the northwest corner of Ninth Avenue and West 51st at 8:00 p.m. without delay just as he and Sharron were about to tuck into their evening meal. Talk about bad timing. But what could he do? The don was doing them a huge favor. Taking issue with the lack of notice might smack of ingratitude...And forever terminate his chance of punishing his wife's attacker.

So, here he was, killing time, doing his best to be inconspicuous.

"Need a jolt to put some bounce into your life, buddy?"

The shock on Nelson's face must have been enough, for the drug pusher said: "Guess not."

Hardly had McCormack recovered his wits when—

"Maybe a warm body, instead? Male or a female? Young or old? Or someone in between?"

Speech deserted him. Oh! the nerve, the nerve of this, this...reprobate. Assuming he—a man of his wealth and stature—would need an artificial stimulant or a stranger's warm body to cope with the vicissitudes of life. Why, he should give him a piece of his mind. But this would be too rich for him, he decided. His self-dignity restored, Nelson politely told the salesman: "No thank you."

Unoffended, the man shrugged as though he had been denied a cigarette and merged with the constant stream of humanity flowing by. McCormack stared after him for a few beats. He shook his head in wonder and resumed pacing.

Cabreezi didn't specify the purpose of their impending meeting over the phone—for good reason. McCormack didn't venture to ask but he was pretty certain what was in play this evening. He was going along for the ride and he hoped it would take him to a place called Closure. Sharron and he needed to reclaim their lives and move on.

Why didn't we meet at his place instead of blocks away? McCormack asked himself, and a cold wind funneled up the man-made concrete canyon and froze his face and ears. He's right around the corner from my building...Maybe he doesn't wish to be seen with me. Is he afraid of being seen with me? It should be the other way around. Then the conversation he had with Cabreezi weeks ago popped up. He knows his place is under surveillance. Bingo! His dilemma solved, he concentrated on the traffic coming his way, willing Cabreezi to materialize before his body froze.

Passersby cast glances his way, probably curious why a well-dressed man was hanging out on a street corner in this neighborhood. He was thankful the mom and pop businesses were open for commerce. Less chance of being mugged, he hoped.

With minutes to spare before the turn of the hour, a gleaming black limo pulled up curb-side. A back door swung open and a bulky suited goon beckoned him from inside.

McCormack entered the warm interior and sank into the plush leather seat next to a silver-haired man who must be the don; he smelled of sandalwood and spices. Two squat men, their suits taut with bulging muscles, sat on the bench seat opposite them, stone-faced. He noticed the goon who had opened the door was wearing pointy snakeskin boots.

"Mr. McCormack, so good of you to join us on such short notice," Cabreezi said with lethal politeness, offering his hand.

As if I had a choice. "Wouldn't miss it for the world."

They shook hands like old acquaintances and Nelson let go of his irritation, for there would be no gain in expressing it.

The Mafia don patted McCormack's knee, real friendly like. "We're taking a trip to the Bronx." A huge diamond ring sparkled on his pinky finger.

"The Bronx?"

"I own a meatpacking plant there. One of several still alive in the borough. You've probably eaten a steak my plant produces at least once in your life. Isn't that so?" he asked, turning to his two brooding gorillas for confirmation.

"Right, Don," they chimed in.

"My sirloin steaks are consumed in many of the finest restaurants in this town."

McCormack merely nodded his head, unsure how to respond.
Polite patter dispensed with, Cabreezi got down to business.
"It wasn't easy, but we captured your wife's attacker."
McCormack pivoted in his seat, his eyes wide with a mixture of amazement and appreciation. "You caught the bastard?"
"I just said so."
"The don just said so," repeated one of the muscle.
McCormack glanced at him, then back at Cabreezi.
"How did you find him?"
"He bragged about his exploit to too many fellow lowlifes."
"Did you teach him a painful lesson?"
Cabreezi reached over and patted his knee again. "Patience, Mr. McCormack, patience," he said, his words invested with suspense.
McCormack sat back, giddy at the prospect of coming face-to-face with his wife's attacker. It's payback time. Just then an idea came to him. "You're entitled to claim the million-dollar reward I offered. Under the table of course," and he gave a chuckle.
"Generous of you," the don said, "but my good deed is priceless, wouldn't you agree?"
McCormack wasn't sure what he was implying. "No amount of money is worth my wife's peace of mind."
"I would imagine so."
They settled into silence. The limo poked its way with purpose through a slalom of winking red and amber taillights in the evening traffic as they headed north on Park Avenue. McCormack couldn't sit still the whole way to their destination. His jitteriness increased when a guard waved the limo through the main gate of a chain-link fence.
Not much longer and justice will be mine, he gloated.
Their vehicle purred to an imperceptible stop by a side door of a hulking building stark against the night sky. "Here at last," Cabreezi announced in an excited tone.
Goon One pushed open a limo door, exited with difficulty and beckoned McCormack to follow him. Goon Two draped a light-weight camel-hair coat over the shoulders of his boss on the other side of the vehicle. Single file, they paraded through a doorway lit by

a naked lightbulb. Multiple pairs of leather soles slapped an out-of-sync staccato cadence on the concrete floor. No one spoke.

McCormack followed Cabreezi and the lead goon through a series of corridors until they came to an unheated cavernous space illuminated by emergency lighting. They halted. The *clack* of large switches being thrown preceded an explosion of light.

McCormack's eyes cast around and stopped wide-opened at someone hanging from a hook.

What in hell's name?

Chapter Forty-Four

Sharron abandoned the special news report and switched off the wall-sized television in the family room. Too distracted by Nelson's unexpected departure, she had trouble following the story about headless bodies popping up around the city. Media spokespeople suspected the murders might be the work of a male white serial killer. Consuming several glasses of wine didn't help her powers of concentration, either. The wine bottle stood stark upright on the table, oozing reproach.

She wasn't supposed to mix alcohol with her anti-anxiety medication. It beats sleeping pills, she justified to herself.

She thought about the headless bodies and shuddered. Then she recalled the victims were non-Caucasian, her dread dissolved. Her one-track mind returned to Nelson's sudden leave-taking hours ago in the wake of a hushed conversation with a mysterious caller. She had asked him about the call. He had gravely informed her he was taking care of her problem so she could regain her peace of mind, and he admonished her not to worry. Everything will work out fine, she remembered him saying to buoy her spirits and belay her anxiety.

Famous last words, she huffed. Despite his well-intentioned blandishments, she worried nonetheless. What wife wouldn't? She examined her reflection in the smudge-free black TV screen and the scar on her cheekbone was visible from her perch on the sofa. Her hand reached for the scar unbidden and traced the ridge. The plastic surgeon will have to be a miracle worker to erase it, she lamented. All she could do was pay and pray when the time came. Once her attacker had been *neutralized*—the ominous ring of the word gave her brief pause—she would make an appointment to have the facial reconstruction surgery performed. The compulsion to look over her shoulder would vanish with him gone from her life.

My paranoid woman days will soon be a distant memory. She managed a brave smile at the thought of being free of the specter haunting her dreams and waking moments these past months. Although her work with Jeannine had paid mental health dividends, she wouldn't be psychologically whole again until her attacker was dead.

One part of her wished she knew how Nelson's friend planned to resolve their special *problem*, and the other part recoiled at the notion. Nelson told her he didn't have a clue what his friend planned to do.

"Would you really want to know?" was how he had put it to her when she had asked him.

And she had replied: "Make sure he is incapable of ever doing to another woman what he did to me."

Sharron pushed herself off the distressed leather sofa, flicked off the light and padded along the marble hallway in her bare feet toward the sanctuary of her bedroom. Dressed in her silk jammies, she threw back the covers, fluffed up a couple of goose down pillows and climbed into bed. Alone in the silent darkness, she huddled beneath the satiny sheets, seeking comfort in them. But solace would not come. She stretched her hand to the night table and retrieved her smartphone.

In the artificial glow of her device she speed dialed Kim, her personal pep-talker; she had agreed to be her lifeline during her recovery for however long it lasted.

"I hope it's not too late," Sharron spoke into the phone sandwiched next to her ear.

"Even if it were, it wouldn't matter. So what's on your mind, girl?"

"I'm all alone in this empty castle. My daring knight departed on a vital mission to slay the evil dragon."

"So tonight's the night?"

Sharron kept Kim abreast of her quest for justice. Or was vengeance the motivating force? Opposite sides of the same coin she repeated to herself to quieten the little voice tugging at her conscience.

"The outcome feels anti-climactic. Anticipation builds and builds to the moment of resolution, then you're left unsatisfied," Sharron complained.

"Like foreplay." They both tittered at her saucy rejoinder. "Any idea who Nelson is working with?"

"His contact operates outside the law." She refrained from telling Kim the full truth.

"Maybe he hired someone like The Equalizer."

"Do such people exist?"

"Plenty of ex-soldiers from the wars in Iraq and Afghanistan offer their unique services online and in military magazines."

"I hope Nelson took precautions. It'd be a miscarriage of justice if he got caught doing what the legal system should have done months ago."

"Don't you worry, Shar. Nelson didn't achieve what he has by being reckless."

Sharron drew comfort from her words. "If you were me, would you...."

"Murder your assailant?" Kim finished for her.

"Yes."

"Good question." A pause took hold. "There's the morality of taking revenge to consid—"

"It's not revenge, it's justice!" Sharron hissed and her vehemence surprised her. "Sorry, Kim. I—"

"Relax, Shar. I understand your view of this situation, but the law views it differently." Kim the lawyer was speaking now. "I'd rather not know how a hypothetical criminal met his fate beyond the purview of our justice system. I would sleep much better."

"This makes two of us." *But my quest for justice still makes me an accomplice to—what?* The unspoken answer clinched it for her. "Nelson was right," she decided.

"About what?"

"What about what?"

"You said Nelson was right."

Sharron mentally backtracked and registered she had been talking out loud. She laughed at herself. "He said: 'Ignorance is best in these matters.'"

"I agree. What you don't know can't be used against you in a court of law."

Sharron yawned. "Thanks for caring, Kim. You're a true friend."

"You'd do the same for me, girl."

"In a heartbeat. I'll call you sometime tomorrow and fill you in—provided Nelson is in a sharing mood."

"Tomorrow your troubles will be over and you can rejoin the legions of the living."

"I sure hope so. This nightmare has lasted long enough."

"One bright future day you'll reflect on this episode in your life and think, 'I attained justice without personal cost.' Trust me."

"Let's hope so."

"Get some sleep, girl."

"I need it. Bye."

Kim didn't know how misplaced her optimism was.

Chapter Forty-Five

Yolanda, consumed with worry for her only surviving sibling, sat with the lights extinguished and stared out the living room window, seeing nothing, her mind elsewhere.

I hope he's safe, she mouthed in silence, picturing her brother lying in wait in the shadows for a mobster named Bronco.

Get a grip, she scolded herself. Bobby survived attacks by ISIS and the Taliban. The Mafia's no match for him. Those goons have no experience in urban warfare. They're skilled at taking out unarmed enemies, but they've never experienced the threat of a battle-hardened marine with a grudge. Besides, Bobby has the element of surprise on his side. So relax. He can take care of himself.

Her brother's stint in the marines had changed him. And not for the better. His friends kidded him for being a recluse. She remembered him being a jokester, someone who saw humor in almost every situation. But the old Bobby was gone. Having seen the brutality and depravity splashed on the evening news night after night, Yolanda appreciated the battlefield horrors he must have borne firsthand in those foreign hellholes. But she couldn't relate to those dangerous experiences. No civilian could. Brother and sister had grown apart. And with the death of Teagan, a casualty of the meth epidemic sweeping the country, they had grown further estranged. Their parents deceased, he was her only family now.

Bobby had blamed himself for their younger sister's early death. He had promised their mom and dad he would watch out for her when they departed this world. But their unexpected demise in a freak car accident two years ago while he was fighting overseas in the 'War on Terror' prevented him from carrying through on his promise. So many times Yolanda had tried to explain to him it wasn't his fault. To no avail. He vowed to avenge Teagan's death, obliging him to leave the marines, a career he didn't always love, but it had afforded him job security and martial adventure, not all of it beneficial though.

So here she was, waiting by the phone, hoping to hear her brother's voice again, a wish much more urgent to her than the success of his quest for revenge.

A whimper from Ali cleared her head. She came alert and listened. Quiet resumed again from his side of the apartment. She eased back into the cushion.

Where are you, Bobby?

Time unspooled at the speed of melting snow. At intervals, sirens wailed in the distance, sometimes near, sometimes far, and muted *thumps* and *bumps* from adjacent apartments eventually ceased, her neighbors succumbing to slumber, some later than others.

Waiting with no word from her brother unnerved her. Not a praying woman, Yolanda reckoned her brother's plan could use help from the Almighty. First, she cleared her throat, then raised her hands.

"Please, God, bless my brother's righteous mission with success. And protect him from evil and deliver him safely home," she prayed in a soft voice. "Amen."

Any prayer is better than no prayer, her mom used to say. The All-Knowing Lord knows what we want beforehand, but He still wishes to hear His servants supplicate Him.

Yolanda's parents had been practicing Baptists, but she had not so much ditched their religion as she had questioned it.

"There's too much evil in the world to believe in a benevolent God," she had debated with her mother more than once.

And her mom always replied in a patient tone: "Yolanda, God created good and evil at the beginning of time, then He granted each human being the free will to choose between these two courses of action. Don't blame God for our choices."

She allowed her mother the last word, partially out of respect and partially for her inability to dispute her mom's wisdom.

And it was her mother's words that helped her deal with her sister Teagan on an October day last year. Yolanda couldn't predict, nor was it possible for her to predict, the lethal impact a decision she made that fateful day would have on her sister.

Bobby wasn't aware their younger sister had visited with her the day before she met her dreadful end in an alley. Yolanda had been too guilt-ridden to inform him of this meeting. She hadn't seen Teagan in weeks when she appeared on her doorstep, begging for a place to stay. She claimed to have quit her habit during a stint in rehab, and for all appearances she had. Her hair was washed, her clothes were clean and her speech was coherent. So Yolanda let her sister sofa surf until she could find a part-time job.

But the pull of addiction, like gravity, is constant. It never lets go of a person. Obliged to run an errand the next day, she left Teagan in charge of Ali. When Yolanda came back through the door, to her horror, she found a strange man in her apartment—probably her sister's dealer—and her sister passed out on the sofa in a drugged stupor. A threat to call the police compelled the stranger to leave and once Teagan came down from her high two days later, Yolanda had no choice but to throw her out on the street. Teagan's irresponsible behavior had placed her son's life in jeopardy, the final straw for her.

It broke her heart to choose between her son and her sister, but it was a choice Teagan had forced upon her. Never did Yolanda expect Teagan's stay to be her last. A visit from the police the following morning to inform her of her sister's death by overdose sent her life into a tailspin for two days of guilt-filled mourning. She didn't remember much from those two days, but somehow, some way, maybe by the grace of God, Ali had survived her period of bereavement.

Once she had regained her emotional equilibrium, she retraced her sister's last known location to a free rehab clinic on Broadway. Among Teagan's meagre possessions returned to Yolanda had been a business card from this clinic. Yolanda paid the clinic a visit and spoke to a blonde-haired volunteer named Sharron who admitted to counselling Teagan the day she died. When apprised of Teagan's overdose, Blondie affected the appropriate gestures of shock and sadness. But Yolanda saw through her artifice and left the place riled at the apparent lack of sympathy from this privileged white woman.

What's one more Black person's drug-induced death? she remembered telling Blondie before storming out of the center. But what could she expect, she told herself, from a woman whose perfectly coiffed hair and immaculately French-polished nails spoke to membership in the private salons of New York's elite, an elite who lived in a rarified bubble of wealth and privilege that protected them from the despair of poverty?

Later, in a more rational frame of mind, Yolanda admitted a good share of her revulsion at her sister's treatment was a projection of her own guilt onto Blondie. With time, Yolanda forgave herself. She wasn't responsible for her sister's poor life choices. Teagan was.

Oh, Teag, why did you overdose?

The phone rang, jarring her, and she lunged for it.

Chapter Forty-Six

Junior's life of crime had caught up to him. He had committed one assault too many. Resigned to his fate, he had ceased hoping for a miracle hours ago, for there was no escape from his current predicament. He could no longer feel his arms and shoulders. He was thankful for this. The pain had been unbearable. If he had known what was coming, he would have never have beaten that blond woman in the park. But hindsight was 20/20.

The slap of leather soles on cement resounding in the hollow space wrenched Junior back to the present. His blood chilled. "No!" he screamed, but the gag in his mouth muffled his voice.

Then bright light flashed beyond his blindfold, signaling the feces had finally met the spinning fan. He bucked his legs insanely, knowing what was coming—his guards had shown him his fate before blindfolding him. A futile action, he continued to thrash wildly about, for stark terror had taken control of him.

Chapter Forty-Seven

McCormack stared bug-eyed at a tall blindfolded man suspended by a cruel hook over a large yellow machine struggling against his restraints while desperate grunts and squeals escaped his gagged mouth. McCormack lowered his disbelieving eyes to Cabreezi and pointed at the prisoner, a mixture of consternation and bewilderment vying for dominance on his features, as if to say, "What gives?"

Cabreezi swept his hand toward the prisoner. "I present to you Junior. Wanted for assault and battery of a pregnant woman."

"Are you sure he's the culprit?"

"We have ways of compelling confessions, Mr. McCormack," and a devilish smile bent his lips. "We also found incriminating evidence on him." He faced Goon Two. "Show Mr. McCormack the evidence."

The hefty goon reached inside his black leather jacket and withdrew a white envelope. He passed it to McCormack.

He opened the flap of the envelope and withdrew a photo. His eyes bulged and he inhaled at the sight of the woman in the snapshot. "How-How did he get this photo of my wife?"

"Junior can point a camera," was Cabreezi's innocent reply.

He came to a startling realization. "The attack on my wife wasn't a random act of violence."

"Appears not, Mr. McCormack."

"But why pick on my wife? Why'd he do it? There has to be a reason."

"Junior is the best person to answer those questions," Cabreezi said. "But he's, uh, tied up at the moment," and the goons shook with mirth.

"What do you plan to do with him?"

"Not *I...You*," and Cabreezi pointed his finger at him.

McCormack stiffened and he threw the don a perplexed look. "*Me?*"

"Yes, *you*." Cabreezi snapped his fingers and Goon One handed McCormack a bulky device resembling a remote control.

"How does possessing the power of life and death feel, Mr. McCormack?" But the don didn't give him a chance to respond. "Doesn't it feel god-like?"

McCormack's hands trembled, the moment of truth dawning on him. "Is this what I think it is?" he asked, holding up the device.

"That device controls the height and angle of the hydraulic hook from which *your* prisoner is hanging. The machine below him is a meat grinder."

Now they were getting somewhere. As though on cue, Goon Two switched on the grinder, and it answered with a deep whirring noise; the tethered man thrashed against his fetters in frenzied terror.

McCormack's mind woke up to the unspeakable horror of the trap set for him and felt his body shudder with massive dread.

"Why so squeamish?" Cabreezi said, smirking. "That punk"—he pointed to Junior—"beat your wife and killed your baby and now you're questioning what's right and what's wrong. Come, come, Mr. McCormack. Time to man up. Your wife wouldn't hesitate if she were in your place," he goaded him.

And still he vacillated.

"Here's the deal, Mr. McCormack. I'm going to make you an offer you can't refuse. If you do not push this button"—he indicated with his finger—"you will trade places with the punk," Cabreezi said, his eyes hard, like ice, and cold. Both goons stole a menacing step toward McCormack. "And I assure you *he* won't hesitate to push the button," Cabreezi warned.

These goons play for keeps, he'd give them that. His senses teetering at the brink of a moral abyss, McCormack gritted his teeth and pushed the green button. He averted his eyes while the hook slowly uncurled and delivered the young man into the voracious maw of the machine feet first. The angry whir of the grinder did not alter in tone while it performed the grisly task of mincing flesh and bones, and the victim writhed against his bonds, muffled screams burbling from his throat. The goons captured it all on video for posterity.

"Congratulations. Your first kill! Not too hard was it?"

The remote control rattled on the floor and McCormack doubled over and retched.

"Don't be distressed, Mr. McCormack. Junior's body won't end up on your dinner plate," Cabreezi said with an evil chuckle. "He'll be fish bait in the East River before the break of dawn."

Bent over, "What've I done?" Nelson said in a hoarse voice barely above a whisper.

"The first kill can be upsetting for many people. Trust me, killing becomes easier with time," Cabreezi said to console him. "But a next time is the least of your concerns. We have a more sophisticated task in mind for a man possessing your special talents."

McCormack unbent himself and wiped his mouth with a silk hanky. "You do?"

"It's difficult for entrepreneurs to earn a decent living these days what with those irksome anti-racketeering laws. Men in my profession have had to go legit to a large degree to circumvent Uncle Sam and his IRS bullies."

"I don't follow."

"You now work for us." Everyone looked pleased except McCormack.

Dazed with incomprehension, he asked, "In what capacity?"

"On the journey here, you said: 'No amount of money is worth your wife's peace of mind.' So, in honor of that sentiment, you are going to transfer your billions as well as your future income to a foundation we established in Canada." He added, "But we'll leave you enough money to live in the style to which you've become accustomed. We aren't greedy."

"How generous of you." All was not lost, he thought. He still had his offshore earnings to fall back on.

Cabreezi shook his head in the way one does when confronted by a man unaware of the deep pile of dung he's stumbled into. Then a patent look of malevolence seized him, and he judged Nelson with cold detachment. "Your sanctimonious attitude is troublesome, Mr. McCormack," he said. "You knew I was no choir boy when we first met and yet you came to *me* for help—a member of the Mafia no less. A mountain of wealth in your possession, yet it was of no use in hunting down your wife's assailant, was it? An impotent multi-billionaire." He let out a harsh laugh. "But I bet billions aren't enough for you. *More* is what your kind crave. More is never enough. But I'm here to teach you *less* is more. So I suggest you bury your sense of self-righteousness, Mr. McCormack. When you open your door to the Devil, expect to sell your soul."

Chapter Forty-Eight

Hands resting on his belly, Rommy sat in front of the TV with Rosie. Bronco had given him the night off. He was glad for the unexpected break. His wife turned away from the commercial and asked him: "You hungry for a snack, dear?"

"What? I'm watching my weight, remember?"

"I didn't think you were being serious."

"For once I am." He cast her a *faux* stern look. "Now get your fanny in the kitchen and fetch me another piece of Cassata."

"Are you kidding me?"

"Rosie, I'm gonna count to three. If there's not a wedge of cake in my hand"—he held up an empty hand—"on three, there's gonna be trouble. One...Two...."

"All right, all right. I'm going." Rosie pretended to scurry away in fright toward the kitchen like her life depended on it.

They both shared a giggle.

"There's too much gratuitous sex and violence on TV," Rosie complained on returning to the living room.

"Gratuitous?" Mr. Romano twisted in his chair and regarded his wife with a mixture of surprise and curiosity. "Where'd you learn that word?"

"A woman used it today on one of the talk shows."

"What does it mean?"

"I suppose it means *too much*."

"You suppose?" Annoyance crept into his tone. "Rosie, if you don't know what a word means, you shouldn't use it. If you use the word in a wrong way, people will ridicule you behind your back."

"The people we socialize with couldn't tell gratuitous from *grazie*," she said, placing a saucer of cake in his outstretched hand.

This got a chuckle out of him. "Ah, Rosie, you're a regular comedian. You missed your true calling," he said, before shoveling a piece of Cassata into his mouth.

"Because I married Mr. Serious," she said, striving to conceal her delight.

"Don't I make you laugh anymore?"

"Rarely."

He swallowed before answering. "My lousy job snuffed out my sense of humor."

"Change jobs," she suggested without reflecting.

"Whose gonna hire this unskilled old man?"

"If you didn't have such a low opinion of yourself, maybe someone *would* hire you?"

He couldn't tell her no one walks away from the Mob. A job with the Mob offered lifetime security, if you kept your nose clean. But even then. *Meno male* (thank God) the children have legitimate careers. "I have a realistic opinion of myself, Rosie," he gruffed. "It's why I am where I am."

"The bleachers are nothing to brag about. You're better than you think you are, my man." She reached over and patted him on the arm. "It's close to ten. I'm going to bed," she announced. "Please be quiet when you come to bed, dear."

Rosie got out of her La-Z-Boy rocker and gave Mr. Romano, reclining in a matching rocker, a peck goodnight.

He watched her broad hips waddle off to the bedroom.

There goes a woman to die for.

A warm sensation overcame him.

He returned his attention to the TV, but he couldn't concentrate, his focus elsewhere. He switched off the TV and stared at a wall covered with framed family photos.

All evening long, the story of his neighbor hovered at the edges of his consciousness. It was his duty to report to Bronco what Rosie had told him about Lorenzo and his girlfriend. But he possessed no desire to involve a young mother and her child in this nasty affair, so he had held onto this explosive information. No one other than Rosie was privy to it, so he felt safe keeping it to himself. Besides, what Bronco doesn't know can't hurt him, Rommy decided.

He couldn't grasp how far from the mark he was. At this same moment, Bronco was on a collision course with a fate name Bobby. Although Rommy had communicated to Bronco earlier in the evening Lorenzo's backpack was nowhere to be found behind the building next door, he had softened this news by suggesting the backpack could have been stolen. Bronco seemed to take his report in stride. He hoped Bronco resisted the urge to snip off anymore of Lorenzo's fingers to satisfy his curiosity…or his cruelty.

His hunger satiated, Rommy placed the crumb-filled saucer on the side table and folded his hands on his round belly.

Bronco's a psychopath. Wise guys with his bent for violence don't usually climb so high in the family. But I gotta hand it to the mook. He's got a few brain cells. Not many, but enough to impress the don, I guess. He'd probably kill his own mother to prove how loyal he was to the don. But he's still a mook.

Rommy shifted his rear-end. The seat padding was worn-down with age, like its occupant.

Bronco would give Rambo the willies, he judged. So never let him think you're going soft on him. Do what you gotta do when he's around, nothing more. The mook's a survivor. He's got more lives than a politician has lies. But just as a politician runs outta of lies, Bronco's gonna run out of luck. He's got to. The universe can tolerate only so many of his kind. Then one day:

Ka-bing, Ka-bang, Ka-boom!

The crap he's tossed at the world is gonna come right back at him. Like a frigging boomerang. I wish I could be there when it happens, to witness him being bumped from his perch. He won't see it coming, either. Cocksure mooks usually don't. They're too blinded by their own superiority. It takes but one fearless renegade to cut them down. Nico got his and one day Bronco will too.

It won't be me, though. It'll have to be someone with little to lose. Someone without a family of his own. He's out there, waiting. And when this dude's had his fill, Bronco better watch his back.

Man, I wish I could escape this horror show and retire. Working for the Mob was like playing a deadly game of survival one day at a time. Violent death was a constant companion. In similarity to his fellow man, he fantasized about retirement, no longer having to answer to the Man. Except he'd have to look over his shoulder the rest of his life if he ever quit his job. The Mob held all the chips. He adopted a posture of resignation.

"Time to turn in."

He performed his toilet, then slid into bed next to his wife. She stirred at his presence but didn't waken. He lay beside her and listened to the rhythm of her breathing.

I swear to God, Rosie, if it weren't for you and the children, I'd quit and to hell with the consequences.

He rolled onto his side and shut his eyes, yearning once more for oblivion to overtake him.

Chapter Forty-Nine

Cabreezi and his bodyguards chatted amiably the whole return trip as if nothing out of the ordinary had gone down at the slaughterhouse. All in a day's work for members of the Mob. From his seat, Nelson, in no mood for idle chatter, watched the cityscape pass by in a blur of motion and blinking lights, haunted by what he had done against his will. Even if the impulse to talk grabbed hold of him, his seatmates were the last people with whom he would entertain a conversation. The experience would probably leave him yearning to be scrubbed with a rough brush.

How can they sit there discussing the merits of Italian restaurants after making minced meat out of a guy? Must be psychopaths. There's no other explanation for their relaxed behavior.

Whether this was true, he was in no position to verify.

McCormack sat squished against the door, keeping as far from the don as physically possible. Despite their laid back postures, a palpable aura of malevolence radiated from them. They reminded him of a pack of slinking jackals, circling a hapless prey. And he was their prey.

Having never known raw terror before, he wanted nothing more in this moment than to curl up into a ball and roll away out of sight. But his desire to disappear wouldn't happen anytime soon. Small and weak and helpless. These crippling sensations were new to him, never even experiencing them as a child. Such was the tangible menace of their presence.

Nelson felt disconnected from reality, from all he knew about existence. He was a stranger to himself. This nightmare can't be real. I dealt a guy a gruesome death tonight. My life is finished. I wish I were dead. What will I tell Sharron?

These thoughts and more treadmilled through his head like a mental ticker tape.

He heard Cabreezi's smooth voice address him, but he ignored it, unconcerned with any retaliation for his reticence. Already dead inside, what did it matter if they snuffed out his life?

"I guess he's not in the mood to chat with his new friends," the don said to his soldiers.

"Maybe we upset him," Goon One offered.

Goon Two snorted. "Not very grateful of him considering the big favor we did him."

The three of them laughed at his expense.

Humiliation seared through Nelson, but he resisted their efforts to bait him. They owned him but why grant them the satisfaction of this awareness? Whatever remained of his tattered dignity, it was all that was left of his former self. And he possessed no desire to trade It away. He had already sacrificed too much tonight. If they hungered for his dignity, they'd have to kill him for it.

Before long, the shiny limousine rolled to a stop in the same spot his misbegotten escapade had begun.

"Home at last, safe and sound," Cabreezi announced. He grasped McCormack's upper arm, he flinched. "I could have forced you to find your way back from the plant through the urban jungle, Mr. McCormack. Fortunately for you, I'm not a cruel man," and his bodyguards laughed.

Nelson remained mute. He would let his tormentor have fun at his expense.

"I have a gift for you, Mr. McCormack," and the don held out to him a smartphone. He gestured for McCormack to take possession of it.

Nelson took the phone and stared at in silence, refusing to make eye contact with his warden.

"We will use this phone to keep in touch," he said, like they were bosom buddies. "Never call me from any other phone. *Capiche*?"

Nelson nodded his compliance.

"I sense this is the beginning of a rewarding partnership," and McCormack recoiled at the touch of Cabreezi's hand on his knee. "A little skittish are we?"

"Can I go now?"

Cabreezi motioned with his finger and Goon One reached over and opened the rear passenger door. Nelson made to skedaddle, but the don restrained him and said: "A word to the wise, Mr.

McCormack. Don't go to the police," and he waggled his smartphone in his other hand as if to say, "We got it all on video."

No second bidding was necessary. Cold fingers of worry worming around inside his head, Nelson could only offer a subservient nod. Scared beyond redemption, he bailed out of the vehicle like it was the Devil's lair itself.

The shimmering black limousine crept away from the curb, a glossy-coated beast on wheels, and an icy finger danced up his spine. His soul was in the belly of that rolling beast, and there was no retrieving it. Not now. Not ever. Even if he killed the beast.

McCormack pulled up his collar, hunched his shoulders and shoved his hands deep into the pockets of his leather jacket while he loitered on the street corner, waiting for the light to change. He copped a glance both ways. To hell with the Walk signal. He crossed Ninth Avenue and made his way to Eighth Avenue; it would become Central Park West further north. He hooked a left, reluctance in his stride. His vaunted status was no longer a haven from the tribulations of the lower world. Evil had found him. And it had stripped him of every defense.

He was alone in the street on his northward trek, the tide of commerce having ebbed hours ago. He had never ventured out this late at night on foot. But what did he care? If a mugger accosted him, he wouldn't resist. Maybe the mugger would do him in. It would be an easy way out. He wouldn't have to explain to Sharron what happened out there and his death might appease whatever deity concerned itself with the matter of the life he had extinguished earlier. A life for a life.

He marched on in misery, and every so often he glanced over his shoulder to check for a cab, but cabs were in short supply on this hellish night. Considering the hour, what could he expect? He didn't relish covering the more than twenty city blocks to his place on foot. Boarded-up businesses—collateral victims of yesteryear's covid skullduggery—on either side of the street pressed in on him, and he hurried past them, his dire need for sanctuary driving him onward.

Without warning, about thirty yards ahead, he spotted a male figure walking toward him. A tremor seized McCormack. Danger incarnate lay ahead.

Where did he come from?

He berated himself for not paying more attention to his environment.

As the man drew closer, an idea seized hold of McCormack.

Maybe he'll be my salvation.

He dug out his wallet and waved it at the advancing figure. "Look what I got, bro."

The man slowed his pace, probably wondering why some crazy dude was doing what he was doing.

"There's at least a thousand bucks in it. Come and get it if you dare, bro," McCormack challenged. He didn't break his stride.

The gap between them closed rapidly.

"What's the matter, bro?" he taunted him. "Too scared to rip it out of my hands?"

McCormack blocked the stranger's path and thrust the wallet in his face. "Here it is, bro."

The man swatted it away and shoved McCormack none too gently against a brick building.

"Get outta my face," he yelled at McCormack. "I have a job!"

McCormack gaped at him. "Shoot me. Stab me. Take my money. *Please.*"

"Get lost or I'll call the po-lice."

McCormack stuffed his wallet back into his coat pocket and scurried away, humiliated, but, alas, still alive.

"And you're not my bro, you crazy fool," the man hollered at him. "I know who my parents are."

You're such a loser, McCormack reproached himself, the distance between himself and his putative executioner growing with each urgent stride. I can't even get myself killed on the mean streets of New York. He chanced a look behind him. The stranger had moved on down the street, muttering to himself.

Many blocks later Nelson spied his building in the distance and his sore feet quickened their pace with renewed energy. Seeming refuge was mere steps away. He nodded at Harvey, the liveried concierge, his youthful countenance sporting curiosity at the sight of him making his way through the lobby to the elevator at this unusual hour of the night.

Sometimes living is harder than dying.

The unspoken words ripped through Nelson's mind, a mind tormented by a predicament from which there was no escape—except death. He couldn't recall who had spouted these words but he appreciated their harsh truth, so much so he wished he were dead.

But it was too late for redos. He had screwed up big time tonight. No two ways about it. His life was now in the maw of an underworld gang, a gang that wouldn't think twice about chewing him up and spitting him out should he hesitate to follow its orders. Even if he wished to—and he didn't—he couldn't go to the police for help; a pair of gang members had filmed an incriminating video of *him* pushing *the* button. An action that caused a grisly fatality.

He was no lawyer, but he wagered a jury might not view too benignly this fatal outcome despite his being threatened with his own demise. *No.* Putting his faith in the justice system wasn't worth the risk to his freedom. The prospect of lifetime imprisonment held less appeal for him than the specter of his present dilemma. He wasn't going to be any Bubba's bitch. Though hemmed in, at least he could still come and go without needing anyone's permission...For now.

Life is all about choices. Some good. Others, not so good. The gang, in its malevolent wisdom, had offered him a choice. And he had done what any sane man would have done. He had chosen life. If he hadn't followed their demands, he'd be fish bait. Damned if he did, dead if he didn't. Some choice. A Faustian pact he never saw coming until it was coiled around him like a viper, fangs bared.

You were ambushed by your own desperation.

Screw you!

You could have resisted and died on your feet. The deed of a moral person.

Cork it!

You took the easy way out. You killed a man to save your own skin. Now you will live on your knees, a slave.

The punk had it coming! By every objective metric, my life is worth more than his. I don't assault people for a living. He did.

Rationalizing?

I prefer to label it *justifying*.

Call it what you will. It doesn't change the facts.

Drop dead.

His inner voice fell silent.

How he had gotten himself into this mess was no mystery. It was his own fault. No question about it. He had been desperate for help. But desperation oftentimes makes for dangerous bedfellows. And nobody was more dangerous than his current bedfellow. He had cashed in a favor never imagining doing so would place his life in permanent jeopardy and probably his wife's too. But he had no way of fathoming his request for help would lead to his involuntary induction into the Mob. Stranger things had happened he was sure. But more perilous? He doubted it.

Complain, complain. You sealed a deal with the Devil, you dumbass. What'd you expect from a mobster? Perhaps a: "We're even now. See you around." This thug plays for keeps. And now he *owns* you. His stomach roiled in acknowledgement his life was in the grip of a ruthless gangster whose tailored wool suits were just so much lambskin on a ravenous wolf.

Despite being blindsided by his present impasse, he couldn't shake the paranoid feeling the frightful circumstances he found himself in tonight did not come about solely by chance. Everything happens for a reason, his inner voice intuited. Despite reviewing his current circumstances in detail, he still couldn't connect the dots leading up to tonight's personal disaster into a causal chain of events. He suspected he was overlooking a factor. Of this he was certain—as rain is wet. He had earned his multi-billion dollar fortune forming patterns out of disparate points of data.

Too rattled to concentrate, he watched the LED panel in terrified silence, the red digits incrementing on each successive floor, and the luxurious conveyance rose soundlessly toward his penthouse. His had always been an ordered life. He marched to his own cadence. No one told him what to do. But now he must march to the beat of someone else's drum, the beat of the wild, the savage, the lethal. And if he didn't—

A pleasant chime went off and the door whispered open. He exited the elevator and stood immobile for a moment in the darkened foyer, noting the exclusivity of his abode hadn't stopped the evil stalking the streets twenty-one stories below from invading what was—had been to all extents —his sumptuous cocoon of security. And now this evil held him tightly in its grasp. He shivered at the thought. The elevator door slid shut behind him with a velvety *swish*, and it reminded him of an old saying: When one door closes, another opens.

Most people assumed this saying conveyed a positive meaning. But it begs the question: Opens to what?

To his horror, a door had opened to an unfolding nightmare, a nightmare from which he would never awaken and from which he couldn't run. No safe harbor, no refuge to shelter in from this raging shitstorm. Nobody ever ran from the Mob and survived for long. The media would have everyone believe this claim. Whether this claim was true or not, he wasn't inclined to test. He had entertained the idea of buying an island in the Caribbean—he still had the money to do it—but they would hunt him down. The Mob never forgets. This he didn't doubt. Without access to the Witness Protection Program, he and Sharron would always be fugitives. The Mob's tentacles reached into every corner of the world. Spending his life looking over his shoulder or lying awake at night listening for strange sounds was not a future he relished. He had made his bed and so now he must lie in it.

He let out a long sigh of resignation.

If only he hadn't found the stupid wallet.

He mentally shook himself and stirred himself to action. What do I tell Sharron? I can't reveal to her what happened. She'll freak out. I'm sure of it. Her mental state is still fragile. It'd be hazardous to her health to burden her with what happened out there. Skip the gory details. The truth might push her over the edge...But—No! Inform her the danger is over. Nothing more. You'll manage the new danger alone. Then perhaps she can begin living a normal life again, one careful step at a time.

Not wishing to disturb Sharron, he removed his Tom Ford brogues in the foyer, padded along the hallway, the marble floor cool to the touch of his aching stockinged feet, and stole into his bedroom. All in vain. Sharron was sitting up in their ornate four-poster king-sized bed fit for a Saxon lord.

"Did you avenge us?" she asked in the semi-darkness, clutching the sheets.

"Give me a minute, Baby. I have to use the bathroom."

He flicked on the light and closed the door behind him. He leaned unsteadily on the marble counter and appraised his reflection in the gilded mirror. Usually a picture of health, haggard described best the image staring back at him. He splashed cold water on his face and patted it dry with a plush towel. A rosy hue now colored his cheeks. After brushing his teeth, he gargled a gulp of mouthwash to wash away the bitter trace of gall. Feeling somewhat human again, he reentered the master suite, tore off his clothes and flung them on an over-stuffed leather wingback armchair. He slid into bed next to his wife and put his arm around her. She nestled against his hairy muscular chest.

"You're shaking, Nels. What happened out there?"

"I took care of business."

"Will that psycho harm anyone again?" she asked small and soft. She rested her cheek on his chest again and relaxed against his firm, lean body.

"Maybe just some fish," and he let out a crazed laugh while he clung to his wife in a cold sweat.

Chapter Fifty

While Nelson was trudging through the mean streets of midtown Manhattan, Bobby happened upon Pepe's Tavern close to midnight. The directions a friend of a friend had given him were spotty but with a dose of good luck, he had found the place. He drove around the block a few times to get his bearings and to plan an escape route. He had yet to spot Bronco's car. A combination of relief and gratitude filled his breast. It meant his quarry hadn't arrived for his usual nightcap. On his second loop, he spotted the dark alley bisecting the tavern and the derelict commercial building next door.

Unlit and concealed. A perfect place to launch an ambush from. Didn't get much better than this.

A former marine reconnaissance officer who had completed two tours of duty in Iraq and one in Afghanistan, reconnoitering enemy territory was second nature to him. He steered his black two-toned Toyota FJ Cruiser around the block for a final tour and parked it near the mouth of the alley. Not too close, but close enough for a quick retreat.

Dark and deserted, the street would rattle any civilian on foot not packing personal protection. But he was no ordinary pedestrian. He had experienced similar settings in his life but in dangerous war zones, places where he and his team of warriors had owned the night. Tonight would be no different. His physical stature alone was enough to intimidate all but the craziest of men. And if this wasn't enough, then the hardware he carried was. A sawed-off ten-gauge shotgun could wipe aside any attack composed of flesh and bone and metal too.

His head covered by a black beanie, he picked his way carefully to the other end of the littered alley and hunkered down in the shadows, his breath condensing in the cold air, and the weight of the stunted shotgun resting in the crook of his arm comforted him. He had machined a choke onto the end of the barrel to concentrate the pellets when they exploded from the barrel so they would hit only the intended human target.

He inspected the kill zone and cataloged it. The brazen illicit activity being conducted in the open on the street stoked a rage in him, the same activity that had ensnared Teagan in its wasting grip. Her drug habit had led to prostitution to pay for the drugs her body craved—an inescapable and vicious downward spiral. Only death had liberated her from her addiction. And so he would avenge her death by taking the life of her killer.

Calm descended on him. Time dragged. Boredom was dangerous to a person lying in ambush. It increased the risk of mission failure. The mind tended to unwind and wander. But he had trained his to run through various scenarios and their potential outcomes for the specific situation he found himself in while he waited. This mental training had earned him numerous triumphs on the battlefield. He had witnessed countless lives lost to haste and an inability to manage tedium. Mastering his mind made him a survivor. Tonight would be no different, he predicted.

Bronco will show, he reassured himself. He has to.

The street action kept his mind busy. Cars rolled by, their drivers checking out the wares of the streetwalkers before striking a deal. He couldn't help but wonder who the losers were paying for sex when it was available for free in any bar in the land.

They must be desperate. The rumble of a brawny engine heading his way rose above the street action and cut short his amusement. His ears pricked up. He shifted his focus in the direction of the mechanical noise. Chrome reflected feeble light. Attached to it was a black Chrysler 300S, and it rolled to a stop a few yards away.

Bingo!

Bobby stiffened. His finger found the trigger on his weapon. A beefy guy struggled out of the car. Mr. Beef walked with a pronounced limp.

Must be him.

He zeroed in on his target. Still aware of his environment, his eyes laser focused on the man approaching him.

"Hey, you Bronco?" Bobby called out to him from the shadows.

"Who wants to know?" Bronco said, slowing to a halt.

"A pissed off big brother," he snarled.

"You must be Tyrone. Lorenzo warned me about you. I assumed he was bluffing, but my assumption was off the mark." His voice didn't waver.

"You killed my baby sister."

"Teagan, right?"

"You still remember her name," further angering Bobby.

"I don't know Teagan from iced tea. I never heard of your sister's name until your friend Lorenzo mentioned it to me before we whacked him."

"So what are you saying?"

"I'm saying your buddy Lorenzo somehow convinced you I did, so he could have you kill me. Appears you swallowed the bait."

Bobby grabbed a moment to think. This matter was no longer personal. His conscience warred against itself. But this hood is still responsible for keeping other girls on the street. He came to a decision.

"Drugs have been the ruin of my people. And it's trash like you who perpetuate this ruin." He pointed his shotgun at Bronco.

"Your people are weak. I met your kind in Spofford. Real badasses when part of a gang, but a bunch of cowards when all alone."

Is he trying to rattle me? Wrong strategy, buddy. "Spofford wasn't real life."

"Call it what you want."

"Revenge is what I want," he snarled.

"You're screwing with the wrong guy. I'm a made man. My associates will hunt you down."

"I dealt with the Taliban in Afghanistan. You wops got nothing on them. And Tyrone isn't my real name." He registered shock on Bronco's face. "Appears Lorenzo played one last trick on you."

"I wasn't responsible for your sister's death. My customers are from my side of the tracks. So let's call this a draw and walk away."

The arrogance of the guy. "You got a lot of brass for a guy staring down a shotgun."

"Comes with the territory. You don't go far in the family without it."

"Some family. I'd rather be an orphan."

"What do you care?"

"Those girls—" he indicated with his shotgun "—are human beings."

"Maybe so. But they're also runaways from broken homes. We give them food and shelter and a chemical boost to help them cope with their lousy past."

Bobby couldn't believe the self-serving rationalizations spewing from this thug's mouth. Enough was enough. It was do or die time. Problem was, he had never shot an unarmed civilian. But his adversary was no ordinary civilian. He was an enemy of humanity, of the values he fought for and his buddies had died for, so he didn't deserve an equal chance in this settling of accounts. Before he could act, the thug sowed his own fate.

Bronco dove sideways, and a gun appeared in his right hand. But Bobby had anticipated such a last-gasp act of self-preservation. His finger already on the trigger, all he had to do was squeeze it. The blast of ten-gauge pellets caught Bronco square in the upper torso and hurled him backwards in mid-air.

Boomerang!

Screams exploded in the street and tires peeled on pavement. Panicked drivers stomped on the gas pedal to get out of Dodge. Bobby didn't stick around to watch his quarry die; he had probably died before he hit the ground.

The shooter tucked the shotgun beneath his bomber jacket and sauntered through the unlit alley. He stopped at the mouth of the narrow passage and peered both ways. All clear. He hopped into his vehicle whose license plates he had covered prior to entering this wretched neighborhood. He would remove the covers once he had cleared the area. Bobby steered away from the scene at peace with himself. Although Bronco's death wouldn't bring back his sister, it might prevent the premature deaths of other innocent young girls. It was a promising upshot he could live with.

As he drove in the darkness, the glow of the instrument panel limning his grim features, he felt the weight of the guilt he had carried around for so long begin to lighten. But, still, he should have been there for Teagan in her direst hour of need. He hoped his deed would bring comfort to his sister's soul. And to his.

"Rest in peace, little sister, rest in peace," he said to the night. "Your big brother avenged your death in the best way he knew how."

Chapter Fifty-One

Yolanda snapped awake on the sofa and grabbed her ringing phone. "Bobby! Are you all right?" She made no effort to quell the anxiety in her voice.

"When have I ever been wrong?" his question punctuated with a rare snicker.

"I've been telling myself repeatedly not to catastrophize your mission and all you can do is joke about it?"

"Sis, I'm back and still in one piece. And the wop won't be pimping young girls anymore."

"You took him out?"

"He tried to get the drop on me, but I dropped him instead. It's over."

She caught the relief in his voice. "Did he admit to killing Teagan?"

"Thugs like him don't confess to their crimes. Despite the absence of a confession, he was still found guilty according to Divine law and I, an avenging instrument of God's will, passed sentence on him and smote him. End of story."

"Did anyone see you?"

"Only if they had infrared vision. It was too dark. I didn't show my face and no one dared follow me."

"How's your conscience, Bobby?"

There was a brief lull.

"When I was in the marines, I killed scores of two-legged animals who preyed on the weak. I never lost sleep over them. Bronco was no different. His execution was a righteous kill."

"So, what are you going to do with the rest of your life now that you've avenged Teagan?"

"I wrestled with this question on the drive back."

"And?"

"The world is divided between good guys and bad guys, and it's behooves the good guys to ensure the bad guys always feel compelled to check who's gaining on them. So I'm rejoining the marines."

"I'm glad to hear this, Bobby."

"You are?"

"You now have a clearer sense of what your purpose in life is. The first time you joined the marines was to escape the tedium of the nine-to-five routine, right?"

"It beat warming a chair in a cubicle for eight hours or more a day."

"Instead of running from something, you're moving toward something now, a goal that will give meaning to your life."

"I never thought of it this way."

"Because I, not you, studied psychology."

"Thanks for the free psych-eval, Sis."

"Hold the praise until you receive my bill."

"Send it to the marines."

They shared a laugh.

"I almost forgot," Bobby said.

"What?"

"Your...Your *friend* Lorenzo is dead."

Yolanda burst into tears, her reaction caught her off guard.

"Why are you crying?"

"How...how can you be sure?"

"Before Bronco drew on me, he bragged about whacking him. You still cared for him?"

"He is—was—the father of Ali."

"Yeah, but you still didn't answer my question."

"You didn't know him like I did, Bobby. Lorenzo could be sweet and zany and—"

"Irresponsible."

"Yeah."

"And he worked for the Mob, Sis. He wasn't selling ice cream cones to kids on a street corner."

"He told me he worked as rent collector for several apartment buildings in Hell's Kitchen."

"A rent collector is Mobspeak for loan sharking."

"What are you saying?"

"Loan sharks beat up people who don't repay their debts on time."

Something clicked in Yolanda's mind. "This explains the cuts and bruises on Lorenzo's hands. He told me he got them doing pushups on his knuckles."

Bobby pondered her moment of clarity. "Our eyes rarely deceive us but our minds often do."

"He wasn't one of them, Bobby. He didn't have a mean bone in his body."

"Then how could he be a member of such a ruthless organization?"

"He may not have been a choir boy but he was no killer."

"So long as the Mob doesn't connect Lorenzo to you, you shouldn't have to worry about the future."

"The last time I saw Lorenzo he told me he had never divulged anything about us to those thugs. Maybe this is why I rarely saw him. It was his way of protecting us. He was probably afraid for me and Ali."

"The Mob has no qualms about silencing the innocent."

"God will keep us safe."

"Let's hope so."

Yolanda sat forward on the sofa. "One thing mystifies me about Lorenzo."

"I'm all ears."

"Why didn't he tell me sooner who was responsible for Teagan's death?"

A pause intervened, then an exhalation traveled across the Ethernet as though Bobby had made a decision.

"Bronco denied any responsibility for Teagan's death. He claimed Lorenzo lied so I would go hunting for him."

"Son of a bitch," she breathed out.

"I applaud Lorenzo for his deception. He had me take out the guy who killed him."

"He played us for his own selfish ends."

"Bronco was a badass, Sis. One of the baddest of the bad. He may not have caused Teagan's death, but I bet he was responsible for the deaths of many other innocent girls."

She sensed she was reaching for moral absolution. "His network might have sold her the drugs that killed her. Good enough for me."

"It's frustrating someone else from his gang will step into his shoes, and the show will go on."

"If folks continue to seek escape through chemical means, the war on drugs is lost."

"The White House should declare a war on mental illness and divert the funds devoted to fighting the futile war on drugs towards combatting mental health issues."

"Too wise for politicians up to their necks in nonsense."

She heard him yawn.

"Well, Sis, we could discuss this issue until politicians get a clue. Not likely. Anyway, it's been a long night. Time for this dude to hit the rack."

"Thanks, Bobby."

"For what?"

"For giving our little sister the justice she deserved."

"It was the least I could do for her."

"Sleep tight, Bobby."

"You too."

Yolanda tapped the red icon on her smartphone to end the call. She leaned back on the sofa and clutched a cushion.

Where ever you are, Lorenzo, I hope you're at peace. There's one less badass in the world because of your self-sacrifice.

If only she knew the whole truth.

Chapter Fifty-Two

"What the hell is going on?" Cabreezi screamed from behind his desk, his face mottled with rage.

The dreadful news of Bronco's murder had reached the don's ears. He appeared ready to blow a head gasket.

Filled with cold terror, Paco watched his boss pace back and forth like a caged lion. But unlike a zoo, there were no wide moats and tall steel fences separating him from the don, only a desk. A large one, but still just a desk. And one Cabreezi could easily skirt. Paco wagered he could outrun him. The don had at least twenty pounds on him, but Cabreezi's bodyguards presented another hurdle. He couldn't outrun them. Hemmed in on every side, he prayed to the Virgin in the silence of his head for protection, the devout Catholic he was.

"First my son and now my best capo. Who's next, me?" he said. He threw up his arms in gesture of alarm while he wore a path in the carpet.

The report of Bronco's violent demise was a kick to the stomach of the family. With his death, the family boasted no one to keep the members in line. Every general relied on a soldier of rank to execute his orders. Bronco's murder sent shockwaves through the family—and through the local newswires.

"Milo and his team have got your back," Paco reassured him from the edge of his seat, referring to the ex-spy on the payroll. "But you should lay low until he can get a read on this crisis."

"Your point?"

"Live in this building for the next week. Milo plans to conduct a counter-surveillance op. Maybe someone other than the police are spying on this place."

"I'm not a coward. I don't hide from my enemies. I feed them their guts."

"This building is secure as a fortress. Your house isn't," the consigliere pointed out. "It has too many access points. There's also the risk of a drive-by shooting." He reminded him of the assassination of a crime boss on Staten Island.

Cabreezi conceded the logic of his argument while he paced back and forth.

"For the good of the family, Don."

"Don't-tell-me-what's-good-for-this-family. *Capiche?*"

Paco wilted under Cabreezi's scarlet-faced glare. He changed tactics. "The family must have you at its head, Don. Without your leadership, this family will be disappear overnight. Nobody can fill your shoes."

"I built this family into a real estate powerhouse and no one is going to take it from me."

"The family's vulnerable without an heir to succeed you."

"So what are suggesting? Father another child?" He chuckled at the idea. "Only if it's conceived in a test tube. A parked car has more drive than Donatella."

Paco clenched his jaw to overcome the urge to laugh. "It's best to appoint an heir and quickly before rival families decide to challenge our position."

"They wouldn't dare."

"Wouldn't we?"

Cabreezi smirked. "War would have been waged and won in the same day."

Paco seized the initiative to bend the don's change in attitude to his advantage. "Allow me to prepare a succession list."

He stopped pacing. "Will your name be on it?"

Paco's face froze in a rictus of contrived fear. "Never, Don. I know my limitations. I serve, not lead."

Placated, Cabreezi said, "We also have to appoint a capo to replace Bronco."

"May I recommend a fella?"

He waved his hand. "Go ahead. Amaze me."

"Tommaso Romano."

"Bronco's partner." He chewed on the name like a termite wasp through wood before he spoke again. "I sold his father's restaurant out from under him over two decades ago. His father dropped dead from the shock." He glowed at the remembrance. "My first foray into real estate, and I made a killing on the sale. No pun intended," he chortled.

Cabreezi parlayed the money from the sale of the restaurant into a real estate empire. And like all empires ruthless at heart, it expanded without regard for rules and laws.

"An inspired choice. But can he be trusted?"

"Romano's loyalty is without question. He iced his own brother a few years back."

"Remind me." Cabreezi listened to the grisly tale with interest. "I bet he's glad he only had one brother."

Paco choked on a laugh. "He's a stand-up guy. Bronco never spilled a bad word about him."

"I'm wondering why he joined our organization after what I did to his parents' restaurant."

Paco shrugged his forehead. He wasn't expecting Cabreezi's hint of wariness. He needed Rommy in Bronco's place for the next phase of their plan. "He didn't blame you for what happened."

"You vouch for him?"

Paco was putting his own life on the line in vouching for Rommy. If Rommy screwed up, Paco would share in the consequences. "I do," he said unequivocally.

Cabreezi came to a decision. "He avenged Nico's death. Good enough for me. Tell this Tommaso fella the job is his and so is Bronco's ride and house."

Paco felt relief calm his insides. Pieces on the chessboard were creeping closer to the king, but they weren't coming to protect him. "Romano will kiss your ring for placing your trust in him." And a whole lot more. But this sentiment could not be expressed out loud.

"One problem solved and another to go. How am I going to find Bronco's killer?"

Paco pretended to consider the Boss' question before he answered. "Give the job to Romano."

"I don't have many good options to choose from." Cabreezi's posture slumped. "Make it happen."

"Romano's a bloodhound," Paco lied. "If anyone can find Bronco's killer, it'll be him. He whacked Nico's killer don't forget."

This news bucked him up. "If he finds Bronco's killer, I'll give him the world."

"I'll pass this on to him, Don."

Cabreezi gripped the back of the chair. "So what am I supposed to do for the next week, Paco? I'll go stir-crazy in this office."

"You could get a manicure."

Cabreezi shot him a sly grin. "Given current circumstances, Donatella will understand my need to camp out. She'll probably kick up her heels at this change in my routine," he said in afterthought. His wife had returned from Italy days ago, her period of mourning for Nico finished.

"So, it's settled then?"

Cabreezi nodded and eased into his chair. "I'll create a list of personal items to retrieve from my home. Send Riccardo for them."

"Will do."

"And if Donatella gives him any lip, tell him he can put her out of my misery." His chest heaved. "I kill myself," he said through his amusement.

If only, Paco wished.

Chapter Fifty-Three

Affecting a sourpuss, Yolanda tapped her mobile to end the call and laid it on the kitchen counter. Her supervisor, Jolene, was less than pleased she was taking a sick day. But who was Jolene to complain? That lazy cow racked up more time off than a hypochondriac with a hangnail. Yolanda could picture her rail-thin boss moaning about her latest ache *de jour*. This was always a prelude to her booking a day off. Yolanda and her coworkers ran a secret betting pool. Winnings went to the person who guessed the correct day their boss would call in sick. The game boosted office morale and offered diversion from the daily grind.

Still groggy-headed from a restless night's sleep, Yolanda schlepped to a prefab desk in her sweats, tabled her misting cup of java and logged into her laptop. The drama from yesterday had overtaxed her nerves. An image of Lorenzo waxed and waned in her brain, the scrolling newsfeed capturing her attention.

A bold headline nabbed her attention, Yolanda came alert in an instant.

Chief Lieutenant of Cabreezi Crime Family
Murdered In the Bronx

She scanned the article. Her eyes bugged out. "Jee-zuz, Bobby," she said. "A shotgun blast to the chest. You sure whipped open a can of wompass on him last night. Teagan would be proud of you." Her throat constricted in pain for a moment. She was relieved to read no witnesses to the killing had come forward. Even if there had been, would they involve themselves in the murder of a mobster? Doing so was asking for a deep pile of dung.

She came to the end of the headline news. No caption about a lanky twenty-something man being found dead caught her attention. He's gone, she consoled herself. At least the a-hole who killed him got his.

Satisfied with the unexpected pick-me-up, Yolanda bent to fulfilling Lorenzo's last wish: mail his envelope to the police.

Luckily for him, she had a stamp. She changed into street clothes and headed out of her apartment. His fever cured, Ali was once again lodged in the daycare, so she wouldn't have to ask Mrs. Romano to babysit him while she mailed the letter.

Yolanda eased into the elevator and pushed #1. To her chagrin the elevator ascended. The door sprang open on the next floor with a loud clunk. The opening was empty. Then a man sprang into view. Yolanda jolted at his sudden appearance.

"Oh, morning, Mr. Romano," she said. "I nearly fainted from fright." She ran into him on occasion when she left Ali with his wife.

Rommy apologized in the cramped compartment. He leaned on the opposite wall, angled to her. "Going down I hope?"

"All the way."

"How's your son?" he asked. The door clanked shut. "Rosie told me he was sick."

Yolanda beamed. "He's doing better. His fever's gone. And his mother is ready for some r'nr."

"Mothers are angels in disguise." His eyes crinkled when he said it. "My Rosie raised our three kids, mostly on her own. They caused her many a sleepless night. Now they're raising our grandkids. The cycle of life never ceases."

By this time, the elevator had lurched to a stop on the first floor and the door cranked open. Rommy shifted sideways to let her pass. They crossed the lobby together. Mere acquaintances, Yolanda stuck to safe a topic.

"You on your way to work?"

"Yeah. Someone has to pay the bills," he said, a hint of world-weariness in his voice.

"Where do you work?" she asked while he held the door for her.

"If I told you, I'd have to kill you."

"You're such a joker, Mr. Romano."

"No joke," he said with a straight face.

Consternation rose in her. He must have noticed, for his lips parted in a grin.

"Had you going, heh? I should've been an actor. I do a mean Don Corleone."

They reached the sidewalk and stopped.

"I work for a security firm," he threw out. "How 'bout yourself?"

"I work in HR."

"Hiring and retiring."

Yolanda laughed. "An original way of putting it. I'm a staff recruiter."

"Interesting. I'm looking for a new partner. Mine up and died on me last night. You have any building security experts in your files?"

"No. We recruit people for software engineering positions." Then curiosity got the better of her. "What happened to your partner?"

"The word is he died suddenly of, uh, a heart attack."

"I'm sorry for your loss, Mr. Romano."

He glanced at the ground, then faced her. "You never know when your time is up."

She conveyed her agreement with a nod. "'Take advantage of what each day offers,' I always say."

"Can I make you an offer you won't refuse?" he said in his best godfather voice.

She heard the wink in his voice, so she counter-offered with: "Go ahead. Make…my…day."

"We're a pair, aren't we?" Without waiting for her reply, he crowed, "My Rosie is making lasagna today. She cooks the best lasagna this side of Sicily. Stop by and tell I told her to reserve you a piece."

"I couldn't. She does enough for Ali and me."

Rommy held up his finger and produced his mobile device with his other hand. "Rosie. Listen. I'm sending our neighbor to you for a piece of lasagna." Short pause. "The one you babysit for. Okay?" Another pause. He ended the call and gave her a thumbs-up. "It's done. She'll be expecting you."

"Thank you so much, Mr. Romano. I'm not in the mood to cook today, so it appears I won't have to."

"Can I offer you a ride?"

"Thanks, but I'm not going far. I have to mail a letter," and she waggled it for him.

"Enjoy your day off."

"You too, Mr. Romano."

He went around the corner to the outdoor parking lot behind their building and Yolanda marched along Bruckner Boulevard toward the mailbox, each oblivious of the looming consequences of their decisions in the other's life.

Chapter Fifty-Four

Later that same day Rommy came through the doorway elated and Rosie was there to greet him.

"So, what's the *big* news you couldn't tell me on the telephone?" she asked.

He watched her hang his jacket in the hall closet. "Remember when you criticized me for being stranded in the bleachers of life?"

"I don't recall saying this."

"You talk too much to remember what you've said."

She pulled a face and shuffled behind him into the living room. "Be glad you're not married to Nina. She talks my ears deaf. I can't slip a word in sideways with her."

"Never mind your hosebag friend. Her husband's a loser," he admonished her. "Find yourself a better class of friends, Rosie." He stopped and faced her. "Your man now has a direct line to the front office."

"You got a promotion?" She clapped with glee.

"The boss promoted me to crew chief," and he tapped his chest with his thumb. "The job comes with a nice set of wheels and a big pay increase. We can move into a nicer place in a nicer neighborhood."

"Oh, my man. I'm so proud of you." She flung her arms around him.

He squeezed her back. "You see, Rosie. Good things come to those who are patient." And cunning, he did not say.

"They took their time in appreciating your value."

"Someone put in a kind word for me."

Rosie released him and craned her neck. "What happened to other crew chief? Was he promoted too?"

"Nah. He got cashiered. Couldn't handle the stress of the job. Created too many enemies."

"Enemies?" She shot him a quizzical look. "How do you make enemies in the security business?"

"Sucking up to the boss. No one can tolerate an ass-kisser."

She shook her finger at him. "Don't use foul language in our home."

He took hold of her finger and kissed it. "All right, all right, Rosie. You asked a question. I gave you the answer."

"I'm not one of those street girls you dated back in the day."

"Which is why I married you," he cooed, still holding onto her hand.

Bashfulness overcame her. "You're such a sweet talker."

"Only to you, my sweetheart."

"This calls for a celebration."

"Break out a bottle of our best grappa." He sniffed the air. "And cut me a big slab of lasagna. Responsibility gives me an appetite."

"Coming right up, my man," she said to him on her way to the kitchen.

Rommy took his seat at the head of the table, pleased with himself. While Rosie banged pots and plates, he contemplated his future. Whoever axed Bronco sure did me a favor. And Paco too. He was going to be whacked anyway, so his murder advances the timetable. Vittrola must be licking his chops at this latest incident. Rommy was referring to Gino Vittrola, the head of a rival crime family with whom he was double-dealing. The takeover of the Cabreezi family was but one heartbeat away. He clapped and rubbed his hands in approval just as Rosie was bringing him his dinner.

She stopped in her tracks and offered a slight bow. "Thank you for the applause."

"I—" Rommy changed course. "You're cooking is worthy of a brass band, Rosie, but unfortunately a clap is all I can offer."

She tabled the lasagna-laden plate and a glass tumbler. "The grappa is on its way, my man."

"You're not going to share a glass of the gods' nectar with me?"

"You know I don't drink."

"Not even on this special occasion?"

"I didn't drink at our wedding. Wine is for communion."

He shot her a glum expression. But his mood didn't last. His mouth watered at the sight of the multilayered pasta feast on his plate. "You outdid yourself again," he called out to her. It was all he could do to restrain himself from attacking his food. Out of politeness, he decided to wait for her to join him.

Rosie reappeared with her plate and the bottle of wine. "You're allowed one glass."

"Ah, Rosie," he said to her in a grumpy tone. "You're too tough with me."

"What did the doctor say?"

"Doctor, shmoctor. God put doctors on Earth to take the fun out of life."

"God put them on Earth to warn us off our unhealthy habits."

Rommy raised his glass in a toast. "Here's to a good fella finishing first."

"You deserve it." She played with her food.

"What's wrong, Rosie?"

"I wished I had known ahead of time. Then I would have prepared you something special for dessert."

"Your sweet lips are my dessert."

Her cheeks flushed. "Stop it. You're embarrassing me."

"Ah, Rosie. You're too Catholic. Those damn priests take the romance out life. But what can we expect from a bunch of eunuchs."

"It wouldn't hurt to come to church once in a while."

He took a swig of grappa before replying: "And listen to those hypocrites preach about morality while they molest young children and each other behind our backs? No. I don't need the Church and the Church doesn't need me."

Awkward silence ensued.

Rommy plated his fork and patted her hand. "Don't get me wrong, Rosie. I don't have a problem with you attending church. If praying makes you a better person, I'm all for it. I never got the call for religion."

His tact brightened her mood. "When can we begin looking for a new place?"

"Right away is fine with me. Our lease expires in a few months."

"I just thought of something."

"What?"

"When we move, who will help our neighbor with her son?"

"Rosie," he said, anger rising in his voice. Then a bolt of compassion shot through him. "Rosie," he began again in a softer tone. "It's admirable of you to consider our neighbors, but sometimes we have to take care of our own interests first. Right?"

"I suppose."

"Is there anyone else in this building who wouldn't mind babysitting a Black child?"

"Why should I mention the child is Black?"

"You know how some people are."

Rosie pursed her lips. "Do I ever." She sifted her neighbors and got a hit. "Maria on the seventh floor lives alone and she's home most of the time. I could check with her."

"Do it then." He gave his teeth a quick swipe with his tongue. "So, where would you like to plant new roots?"

"I've always wanted to live in Queens—or Brooklyn." Her eyes came alive. "Can we afford to rent there?"

"Nothing's too good for you, Rosie." His eyes smiled. "There's a nice house available on a tree-lined street in Floral Park, Queens."

"When can we visit?" she gushed.

"I'll have to make some calls first," he said with a self-important air. "Now finish eating. Your lasagna's getting cold."

Part VI

Days Later…

Chapter Fifty-Five

An immaculate Lincoln Town Car rolled to a stop in the Central Park Police Precinct parking lot. Sam jumped out of the vehicle and held open the rear door. Nelson alighted first and offered his hand to Sharron who stepped flamingo-like onto the pavement with her long slim legs. Anyone present must be wondering why such a well-heeled couple were slumming at a copshop.

"I'll call you when we're done," Nelson said to Sam. He advised him not to wander too far away with the Lincoln. Hand-in-hand, husband and wife headed toward the soaring atrium sheathed in bullet-resistant glass dazzling with reflected sunlight.

We got a break in your wife's case, Detective Ambrose had gushed to him earlier on the phone while he was neck deep in market data. This news unsettled Nelson. For good reason. Ambrose insisted he and his wife pay him a visit this afternoon. Nelson wanted to refuse the request, but a refusal might have provoked suspicion. So he cleared his schedule and rushed from the office to meet with the detective and his attractive partner whose name he had forgotten. On the way, he swung by his place to pick up Sharron. Ambrose needed her to ID a suspect in her case.

"I thought you dealt with my attacker," Sharron said to Nelson on their way to the precinct.

"So did I," Nelson said. "I have no idea what's going on. We need to play dumb and you need to put on a good show for the cops."

Sharron agreed with his plan.

They entered the modern, airy lobby and strolled to the reception counter. Nelson announced himself. They were asked to take a seat while they waited for Detective Ambrose to show. Every seat was occupied, so they stood off to one side and tried to be inconspicuous, difficult to do decked out in fashionable tailored clothing. Everyone else look rumpled in comparison.

The area buzzed with activity. People moved with purpose. Serious purpose. No one smiled. Patrolmen paraded by, escorting handcuffed suspects looking like they wished to be any place else. There but for the mercy of Cabreezi go I, Nelson mused. Whispering clusters of visitors, heads leaning inward, huddled against the outer walls. Probably lawyers and the relatives of the arrestees. So glad I'm here for a different reason. But his proximity to the criminal justice system still gave him the jitters. God forbid I should ever fall into its clutches, and he shuddered at the possibility, remote though it was.

Nelson spied Ambrose first. His height and bulk were not hard to miss. He adopted a neutral expression to mask the poker of fear stabbing his gut. He prayed Ambrose couldn't read minds. Relax, he told himself. You didn't kill the loser. The machine did. The detective approached him with his right hand extended. They pumped hands, neither one out-squeezing the other.

"Thank you for coming." He smiled at both of them. "I'm glad you could appear on such short notice."

Unmoved by the detective's cheerfulness, Nelson went on the offensive. "We're hoping for closure in this case. It has dragged on for far too long."

Sharron backed him up with a haughty look.

Ambrose's enthusiasm faded like the sun passing behind a cloud. "With no leads, a case won't solve itself," he said in self-defense. He brightened up. "But your case is about to change. Hopefully for the better."

"So what new evidence has come to light?" Sharron tossed out.

"Follow me," he said. "This won't take up too much of your time. I promise."

"Promise, promises," Sharron whispered to Nelson.

If Ambrose heard her, he didn't let on.

They followed the detective as he plowed through the noisy squadroom past fellow officers tapping on keyboards, phones shouldered against their ears. Ambrose nodded to colleagues they passed. His lumbering frame stopped at a glass-walled conference room and gestured for them to enter. Sandanos, backlit by natural light, sat at a table with a row of photos arrayed before her. She rose and extended her greetings to them. They exchanged awkward handshakes. She asked if they wanted coffee. They declined her offer absent a thank you tag.

Ambrose closed the door and gestured to two empty seats. Nelson and Sharron folded themselves into the roll-away chairs. Sharron fussed with the folds and seams of her clothing.

Sandanos assumed control of the meeting. "I'm sure you're both busy, so I'll come straight to the point. A new piece of evidence points to a suspect who is no stranger to us."

Sharron focused her attention on the female detective.

"Mrs. McCormack," Sandanos continued, "Please examine these mugshots. Perhaps one of them matches your memory of the person who assaulted you." She slid the photos across the table and arranged them in a neat row in front of her. "Take your time. We're in no hurry."

Sharron glanced at Nelson who urged her on with a jut of his chin. He watched her. She swallowed hard. Mugshots not even a mother could love glared back at her. She took her time scrutinizing them. Then she stabbed her finger at a photo. The perp's eyes convicted him. Laughing eyes. "He's the son of a bitch," she shrilled, and she leaned against Nelson. He put his arm around her and consoled her with soothing words. The suspect's the guy I killed, he realized. Sandanos threw Ambrose a winning smile.

"Good job," Ambrose said to Sharron. "The person you chose has a rap sheet."

"Not so hard was it?" Nelson said to his wife. She eked out a feeble smile for him. "How did you pick up this scumbag's trail?" he said to the detectives.

Ambrose piped up. "All I'll say is we received an anonymous tip in the mail."

The revelation knocked McCormack back in his chair. "Who is this punk?"

"We can't divulge this information right now. We're going to round him up and bring in him for a lineup first," Sandanos said with confidence. "Mrs. McCormack, would you be willing to identify your attacker in person?"

Sharron nodded her head vigorously, and she dabbed at her moist eyes with a tissue. Her performance was worthy of an Oscar.

"This convict will lead us to bigger fish. Thank you so much for coming," Ambrose said, ending the meeting. He opened the door and led them through the labyrinth of corridors back to the reception area. "We'll be in touch," he said to both of them. A brief round of handshaking and they went their separate ways.

Nestling against him in the backseat of the Lincoln, "How was my performance back there?" Sharron asked.

"Two thumbs up, Baby. The cops will never discover the truth. As far as I can tell, the guy in the mugshot is the same guy my acquaintance and I took care of the other night. Scumbag is gone. Forever. There will be no future line-up. Ever." He held on to Sharron and watched the skeletal trees of Central Park flash by their rolling sanctuary. Thank God fish can't talk.

Chapter Fifty-Six

Paco removed the phone from beside his ear and stuffed it into his suit jacket, the carpet absorbing the urgency of his footfall propelling him along the hallway toward Cabreezi's office. The don needed to be brought up to speed without delay about what he had learned. He halted outside the double doors, his broad chest heaving, and with a nod of his head he signaled Riccardo to announce his unexpected presence with a knock.

"Later!" Cabreezi's voice bellowed from within.

Paco jerked and he cast a nervous glance at Riccardo who was guarding the entrance. Fear knotted his face. "Don't worry," Paco told him with his eyes. He signaled for the guard to knock again.

"Hold on," Cabreezi said.

An eternity seemed to pass.

"Come in."

Better you than me Paco heard Riccardo whisper to him when he slipped past. The consigliere swallowed and plunged into the don's lair.

His eyes ablaze, "This had better be good," Cabreezi said from behind his desk, while an attractive young woman straightened her clothing, her curly blond hair askew. "You interrupted my, uh, manicure."

"Please excuse the interruption, Don." Paco missed nothing. No tools of the manicure trade were in sight, so far as he could tell. He stood on the carpet, pretending to be oblivious. "I need to speak with you. Alone."

Cabreezi dithered while the manicurist fluffed up her hair. "Run along now, Nina. You can, uh, finish trimming my nails later." She pouted at him. He fluttered his hand to send her on her way.

Paco desired nothing more than to throw her a knowing wink that said: "Manicure, heh?" But his life was worth more than a naughty gesture, so he stared straight ahead while she scurried past, and his nose caught a whiff of an exotic scent following in her wake. Without a doubt, she possessed the right stuff to cure a man of whatever ailed him, even long fingernails. He waited for the door to shut. Assured they were alone, Paco didn't waste time with a preamble. "Milo spotted our fish with his hand in the donut box minutes ago."

Cabreezi shot forward in his over-sized chair and beheld his consigliere with a mixture of anger and disappointment, his *manicurus interruptus* all but forgotten.

"Is our man certain?"

Paco offered him a grim nod when he took his seat. He sat stiff-backed in the overstuffed leather chair. "He followed our fish to the main donut shop and saw him enter the premises with his mate."

Cabreezi drummed his fingers on the desk. "I wonder if he confided in her."

"Sorry, Don, I have no answer."

"I would love to have been a fly on the wall."

"He probably turned state's witness."

His fingers stopped drumming. "It's his word against ours. There's no corpse, and the men stripped and cleaned the machine?"

"Per your orders."

"Ambrose is probably huddling with the DA as we speak. A search warrant can't be far behind."

"No worries, Don. He'll have as much luck finding evidence of a crime at the slaughterhouse as he would finding evidence of Russians in the White House."

Cabreezi nearly burst a blood vessel stifling a laugh. "A real tough assignment. A mission impossible."

The consigliere wished to carry the banter further, but there was no time for levity; it was time to circle the wagons. He steered the conversation back on track. "So what do we do with the fish?" He possessed a plan, but the decision was not his.

"Why did he run to the police?" Cabreezi asked the air. "We didn't mistreat him. We left him enough money to live on until the end of his days. And this is how he thanks us? Such ingratitude. Such *treachery*." His cheeks reddened, but he maintained his sang-froid. "Profound pain in his dying moments is his reward. Physical *and* psychological."

"Do you have something special in mind?"

Cabreezi sat back, linked his hands on his stomach and tapped his thumbs. "Grinding a fish into minced meat has lost its shock value." He meditated for several beats. "His kind endeavor to insulate themselves from the masses. No buses or subways for the limousine set. God forbid they should brush up against the common man and contaminate themselves. Seclusion and exclusion are their bywords."

"Why don't we introduce our fish to their opposite?" the consigliere proposed. "Have him mix it up with undocumented aliens."

The Mob boss considered Paco's proposal. "Your suggestion has merit."

"Our fish deserves a chance to shine beneath a bright spotlight before an audience thirsting for blood."

"Ahhh," Cabreezi said. "I see where you are venturing." His eyes gleamed. "Anything else?"

"How if we record a special video and courier it to his mate. A souvenir of his cinematic debut?"

"Imagine his mate's horrified reaction when she sees him in living color." Cabreezi reveled in the viciousness of their plan. "I wish I could be present when she's watching his performance. Witness every howl, every tear she sheds for her fink of a mate."

"The female mate is always the last to know," Paco said.

"So true."

Paco puzzled over this remark, but he wasn't about to press for clarification. Was Cabreezi referring to his "manicurist"? Did his wife know of his affair? These thoughts zipped through his mind at lightning speed. "So what remains to be done?"

"We've already plucked him clean, so it's time to sacrifice the goose that laid the golden egg. The DA won't have a case without the star witness."

"It's a go, Don?"

He nodded. "Pick up our fish tonight. Let's see if he's a better scrapper than a tattler."

Chapter Fifty-Seven

Another day of drudgery had come and gone at McCormack and McCormack, and Nelson plunged to the ground floor in the executive elevator in a morose mood. Since he had become Cabreezi's poodle, the zest for wheeling and dealing had died a pitiless death and with it his dream of becoming the world's richest man. Harsh reality had stolen a march on it. As a newly minted member of the working class, he now understood what it meant to work for a living, his human capital exploited for the enrichment of the Man. No longer the master of his own universe, he felt trapped, powerless to alter the circumstances of his grim fate. And how he wished to quit his job, but like other members of this class, he couldn't step off the treadmill of labor. Working was now a matter of survival, for him and for them.

To add to Nelson's misery, Cabreezi demanded daily performance reports. Never in his life had he been micro-managed. Accounting for his time taxed his nerves to the limit, but there was no way of escaping—other than death—Cabreezi's management regime. His new life had become a prison, and no crueler a warden than the don existed.

As Nelson watched the digits on the display panel decrement, he hoped he wouldn't have to work the coming weekend. Then he remembered all the times his employees put in long hours, even on weekends, to meet a deadline with nary a protest. But their acquiescence, he saw with new eyes, sprang not from a spirit of teamwork but from a position of powerlessness. And now he was one of them, his downfall total. From here on out he would dance to the tune of Yes, Sir! No, Sir! Three bags full, Sir!

Although he still occupied an exalted perch in his company, Nelson admitted Cabreezi could topple him from it with a flick of a finger. And no golden parachute would be offered to ensure a soft landing. Nelson wondered if he could make it to retirement age. The door opened before an answer revealed itself.

It was close to 8:00 p.m. when Nelson exited the rarified confines of the executive elevator on the ground floor and passed through a secure turnstile. From behind a row of monitors mounted on a semicircular counter, two uniformed security guards, armored up with enough protective gear to stop a slobbering mob of grievance mongerers from rushing the lobby, wished him a good evening.

He acknowledged the guards with a dejected nod, his leather-soled shoes scuffing the polished granite in the empty lobby as he trudged toward the wall of glass doors blackened by nightfall. Most of his employees had bolted hours ago. Now it was his turn, and he was glad for it.

Crisp, cold air greeted him outside, and it failed to revive his spirits. He rounded the corner of the limestone building and waiting for him in its usual spot at the curb beneath the glow of a street lamp was his company vehicle, a black Lincoln Town Car. It gleamed in the wash of light. A chauffeur he didn't recognize hopped out of the front seat.

"Where's Sam?" Nelson asked.

"Beats me, sir," the driver said, holding open the rear door. "Maybe he called in sick."

"Sam was fine this afternoon."

The driver shrugged. Without further comment, Nelson ducked into the warm interior.

"Move over," a voice ordered.

Disconcerted, Nelson attempted to look at his intruder but something cold and metallic pressing against his left temple prevented him. Tendrils of icy fear crept up his spine. He slid over to the next seat and whatever was stuck against his skull did not budge. Out of the corner of his eye, a hefty man with a flushed face and thinning hair dressed in a black leather coat squeezed into his just-vacated seat. The door clunked shut and the courtesy light blinked off.

"We're going for a drive." The man with the gun produced a black hood and tossed it into Nelson's lap. "Put it on."

"If you want money, I have piles of it."

"Once more from the top. Put-the-hood-on-now!"

Nelson jerked at the last word. He pulled the hood over his head and his world went black.

"So typical of your kind. You like to bribe your way out of every tight spot. This may happen in your world. But that guff got no currency in my world."

The man's indifference to money caught Nelson off guard. "W-What do you want?" He couldn't control the tremor in his voice.

"For starters, put your hands behind your back. No heroics or I'll shoot you."

Nelson complied without a fight.

"Put your wrists together."

The leather seats protested their movements.

"Hold still."

Something hard and narrow snugged around his wrists, the action sounding like a zipper zipping. A muffled whimper escaped Nelson's throat.

"Where are you taking me?"

"You into cage fighting?"

Nelson paused a beat to respond. "You mean mixed martial arts?"

"What else?"

"I-I've seen a match or two in my life."

"Excellent."

His kidnapper seemed pleased with his response.

"I hope you paid attention to the fighters when they got it on."

"What if I didn't?"

"Then I ain't placing no bet on you."

"You a gambling man?"

"Only with other people's lives. What about you? I bet you gamble. In fact, I know you gamble."

"What's it to you?"

"Everything we do in this life *matters*," and he emphasized the last word. "You gambled by going to the police earlier today. This mattered a great deal to the people I work for."

Stunned, Nelson took a breath and the hood came with it. He blew it out of his mouth with a puff of air. "You work for Cabreezi?"

"Yeah."

"I didn't rat your boss out to the police if that's what he's thinking."

The kidnapper snorted. "You were being tailed, bub. Don Cabreezi trusted you. But he always verifies the trust he places in people. You failed the test."

Nelson bounced in his seat, the heavy vehicle meeting a bump in the road.

"The detective handling my wife's case called me. They said they had new evidence about my wife's assault."

"Whatever. You played with fire and so you must burn." His tone brimmed with pleasure.

Nelson issued a low moan.

The kidnapper took pity on him. "It's not all bad, bub. You've got a fifty-fifty chance of living beyond this evening."

"Those are terrible odds."

"Better than a bullet in the back of the head."

"You plan to kill me?"

The man clicked his tongue. "No. Someone else takes out the trash tonight."

Nelson caught a note of relief in his tone. "You don't like to kill do you?"

"I do what I'm ordered to do."

Nelson had to figure a way out of his predicament. So he kept talking to keep himself from full-blown panic.

"I didn't tell the police anything about your boss."

"Not for me to decide."

"Do you ever make decisions?"

"Only when I'm given them."

"Don't you hate being someone's lap dog?"

The man cold-cocked him with a hard object and Nelson cried out. Fireflies danced inside the hood.

"I ain't no one's lap dog. Got it?"

Nelson's head throbbed with pain. "The price for doing a good deed is too high."

"What? Speak up. You're hard to hear."

"A stupid wallet is responsible for this mess I'm in," and he stifled a sob. "I should've minded my own business."

"Should've, could've, would've. The holy trinity of never-rans."

"I found your boss' wallet last fall."

"No kidding. Were you aware the wallet belonged to a Mafia don?"

"I knew Cabreezi was a mobster, but so what?"

"And you returned the wallet?" His question came out more like, "Are you an idiot?"

"What was I supposed to do?"

"Haven't you heard? No good deed goes unpunished. When you come into contact with evil, some of it will rub off on you."

"Speaking from experience?"

"It's a long story."

"We have time. I'm not going anywhere. I'm, uh, tied up at the moment." Nelson didn't hide the sarcasm in his voice.

Silence reigned. Then a breath issued from the kidnapper.

The gunman found a starting point for his tale. "My father and mother, may God's mercy be upon their souls, owned a restaurant decades ago. They served traditional Italian food. Homemade pasta. Homemade sauces. Nothing came out of a can. The restaurant was a success. My papa planned to expand it. But no bank would lend him the money to finance the expansion. So a cousin of his said he knew someone who knew someone who could loan him the money."

"I see where this story is going."

"Interrupt me again and I swear I'll whack you."

Nelson cringed against the door.

"So where was I?"

Nelson was about to speak, then he remembered his kidnapper's threat.

"Yeah. So two fellas came by my parents' restaurant one afternoon. One of them was Cabreezi. The other fella was a brute named Bronco. He's dead now. Got whacked. Didja hear about it? In the Bronx. Took a shotgun blast to the chest. Bastard had it coming."

Nelson remained mute.

"I-asked-you-a-question-bub."

"Uh, no. I must have missed it." Nelson wasn't about to tell him The Wall Street Journal didn't peddle sordid stories about petty criminals.

"Anyway, Bronco and Cabreezi agreed to loan my papa several grand. With conditions." The gunman paused, telegraphing the tale was about to take a tragic turn. "Weeks later, my papa suffered a heart attack. He couldn't work. Business declined. My brother and I worked there, but my papa had a special way with customers. They quit coming 'round. Bills piled up. My papa got behind on the juice—Mob lingo for interest on a loan. Anyway, soon enough Cabreezi and Bronco came knocking. My papa explained the situation to them. They were understanding. As understanding as hungry wolves circling a bleating lamb."

His voice caught, but he continued, "They forced him to sell the restaurant. Every penny went to those wolves. The restaurant was my parents' life work. It was the death of my papa. A second heart attack killed him."

"I-I'm sorry."

"Yeah."

Muted street sounds penetrated their glass and metal cocoon as they drove on through the night, and the tension rose.

Unable to resist, Nelson said: "May I ask a question?"

"Sure."

"Why do you work for the guy that caused your father's death?"

"Two reasons. One, with the closing of the restaurant, my brother and I were out of work, so we joined the Cabreezi gang."

"If you can't beat 'em, join 'em," Nelson said and Rommy grunted in agreement.

"And, two, cold, hard revenge."

"You're a patient man."

"Yeah. Your father still alive?" the kidnapper asked.

"Yes."

"You visit him much?"

No different than many workaholics, Nelson was guilty of being an absentee son. "Not as often as I should."

"Children have no time for their parents. You raise them, you love them, you educate them. Next thing you know, they fly the coop and you rarely hear from them again."

A horn blared long and loud and Nelson's body slammed against the passenger door.

"Watch it!"

"Sorry, Rommy."

"Sorry's going to get us killed, you stupid schmuck. Step off the gas. We're in no hurry."

Nelson wished for a car accident. It would attract the attention of the police. But he was in no position to cause one. He sat in wary silence and listened to the steady hum of the vehicle rolling over the streets of Manhattan, a counterpoint to the heavy beating of his heart. Out of nowhere the theme to *Mission Impossible* shattered the quiet.

"Shit," Nelson heard Rommy say. "Where's your phone?"

"Left jacket pocket." He felt Rommy rummage in his jacket.

"You can be traced with your phone." Traffic noises loudened and Nelson felt a wisp of cold air. "Out you go." The noises lessened again. "Almost got busted."

Nelson's despair deepened. His lifeline had been severed. Time rolled on and he soon lost track of it.

"Pull up to the door," broke the suffocating quiet, at least for Nelson.

Nelson felt the car decelerate, then jerk to a halt. A shot exploded. He screamed and couldn't stop.

"Shut up! You're alive...Shut! Up!" Rommy yelled at him.

Nelson pulled himself together. His ears rang and his nose caught the scent of burnt gunpowder. "Who got shot?"

"The driver," Rommy said, his tone matter-of-fact.

"You shot the driver?"

"He overheard too much."

"You're an animal."

"Life is a jungle. You're either the predator or the prey. From what I've heard, you're the prey."

Chapter Fifty-Eight

Sharron fussed with the silver place settings on the dining room table while she waited for Nelson to show. No matter how precisely Renalda had arranged the cutlery and glasses, Sharron felt compelled to make imperceptible adjustments every time. She suspected her maid repositioned them behind her back.

Sharron surveyed the table once more, pleased with her efforts. Beads of sweat trickling down the smooth flank of a Grand Cru Montrachet chilling in the silver ice bucket caught her attention. She swept her finger along the stem of the bottle and caressed her neck with the cool moisture. How she longed to sip a glass of the buttery nectar squeezed from the exclusive green grapes cultivated in the rich brown soil of the Burgundy wine region of France. Her mind took flight and golden creamy liquid trickled its way down her parched throat and settled contentedly in her stomach. But anti-anxiety medication and alcohol didn't mix she had learned the other night, so she demurred. Once more, she checked the time on her diamond-and-emerald encrusted Piaget watch.

What's keeping him?

The tableware set to perfection, she sniffed the air and tantalizing aromas wafting from the kitchen set her mouth to watering. For all of Renalda's imagined faults, her cooking whetted Sharron's appetite like nobody's business. Her maid's talent with a skillet had rescued her from the unemployment line on many occasions when Sharron lost her composure over a trivial infraction. A daily banquet was worth the aggravation.

Fed up with waiting, Sharron snatched her phone off the table and speed dialed Nelson. She tapped her toe while she studied a vibrant Japanese watercolor positioned on the wall, the dial tone droning in her ear. Her annoyance rose with each ring.

"Answer your damn phone," she willed, and on a busy street somewhere in New York City, Nelson's phone rang.

The abstract artwork of slapdash splashes of color brought to mind the image of a person fighting invisible forces.

Her phone landed on the table with a bang.

He'll pay when he comes through the door, she vowed. Dearly. I'll tear a strip off him and whip him with it. A wicked smile adorned her.

"Renalda!"

"Yes, Missus McCormack," she said, magically appearing at the entrance to the kitchen, her hands busy on her apron.

"I will dine in the den this evening. Fix me a plate of food and throw out the rest." Sharron made to leave then stopped herself. "Something wrong?"

Her maid, now a picture of neutrality, replied: "No, no. Everything fine."

The feast Renalda had prepared could feed a large family back in the Philippines.

"Get moving then."

Sharron grabbed her phone off the table and marched toward the den, her high-heels clacking on the marble like gunfire. Nelson can starve for all I care. Serves him right. He'll think twice before he ignores me again. She flopped onto the couch and thumbed through the offerings on the TV with the remote control.

Unbelievable! Hundreds of channels and nothing worth watching. Her thumb paused its search. *All in the Family*? Sharron read the synopsis of the popular Seventies show and a thrill shuddered through her body. Love at first site. She settled back in her seat, kicked off her heels and propped her bare feet on the table.

Minutes later Renalda breezed in with a tray of food.

"Where I should put this, Missus McCormack?"

Focused on the TV, Sharron frowned and flicked her hand. "Find a place on the table. And don't dare block my view."

Renalda went about her task with the illusion of docility.

"Oh. My. God!"

Renalda jolted upright. "What is wrong? I do something wrong?"

"Huh?" Sharron eyed her maid. Alarm showed. "No, no. This comedy is a real gem. I'm surprised the commissars of political correctness haven't canceled it."

"I no understand you."

Sharron stared at a distant wall in search of an explanation. She then locked eyes with Renalda. "This comedy show teaches people like *you* to know your *place* in my country."

"My place?"

"Never mind. It's way over your head," she said, miming her point with a popular hand gesture.

"My ancestors once belong to Filipino royal family. Before white men came and ruin my beautiful country."

Thrown off guard, Sharron rallied quickly. "My people belong to the noble class of one-percenters."

"I hear of this class on TV."

"Oh."

"A rich woman die and leave millions to her dog."

"So. Happens all the time."

"This help me understand a common expression."

"Which one?"

"America is going to the dogs." Renalda, her head held high, offered Sharron a smug smile. "In my country, dogs know their place."

Sharron remained speechless.

"Is this be all, Missus McCormack?"

"Uh, yes. You're dismissed." Her eyes followed the maid out of the room. "Why the attitude?" Sharron shrugged and resumed watching her show.

So absorbed was she in a bigoted world from a bygone era, hours passed unnoticed. Out of nowhere, an unbidden dispatch welled up from her subconscious and prodded her out of her high-definition-induced stupor. She glanced at her timepiece. A litany of swear words ran through her mind.

She called Nelson while in the background Archie Bunker railed at Meathead, his son-in-law, over a silly misunderstanding. No answer. Bastard. She muted the TV to think. Do I call the police? She gave this impulse careful consideration. And dismissed it. Those jelly donut junkies are too low on the ladder of responsibility to give a damn. Their jobs aren't on the line, so why should they care? Those buggers forget they're paid to protect our rights and interests. To hell with them. Her mind ranged when a bold idea invigorated her. Nelson and I don't spread money around town for kicks. To hell with the hour. Time to light a fire under the mayor and remind him who pays his campaign bills.

Chapter Fifty-Nine

Rommy muscled Nelson out of the car and murmured to someone nearby, a conversation he didn't catch. Rommy then gripped him by the arm and guided him down a metal staircase.

"You're shaking. Something scare you back there?"

"Being party to an execution wasn't on my wishlist."

"Watch your step, bub," Rommy said. "I might not stop you from falling."

Still blindfolded, Nelson placed each foot with care in his descent. He didn't relish dying from a broken neck. Or from a bullet in the back of his head.

The shock of the shooting had worn off and cold fear had taken hold of him again. "Where are you taking me?" he asked over the clanging of their footsteps on the metal treads.

"To a far better place than you have ever known."

"Doesn't smell like it."

Rommy chuckled. "Hopeful people have come from foreign lands to this joint for a shot at freedom. You should feel privileged to be in their company."

"Forgive me if I decline the honor."

"But you're the main event tonight."

"I don't like the ominous ring of those words."

"Relax. It's all good."

"For you or for me?"

"Both," was Rommy's terse reply.

They descended a few more stairs.

"My offer is still on the table."

"What offer?"

"Money for my freedom."

"How much we talking?"

"Tens of millions."

"I'm listening."

"Not another word out of me until you remove this hood and cut my bonds."

"You're a tough negotiator. Hang tight. We're almost there."

"Where is there?"

"A room without a view."

"Sounds inviting."

"Depends on the eye of the beholder."

As they descended, faint strains of cheering filtered into their space. He wondered at it. "Is that a television I hear?"

"People above us are celebrating the end of a pay-per-view fight."

"Is there a bar upstairs?"

"You ask too many questions."

The staircase ended and they walked down what must be a hallway, McCormack reckoned.

"Here we go."

A door opened with a squeal. The hood came off with a yank and Rommy shoved Nelson forward. He stumbled and blinked at the harsh light. When his sight had adjusted, he inventoried the windowless room. The cinderblock walls stood bare and so was the space except for a lone chair. A pair of white shorts and a plastic bag lay on the seat.

"What is this place? A dungeon?" Nelson cast about for an escape route. He couldn't detect one.

"Depends on your perspective. Grab a seat."

Nelson complied and the bag crinkled beneath him. Rommy stood guard at the doorway.

"So how do I get my hands on those millions?"

"Before I tell you, how can I be certain you'll free me?"

"You have everything to gain by trusting me."

"Famous last words."

"I'm your best hope."

Nelson studied the floor while he sifted his kidnapper's words for truth. Out of options, he resigned himself to trusting this guy. "Here's the low-down," and he pitched the details of his scheme to Rommy who listened with amazement and probed with exactitude.

When Nelson finished, Rommy said: "And here I pegged you for a softie. You had me fooled. I'm impressed."

Nelson waved off the compliment with a toss of his head. "I'm a survivor. There's no 'women and children first' bullshit in my world. Every man for himself."

Rommy copped a glance at the hallway.

"The coast is clear. I'm going to keep my part of the bargain. You can't go back the way we entered. There's a guard at the door. But there's unguarded rear exit."

"Lead the way."

"First, change into the shorts and stuff your clothes in the bag."

"What for?"

"In case we run into another guard. It's for the sake of appearances. At the exit, I'll give you back your clothes. You'll get dressed in the alley. And don't mind Earl," he tacked on.

"Who's Earl?"

"A homeless dude who lives in the alley. He keeps the rats company." Rommy laughed at Earl's expense.

"Should I be worried about him?"

"Nah. He's harmless."

"Great. Cut my hands free."

"Don't be a hero. I won't hesitate to shoot you."

Nelson nodded his compliance. He got up and gave his back to his kidnapper. A tug on the ligature and his hands were free. He rubbed his chafed wrists.

"I wouldn't go home when you leave here. It's the first place they will come for you."

"Thanks for the advice."

"Part of sticking to my word." Rommy resumed his vigil at the door.

While Nelson changed into the shorts, he heard Rommy speak to someone in hushed tones. He dared not ask what the conversation was about. He stowed his clothes in the bag and faced his captor.

Rommy appraised him. "You pump weights?"

"Three times a week in the company gym."

"It's a shame I'm setting you free. I would have bet money on you."

"For what?"

"To win a fight."

"Which fight?"

"It doesn't matter now. You got lucky. And so did I."

"Cheers all around."

"Lose the socks."

Nelson wiggled his toes. He shrugged. "Whatever you say."

"Ready?"

"Let's get the hell out of here."

"Give me your bag of clothing. I'll hold it for you until we reach the back door."

Quiet reigned in the hallway as they walked. Must be intermission time, Nelson supposed.

"How are you going to explain my escape?"

"I'll tell my boss you overpowered me and took my gun," he said to Nelson's back.

"Let's do it." Nelson's spirit rose, his bare feet propelling him toward freedom.

"The door's up ahead," Rommy said.

They walked several more yards then Rommy called a halt to their march. He rested his ear against a door for a moment. He put his finger to his lips, cracked open the door and took a peek. Satisfied, he gave the thumbs up signal. Rommy held the door for him. Blackness stretched beyond it. Nelson stood on the threshold of escape, and his nerves tingled. He sensed an unsettling presence in the void and a foul odor, like a slaughterhouse. He angled himself toward Rommy. "What's that smell?"

"Freedom," and he gave Nelson a shove. Bright light burst and a raucous cheer broke out.

Chapter Sixty

No matter what sleeping position Sharron adopted, she couldn't fall asleep. Nelson's disappearance had pushed her to the edge of panic. She tossed and turned in the empty bed like a spastic marionette. Desperate for respite, she got up and wandered through her palace in the sky, visiting darkened rooms, each one silent as a crypt. But each comfy space, instead of calming her beleaguered mind, reminded her of happier times, and the recollections compounded her anguish.

A late-night chat with Kim, her go-to remedy for resolving personal crises, had also failed to quell her anxiety. Grasping at straws, Kim suggested Nelson might have made a spontaneous pit stop for a nightcap. Sharron was having none of this. Nelson wasn't impulsive and he never frequented bars, she had told her. However, she had smelt alcohol on Nelson's breath the past few evenings. And he seemed depressed, like something was weighing on him. Not to mention his lack of libido. She had probed, but he didn't want to discuss it. Problems at work, was all he said. Short on patience, Kim ended the call with a plea for optimism, and Sharron got back in bed in no better mood than before her walk-about.

Time dragged and Sharron's anxiety intensified. Midnight passed without fanfare or fireworks and still no word from the police. She debated how earnest their search for Nelson really was. Were they busting their asses on the beat or cramming their craws with crullers? She expected his case to be assigned top priority in the missing persons queue. And why not? Her husband was America's wealthiest man, reason enough to receive special treatment from law enforcement personnel.

Problem was, Nelson had been AWOL for less than five hours. So the police weren't legally obligated to launch a missing person investigation until twenty-four hours had elapsed. Prestige, however, possessed the power to concentrate minds and amplify concerns of public officials, especially those whose precious campaign coffers relied on financial contributions from her husband. Elections, after all, don't run on fresh air. But hot air? Definitely.

Mayor Banks had responded with alacrity to her appeal for swift action. He worked the phones, browbeating police brass, but there was only so much pressure he could bring to bear on them before rank-and-file pushed back. Unions! She contemplated placing another call to Banks when her smartphone rang. She jumped out of her skin. The caller ID informed her Harvey the doorman was calling.

"What is it?" she snapped.

"A-A courier delivered a package addressed to you."

"It's past midnight! Who the hell delivers packages at this hour?"

"I didn't think to interrogate him."

"Of course not. You're just a dumbass doorman." Harvey, a part-time university student, was about to respond when she cut him off. "Dammit to hell." She flung aside the bedsheets and hopped to the floor. "Get your ass in gear and bring the package to me." She cast her smartphone onto the bed.

Slipping under Sharron's radar, Harvey's interruption evaporated her anxiety. She padded to the elevator door without slippers and paced in the darkened foyer, the lava floor cooling her bare feet. A chime stilled her. Hands on her hips, she watched the door slide open and flood the space with light. Highlighted in the glow of the compartment, Harvey's eyes ballooned, seized with the apparition of her dressed in a skimpy silk camisole and short shorts.

"What are you ogling at?" she snarled. "Give me the damn package."

He thrust a cardboard envelope at her. Sharron snatched it and spun on her heel, her feet spanking the marble. She didn't see him leer at her wiggling derriere before the elevator door glided past his pimply face.

Sharron fingered the package, and her heels pounded her irritation in a steady rhythm along the unlit hallway back to her bedroom. She flicked on a lamp and jumped onto the bed. The small square envelope bulged, and it was indeed addressed to her. She searched for a return address. None...Odd. She tore off the perforated cardboard strip and squeezed open the envelope. Nested inside was a USB flash drive.

"That's it?"

Sharron withdrew the electronic device and peeked inside again for a note. Empty. She tossed aside the envelope and studied the flash drive. Pessimism soon got hold of her.

A digital ransom note?

Fear clutched at her insides.

Where the hell's my laptop?

The answer came to her, having already discounted several other possibilities. She hopped off the bed and sprinted for the den. Navigating in the gloom to the edge of the leather couch, she stubbed her baby toe on a table leg. A string of expletives ejaculated from her mouth while she hobbled around, careful not to bang into other objects. The pain in her toe now bearable, she flopped onto the couch, flipped open her laptop and pressed the power button.

"Come on, come on," she growled. "Wake up you piece of crap."

After what seemed like an eternity, the desktop appeared. Several frantic attempts later, she rammed home the flash drive and waited for the operating system to recognize it. A click of the mouse and a video window popped open.

Ignoring the wild cheering, two men in matching white shorts circled one another in a small dirt pen, their fists raised in a defensive posture, ready for combat. No referee kept them apart. Only fear separated them, and not for much longer, the distance between them closing step by cautious step.

Sharron forgot her irritation while the video played. Worry soon wormed its way back into her cranium. Her fingers moistened and her lungs shrank as her apprehension mounted.

The combatants were a study in contrast. One man was dark-skinned and worse for wear, the other, white-skinned and groomed. But both men were lean and muscular. She noted something familiar about the second man's backside. Sharron leaned in, transfixed, her face reflecting the luminosity of the screen. He circled, and the camera zoomed in; his profile sharpened.

Sharron bolted upright and her sweaty hand flew to her mouth. "Oh my God!"

Chapter Sixty-One

Dappled sunlight burned through the naked branches of mature hardwoods lining the narrow street and flickered off the tinted windows of the limo as it rolled along Mapleview Road beneath the crooked skeletal canopy in the posh neighborhood of Alpine, New Jersey. Secure in his armored limousine, Cabreezi, happy to be out of his cage, had been given the all clear signal from Milo, his head of security, and was now on his way home after hunkering down in his cramped Manhattan office for the past week. He looked forward to tooling around in his roomy chateau-styled house and its expansive grounds. There were only so many *manicures* a man his age could bear.

As his ride approached the end of his street, Cabreezi took notice of a large white van parked on the grassy shoulder. Suspended twenty-five feet above the ground in the vehicle's roof-mounted cherry picker, a hard-hatted technician outfitted in navy blue coveralls fiddled with a box attached to one of the many wires strung between telephone poles like strings on a violin. If the worker heard them coming, he gave no sign. *CableCom* plastered the side panel of the vehicle, the don noted as he slid past it on his right. He then remembered his wife had mentioned a freak winter thunderstorm had rumbled through the neighborhood earlier in the week, so perhaps lightning damaged the cable lines. Too bad lightning hadn't struck *her*, and he chuckled to himself.

What did I do to deserve her? Cabreezi sulked. Married for over thirty-five years, those years felt more like a prison sentence than a marriage. But at least he could come and go as he pleased and see whoever he wanted. The house was spacious enough for them to live separate lives.

If his wife knew about his liaisons, she kept this knowledge to herself. He didn't care if she suffered, so long as she did so in silence. And her silence cost him dearly. Now and then she reminded him the price of her happiness was cheaper than a divorce. Having contributed not one cent to his wealth, yet she was entitled to an equitable share of it should he dissolve their marriage. Damned if he remained hitched, damned if he didn't. God-forsaken divorce laws, he fumed.

The ill-gotten gains he had squeezed out of McCormack would be kept hidden from her. Almost three hundred billion dollars were now at his disposal. Three. Hundred. Billion! An unimaginable sum. More than many countries' national budgets. Cabreezi had already spent a mere pittance of it—in his imagination. An extravagant sea-going yacht was first on his list. He would dock it in Monaco, a playground for the super-rich, and he marveled at being a secret member of this exclusive group. Next on the list was a parcel of real estate befitting a man of his newfound wealth. He coveted forested land and a castle. Britain or Ireland was the best location for achieving this end.

The sturdy steel gate blocking access to his property soon appeared. He relaxed and thought nothing more of his planned spending spree. A transponder in the limo unlocked the barrier. It swung open, and the long vehicle entered the property without slowing down. The barrier closed behind it. Cabreezi admired the lawn dotted with leafless trees and evergreens spreading toward his grey stone house topped with black slate. Up to this point he had never tired of this view, but he was expecting grander views in his future.

The driveway curved around to the front of his residence. The limo came to a halt before a set of tiled stairs. The chauffer left the motor running and opened the rear door. Cabreezi stepped out and climbed the steps while the chauffeur drove away to park the limo in the detached garage. On the wide porch, like always, he turned to admire the panoramic scene. Whoever said crime doesn't pay was a fool. Barely had he composed this judgement when he heard a *crack!* and collapsed bonelessly in the next instant.

Chapter Sixty-Two

Outside her patio doors a row of palm trees soughed in the tropical breeze and beyond them the aquamarine surface of the sea sparkled with reflected sunlight beneath a flawless cobalt sky. In her air-conditioned hotel suite, Deeanna reached down and chose a pair of white deck shoes from the selection in the closet to match her all-white outfit. Sandals wouldn't be appropriate for her island-hopping real estate adventure she had planned for today. She slid her petite feet into the shoes. A wide-brimmed floppy white hat set at a tilt on her head completed the picture. She admired herself in the large dresser mirror. The hat complemented her angular unlined face and the sleeveless blouse set off the toned and tanned flesh of her long upper limbs.

I should be on the cover of Vogue. A conceited smile twitched the corners of her mouth.

Her tenure at McCormack & McCormack had become a distant memory. And so was the strain of living in the anthill colony of Manhattan. Gone were the constant press of people and the perpetual clash of cultures. Deeanna lived by island time now. *Take it slow, mon,* the mantra of the Bahamas, were words she strove to live by. She boasted no people to see and no place to go. And the ready-to-please staff of the Royal Empress Hotel attended to most of her needs.

An unexpected knock broke her daydream.

She approached the door. "Who is it?" she asked in a raised voice.

"Flower delivery, ma'am."

"I didn't order flowers," she said. She removed her hat and spied through the peephole. A stout ruddy-faced man in hotel livery stood with a grand bouquet, sporting a neutral expression.

"They were sent courtesy of Percy Hughes Island Real Estate."

Delight lit up her features. Percy, a grizzled British ex-pat who had settled in Nassau decades ago, seeking prosperity and life in the slow lane, had regaled her with tales of his checkered past at their first meeting. What Deeanna couldn't know was Percy's life had slowed to a permanent halt earlier in the day courtesy of the delivery man.

Deeanna unlocked the door. She rotated the handle and was thrown off her feet by the force of the door swinging violently inward on her. The delivery man ducked in and closed the door quietly behind him. A sound-suppressed gun appeared in his right hand. He chucked the flowers on the unmade bed. Fear choked off her scream.

"Keep your mouth shut," he ordered, "and you'll live."

Bowl-eyed with terror, Deeanna pantomimed her compliance by bobbing her head.

The man sat on the edge of the bed, the gun pointed at her. He didn't waste any time with pleasantries. "Here's what you're going to do," and he explained to her how she would, on pain of death, transfer forty-eight of the fifty million dollars in her Nassau bank account to another account in the Cayman Islands. He allowed her to keep two million.

"Who told you about the money?"

"Lover boy told me."

"Lover boy?" she said to herself. Then awareness exploded in her head. "Nelson sent you," she rasped out.

"This information was—" he paused to consider his next words"—McCormack's going-away gift before he checked out."

"Where is he?"

"Maybe this will help you." He produced a mobile phone from his jacket pocket and manipulated its screen with his thumb. He showed her a video in play. "Pay close attention."

To the accompaniment of raucous cheering, a bruised and bloodied brown-skinned man dressed in white shorts, brandishing a sword, approached a white man lying on his stomach in matching shorts on a dirt floor. A gray circular wall surrounded the two men. It dawned on her she was viewing the climax of a brutal fighting match. But what's with the sword?

She didn't have to wait long for an answer. The man with the weapon crouched and grasped the other fighter by the back of his head and jerked it up. The camera angle changed. She couldn't identify the prone man's face at first; it had been beaten to a bloody pulp. Eyes, swollen and bruised, blinked in pain. She focused on them. Something about those eyes. Then recognition jolted her.

The fighter released the man's head; it flopped into the dirt. "Nelson!" She cringed in horror, but was unable to look away. The opponent raised the sword, and the crowd held its collective breath. The camera zoomed in on the gleaming blade and followed its lethal plunging trajectory. The sword performed its death-dealing role with cruel efficiency. Deeanna shut her eyes and gulped for air. Voices exploded in frenzied cheering.

"Turn it off. Turn it off!" she wailed, writhing on the carpet, her hands covering her ears. Through her hysteria, she heard her captor say: "Now you know we mean business."

Deeanna struggled to regain her self-control while she wiped her wet eyes.

"Show's over. Get up."

She slowly got to her feet, whimpering. Her hat remained on the carpet, crumpled.

"Dig out your financial documents. We're going for a drive."

On autopilot, she opened the safe in the closet and withdrew the papers.

"Don't move."

Deeanna froze. Clothing rustled.

"Turn around."

The man had shed the hotel jacket and held it out to her. "Stuff this in one of those drawers," he indicated with his weapon, and he threw it at her.

"This is how it's going to go down." He gave her a hard stare before continuing. "We're going to visit your bank where you will execute a transfer of funds." He advanced on her and gave her a white envelope. Then he backed away. "The instructions are in there." Waggling the gun, he said: "Don't cause any disturbance in public. If the police arrest me, others are ready to take my place. You cannot escape. We found you once. We will find you again. Are we clear?"

Deeanna shook her head, and she fought to control her trembling limbs.

The man tucked his gun in his waistband and concealed it with his tropical-patterned shirt. He then grabbed hold of her arm and guided her out of the suite through the patio doors.

The ride to the bank was a blur in motion. The kidnapper's partner drove them in a rented jeep through lazy sun-splashed streets bordered by whitewashed colonial buildings and palm trees. They sat in tense silence the entire brief journey.

In the dappled shade of palm fronds, the tiled path to the large glass doors of the colonially architected bank stretched away from Deeanna, surreal-like. Palm trees bordering the path converged on the entrance in the distance. Her legs quivered, and the envelope dampened in her sweaty grip. She dared not glance back. They were watching. She could feel their piercing eyes boring into her. She forced her feet to move, planting one in front of the other. It was the hardest journey she ever took. But not her last, she trusted.

The driver twisted around in his seat. "Will she cough us up?"

Rommy cut away from Deeanna. "Don't worry. I let her keep two million. A sign of goodwill."

"You did what?"

Patting the air with his hand, "Relax, Paco," he said to calm him. "It's insurance money. Except she won't live to collect it."

Paco grinned. "Ooo, you're evil, Rommy. Undeniably evil."

"I learned from the best. Leave no loose ends."

Chapter Sixty Three

Detective Ambrose went through the bittersweet ritual of filling the banker's box on his desk with personal doodads. There weren't many despite three decades plus of police work. He paused to appraise a plaque awarded him by a former mayor for bravery in the line of duty. He blew dust off the surface. (Housekeeping wasn't his thing.) The jaw was lean, the skin smooth, the tightly curled sideburns still blacker than his skin. Where had the years gone? he asked the stouter version of himself, not for the first time today.

Nigh on thirty-three years of apprehending criminals of all stripes, Ambrose was pulling the plug on a storied law enforcement career short a round of fireworks. He had hoped to go out in a blaze of glory with the arrest of Vito Cabreezi; instead, he had to be content with the don's unexpected demise, the victim—deservedly so many agreed—of a daylight assassination.

Ambrose felt Sandanos' eyes on him. "Not much to account for after three decades of collaring criminals."

"Your achievements are accounted for not in the number of honors but in the number of cases you solved. A record in this precinct," she added to buck him up.

"Except for one."

"It's not the outcome you staked your retirement on," Sandanos said, facing him at her desk, "but Cabreezi's out of your misery now."

He drew himself up. "Cabreezi should have rotted to death in prison, not die of an assassin's bullet."

Sandanos waxed philosophical. "He lived by the gun, he died by the gun."

"Assassination was too good for him." Ambrose paused loading the box. "Men like Cabreezi are animals. Caging them drives them mad. He deserved to spend the last years of his life climbing the walls of his concrete cage, day and night. It's the ultimate punishment for his savage kind."

"Astute insight into the criminal mind."

"Comes with the territory," he said. "When you've been in the trenches for as long as I have, you'll gain a better understanding of what makes criminals tick."

Sandanos changed course. "Any regrets?"

"About?"

"Your years on the force."

"Other than failing to nab Cabreezi...." He ruminated for several beats then his face assumed a pained expression. "Wife number one."

Sandanos urged him on with her eyes. Ambrose rarely talked to her about his personal life.

He let out a breath as if to say, "What the hell." He plunked into his chair and pushed aside the box to clear his view. "I was a rookie. And a newlywed. I desired nothing more than to be New York City's biggest, baddest crime stopper. I guess every rookie cop launches into his—or her—career with the same sort of fire in the belly. You know, before cynicism extinguishes it." His eyes misted in remembrance of his naiveté. Then he fastened his eyes on her again. "I believed I could balance career with marriage, but my marriage took second place to my ambition. You don't make detective in five years without sacrificing something."

"Then what happened?"

"By this point, I was a husband missing-in-action. Marcy got tired of the lonely nights and empty spaces, both emotionally and physically."

Sandanos nodded her head in understanding.

"She filed for divorce in year six of my career." He sat back in his chair. "I-I didn't fight for her, for our marriage. I loved her. But I loved the kick from the adrenaline high of police work so much more. Of sifting clues and catching badasses—and the odd bad girl."

"Not so unusual. It comes with the territory," she reminded him. "But you remarried. What changed for you?"

He cast a wary glance around. "Like any drug, you eventually crave more of it to achieve the same high. I stumbled around in the undergrowth of police work before I realized my life had veered off course. You know the deal: all work and no play. So I mustered the courage to visit a private psychologist," he confessed. "I avoided the department shrink. No one on the force needed to know I was battling mental health issues."

"Admitting you had a psychological problem is not a sign of weakness."

"Back then it was. Still is. But no one will admit it." He pulled a face. "Anyway, I straightened things out up here"—he gave his shiny head a tap—"and the rest is history as They say. Then I met Shanice. She's my rock. Being a super husband beats being a super cop."

"I'll keep this to myself." A novel idea came to her. "Have you ever considered speaking to the rookies about your experiences?"

Ambrose mentally kicked the suggestion around before answering. "I was wondering what to do in my spare time. I don't have any hobbies. Would the brass go for it?"

"In case you don't realize it, Terrell, you're a legend around here. Only someone of your stature can speak to the mental health problems cops experience daily on and off the job."

The din of office noise compensated for his momentary reticence.

"I'm not sure the machismo culture of fighting crime is ready to have its collective head examined."

"It has to start somewhere, sometime."

"I'll run it by Shanice. Maybe she'll be willing to share me in my retirement." She'll resist the idea outright, he thought.

"Someone needs to take the stigma out mental illness in Copland."

Just then Sandanos smacked her desk and Ambrose jumped in his seat like it were electrified. "Jeezuz, Camila." His eyes flashed. "You scared the crap out of me!"

"Have you noticed what's been missing in the news since Cabreezi bit the bullet?" she lobbed at him.

Ambrose, still shocked, had no chance to reply.

"Headless corpses."

Regrouped, he said, "Could be just a coincidence." But his tone implied otherwise.

"I doubt it."

Then Ambrose fixed her with a care-free air. "I look forward to reading the outcome of the FBI investigation in my pajamas one lazy day in the future."

"The outcome won't bring back McCormack or restore his wife's sanity," she lamented.

"No good deed goes unpunished."

"And the road to hell is paved with them," Sandanos rejoined.

"Aren't we a couple of cynics?"

On the cusp of responding, Sandanos stopped herself and her eyes slipped past him. He was about to swivel—

"Detective Terrell," his superior officer said. He took his time rising out the chair. "So, today's the big day, is it?"

"Appears so, Lieutenant."

"This precinct owes you a debt of gratitude, Detective. You had a 92% homicide solution rate over the course of your career. I would venture this is the highest rate not just in this city, but in the entire country."

Ambrose mumbled some perfunctory words of appreciation.

"Your record will probably never be broken."

He made a noncommittal noise and offered up a humble smile.

"I heard through the office grapevine there's a celebration for you tonight at *Monty's*."

The lieutenant was referring to a watering hole for cops over on 54th.

"You heard right." He was on the verge of asking her if she planned to join them but he caught himself. Why encourage her? Instead, Fate intervened and saved him the trouble.

"I'd come to your send-off but duty calls. I'll be there in spirit, though." Her voice strained to conceal the insincerity in her words.

Ambrose favored her with a barefaced *I'm-too-polite-to-call-you-on-your-bs* look. He held out his hand to terminate her awkward tribute. "It was a pleasure working with you, Lieutenant." It was the best farewell he could muster.

They shook hands like lepers, and she went on her way.

Ambrose's aspect conveyed relief. "Glad that ordeal is over with."

"You won't be seeing her ever again."

He gave her a high-five. While Sandanos watched, Ambrose finished packing the box. "Why don't we duck out early?" he suggested.

"Sure. Let me check my messages first."

Ambrose tucked the lidded box of doodads under his massive arm while Sandanos fiddled with her phone. He noticed her frown.

"What's the matter?"

"My cousin went island shopping in the Bahamas. She was texting me daily until a few days ago."

"Island shopping? Your cousin must be loaded."

Sandanos lowered her voice. "She settled a sexual harassment lawsuit out of court. Her former employer paid her millions to settle the suit."

"Who was her employer?"

"It's confidential."

"She told *you*."

Sandanos paused to decide. "I guess I can trust you," and she giggled.

"Very funny."

"My cousin was the Chief Investment Officer at McCormack's firm."

Ambrose's eyes bulged. "What the—"

"I know. Freaky, isn't it?"

"And when did you plan on sharing this news with me?"

"Never. It had no bearing on our work."

"Still."

"Are you hurt I didn't tell you?"

"Kind of."

She clapped him on the arm. "You'll get over it."

Ambrose lightened up. "I wouldn't worry about your cousin. The islanders have a saying: *Take it slow, mon*," he drawled in his best Caribbean accent. "She's probably sipping piña co-la-das at a seaside bar, watching the sun sink into the sea."

"You're probably right." Sandanos slipped her phone into her back pocket. "Shall we go?"

"Retirement, here-I-come!"

***

A muffled scream shattered the air but was quickly cut short by a *splash*. Tied up and weighted down, Deanna sank like a stone in the clear blue waters of the Caribbean, and sunlight filtering through the water quickly faded to black above her. The water grew cold as her body made its rapid descent into the deep, and she held her breath for all she was worth, knowing what was coming. Her lungs burning for oxygen, and no longer able to resist, she involuntarily inhaled a lungful of seawater, and at the same instant her mind screamed "See you in Hell, Nelson!"

Endings

To the din of cheering in the background—the home team must have scored—Bronco ignored his underling's jest and in a loud voice said: "Take care of this," and his hand whipped out of his creaky leather jacket. With a deft flick of his wrist, he flung a photograph across the marred surface of the table. The kid stopped the color photo from flying off the edge with a quick hand movement.

"Mm-mmm. She's a looker," he said, holding the photo in the air.

"Put your eyes back in your head," Bronco said in a tone that commanded respect, if not fear.

"How much does she owe?"

Bronco scowled at the intrusive question, but contained his rising anger. "None of your damn business. She's bait. Nothing more."

"I'll say she is," he drooled, indifferent to his overling's irritation. "I wouldn't mind hooking up with her."

Bronco considered giving the kid a wallop but judged better of it. He swallowed his anger. He needed the kid's full cooperation in this latest ruse. "No chance of that happening."

"What'd she do?"

"Nothing. It's what her husband did."

"Okay, so what did her husband do?"

"A good deed that can't go unpunished."

"You don't say. Stupid putz doesn't deserve her."

"And neither do you. So don't get any ideas."

"I'm out of her league." He snickered in spite of himself.

"Sure. You're a real lady's man."

"So I'm told," he agreed, but there was a noticeable lack of conviction in his words.

"Listen up. She's your target. She speed walks in Central Park with her snooty high-society friends every weekday morning."

"Oh, one of *them*." The kid's features hardened. "My mama used to clean their cribs. They treated her like dirt. If I didn't need the money, I'd do the job for free."

"No one wants to volunteer anymore."

"Life's expensive," the kid fired back. "So what's the plan?"

"Put the boots to her. Her face. An arm. Some ribs." Bronco spoke with the gravitas of a guy reading off a grocery list.

"Throw in some groping and you've got yourself a deal."

"Sure. Wouldn't want to deny the broad her #MeToo moment in the sun. But don't kill her. We need her alive."

"No worries there. Not my m-o."

Which makes you disposable. "We all got our boundaries," Bronco said.

The kid leaned forward and placed the photo back on the table. "I'll do it for the usual fee." He rubbed his hands in anticipation.

"Good. Because the *usual* is all you're getting." Bronco pushed a thick white envelope toward him. "Half now and the other half later, if the job is done right. *Capiche*?"

"Money in the bank."

"The address of her building is on the back of the photo. Memorize it, then destroy it."

"When do I dance with her?" the underling asked, once again fixated on the woman in the photo.

"Within the month. But the sooner, the better." Bronco was about to heft himself up when he stopped himself. "And, Junior."

Tearing his eyes away from the photo, "Don't call me Junior. My foster father used to call me that," he protested, a momentary flush of anger coloring his cheeks.

"Don't screw this up, *Lorenzo*. Remember, you're an expendable in the Cabreezi family. *Capiche*?"

Fear crossed Lorenzo's features quickly supplanted by bluster. "What do I look like, an amateur?"

If all goes well, you'll look like ground beef none too soon, you dumb schmuck. But Bronco kept this privileged information to himself. "When you're done dancing with the lady, go to ground in the bolt-hole in Port Morris. You remember the joint?"

"How can I forget it?" his tone neutral.

"Stay there until you're told otherwise. Someone will make grocery deliveries once a week."

"So long as you keep me in smokes and Netflix you'll have to drag me out."

If you knew what was coming, we'd probably have to. He smiled at Lorenzo and there was cruelty in it. A twinge of morality pinged his conscience, then it was gone. Condemning one of his underlings to a painful death wasn't so hard, was it? His face hardened. "We're done here."

The pendulum of Lorenzo's fate was now in full swing.

Bronco slid over and shoved his bulk off the vinyl banquette, and his jacket creaked with the movement. He left the tavern without looking back.

Lorenzo watched him go. "Muscle-bound prick," he muttered. He returned his attention to the photo. "Whoever you are, lady, I can't wait to meet you."

THE END

Author's Notes

This novel is dedicated to my second grade remedial English teacher Mrs. Nancy O'Reilly (RIP) with whose dedication and support all those decades ago helped make this story possible.

NO GOOD DEED GOES UNPUNISHED started life several years ago as a 4000-word short story I entered in a literary contest. Although my story didn't make it to the winners' circle, I liked the characters so much—especially Rommy—I believed they deserved a full novel-length treatment. As the sages' are wont to say: The rest is history. I hope you enjoyed reading my cautionary tale about the follies of greed and revenge. If you did, please leave a review on Amazon and Goodreads. I assure you your leaving a review is one good deed that will go unpunished.

Read on for an excerpt from

THE PACKAGE

The internationally acclaimed conspiracy thriller by
Bryan Quinn

Beginnings
Istanbul - Present Day

Leave *now* with the package or end up dead like the other two.

Delivered moments ago by his terrified friend, the grim warning haunted Marco Arrigoni as he scrambled to plot an escape route across a crumpled map of Turkey he had smoothed out to the edges of the kitchen table. So much for this day being one he wanted to remember rather than one he wished to forget. But remembering or forgetting today paled in importance to surviving it, and there was no guarantee he would—all because he had pinched from a sacred tomb a holy relic he probably shouldn't have.

So now here he was, holed up in his apartment like a common fugitive, cowering from a vicious killer who hungered after the stolen relic. Hungered after it badly enough to gun down two innocent men last night—one of whom had been his friend's lover. A sure sign the killer was close on his heels.

Or maybe he was a tad paranoid.

Perhaps. But paranoia didn't waste those unlucky victims, Marco reminded himself as he struggled to concentrate on the map.

If nothing else, he now understood how a fugitive must feel—an understanding he would gladly give away in charity if he could, generous soul that he was. Beyond that, Marco knew diddly-squat, and not knowing so unnerved him he couldn't stop himself from flinching at every ominous *thump* and *creak* while he studied the map in the confines of his tiny kitchen which seemed more animated than usual. Time was short—he expected a private courier to collect the packaged relic at any moment. Then he would skedaddle, preferably before the shooting started.

Funny thing how the passing decades had tamed his wild side. Back in the day, he had cut a broad swathe through his feral Bronx neighborhood cracking skulls and breaking bones. But twenty-plus years of shilling sermons on turning the other cheek had dulled his fighting edge. A guilty consolation to him. Guilty because he earned his daily bread preaching a philosophy of life totally at odds with his less-than-stoic behavior of the moment. So what? Failing to walk the walk wasn't the end of the world. A desperate killer was stalking him after all. So his friend had warned. Reason aplenty to excuse this minor episode of backsliding and cut himself some slack. Besides, practicing what he preached wasn't his strong suit. Never had been. Especially the practicing part.

Done justifying his skittish behavior to himself, Marco tore his eyes away from the map and flicked a nervous glance at the clock suspended high on the opposite wall. A double-take, a hard swallow, then fear and anger soared in tandem. The blasted courier was late. The odds of the relic falling into the hands of the gunman shot higher.

His mind in turmoil, Marco sat gaping at the timepiece while the rotating second hand ratcheted up his sense of doom. Just then a horrible awareness rocked him.

If I'm killed, the secret of the relic will die with me.

His senses reeled.

The shooter can't win.

Too much is at stake!

Not one to panic at the first sign of disaster, Marco showed anxiety the door and rallied himself. When you get out of this jam alive, you're gonna buy that backstreet courier the biggest damn clock in the city and chain him to it. Let him then dare lose track of time again. Bong! Bong! Bong!

Despite his dour mood, a sly grin stole over his kisser.

Doubt if the courier will find it funny.

Tough.

As much as he wanted to flee, running from danger wasn't listed in the code that governed his conduct. (A double-check confirmed this.) If he did, his conscience would plague him like an incurable itch. Nah, he'd rather grapple with a psychotic cage fighter than tangle with his nag of a conscience. He had promised to deliver the package, so despite the potential threat to life and limb, deliver it he would.

This wasn't the first time Marco's take-it-to-the-mat sense of moral obligation had placed his life in jeopardy. He simply ached for it to be the last. It had better be. At forty-eight, "Dead Hero" wasn't an epitaph he hankered after, but it might come to that since he wasn't packing a weapon.

Except.

He flexed his scarred ball-peen-knuckled hands and examined them as though seeing them for the very first time...Fingernails could stand a trim...Not solid enough to stop bullets but strong enough to break bones. Better than nothing, he conceded. Marco hadn't clobbered anyone since becoming a priest over two decades ago. But that's not to say the impulse had vanished altogether. Uh-uh. He had lost count of the number of times he felt like hurtling himself through the flimsy latticed divider in the confessional to knock some sense into the heads of wayward congregants committed to perpetrating the same debaucheries again and again, and who then possessed the gall to wonder why the outcomes were no different from the last. The insanity of it all. Luckily for them, he feared prison more than he loathed the priesthood. Retirement couldn't come soon enough.

Marco's lapses of compassion aside, his fists and hard-earned street smarts had rescued him from countless scrapes in his past. And then some. He possessed the scars to prove it. Scars or no, the wary voice in his head, the one that had kept him alive in the mean streets of his youth, reminded him he was going to need his fists and his wits if he expected to outfox the hitman. Once more, consequences be damned, he'd trust in his weapons fashioned from flesh and bone to live beyond the end of the day. What else could an unarmed priest do?

Pray?

He mentally shook himself and turned his restless attention to the bulky package positioned at the edge of the map. It drew him as a wave drawn to the shore. Unable to look away, he regarded it with awe. For the truth was alive in there, with a capital *T*. That much was certain. Unbidden, his hand whispered over the map to the packaged relic and awarded it a gentle pat.

So many innocents slaughtered across so many centuries for the sake of some well-spun lies. Never again! he vowed. The message in this package will expose the biggest hoax ever foisted upon huma—

"Enough!" He glared at the window, and if looks could shatter, the glass would've burst.

Shrill for the time of day, unusual since rush hour hadn't yet slipped its straining leash, the din of traffic flaring up from four stories below sprang him from his chair, sending it crashing across the linoleum floor into the fridge. He rushed to the window to investigate....

Lined up bumper to bumper, cars crept past his building in horn-blaring protest. Farther down the road he spied a double-parked car, its taillights flashing.

"Way to go, buddy," he yelled into the noise. "Those flashers will speed things up real fast." He ducked in and slammed shut the window. "Takes just one selfish jerk to cause a stretch of chaos."

Too preoccupied with the fix he was in to latch onto the illegally parked vehicle as a harbinger of something more than a mere case of self-centered behavior, Marco spun away from the window, none the wiser.

"Damn natives have got nothing better to do than pound on their horns," he griped as he went to retrieve his chair. If time permitted, he would've liked to pound on the drivers just to hear *them* wail.

He shoved the chair home with his foot and plunked himself down in it. Powerless to stop the manic traffic noise, he rubbed his hands through his wavy jet hair then let them flop onto the table, and another glimpse at the burning clock did little to cool his annoyance.

He grunted in frustration. To distract himself, he ranged through the rudimentary escape plan he had devised. He could find no hiccup in it. Must be perfect. Like him. Stealing a final look at the location he had circled on the map, he thought, Should be a quiet refuge to hunker down in until things blow over. No one will think of searching for me there. Any place is better, not to mention safer, than this crib. And if it isn't, well, I'll discover that soon enough.

The escape route Marco would travel to reach the secluded Sümela Monastery in the northeast part of the country settled, he gathered the crumpled map, refolded it after several maddening attempts and finally rammed it into his back pocket for future retrieval.

A futile expectation he would later discover.

With nothing left to do, he stared out the filmy kitchen window at the Hagia Sophia, its massive brick-and-mortar dome seemingly propping up the leaden sky like a giant umbrella. His gaze turned inward while his fingers probed the jagged scars on his knobby knuckles, the crude braille of a troubled past etched in his flesh, if not in his soul.

How did the shooter get wind of the relic? he asked himself and not for the first time today. Only three other people are aware of its existence. Two of them are trustworthy. They wouldn't say a word. Would they? But the third. Could he have informed the gunman from jail…? But how?

He would give much for the answers to these questions. Even his vows? Worth considering. Too overwrought to think straight, he let the matter drop. The answers wouldn't change his predicament anyway.

The horns blared on, but Marco's gaze did not waver.

Steely you might call it. And you'd be right.

Doing his best to ignore the shrill protest percolating up from the traffic-snarled street thirty-feet below, and containing his gut instinct to lay down some scuffed-up shoe leather and beat a path to safety, he sat tight and willed the courier to materialize. Only then would he put shoes to pavement and disappear. And with no trail to follow, perhaps the unknown killer would too.

He hoped.

That was the plan. Such as i—

The doorbell went off, detonating the tense atmosphere in his apartment. Marco bolted upright in his chair.

Must be the courier. So he deigned to show up. About damn time.

Hurrying toward the front door, he welcomed a surge of relief.

It didn't last.

An obvious question rattled his brain: What if it's not him?

Marco froze and time with him. The living room seemed to shrink and fade away until nothing but the front door loomed before him. If he remained still, maybe the caller would give up and leave.

The buzzer detonated again; he jumped out of his skin.

Caught in the amber of indecision, Marco fixated on the door, knowing there was no going back once he opened it.

His senses on full alert, he found his courage and reached for the deadbolt with utmost effort, as though in a nightmare, and at that same moment a shudder ripped through him—the fuse on the most explosive secret in history was about to be lit.

The time for him to skedaddle had come.

He didn't know how wrong he was.

His ordeal wasn't over. It hadn't even begun.

CPSIA information can be obtained
at www.ICGtesting.com
Printed in the USA
LVHW050011231220
674915LV00032B/964